and *Grooms*

*Weddings worth waiting for...*

# Acclaim for Rebecca Winters, Leigh Michaels and Helen Brooks

## About Rebecca Winters
"Rebecca Winters is a woman for all seasons with her ability to write fantastic romance novels."
—*Affaire de Coeur*

## About Leigh Michaels
"Leigh Michaels gives fans a wonderful reading experience."
—*Romantic Times*

## About Helen Brooks
"Helen Brooks creates an emotionally intense reading experience."
—*Romantic Times*

# Brides and Grooms

**BOTH OF THEM**
by
Rebecca Winters

**TEMPORARY MEASURES**
by
Leigh Michaels

**AND THE BRIDE WORE BLACK**
by
Helen Brooks

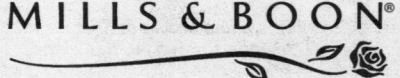

**DID YOU PURCHASE THIS BOOK WITHOUT A COVER?**
If you did, you should be aware it is **stolen property** as it was
reported *unsold and destroyed* by a retailer. Neither the author nor
the publisher has received any payment for this book.

*All the characters in this book have no existence outside the imagination
of the author, and have no relation whatsoever to anyone bearing the
same name or names. They are not even distantly inspired by any
individual known or unknown to the author, and all the incidents are
pure invention.*

All Rights Reserved including the right of reproduction in whole or in part
in any form. This edition is published by arrangement with Harlequin
Enterprises II B.V. The text of this publication or any part thereof may not
be reproduced or transmitted in any form or by any means, electronic or
mechanical, including photocopying, recording, storage in an
information retrieval system, or otherwise, without the written
permission of the publisher.

*This book is sold subject to the condition that it shall not, by way of trade
or otherwise, be lent, resold, hired out or otherwise circulated without the
prior consent of the publisher in any form of binding or cover other than
that in which it is published and without a similar condition including this
condition being imposed on the subsequent purchaser.*

MILLS & BOON and MILLS & BOON with the Rose Device
are registered trademarks of the publisher.
Harlequin Mills & Boon Limited,
Eton House, 18-24 Paradise Road, Richmond, Surrey, TW9 1SR

BRIDES AND GROOMS
© by Harlequin Enterprises II B.V., 2000

*Both of Them, Temporary Measures* and *And the Bride Wore Black*
were first published in Great Britain by Harlequin Mills & Boon Limited
in separate, single volumes.

*Both of Them* © Rebecca Winters 1992
*Temporary Measures* © Leigh Michaels 1991
*And the Bride Wore Black* © Helen Brooks 1993

ISBN 0 263 82420 9

05-1000

*Printed and bound in Spain
by Litografia Rosés S.A., Barcelona*

**Rebecca Winters**, an American writer and mother of four, is excited about the new millennium because it means another new beginning. Having said goodbye to the classroom where she taught French and Spanish, she is now free to spend more time with her family, to travel and to write the Mills & Boon® novels she loves so dearly.

# *BOTH OF THEM*
## by
## REBECCA WINTERS

## CHAPTER ONE

HE WAS THE BABY'S FATHER all right! The same olive complexion, the familiar obstinate chin, the identical hair, black as India ink. Even from the distance separating them, the resemblance seemed to shout at Cassie.

She leaned against the doorjamb in disbelief. Her sister's motherly intuition hadn't failed her, after all.

*Cassie, from the first moment I held Jason in my arms, I thought there was something...different about him. If Ted was still alive, he'd say the same thing. Jason's not our son! I'm convinced of it!*

*Remember I told you how he was rushed to the intensive-care unit as soon as he was born? And remember my telling you about a disaster that brought all those victims to the hospital at the same time? There was so much commotion that morning, I honestly think a mix-up occurred and they brought me back the wrong baby from intensive care.*

*Jason belongs with his natural parents. Promise me you'll find my baby and take care of him for me, Cassie. Then I can die in peace.*

Faced with the irrefutable proof of Jason's true paternity, Cassie went alternately hot and cold. Down to the smallest detail, like the shape of the long, square-tipped fingers, or the way one dark brow lowered with displeasure, nine-month-old Jason was the robust replica of Trace Ellingsworth Ramsey III, the autocratic male she could see through the doorway seated behind the desk. He was rapping out edicts over the phone to some no doubt terrified underling of the Greater Phoenix Banking Corporation.

Her eyes closed in reaction, because it meant Susan's natural son had left the hospital with this prominent, high-powered banking executive and his wife. Susan's baby would now have the Ramsey name, would now be assured his place in life as one of the Ramsey heirs.

Had the Ramseys, like Susan, ever wondered about that day nine months ago? Had they ever sensed anything about their baby that didn't seem right? Any physical characteristics, for instance, that didn't appear in their families?

"Come in, Miss Arnold!" Trace Ramsey called out, not bothering to hide his impatience as he put down the receiver. Before entering the room Cassie darted a nervous glance at Jason, who was still asleep in his carryall next to the secretary's desk.

Though high heels added several inches to her five-foot-three-inch frame, Cassie felt dwarfed by the dimensions of the walnut-paneled office. To her disappointment there were no mementos or framed photographs of Ramsey's wife and son. Except for some paintings on the walls and a bonsai tree placed on a corner of his desk, the suite was immaculate, and blessedly cool.

She sat down in one of the chairs opposite his desk. "Thank you for taking time out of your busy schedule to see me this morning, Mr. Ramsey. I realize it was short notice."

His dark brows furrowed in undisguised irritation. "According to my secretary, Mrs. Blakesley, you have a highly confidential matter to discuss with me, which you refused to disclose to her."

"I couldn't say anything to her," Cassie said immediately, her guileless, leaf-green eyes pleading with him to believe her. "It's no one's business but ours. When I say ours, I'm including your wife, of course," she added in a soft voice.

He sat forward in the chair with his hands clasped on top of the desk, gazing directly at Cassie. She stared into his eyes, deep blue eyes set between impossibly black lashes. Like Jason's... The Ramsey eyes reminded Cassie of the intense blue in a match flame.

"My secretary never arranges appointments without first obtaining background information, Miss Arnold. She made an exception in your case. I hope for your sake you were telling her the truth when you said this was a life-and-death situation. Lying to gain entry to my private office is the surest way to find yourself slapped with a lawsuit for harassment. As it is, I'm taking time from an important board meeting to accommodate you."

His arrogance took her breath away. If all this

weren't for the ultimate happiness of everyone concerned, she would've relished storming out of there and slamming the door in his good-looking face.

"This concerns your son," she said quietly.

The menacing look that transformed his taut features made her heart leap in apprehension. With dangerous agility, he got up from his seat and placed both hands on his desk, leaning forward. "If you're part of a kidnapping scheme, let me warn you I've already activated the security alarm. When you walk out of here, it'll be with an armed guard."

"Are you always this paranoid?" She was aghast; until now it hadn't occurred to her that his wealth made him a target for kidnappers. At the mere thought, a shudder ran through her body.

"You've got thirty seconds to explain yourself." The implicit threat in his voice unnerved her.

"I-I think you'd better sit down," she said.

"Your time is running out."

In an attempt to feel less vulnerable, Cassie rose to her feet, clutching her purse in front of her. "It's not easy for me to explain when you're standing there like...like an avenging prince ready to do battle."

He flicked a glance at his watch. "You're down to ten seconds. Then you can explain all this to a judge." From the forbidding expression on his face and the coldness of his voice, she knew he meant what he said.

As worried and nervous as she was about confronting him with the truth, she had to remember that this man and his wife were her only passport to Susan's son. That knowledge gave her the courage to follow through with her plan.

Taking a deep breath, she said, "I happen to know that you and your wife have a nine-month-old baby boy who was born to you on February twenty-fourth at the Palms Oasis Health Center. My sister, Susan Arnold Fisher, also delivered a baby boy there on the same day.

"Until the moment she died, she believed that there was an upset in routine because of the catastrophe—the chemical plant explosion. It brought a flood of injured people to the hospital, and somehow the wrong name tags were put on the babies' wrists in the intensive-care unit. The result was that my sister was presented with your baby, and you and your wife went home with hers."

The silence following her pronouncement stretched endlessly. His face looked impassive, hard and cold as stone. "All right," he finally muttered. "I've listened to your tale. Now I hope you have a good attorney, because you're going to need one."

"Wait!" she cried when he pressed the intercom button. She had expected this encounter to disturb him, but she'd never dreamed he would call in the authorities before she had convinced him of the truth!

"It's too late to backtrack, Miss Arnold."

A knock on the door brought Cassie's head around and she saw an armed security guard and a police officer enter the room with their hands on their unsnapped holsters. Behind them stood an anxious Mrs.

Blakesley. She held a wriggling, squirming Jason, who was bellowing at the top of his lungs.

"What in the—?" Trace Ramsey stopped midsentence and raked a hand through his black hair, shooting Cassie a venomous glance. But she was too concerned to be intimidated; dropping her purse, she made a beeline for Jason.

Since Susan's death two months earlier, Cassie and Jason had become inseparable. She might not have been his biological mother, but she loved him every bit as fiercely. She felt guilty for leaving him in Mrs. Blakesley's care, even for such a brief time. He must have awakened after his morning bottle and been frightened by the unfamiliar face hovering over him.

"What's the trouble, Mr. Ramsey?" asked the guard. But Cassie didn't hear his answer, because Jason had caught sight of her. Immediately his lusty cries intensified, resounding through the suite of offices. "Ma-ma, Ma-ma," he repeated, holding out his hands.

Despite the gravity of the situation, Cassie couldn't repress a tiny smile, because it was Trace Ramsey's own noisy son creating all this chaos.

"Mommy's here, darling." With a murmured thank-you, she plucked him from the older woman's arms and cuddled him against her chest, kissing his damp black curls, rubbing his strong sturdy little back with her free hand.

Jason had made it clear that he wanted Cassie and no one else. He clung tightly to her and calmed down at once. Cassie felt a wave of maternal pride so intense she was staggered, and at that moment she knew she could never give him up. She knew she'd made a mistake in coming here.

With the best of intentions, Cassie had walked into Trace Ramsey's office and upset his comfortable, well-ordered life. If his reaction to a possible kidnapping attempt was anything to go by, his love for the son he'd brought home from the hospital was as great as hers for Jason. She wanted to honor her sister's dying wish, but she *couldn't*. She realized that now. It was wrong, unfair—to all of them.

"Mr. Ramsey?" she started to say, but the second she caught sight of his ashen face, the name died on her lips. In her preoccupation with Jason's needs, she hadn't noticed that everyone except his father had left the room. He stood motionless in its center.

Swallowing hard, she loosened Jason's fist, which was clutching her hair, before turning him around to face his father. Only seconds later, she heard his shaken whisper. "Dear Lord, the likeness is unbelievable."

Cassie's compassionate heart went out to him. She couldn't imagine what it would feel like to learn that she'd been nurturing the wrong child since his birth, let alone to see her own baby for the first time.

"That was my reaction as soon as I saw you," she said quietly. He looked away from the child then, and gazed at her, his eyes dark with emotion.

"He's called Jason," Cassie added. The sound of his name brought the baby's dark head around and he clamored to be held in his favorite position, with his face buried in her neck, his hand gripping the top of her dress for dear life.

"May I hold him?" Trace's voice sounded strained. He lifted his hands instinctively to take Jason from her.

"Yes, of course. But don't be surprised if he starts crying again. He's going through that stage where he won't let anyone near him but me."

Jason immediately protested the abrupt departure from Cassie's arms. His strong little body squirmed and struggled, and he kicked out his legs, screaming loudly enough to alert the entire building. But not for anything in the world would Cassie have intruded on this private moment between father and son.

They looked so right together, so perfect, it brought a lump to her throat.

Trace's gaze swerved to hers as he bounced his unhappy son against his broad shoulder, apparently unconcerned about his elegant, stone-gray silk suit. "Do you have a bottle I can give him? Maybe it'll quiet him down."

She should have thought of that. She began to rummage in the bag Mrs. Blakesley had brought in. "Here."

Gently but firmly he settled Jason in his arm and inserted the nipple in his mouth. He performed the maneuver with an expertise that would have surprised her if she hadn't known he'd been fathering Susan's son for the past nine months.

But Jason wasn't cooperating. He just cried harder, fighting the bottle and his father with all his considerable might. Cassie could tell that Trace was beginning to feel at a loss.

"Why don't you let me change him?" she suggested softly. "It might do the trick."

He slanted her a look she couldn't decipher and with obvious reluctance put a screaming Jason back in her arms. While Jason snuggled against her once more, his father reached for the baby quilt lining the carryall and spread it on top of his desk, pushing the telephone aside. Never had she imagined she'd be changing Jason's diaper there!

"Come on, sweetheart. Mommy's going to make you comfortable." Though Jason continued to protest vociferously and eye his father as if he were the enemy, she managed to make him lie still long enough to unfasten his sleeper and peel it off along with his damp diaper.

As she put on a clean disposable diaper, Trace murmured something unintelligible beneath his breath, and almost as if he couldn't help himself took Jason's right foot in his hands. For some reason the baby didn't seem to mind and actually relaxed a little, no doubt because he was receiving so much attention. His extremities had become of paramount importance in his young life.

Cassie had always been intrigued by Jason's right foot. The third and fourth toes were webbed, a characteristic never seen in either Susan's or Ted's families. His father seemed to find it of inordinate interest, as well.

"He's my son!" Trace proclaimed solemnly, then

let out a cry of pure delight. Fierce pride gleamed in his blue eyes.

"We probably ought to take the babies to the hospital and have their blood types checked against the records."

"We will," he muttered, "but the truth is sitting right here." He grasped Jason's fingers and pulled experimentally to test the baby's strength. Jason caught hold with a firm grip and lifted his head and shoulders from the desk to sit up without help, producing a satisfied chuckle from his father. Jason had become equally curious about the black-haired stranger who seemed to take such pleasure in playing with him.

Because it was cool in the room, Cassie searched for a clean sleeper in the diaper bag. No sooner had she found one than it was taken from her hands.

"I'll dress him," Trace stated. There was an unmistakable ring of possession in his tone as he proceeded to fit Jason's compact body into the arms and feet of the little white suit.

After snapping the front fasteners, he picked up his son, who had by now stopped fussing, and held him against his shoulder, running his fingers through Jason's wild black curls. Cassie noted that even their hair seemed to part naturally on the same side.

Needless to say, she'd been forgotten as Trace carried Jason over to the window where the great city of Phoenix lay sprawled before them. Whatever he said was for his son's ears alone. She knew that Trace Ramsey had already taken Jason to his heart.

Now there were two people in the world who loved Jason intensely. And as soon as his wife was informed, there would be three. Everything had suddenly become much more complicated. Cassie understood instinctively that Jason's father wouldn't give up anything that was his. But in this case they would have to work out vacation schedules, because she wasn't prepared to lose Jason. She had come to love him too much.

"Mr. Ramsey? I have a plane to catch later today. Do you think we could meet with your wife this morning and tell her what's happened? I can hardly wait to see my nephew, and I'd like some time with him before I go back to San Francisco with Jason."

*"San Francisco?"* He wheeled around, a grimace marring his features.

"We live there, Jason and I."

Her voice must have attracted Jason's attention because he cried out and reached for her again. When Trace continued to hold him, Jason wailed piteously and tried to wriggle out of his father's grasp. He had been a determined, headstrong child from birth. Now she knew why.

"It's time for his lunch, but a bottle will have to do." The gentle reminder forced Trace to close the distance between them and deposit Jason in her arms. But with every step he took, she could tell he rebelled against the idea of relinquishing his newly discovered son even for a moment.

Cassie couldn't blame him. The situation was so emotionally charged she was afraid she would burst into tears any second. Comforted by the familiar feel of Jason's warm little body, she sat down in a leather wing chair Trace positioned for her. Jason grabbed the bottle with both hands and started gulping down his milk.

Actually he'd been attempting to drink from a cup for the past week. But her pediatrician had said to use a bottle while they were traveling because it would give him a greater sense of security. Jason was such a noisy drinker, Cassie couldn't help smiling and felt Trace's eyes on both of them.

"My wife and I divorced soon after the baby was born," he said abruptly. He paused, then went on, speaking quickly. "She gave me custody and went back to her law practice in Los Angeles. I have my housekeeper, Nattie, to help raise my son. She and her husband, Mike—who looks after the grounds— have worked for me for years. Nattie's wonderful with children, and Justin adores her."

*"Justin!"* As she said his name, her mind grappled with the unexpected revelation that Mrs. Ramsey was no longer a part of this family's life. She lifted her head and fixed imploring green eyes on Trace. "Tell me about Susan's son—your son," she amended self-consciously. "What does he look like? I-I can't wait to see him."

Without hesitation he strode swiftly to his desk and buzzed his secretary. "Mrs. Blakesley? Cancel all my appointments for today. I'm going home and won't be back. Tell Robert to have my car waiting in the rear. We'll be down shortly. If there are any urgent phone messages, give them to me now."

While he dealt with last-minute business, she felt his gaze linger on her slender legs beneath the cream cotton suit she was wearing. Cassie's heart did a funny little kick, and she forced herself to look away, studying the paintings hung on the walls of his office. Until now, Trace Ramsey had been the focal point of her attention.

If the decor was a reflection of his personal taste, he tended to enjoy the watercolors of an artist unknown to her. The paintings depicted a variety of enchanting desert scenes, in a style that was at once vibrant and restrained. She would have liked one for herself.

A loud burp from Jason brought her back to the present. Trace's spontaneous laugh made him look, for a moment, more carefree, and Cassie chuckled, too. Obviously Jason had finished his bottle without stopping for breath.

"Shall we?" Trace stood at the door holding a briefcase and the carryall, indicating she should join him.

"That's a beautiful boy you have there," Mrs. Blakesley commented to Cassie as they passed her desk on their way out.

"Mrs. Blakesley," Trace said to the older woman, his eyes still glowing in wonder, "I'd like you to be the first person to meet my son, Jason. When I'm in possession of all the facts, I'll explain how this came about, but for the time being I must ask you to keep it to yourself.''

''I knew it!'' The matronly woman jumped to her feet. Hurrying around her desk she shaped Jason's face with her hands. ''Even before she said it was a matter of life and death, I knew it. He bears an amazing resemblance to you, Trace. I never saw anything like it in my life!''

A satisfied smile lifted the corners of Trace's mouth as he gazed down on his son.

Cassie could imagine all too easily what his secretary was thinking—that at one time Cassie and Trace had had an affair and Jason was the result. She wanted to set the matter straight, but Trace was already whisking her out of his office and around the corner to a private elevator.

When he'd ushered her inside and the doors were closed, he asked, ''How did you get to my office?''

''A taxi.''

''How long have you been in Phoenix?''

Jason's curious eyes darted back and forth as they spoke.

''Only two days this time.''

''This time?'' His black brow lifted in query. The elevator arrived at the ground floor and they stepped out, but Trace remained standing in the hallway as he waited for Cassie's answer.

''I've made several rushed trips to Phoenix in the past two months trying to find out if Susan was right about the switch. There were five couples who'd had a son at that hospital the same day Susan gave birth to Jason. I mean Justin."

Trace blinked. "I didn't realize there were that many. Palms Oasis is a small hospital."

"I know. I was surprised, too. Anyway, I visited each family in turn but came to a dead end each time. I began to think Jason was one of those rare accidents of nature, after all—the odd gene producing a throwback in the family. That is, until I saw you." She ventured a look into his eyes and wondered why she'd ever thought them glacial. "When your secretary told me you wouldn't see me without knowing the reason for my visit, I almost turned around and walked out."

His eyes turned an inky blue color and he sucked in his breath. "Thank God you didn't."

She gave a quick half smile. "You're not exactly an easy man to reach, Mr. Ramsey. No home phone. Security guards. I didn't have a choice except to meet you without an appointment. You'll never know how close I came to giving up. You were the last person on my list and it seemed like an unnecessary gesture, another exercise in futility."

"What made you so persistent?" he asked soberly.

"I have to admit that since I started looking after Jason, I've entertained some doubts about his parentage, too. I made up my mind to be as thorough as possible, so there'd be no lingering shadows when I returned to San Francisco to raise Jason as my son."

On impulse she lowered her head to kiss the child's smooth cheek. "And something told me that if I left without seeing you, I would always have these doubts...."

Just as she spoke, Trace moved closer. He cupped her elbow and guided her through the hall to a back door. A BMW sedan stood waiting in the drive. "Come here, Tiger," he said to Jason, lifting him from Cassie's arms and strapping him in the baby seat.

Jason took one look at the unfamiliar surroundings and began to scream.

"I think I'd better stay with him or you won't be able to concentrate on your driving." She climbed in back, then handed Jason one of his favorite toys, a hard plastic doughnut in bright orange. That calmed him and he soon grew absorbed in chewing it.

Trace leaned inside to fasten her seat belt. His action brought their faces within an inch of each other, and she was painfully conscious of his dark glossy hair, his clean-shaven jaw and his fresh scent—the soap he used? To mask her awareness of him, she pretended to adjust Jason's seat belt. Trace backed away from her and closed the door. In seconds he had gone around to the driver's seat.

"Thanks, Robert," he called to the garage attendant, and they were off. If the older man found the situation somewhat unusual, he didn't let on. But she could tell he was curious about Trace's little black-haired look-alike sitting in Justin's usual spot.

Despite the way he had treated her earlier, Cassie found herself warming to Trace. She liked the fact that he took his fatherhood role so seriously. And she liked the way he accepted a child's presence in his life, not worrying about his costly suit or his expensive car. She knew a lot of men who never allowed children inside their luxury cars.

They left the busy downtown center and drove north toward the foothills, where she could see Camelback Mountain in the distance. What impressed Cassie most about Phoenix was the cleanliness of its streets and the beauty of the residential lawns and gardens. The vivid flowers and shrubs, the sparkling blue of swimming pools...

This was the first time in months that she'd been able to appreciate her surroundings. The pain of her broken engagement, plus the trauma of trying to cope with Susan's death and Jason's needs—on top of running her home handicrafts business—had drained her. She couldn't remember when she'd been able to relax like this.

But her pleasure was short-lived. When she turned her head to find another toy in her bag, she discovered a pair of narrowed eyes watching her through the rearview mirror. If their guarded expression and his taut facial features were any indication, something unpleasant was going through Trace Ramsey's mind. She couldn't understand it, because only moments before everything had been so amicable.

Inexplicably hurt by his oddly hostile look, she closed her eyes and rested her head against the leather upholstery.

In fairness to him, she supposed, it wasn't every day a man kissed the child he thought was his son goodbye, only to be confronted with his *real* son a few hours later.

Again Cassie tried to imagine his feelings and couldn't. Only once in her twenty-five years had she heard of a case involving a switched baby. That instance, too, had been a mischance, sending two families home with each other's babies. Cassie didn't know the statistics, but figured such an accident had to be in the one-in-a-billion category.

Until now, most of Cassie's thoughts and concerns had been for Jason. But the closer they drew to Trace's home, the more excitedly she began to anticipate her first look at Justin. She found herself speculating on why the Ramsey marriage had fallen apart so soon after the baby was born. How could his wife have left her child and gone to another state to pursue a career? Didn't her heart ache for her son?

Cassie couldn't fathom any of it. She was so deep in thought she didn't realize the car had left the highway and turned onto a private road. It wound through a natural desert setting, dotted with saguaros and other cacti, to a breathtaking Southwestern house—a house that looked as if it had sprung from the very landscape.

The house appeared to be built on two levels, with a whitewashed stone exterior and pale wood trim.

The architect who had designed Trace Ramsey's home had not only succeeded in reflecting the environment but had caught the essence of the man. The clean yet dramatic lines, the soaring windows, the quiet beauty of the wood, created a uniquely satisfying effect.

He continued driving around the house to a side entrance where Cassie caught sight of a rectangular swimming pool. Immaculate, velvety green lawns flanked the water, which was as blue as a deep-sea grotto.

Cassie gasped at the sheer size and beauty of Trace Ramsey's retreat, tucked only minutes away from the center of his banking empire. Cassie had never seen anything quite like this place. She'd spent the whole of her life in San Francisco, living with her widowed mother and sister in the bottom apartment of a flat-fronted Victorian house on Telegraph Hill. Cassie couldn't remember her father, who'd died when she was very young.

While she lifted Jason from his car seat, Trace came around and opened the door to assist them. The air smelled of tantalizing desert scents and was fresher than in downtown Phoenix. Cassie thrived in cooler temperatures; she estimated that it couldn't be much warmer than seventy-five degrees. Perfect weather for early December, just the way she liked it.

"Shall we go in?" He didn't seem to expect an answer as he gripped her elbow and helped her up the stairs to the entry hall, carrying the baby bag in his other hand. He didn't attempt to take his son from her, probably because he didn't relish a repeat of Jason's tears. But she could sense Trace's impatience to hold him.

Jason was fascinated by the click of her high heels

on the Mexican-tile floors and kept turning his head in an attempt to discover the source. It was a fight to keep him from flipping out of her arms, especially since Cassie found herself so distracted by the beauty around her. Every few steps, she had to stop and stare at the dramatically cut-out white interior walls and bleached wood ceilings.

They walked along a gallery filled with lushly green trees and local Indian art. It looked out on the swimming pool, part of which was protected by the overhanging roof.

"Nattie? I'm home, and I've brought someone with me for lunch. Where are you?" Trace called out as they went down a half flight of stairs toward the indoor portion of the patio.

"Justin's been helping me water the plants. I didn't know you'd be back to eat. I'll get something on the table right away."

They entered a charming courtyard reminiscent of old Mexico, with a profusion of plants and colorful flowers. But Cassie hardly noticed the wrought-iron lounge furniture or the retreating back of the auburn-haired housekeeper. Her eyes fastened helplessly on the child in the playpen who had heard his father's voice and was squealing in delight.

The slender lanky child, dressed in a sleeveless yellow romper suit, was standing, a feat Jason hadn't yet mastered, as he clung to the playpen webbing, rocking in and out as he watched his father's approach.

Round hazel eyes shone from a fringe of fine, straight, pale-gold hair that encircled his head like a halo. His total attention was fixed rapturously on Trace.

Cassie came to a standstill. It was an astonishing sensation—a little like putting the final pieces in a jigsaw puzzle. The frame of this child's body was Ted's, but his complexion was Susan's. The shape of his eyes was Ted's, but the color was Susan's. The texture of the hair was Ted's, but again, the coloring was Susan's. The straight nose and cheekbones were Ted's, but the smile...

Cassie's eyes filled with tears. Her adored sister, who only eight weeks before had lost a valiantly fought battle with pneumonia, lived in her son's glorious smile.

"Oh, Susan!" She sobbed her sister's name aloud and buried her face in Jason's chest. She was overcome with emotion, with feelings still so close to the surface that she couldn't contain them any longer.

Jason fretted, patting her head agitatedly. Cassie fought for control and after a few minutes lifted her tear-drenched face to discover a pair of angry blue eyes staring at her, not only in silent accusation but contempt.

"What's wrong?" she whispered, attempting to wipe the tears from her cheeks. "First in the car, and now here. Why are you looking at me like that?"

## CHAPTER TWO

IN THE SILENCE that followed, he reached for Justin and hugged him protectively, rubbing his chin against the fine silk of the child's hair. "I was counting on that reaction and you didn't disappoint me," he said bitterly.

They faced each other like adversaries. Cassie shifted Jason to her other arm. *"What reaction?"* She couldn't imagine what had caused such hostility.

"It's too late for pretense. Justin needs people around who see him for the wonderful person he is."

She shook her head in total bewilderment. "He *is* wonderful!"

"But—"

"But what?" she demanded angrily, feeling a wave of heat wash over her neck and cheeks. Jason could sense the charged atmosphere and started to whimper.

"You're no different from my ex-wife! She was so repulsed by Justin's deformity, mild though it is, that she wouldn't even hold him."

*Deformity?* "I don't know what you're talking about! Two months ago I watched my sister's body laid to rest and I thought her lost to me for the rest of my life." Her voice shook, but she hardly noticed.

Without conscious thought she lowered Jason into the playpen and reached for her tote bag. Oblivious to his sudden outburst, she pulled one of Susan's wedding pictures from the side pocket and held it up for Trace's scrutiny. It was her favorite picture of Susan and Ted, smiling into the camera just before they left on their honeymoon.

"When Justin's face lighted up just now, it was as if God had given Susan back to me. Take a good look at the picture, Mr. Ramsey. See for yourself!"

Grim-faced, he set Justin in the other corner of the playpen and took the photograph. Immediately Justin, too, began to cry. In an effort to distract the howling infants, Cassie knelt beside the playpen and started to sing "Teensy Weensy Spider," one of Jason's favorite songs. Within seconds, both babies grew quiet. Jason crawled toward her, while Justin clambered to his feet.

It was when he put out his left hand to grasp the playpen's webbing that she noticed the depression—like a band around the middle of his upper arm. Below the depression, his arm and hand were correctly shaped, but hadn't grown in proportion to the rest of his body. The deformity was slight, but it was noticeable if you were aware of it.

"You dear little thing." Unable to resist, she stood up and leaned over to take Justin in her arms. "You precious little boy," she crooned against his soft cheek, rocking him gently back and forth.

"Your mother and daddy would have given anything in the world to hold you like this. Do you know that?'' she asked as he stared quietly at her. The seriousness of his gaze reminded her of the way Ted used to look when he was concentrating. "Susan made me promise to find you. I'm so thankful I did. I love you, Justin. I love you," she whispered, but the words came out a muffled sob.

She wanted to believe the baby understood when she felt his muscles relax and his blond head rest on her shoulder. For a few minutes Cassie was conscious of nothing but the warmth of her nephew's body cuddled against her own.

"I owe you an apology."

Cassie opened her eyes and discovered Trace standing not two feet from her, with Jason riding his shoulders. His sturdy little fingers were fastened in his father's black hair, a look of fear mingled with intense concentration on his expressive face.

She smiled through the tears. "He's never seen the world from that altitude before."

Miraculously Trace smiled back, their enmity apparently forgotten. Cassie's heartbeat accelerated as she found herself examining the laugh lines around his mouth and his beautiful, straight white teeth. She raised her eyes to his, and the pounding of her heart actually became painful.

"Trace?" the housekeeper called out just then, jerking Cassie back to reality. "Do you want lunch served on the patio or in the dining room?"

"The patio will be fine, Nattie." To Cassie he said, "I'll get the high chair. The boys can take turns having lunch."

*The boys.* Those words fell so naturally from his lips. Anyone listening would have assumed this was an everyday occurrence.

"Since Jason and I will have to leave for the airport pretty soon, I'd like to spend this time with Justin. Do you mind if I hold him on my lap to feed him?"

A scowl marred his features. "When's your flight?" he demanded, not answering her question.

"Ten after four."

"I'll get you to the airport on time," was the terse response. "Right now the only matter of importance is getting better acquainted." He grasped Jason's hands more tightly. "Come on, Tiger. We'll go get Justin's chair and surprise Nattie."

Jason forgot to cry because he was concentrating all his energy on holding on to his father. The two of them disappeared from the patio, leaving Cassie alone with Justin, who seemed content to stay in her arms. Compared to the sturdy Jason, Justin felt surprisingly light.

She sat down on one of the chairs at the poolside table and settled him on the glass top in front of her. Though taller and more dexterous than Jason, he hadn't started talking as well yet. Probably because he was too busy analyzing everything with that mathematical brain inherited from Ted.

Jason, on the other hand, never stopped making sounds and noises. He liked to hear his own voice and adored music of any kind, which was a good thing since Cassie played the piano and listened for hours to tapes of her favorite piano concertos while she designed and appliquéd her original quilts, pillows and stuffed animals.

"I know a silly song your grandma Arnold would sing to you if she were here." She kissed his pink cheek and took his hands, touching each finger as she sang. "'Hinty, minty, cutie, corn, apple seed and apple thorn, Riar, briar, limber lock, six geese in a flock, Sit and sing, at the spring, o-u-t out again!'" She made his arms fly wide and he began to laugh, a real belly laugh that surprised and delighted her. They did this several times before Cassie heard a woman's call from another part of the house. Not long afterward, the trim sixtyish housekeeper appeared on the patio carrying two heaped plates of taco salad. Trace followed with the high chair in one arm and Jason in the other.

"I've got to meet the brave young woman who made it past Mrs. Blakesley and presented you with your son!"

She beamed at Cassie, who rose to her feet and balanced Justin against her hip while the older woman put the plates on the table. After wiping her fingers on her apron, she held out a hand, which Cassie shook. "I'm Nattie Parker and I have to tell you this is probably the most exciting day of my life! Talk about the spitting image!"

Cassie's eyes filled with tears as she looked at Jason. "He is, isn't he? And Justin is so much like my sister and her husband, I'm still in a daze. In fact, none of this seems real." She couldn't resist kissing Justin's silky blond head.

Nattie nodded in agreement. "That was a switch for the books. And to think you've been looking for Jason's daddy all this time, and Trace almost sent you away with the police. Shame on you, Trace," she said in a stern voice, but love for her employer shone through.

The woman's raisin-dark eyes fastened on Jason. "I can't wait another second to get my hands on him. He has the kind of solid little body you just want to squeeze, d'you know what I mean?"

"I know exactly," Cassie said, loving Nattie on the spot. She let her gaze wander to Trace, who was tenderly eyeing both his sons. One day Jason would grow into the same kind of vital, handsome, dynamic man....

At the moment, though, Jason was struggling with Nattie. He stopped when she handed him a cracker from her pocket; she gave another one to Justin with a quick kiss. "Come on, young man," she told Jason. "You can go with me to get the baby food. What would you like today? Beans and lamb? That's what your brother's having."

As she walked away chatting, Trace motioned Cassie to a chair. "Are you sure you want to feed Justin?"

"Positive," she asserted, placing him on her lap. Despite the cracker halfway in his mouth, he reached for the salad, which she pushed out of his way.

Turning her attention to Trace, who'd gone to the bar behind them, she said quietly, "Do you know what thrills me? He uses both hands in all his movements. That means he has the full use of his arm. He'll be able to do any sport or activity Jason can do." She paused to remove her fork from Justin's eager clutches. "Tell me what the doctors say about him."

Trace supplied napkins and iced fruit drinks before taking his seat. Their eyes met. "It's called an amniotic band. It tightened around his arm in the womb, cutting off some of the blood supply. The specialist says physical therapy to build up his muscles can begin when he turns three. By the time he's an adult, the defect will hardly be noticeable."

She leaned down and kissed Justin's smooth shoulder. "Well, aren't you the luckiest little boy in town. I wonder if you'll turn out to be as great a tennis player as your father. You're built just like him."

Trace looked pensive as he ate a forkful of salad. "Genes don't lie, do they?"

"No." She ate a mouthful of cheese and guacamole, then let Justin try a little of her pineapple drink.

"When did your sister first suspect Jason wasn't her son?"

"Her baby was rushed to the infant intensive-care unit as soon as he was born. A little later, the pediatrician told her he'd had trouble breathing on his own. She didn't actually hold him for about eight hours.

"When he was finally brought to her, his black hair and olive skin were so different from what she'd expected, she couldn't believe Jason was hers and told me as much over the phone. But since Susan's and my baby pictures show us with dark hair, I assumed Jason's hair would turn blond after a few months and didn't take her seriously. Until I saw him for the first time, that is."

Trace let out an audible sigh. "Unfortunately, I wasn't there for the delivery. The baby came sooner than we expected, and by the time I arrived at the hospital, Gloria was in her room and the baby was in the intensive-care unit. About a half hour later the pediatrician came to tell us about Justin. I went down to the nursery with the doctor and saw Justin for the first time lying in one of those cribs. The switch must have occurred in the unit."

She nodded. "Susan said the baby was born at 9:05 a.m."

Trace put down his fork and looked at her solemnly. "Our son was born at 9:04. And your sister was right. There were ambulances all over the place when I arrived. The chemical plant outside Phoenix blew up, killing a dozen people and sending dozens more to various hospitals. The place was swarming with hospital personnel, relatives, reporters. Because of all the confusion, I was delayed getting to Gloria's room."

She closed her eyes. "It sounds so impossible, so incredible, and yet that must explain why there was a mix-up. Do you think we should demand an investigation and lodge a formal complaint to prevent this from happening to anyone else?"

He was quiet so long she didn't know if he'd heard

her. "Part of me says yes. Another part says accidents do happen, even when the greatest precautions are taken. Probably the chances of such a thing occurring again are something like a billion to one."

"I've thought that myself. We know it wasn't intentional."

After a pause he said, "In principle, I'm opposed to unnecessary litigation. This has become a sue-happy society. So, on balance, I'm against suing."

Cassie didn't realize she'd been holding her breath. "I'm glad you said that. I don't think I could handle an official investigation after everything I've been through in the last year with Ted's death—he was killed in an accident—and then Susan getting sick and...and dying." Not to mention Rolfe's recent engagement to a woman overseas, which had come as a painful shock to Cassie. She and Rolfe—her life-long neighbor—had always been close, although she'd put off making a decision about marriage. But she'd assumed that when his studies were over, he would come home and they'd work things out.

"The newspapers would get hold of it and the publicity would be horrible," she said, shuddering at the prospect. "In the end, all it would do is damage the hospital's reputation and ruin people's lives. I don't want this to affect the boys."

"I agree," Trace concurred in a sober tone. "However, we will get those blood tests and I'm going to write the hospital board a letter informing them what happened. I'll let them know that, though we're not pressing charges, we are requesting an unofficial inquiry to satisfy our questions. Indirectly it might prevent another mistake like this in the future."

"I think that's best, and I know Susan and Ted would have felt the same way. Mr. Ramsey, did you or your wife ever have any suspicions that Justin wasn't your son?"

He cocked one dark eyebrow. "I think at this stage we should dispense with the formalities. My name is Trace, and the answer to your question is a definite no. Gloria is a tall willowy blond with hazel eyes. Everyone assumed Justin inherited her coloring and slender build. But after looking at your sister and brother-in-law's photograph, I can see the resemblance to Gloria is superficial at best. Justin bears an unmistakable likeness to both his parents."

Cassie nodded in agreement. She wanted to ask him more questions about his wife, but Nattie's entry with Jason and the baby food prevented her. Jason now sported a bib, which he was trying to pull off.

While Trace relieved her of his son and slipped him into the high chair, Nattie put the food on the table. "Here's a bib for my golden boy." She tied it around Justin's neck. "Now all of you have a good lunch. I'll hold any phone calls to give you a chance to talk."

Trace didn't let Nattie escape until he had pressed her hand in a gesture that spoke volumes about their relationship. Justin was surrounded by people who loved him, and that knowledge brought the first modicum of peace to Cassie's heart.

For the next while Cassie told Trace about Ted's

fatal car accident en route to summer camp with the army reserve and Susan's subsequent depression, which led to one of her chronic bouts of pneumonia after a troubled pregnancy. Without Ted, she couldn't seem to endure.

Justin behaved perfectly while they talked. Half the time he managed the spoon by himself without making any mess. Cassie wished she could say the same for Jason. Though he loved the lamb, every time Trace gave him a spoonful of beans he'd keep them in his mouth for a minute, then let them fall back out. And worse, he smeared the top of his high chair so it resembled a finger painting.

Trace surprised her by being highly amused rather than irritated. She could hardly equate this patient caring man with the forbidding bank official who would have sent her from his office in handcuffs without a qualm.

Halfway through his peaches, Justin showed signs of being tired and his eyelids drooped. Jason was exhausted, as well. Unfortunately he tended to become even more restless and noisy before falling asleep.

She looked over at Trace who was chuckling at the funny sounds Jason made as he practically inhaled his fruit. "May I put Justin to bed?" she asked.

Trace flicked her a searching glance, then gently tousled Justin's hair. "Has too much excitement made my little guy sleepy? Why don't we take both of them upstairs? While you deal with Justin, I'll put Jason in the tub."

Cassie tried to smother a smile but failed. "I wish

I could tell you Jason isn't usually this impossible at meals, but it wouldn't be the truth.''

His lips twitched. ''I'm afraid when my mother finds out about this, she'll tell you I was much worse. Like father, like son.''

Carefully lifting Justin, she rose to her feet. ''Does your mother live here in Phoenix?''

''Not only Mother but the entire Ramsey clan.''

''You're a large family, then?''

''I have two brothers and a sister, all of whom are older with children,'' he informed her as she followed him to a hallway on the other side of the patio.

By now Jason's bib had been removed and Trace held his food-smeared son firmly around the waist. ''Ma-ma, Ma-ma,'' Jason cried when he realized he was being swept away from their cozy domestic scene by this dynamic stranger.

''Da-da's got you, Tiger,'' Trace said, mimicking his son. Cassie's heart leapt in her chest. No man had ever had this physical effect on her, not even Rolfe. She'd loved him from childhood; he was the man she'd planned her future around. But the grief Cassie had suffered over her mother's death, followed by Ted's fatal accident and Susan's illness, had taken its toll. She wasn't ready to set a wedding date. Rolfe, hurt and disillusioned, had accused her of not being in love with him and had broken their engagement. The next thing she knew, he had gone abroad to study music. He was a gifted musician who'd been offered more than one prestigious scholarship.

Before Susan died, she'd said that a separation was

exactly what Cassie and Rolfe needed. They'd never spent more than a week or two away from each other, and a year's separation would clarify their feelings. When they came together again, there'd be no hesitation on either side if a marriage between the two of them was meant to be.

Susan's remarks made a lot of sense to Cassie. But she hadn't considered the possibility that Rolfe would fall in love with someone else in the interim, nor that it would hurt so much. Now Susan was gone and Cassie would never again be able to confide in the sister who'd always been her best friend and confidante.

"Cassie?" Trace called over his shoulder with a puzzled expression on his face. "Are you all right?"

"Yes. Of course." She smiled. "I had to stop for a minute and look at all these watercolors. They're fabulous, just like the ones in your office."

"My sister, Lena, is one of the most talented artists I know, but she's so critical of her own work, she refuses to display any of her paintings in public."

"So you do it for her," Cassie murmured. She couldn't help but be touched by his loyalty to his sister. It was ironic, and somehow pleasing, that while she'd been reliving bittersweet memories of her own sister, she'd been gazing at *his* sister's work—a sister he obviously adored. There were many surprising and wonderful facets to Trace Ramsey's personality, as she was beginning to learn. "How many of Lena's paintings have you sold?"

"None," he said as they reached the second floor.

"She made me promise. In fact, she hasn't signed them. But if she ever changes her mind, my walls will be bare."

Cassie could believe it. In fact, there were several paintings here that gave her ideas for wall hangings and rugs, but they were fleeting images and she couldn't do anything about them now.

Justin's suite of rooms had the Southwest flavor of the rest of the house, but concessions had been made to practicality, creating a more traditional child's decor. Chocolate-brown shag carpeting covered the floors, and baby furniture filled the spacious room. A huge hand-painted mural took up one whole wall.

It was an enchanted-forest scene, with each little animal and insect possessing a distinct personality. Cassie was completely charmed by it and easily recognized the artist's hand. "Your sister painted this."

"Yes. That was Lena's gift to Justin," he called out from the bathroom. The minute the water started filling the tub, she could hear Jason's protests turn to squeals of delight. He always enjoyed his bath.

Cassie wondered if Justin liked the water, but she'd have to find out another time, because he was sound asleep, lying limp against her shoulder.

She gently placed him on his stomach in the crib and covered him with the cotton blanket. Automatically his thumb went to his mouth. He looked so blissfully content she didn't have the heart to pull it out again and risk waking him.

After leaning over to bestow one last kiss, she headed for the immaculate white bathroom accented, like the downstairs rooms, in natural wood. It was difficult to tell who was having a better time, Jason or his father.

Trace's white shirt-sleeves were rolled up above the elbows to display tanned forearms with a sprinkling of dark hair. His smile made him look years younger as he urged Jason to float on his back and kick his sturdy little legs. "That's it, Tiger. Make a big splash."

When water hit him in the face, he burst into deep-throated laughter. He sounded so happy that Cassie hated to disturb them. However, Jason had already caught sight of her standing there holding a fluffy tangerine-colored towel. He immediately tried to sit up, plaintively crying, "Ma-ma," and stretching out his arms.

"I'm afraid we've got to get going," she said apologetically to Trace who looked distinctly disappointed by the interruption. With undisguised reluctance, he wrapped Jason in the towel and started to dry him. "My luggage is being held at a motel in West Phoenix," Cassie went on. "We'll have to stop there on our way to the airport."

Trace frowned and she knew why. But he didn't understand what it was like to live on a budget. Even when her mother was alive and Susan was at home, they had all worked hard to make ends meet. And now that a future with Rolfe had slipped away, and with little Jason to support, she had to be more careful than ever how she spent her money.

In the short year and a half Susan and Ted had been

married, they had acquired some insurance and savings. But before her sister's death, Cassie and Susan had agreed that any money would be invested for Jason's education. Cassie wouldn't have dreamed of touching it.

When she started to gather up Jason's soiled outfit, Trace told her to leave it for Nattie to wash. "He can wear something of his brother's for the flight back, can't you, Tiger?"

After diapering him on the bathroom counter, he reached into the drawer for a pale green stretchy suit with feet and put Jason into it. Then he playfully lowered his head to Jason's tummy and made a noise against it, producing a gale of infectious laughter from his dark-haired son.

In a very short time, Jason seemed to have overcome his fear of Trace. Much more of his father's attention and he wouldn't want to leave, a thought that troubled Cassie more than a little. This was his first experience with a man and he appeared to be enjoying it.

Cassie couldn't help wondering if her letter telling Rolfe about her plan to raise Jason as her own son had something to do with his recent engagement. His fiancée was another violinist, a woman he'd met in Brussels. Cassie was tempted to phone him long-distance, despite the cost; that way, they could really talk. Maybe expecting him to take on Jason if he married her was asking too much.

Then again, maybe he was truly in love with this other woman. Cassie was so confused she didn't know what to think. They'd been childhood sweethearts and had turned to each other whenever problems arose. She'd never stopped loving him and didn't think he'd stopped loving her, either.

Peeking in on Justin one more time, Cassie had to resist the impulse to kiss him, for fear of waking him. He looked like Susan while he slept, a fair-haired angel with flushed pink cheeks. Once again she felt that tug of emotion and hoped, somehow, that Justin's parents knew their little son was happy and well in Trace's home and heart.

In no time at all, Cassie had thanked Nattie and was following Trace outside to the BMW. Without giving her a choice, he ensconced her in the front seat. As he strapped his son in the back, she could tell he had some serious concern on his mind.

Once again he wore that look of determination. It made her uncomfortable, and she wished Jason was fussing so she'd have a reason to hold him in her arms as a buffer against Trace. But Jason's eyelids were fluttering, which meant he was ready to fall asleep any second.

When they had driven away from the house and were headed for the motel, Trace darted her a swift glance. "I want Jason close to me, Cassie," he said, using her name for the first time. "I've already missed his first nine months, and I refuse to lose out on any more time. I can tell you want to be with Justin just as badly. Let's be honest and admit the odd weekend here, the three-day holiday there, will never be enough for either of us."

Cassie had been thinking hard about that, too. Already the wrench of having to leave Justin hurt unbearably. But how soon would she be able to break away from her work to fly here again? With Christmas only three weeks away, this was her busiest time.

The money made from holiday sales would support her and Jason for at least five or six months. She didn't dare lose out on her most lucrative time of year. And her other job, playing piano for ballet classes four mornings a week, made it impossible to get away for more than a couple of days at a time.

"I agree with you, Trace, but I don't have any solutions, because I'm swamped with work and I know you are, too. I was going to suggest we trade the children from time to time."

The angry sound that came out of him made her shiver and immediately told her she'd said the wrong thing.

"Out of the question. As far as I'm concerned, six months with one parent, then six with the other is no alternative."

"I don't see that we have a choice."

"There's always a choice," he muttered in what she imagined was his banker's voice. "You could move to Phoenix with Jason."

She jerked her head around and stared at him in astonishment. "That would be impossible. I may not own a banking corporation, but my business is just as important to me. It relies on a clientele that's been built up over two generations of sewing for people. My mother taught Susan and me the business. Now

I've branched into handicrafts. I wouldn't even know where to start if I had to relocate to a different city."

At this point they arrived at the motel. Without responding to her remarks, he got out of the car and went into the office to get her luggage. Within minutes he'd stashed it into the trunk and was back in the driver's seat. Before starting the car, he pulled a little black book from his pocket and asked for her address and phone number in San Francisco. Grudgingly she gave him the information; then they drove in painful silence to the airport, where he found a vacant space in the short-term parking lot.

He didn't immediately get out of the car. Instead he turned to her with a dangerous glint in his eye. "I'm warning you now that if we can't work this out, I'll take you to court and sue for custody of Jason."

*"You don't mean that!"* she burst out angrily, but the grim set of his jaw told her he did. Her heart was pounding so fiercely she was sure he could hear it.

"I'm his natural father and I'll be able to provide for his financial well-being in a way you never could. There isn't a judge in the state who would allow you to keep him. Bear in mind that the hospital will be called in to prove paternity and it could get messy."

"You told me you didn't approve of people who sued other people," she said, her voice shaking in fear and fury.

His eyes narrowed menacingly. "If you recall, I said, 'in principle.' But we're talking about Jason here, and what's best for him. You've already told me you're not married or even engaged." *But only because she'd put off Rolfe one too many times. Maybe it still wasn't too late.* "In fact," he continued, "I gathered from our conversation at lunch that you're not even dating anyone special who could help you raise him. You've only taken care of him for two months. You're not his parent. You're not even related."

"Now you listen to me!" Cassie whispered hoarsely, trying not to wake Jason by shouting. "I love that child with every fiber of my being. You're not related to Justin, either!"

"Justin's been my son since birth, and no judge will take him away from me. As his aunt, the most you can expect will be liberal visitation rights and a bill for exorbitant court costs and attorney's fees. Think about it, and give me your answer tomorrow night. I'll phone you at ten."

"Give you *what* answer?" she lashed out. "Do you know what you're asking? That I leave my whole life behind and move to a strange city with no friends, no support system, just so you can have your cake and eat it, too?"

"Naturally I'll provide for you and make sure you're comfortably settled until you can get your business going here. With my contacts, you would have no problem. Would that be such a penance when it means we would both have daily contact with the boys for the rest of our lives?"

Cassie didn't want to hear another word. "Aside from the fact that the idea is ludicrous, has it occurred to you what people would say? People who don't know the true situation? I noticed you didn't bother to explain anything to Mrs. Blakesley. She probably thinks I'm one of your mistresses who suddenly showed up to ask for money."

"I'm not particularly worried about what Mrs. Blakesley thinks," he countered smoothly.

"Maybe you're not concerned about your reputation, but I value my good name more than that!"

"More than you value a life with Jason and Justin?" His question was calculated to reduce her arguments to the trivial. But by now she was on to his tactics.

"You can phone me all day and all night, but it won't do you any good. I guess I'll have to take my chances and let the judge decide when I can spend time with Jason and my nephew. See you in court!"

She didn't, couldn't, hide the disgust and anger in her eyes or her voice. Jumping from the car, she yanked the back door and reached for Jason, who was still sleeping soundly. Trace finally got out of the car to collect her bags from the trunk.

Unable to bear his presence another second, she walked toward the terminal with the baby in one arm, her tote bag in the other. Right now she wanted to put as many miles as possible between them. All the way back to San Francisco, she regretted her trip to Phoenix and wished she'd never heard of Trace Ramsey.

## CHAPTER THREE

CASSIE TAPPED on her neighbor's door and let herself in. "Beulah? I'm back."

After climbing all those steep streets from the ballet studio in the bitter cold, the apartment felt toasty and inviting. San Francisco had been locked in fog since the night she'd flown in from Phoenix more than a week ago. It seemed to penetrate everything, including the ski sweater she wore over her sweatshirt.

"I'm in the studio," Beulah Timpson called out. The older woman had been like a favorite aunt to Cassie and Susan, and had come close to being Cassie's mother-in-law. For as long as Cassie could remember, Beulah, a talented ceramist, had lived with her three children in the apartment above the Arnolds'.

Cassie and Susan had been best friends with Beulah's two daughters and her son, Rolfe. It was in her late teens that the close friendship Cassie shared with him gradually changed into something else. When Susan's and Cassie's mother fell ill with cancer, Rolfe became a source of strength. Cassie turned to him more and more, and learned she could always depend on him to offer help and compassion.

Soon after her mother's death, he told her he loved her and wanted to marry her. Cassie happily accepted his modest engagement ring; by that time they were both seniors at the university, studying music theory. He played the cello and she the piano.

Rolfe wanted to get married immediately after graduation, but Cassie couldn't see any reason for urgency, since they were constantly together, anyway, and had no money. She encouraged him to get his master's degree in music while she worked on expanding her home sewing business. A year down the road as a Ph.D student, he'd be able to earn extra money teaching undergraduates. By that time, she would have saved enough money for a small wedding and a honeymoon. They'd live in her apartment, since Susan had already married and moved to Arizona.

Unlike Susan, who married Ted within eight weeks of meeting him, Cassie wasn't in any hurry. She needed time to regain her emotional equilibrium first. The loss of their mother had been bad enough. But when she received the horrifying news of Ted's untimely death, Cassie went into a severe depression. At that point, her constant worry about her pregnant sister, whose history of chronic pneumonia put her at risk, made it impossible for Cassie to think about her own needs, or Rolfe's.

Then came a night when everything changed. For the first time since she'd known him, Rolfe didn't seem to understand. In fact, he refused to hear any more excuses and demanded that she set a wedding date—the sooner the better. Since they'd already been over that ground more than once, Cassie was surprised by his demands. She'd never seen him so insistent and unyielding. She asked him to leave the apartment, saying they'd talk again in the morning, when their nerves weren't so frayed.

But he stayed where he was. In a voice that shocked her with its anger, he accused her of using him. Cassie shook her head in denial, but he was obviously too hurt to listen to reason and asked for his ring back. When she begged him to be patient a little longer, the bitterness in his eyes revealed his hurt and disillusionment. He retorted that he hadn't pressured her to live with him because she didn't approve of premarital sex. And since she couldn't set a date for the wedding, he had to conclude she wasn't in love with him.

Cassie hadn't been prepared for that, nor for his declaration that he'd been offered a fellowship to study in Belgium and had decided to accept it. He held out his hand and Cassie wordlessly returned the ring.

He left at spring break, plunging her into a different kind of despair, one of profound loneliness. But by then Jason had been born and Susan was seriously ill. Looking back on that dreadful period, Cassie wondered how she'd survived at all. If Jason hadn't needed a mother's love and attention even before Susan died, Cassie might have died of grief herself. And still Rolfe stayed away.

Through it all, Beulah never pried or made judgments. As a result, the two of them were able to remain firm friends. Now that her children lived in other parts of the state, Beulah seemed to encourage Cassie's friendship, even volunteering to tend Jason in the mornings.

Walking through the apartment to the workroom, Cassie found the older woman at her potter's wheel. She stopped short when she didn't see the playpen. "Where's Jason?"

Beulah was throwing clay and didn't pause in her movements. "He's downstairs in your apartment with his daddy."

"Beulah! You didn't!"

"I did." She concentrated on her work for a moment. "First of all, he's not here to kidnap Jason. He assured me of that and I believe him." Her voice was calm and matter-of-fact. She glanced up at Cassie, smiling. "The two of them are carbon copies of each other, just like you said. Since Jason seemed perfectly happy to go with him, I couldn't see that it would hurt. I never saw a man so crazy about a child in my life. Watching them together made my Christmas."

All the while she was talking, Cassie held on to the nearest counter for support. *She should have known he would come.* Hanging up on him every time he called had probably infuriated him. But she had none of the answers he wanted to hear.

After agonizing over the situation for endless hours, Cassie had decided a judge would have to sort it out. Though she ached to know and love Justin, it was clear that her nephew's world was complete and revolved around Trace. If she was patient, the law would eventually dictate visitation rights so she could get close to Susan's son.

As for Jason, she'd hang on to him as long as possible. There was no doubt in her mind that she'd lose him in the custody battle Trace was planning. In fact, he'd probably come to San Francisco to make sure she'd given him the right address before he had her served with papers. His presence meant she couldn't prolong the inevitable confrontation.

"Well? Aren't you going to go find the man and say hello? He flew all the way from Phoenix early this morning to see you. What are you afraid of?"

"I'm going to lose Jason."

"Nonsense. From everything you've told me about him, he isn't the kind of man who'd cut you out of Jason's life. Especially once he knows the personal sacrifice you went through trying to find him in the first place. Cassandra Arnold, it's because of you that he's been united with a son he didn't know existed. Do you think he's going to forget a thing like that? Or the fact that Justin is Susan's child?"

"You weren't there when he threatened me with a custody suit." She shuddered at the memory.

"No, I wasn't. But that was a week ago, and he's had time to think since then. So have you. The least you can do is hear what he has to say. You owe him that much after refusing to take his phone calls."

Since there was no help from that quarter, the only thing left to do was go downstairs and see him, get it over with.

A feeling of dread formed a knot in her stomach

as she thanked Beulah and headed for the ground-floor apartment, which was the only home she'd ever known.

After their mother's death, Cassie and Susan had taken over her business and pooled all their resources so they could continue to live there. When Susan and Ted moved to Arizona because of his job, Cassie stayed in the apartment. Although half the contents went off to Phoenix in the moving van, the place was still crowded to overflowing with furniture and mementos accrued over a lifetime. Cassie took the opportunity to clean house and quickly turned her home into a crafts shop of sorts. Right now, it was filled with Christmas orders—quilts, afghans, wall hangings, pillows, rag dolls, hand puppets, stuffed animals... The list went on and on.

Every nook and cranny of the small living and dining room contained evidence of her handiwork. Trace wouldn't be able to find a place to sit down. Even the top of the upright piano and bench were covered with stuffed Santas, reindeer and gingerbread men.

The two bedrooms were even worse. She kept her sewing machine and all the patterns and materials in her room, which hardly left enough space for her to crawl into bed at night.

Jason's room had become the depository for the larger stuffed animals and figures. They stood side by side, lined up against all four walls.

By Christmas Eve she should be able to find her furniture again. She'd had to put their two-foot Christmas tree with its homemade ornaments in the middle of the kitchen table. Jason loved the miniature lights and stared at them in fascination while he played with his food.

Taking a deep breath, Cassie entered the kitchen through the back door. She could hear Jason's shrieks of delight coming from the vicinity of his room. He was obviously thrilled to have his father there, and Cassie had to admit that fatherhood seemed to come naturally to Trace. It was possible that he'd already been given a court date; in that case, it wouldn't be long before Jason went to live with him and Justin.

She felt a pain in her heart as real as if she'd been jabbed with a knife. Maybe it was best he had come, after all. She couldn't live with the anxiety any longer.

Pushing the bedroom door open a little wider, she peeked inside. Jason was sitting in front of Trace, who was dressed in cords and a crew-neck black sweater, lying full-length on the carpet with his back toward her. His dark head rested on the five-foot-long green alligator Cassie had made for Susan. She'd added yellow yarn, to represent Susan's blond hair, and sewn the word "mommy" on the tail.

In Trace's hand was the eighteen-inch baby alligator with a green-and-yellow body and black yarn for hair; it bore Jason's name on the tail. He continued to tease Jason, tickling him gently and making him laugh so hard he was thrashing his arms and legs.

Suddenly Jason saw Cassie. He pointed a finger and tried to say, "Ma-ma," but couldn't get the words out and laugh at the same time. Alert to his every movement, Trace turned over on his back, resting his hand on the alligator's head.

His blue eyes searched hers for a long breathless moment. At least they didn't freeze her out as they'd done at the airport. "Hello, Cassie." Slowly his gaze traveled from her sweater-clad figure to her windblown hair and cheeks turned pink from the cold outside. "Your neighbor let us in. She seemed to think it would be all right."

Strangely affected by the intimacy of his look, Cassie smoothed the curls from her forehead in a nervous gesture. "I'm sorry you couldn't find a place to sit."

A smile lurked at the corner of his mouth. "Since Justin came into my life, I've discovered the floor is a wonderful place to be. You meet all kinds of fascinating creatures." He rubbed his thumb over the alligator's glassy eyes. "Do you know I'm feeling deprived? There's no daddy alligator. I'm putting in an order for one right now. About six feet long with wild black hair and a scary grin, just like Jason's."

It sounded very much as if he was extending the olive branch. How could he be talking this way when they had resolved nothing? She was still reeling from the bitterness of their last encounter.

"Come on, Jason. It's time for a nap." She stepped over Trace and scooped the baby up from the floor. Trace stayed where he was while she changed Jason's diaper and put him in his crib with a bottle. It was actually time for his lunch, but she'd feed him later, after his father had left.

Right now she needed to know what Trace had on

his mind, and she didn't want Jason upset if the conversation turned into another angry battle. "Let's go into the kitchen. Jason will settle down in a little while."

By tacit agreement they left him crying. She knew he was wailing out his disappointment and fury; he'd been having such a wonderful time, and then she'd come along and spoiled everything. It didn't make Cassie feel any better. But this talk with Trace was crucial—and there was no sense in postponing it.

When they reached the kitchen, she offered him a seat and began to fix cocoa for both of them. Nobody was going to say she was uncivilized on the way to her execution!

Because of the fog, the room was darker than usual, and the lights on the tree twinkled all the more cheerfully. Suddenly she felt too warm, with Trace so close and vital and alive. She pulled off her ski sweater and hung it over a chair back.

When she'd prepared the hot chocolate, she placed their mugs on the table and sat down opposite him. Briskly pushing the sleeves of her navy sweatshirt up to the elbows, she began, "I shouldn't have hung up on you—" she paused for a deep breath "—even though I was angrier than I've ever been in my life."

"I wasn't exactly on my best behavior last week," he admitted gravely. "Court isn't where I want to settle our problems."

Cassie had been expecting to hear anything but that. "I—I know how much you love Jason. He's your flesh and blood. The problem is I love him, too." Her voice had that awful quiver again. "And I love Justin because he's part of my flesh and blood."

"I know." He sounded totally sincere.

She raised tortured eyes to him. "No matter how I try to come up with a satisfying compromise, it sounds horrible becau—"

"Because that's precisely what it is. A compromise," he finished for her. "The only way I see out of our dilemma is to get married. That's why I'm here. To ask you to consider the idea seriously."

*"Married?"* She felt the blood drain from her face. In the interim that followed, Jason's cries sounded louder than ever.

Trace took a long swallow of cocoa. "Surely I don't have to point out the advantages to you. With everything legal, your reputation won't suffer, Justin and Jason will have a mother *and* a father, and we'll have the joy of raising the children together in our own home."

"But we don't love each other!"

He gazed steadily into her eyes. "Our marriage will be a business arrangement. Separate bedrooms. You'll be able to start up your crafts shop in Phoenix without the worry of having to meet the monthly bills. And I'll have the satisfaction of going to work every day knowing the boys are with the only person who could ever love them as much as I do."

Her hands tightened around the mug. "But you're still young, Trace. One day you'll meet someone you truly want to marry. Just because your first marriage didn't work out doesn't mean there isn't someone else in your future."

"That works both ways, Cassie," he said in a deceptively soft voice. "You're a very attractive woman. I'm surprised you didn't get married years ago." *Rolfe tried,* a niggling voice reminded Cassie. "But the fact remains, I've been married once in the full sense of the word and have no particular desire to repeat the experience. As far as I'm concerned, the only issue of importance here is the children. They need *us,* you and me. And they need us *now!* Some experts say that the first three years of a child's life form his character forever. If that's true, I would prefer if you and I were the ones guiding and shaping the boys' lives."

She couldn't sustain his penetrating glance and pushed herself away from the table. In two steps she'd reached the window, but even if the mist hadn't been so thick, she wouldn't have seen anything.

What Trace Ramsey had proposed was a marriage in name only. A marriage of convenience, her mother would have called it. Cassie had heard the term, but she'd never known anyone who had entered into such an arrangement. It sounded so cold-blooded. No expectations of physical or romantic love. Just a convenient solution to a problem that concerned them both. The children needed parents, and she and Trace Ramsey could honorably fill that need and still stay emotionally uninvolved.

She heard the scrape of Trace's chair against the linoleum as he stood up and came to stand next to her. "I know what you're thinking, Cassie. You're considerably younger than I am, and you have a right to a life of your own. But as long as we're discreet, we could see other people on the side, no questions asked. If some time down the road either of us wanted out of our contract to marry someone else, well... we'd face that when it happened."

She gripped the edges of the sink so hard her knuckles turned white. "I think you're forgetting your ex-wife. Maybe she never bonded with Justin because, like Susan, she sensed he wasn't her baby. If she was to see Jason, isn't it possible she'd fall in love with him? I could certainly understand if she wanted another chance at marriage with you under those circumstances."

Cassie wheeled around so she could read his honest reaction, but that was a mistake. Her kitchen was minuscule even with no one in it; now, with Trace blocking her path and the faint scent of his soap filling her nostrils, she felt almost claustrophobic.

"I'm way ahead of you, Cassie," he replied evenly, his hands on his hips. "I phoned her the evening you left Phoenix, but she was still in chambers so I sent her an overnight letter."

"And?" She held her breath, unsure what she wanted Trace to tell her.

"She never responded."

"Maybe she hasn't had time, or hasn't even seen the letter."

"You're very generous to make excuses for her,

but no." He shook his head. "I talked with Sabie, her housekeeper. Gloria read the letter."

"And she didn't want to see Jason immediately?" Cassie cried, incredulous.

"I knew she wouldn't. But on the off chance that she'd gone through a complete character change, I told her to let me know and I would make it possible for her to spend time with Jason. Otherwise, if I didn't hear from her, I would assume it made no difference to her."

"But Jason is her own baby!"

Something flickered in his eyes. "Not all women have motherly feelings, Cassie. She never pretended to be anything but what she is, a remarkable attorney who is now a city-court judge and hopes to one day sit on the Supreme Court."

Cassie couldn't comprehend it. Talk about opposites attracting! She might search the earth and not come up with a more caring, devoted father than Trace. "Did you know she felt this way before you married her?" she asked in a quiet voice.

"If I hadn't made her pregnant, we would never have married."

She swallowed hard as she tried to take in what he was saying. "Didn't you love her?"

"We cared for each other. We also understood each other. Marriage was never in our plans, and I knew she'd give up the baby for adoption. I found I couldn't let her do that, so I struck a bargain with her. We would stay married long enough to satisfy protocol, then divorce with the understanding that I received custody of the child."

She blinked. "How often does she visit Justin?"

"She doesn't. She never has."

"Not once?" Her eyes grew huge.

He reached out and smoothed a stray curl from her forehead. At his touch her body trembled. The same gesture from Rolfe had never affected her this way. "That's why her lack of response to my letter doesn't surprise me. Is there anything else I can clear up for you?"

Needing to put distance between them, she slid past him and gathered the mugs from the table. "What would your family think?"

His wry smile seemed to mock her. "Whatever we want them to think. We can tell them that the moment we met, it was love at first sight. Or we can say nothing and let them draw their own conclusions. I'm a big boy now. I don't need my family's approval for what I do."

Her mouth had gone so dry she could hardly swallow. "I don't like lies."

"Then we'll tell them the truth. That we've decided to get married to provide a home for Justin and Jason. Period."

When he put it like that, so bluntly, she didn't know what to say. "E-Excuse me a minute, I have to check on the baby."

To her surprise he shifted his position, preventing her from leaving the kitchen. "I have a better idea. I'll leave—to give you time to think over my proposal. I'm at the Fairmont. Call me there when you've made your decision."

Her heart started to hammer. "How long will you be in San Francisco?"

"As long as it takes to get an answer from you."

She averted her eyes. "If the answer's no, what will you do?"

The muscles of his face went taut. "You're going to say yes. The boys need you too much. In your heart, you know it's the only solution. What was it your sister said before she died—*Find my son and take care of him for me?* Now you can honor her request and be Jason's mother at the same time."

On that note he disappeared from the kitchen and out the front door of the apartment.

So many thoughts and emotions converged at once that Cassie couldn't stand still. As if on automatic pilot, she tiptoed to Jason's room and discovered him sound asleep in a corner of his crib, with his cheek lying on his bottle.

The poor darling had finally worn himself out. Gently she pulled the bottle away and covered him with a light blanket. She thought of seeing him only on holidays, of missing his first steps and not being able to take him to kindergarten on his first day of school....

If she married Trace, she would have the luxury of being a mother to Justin, as well. The four of them would be a real family, in almost all the ways that mattered. Many things about Trace still remained a mystery, but the one thing she knew beyond any doubt was his devotion to the boys.

Not every man would have married his lover to obtain custody of his unborn child. And a small voice told her not every man would have wanted Jason on sight—no matter that Jason was the son of his body, no matter how precious he was. In that regard Trace Ramsey was a remarkable man.

*Was it enough?* Would it be enough for her? Could she marry him knowing the most important ingredient in the marriage was missing? Knowing that because of their loveless arrangement, she would never have a baby of her own?

Maybe Trace could conduct an affair on the side; in all probability he was seeing someone right now. But Cassie wasn't made that way and knew herself far too well. Perhaps her ideas were old-fashioned and out of date, but if she took marriage vows, she would hold them sacred until she died. Or until Trace asked her for a divorce....

Was that what worried her most? That one day he would fall deeply in love and want a real marriage with the woman who had captured his heart? The thought left Cassie feeling strangely out of sorts and depressed, which made no sense at all.

She'd wondered more and more about the things Rolfe had said to her the night he'd walked out. With hindsight, she could see how much she'd hurt him by putting him off. But during that long dark period, she hadn't been capable of making a decision, hadn't been ready to make a commitment. Instead of clinging to him as his wife, she'd left him hanging while she dealt with her grief.

And her refusal to go to bed with him had probably planted more seeds of doubt. But Cassie's mother had raised her girls to value their virginity, to reserve physical passion for their husbands. That was why Susan was so eager to get married. In fact, Susan's intense feelings for Ted were so different from Cassie's easygoing, comfortable relationship with Rolfe they weren't even in the same league.

Susan and Ted couldn't stay away from each other, couldn't keep their hands off each other. Cassie had never been able to relate to those feelings. She loved Rolfe and always would, but she could wait until their honeymoon to express her love.

If she married Trace, there would be no problems in that area because he wouldn't be making physical demands on her. He'd be seeing other women. She was sure he'd be the soul of discretion. The little she knew about Trace told her he'd go to great lengths to keep his private life private, so no gossip could hurt the boys. They meant everything to him.

So why was she hesitating? Was she hoping against hope that Rolfe would break his engagement and come back to San Francisco to take up where they'd left off? How had Rolfe been able to fall in love with another woman so fast? Was it because his fiancée was willing to sleep with him? Cassie tried not to think about him sharing intimacies with anyone else, because it hurt. And, she supposed, because it was humiliating.

If they *were* sleeping together, that meant Rolfe wasn't really missing Cassie. And if that was true, then he'd gotten over the pain of Cassie's rejection and was making plans for a future that didn't include her. But it hadn't been a rejection, only a plea for more time.

So where did that leave Cassie? She had no guarantee that a man would ever come along to love her, body and soul. At least if she married Trace, she'd be able to indulge her longing to be a mother. Otherwise she would remain on the fringes of Jason and Justin's lives, never really involved. She couldn't bear that.

For the rest of the day she kept busy playing with Jason and putting the finishing touches on an order for a pear tree with partridges. After six o'clock, the doorbell rang continuously with customers placing and picking up orders.

Not until she'd tucked Jason into bed and cleaned the kitchen did Cassie work up enough nerve to reach for the phone. It was almost eleven and she'd run out of reasons not to call. She'd made her decision.

Her heart pounded in her ears as she asked to be put through to Trace Ramsey's room, but after ten rings and no answer she hung up. Maybe he was out, or had gone to bed. Whatever the case, she'd have to wait until morning.

Perhaps it was just as well. If she awakened tomorrow still feeling she was doing the right thing, then she'd try to call him again.

Feeling oddly deflated despite her tension, she unplugged the Christmas-tree lights and took a long hot shower. She checked on Jason one final time, then hurried into her own bedroom, eager for sleep. As she turned down the covers, she thought she heard a knock at the door.

Beulah was the only person who ever bothered her this late at night, and she always phoned first. Cassie had never had trouble before, but there could always be a first time. With the stealth of a cat she tiptoed to the living room and listened to see if she'd been mistaken.

After a minute she heard another rap. "Cassie?" a voice called out in hushed tones. "It's Trace. Are you still up? I didn't want to wake Jason if I could help it."

*Trace?*

A kind of sick excitement welled up inside her. She braced her hand against the door for support.

"Just a minute," she whispered and rushed to the bedroom for a robe. After opening the door she belatedly remembered that her hair was still damp from the shower. Her natural curls had tightened into a mop of ringlets that only a good brushing could tame.

He stared down at her, the hint of a smile lurking in his startling blue eyes. The moist night wind off the bay had tousled his hair, and he wore a fashionable bomber-style jacket made of a dark brown suede. Cassie had no idea he could look so...so...

"The answer's yes, isn't it?" he said matter-of-factly. "Otherwise you'd have called me hours ago and told me to go back to Phoenix and start court proceedings. Because one thing you're not, Cassie, is a coward."

## CHAPTER FOUR

"Miss Arnold?" Nattie's voice carried to Justin's bedroom, which now contained a second bed for Jason.

Cassie turned as Trace's housekeeper entered the nursery. "Can't you and Mike bring yourselves to call me Cassie? I realize Trace only brought me and Jason to Phoenix twenty-four hours ago, but you and your husband have been so wonderful helping us to settle in, I feel like we're good friends already."

The older woman's eyes lit up. "If you're sure."

"I am. So, what is it?" She returned to the job of fastening an uncooperative Jason into his new outfit.

"Trace asked me to take over in here so you can finish getting dressed. He's one man who likes to be on time—particularly for his own wedding. I'll finish doing those buttons and take Jason downstairs to Justin and his daddy."

"I appreciate the offer, but he's dressed now," Cassie murmured as she slipped on his little white shoes and tied them with a double knot so he wouldn't kick them off. She gave him a kiss on the cheek and handed him to Nattie, who promptly carried him out of the room.

Cassie followed her more slowly and then headed to her own room. There were three guest bedrooms on the upstairs floor of the house, with the nursery at one end and Trace's private suite of rooms at the other. Since he'd told Cassie to choose a bedroom for herself, she'd picked the one closest to the children. That way she'd be able to hear them if they cried during the night.

Though the smallest of the three, her room had its own ensuite bathroom, and the wicker furniture plus the charming window seat created a cozy feeling that immediately made her feel at home. She'd already spent several hours gazing out over the fascinating desert landscape, with the mountains in the distance.

Off-white walls and soft yellow trim blended beautifully to give the room a timeless dreamy feeling. Large green plants stood grouped in one corner; they were reflected in the sheen of flawless hardwood floors stained a warm honey tone.

Cassie couldn't wait to design an area rug that would incorporate the room's colors in all their subtlety. But her thoughts were far removed from that particular project as she finished dressing for her wedding.

If the image in the mirror didn't lie, she *looked* like a bride. She wore the trappings of a bride—large, marquise-shaped emerald ring on the third finger of her left hand, matching emeralds on her ears, which were a wedding present from Trace, a cascade of orange blossoms on the shoulder of her simple white Thai silk dress with its scooped neck.

Five weeks ago she'd been living with Jason in San Francisco, heartbroken over her sister's death and Rolfe's engagement, working furiously at two jobs in order to build a business that kept her busy all hours of the day and night.

Right now, that Cassie seemed a different person. Trace had pampered her so thoroughly she hardly recognized herself anymore. Once she'd agreed to marry him, he had taken time off from his banking affairs to stay in San Francisco both before and after Christmas. He'd helped her with Jason and made all the preparations for the marriage and her move to Phoenix. Meanwhile she'd wound up her business and called her old friends with the news—friends she'd hardly seen in the past three years. Her responsibilities had made a social life impossible.

Not since Rolfe's tenderness at the time of her mother's death had she experienced anything approaching this extraordinary feeling of being looked after, taken care of. In fact, Beulah—who to Cassie's surprise approved of their forthcoming marriage—commented that all Cassie had to do was mention something and Trace had it done before she turned around.

When Cassie asked if they could be married before she met his family, with only the babies and Nattie and Mike for witnesses, Trace agreed to her wishes and arranged a private ceremony at the county clerk's office.

In certain ways, Trace was the equivalent of a fairy godfather, and even if their marriage wasn't a normal one, she knew she was a very lucky woman. She told herself not to dwell on the past or reminisce about what might have been. But it was impossible to forget that for most of her life she had imagined walking down the aisle with Rolfe.

Without conscious thought she pulled his framed picture from a box of mementos she hadn't yet put away. She sank down on the bed to study his lean, ascetic face one more time. She couldn't help wondering what he'd thought when he received her letter. She'd informed Rolfe that she was planning to be married after Christmas. She'd told him the truth—that she'd accepted Trace's proposal in order to be a legitimate mother to both boys. She also admitted that she still loved him, that she would always love him and hoped he'd forgive her for ever hurting him.

When there was no return letter from Belgium, Cassie had to accept the fact that he was truly lost to her, but it still hurt. "Oh, Rolfe..." She wept quietly for the many memories and the dream that was gone.

"*Cassie?* Are you ready yet?"

At the sound of footsteps she panicked and thrust the picture beneath one of the pillows on her bed. But she was too late. Trace had seen the betraying gesture and in a few swift strides crossed the room and reached for the frame.

After studying the photo for several seconds, he raised his head and stared at the moisture beading her eyelashes. "I've seen this man's picture before. In Beulah Timpson's place."

His face hardened and a dull red tinged his smooth-shaven cheek and jaw. She was immediately reminded of the implacable man she'd originally met, the one who had accused her of being part of a kidnapping scheme. "What's going on, Cassie? When I brought you here to see Justin that first day, you told me you were unattached. I assumed you were telling the truth." His voice barely concealed his anger.

Cassie slid off the bed, furious with herself for having inadvertently caused this friction when he'd gone out of his way to make everything so wonderful. From the beginning Trace had been completely honest with her; he deserved the same consideration.

"I grew up with Rolfe," she began in a low voice. "We were once engaged, but things didn't work out. He asked for his ring back, and now he's engaged to someone else, someone he met in Europe. I was saying goodbye to past memories. That's all." She gazed straight at him as she spoke.

Trace searched her eyes, as if looking for some little piece of truth she might have withheld. "The ceremony takes place at eleven. We still have forty-five minutes. It's not too late to back out."

*"No!"* she cried instantly, surprising even herself with her vehemence.

He pondered her outburst for an uncomfortably long moment. "Be very sure, Cassie—and not just for the boys' sake."

For some reason his comment sent her pulses racing. "I am," she answered without hesitation, realizing she meant it.

He squared his shoulders and the tautness of his

facial muscles seemed to relax. He tossed the picture onto a stack of photos piled in a cardboard box beside her bed. "Let's go, shall we?"

The next hour flew by as Mike took pictures of Cassie and Trace holding the children, both before and after they arrived at the courthouse. Justin fussed because he'd come down with a cold. When the justice of the peace appeared and announced that it was time, Justin didn't want to let go of Trace, and that started Jason crying, too. Poor Nattie and Mike had to hold the children and try to pacify them while Trace grasped Cassie's hand and led her to the center of the room.

Despite the noise and impersonal surroundings, Cassie felt the solemnity of the occasion and wished more than ever that her mother and Susan were alive to share this moment with her. They would have loved Trace on sight. Not even Beulah was immune.

Out of the corner of her eye she darted a glance at her husband-to-be, who stood erect and confident. His snowy white shirt and midnight-blue suit not only enhanced his attractiveness but underlined his power; the red carnation he wore in his lapel added a note of festivity and joy. *I'm actually marrying this man*, she mused in awe and felt her heart turn over.

The justice of the peace bestowed a warm smile on them. "Cassandra Arnold and Trace Ellingsworth Ramsey, after this ceremony, today will be the first day of your life as a married couple. You've come together in the sight of God and these witnesses to pledge your troth. Do you know what that means?"

He eyed them soberly, capturing Cassie's whole attention.

"It means commitment and sacrifice. It means enduring to the end, long after the fires of passion are tempered with the earning of your daily bread. It means forgetting self and living to make the other person happy, no matter the season or circumstances. Will you do that, Cassandra? In front of these two witnesses, do you take this man, of your own free will, to be your lawfully wedded husband?"

Cassie felt Trace's heavy-lidded gaze upon her. "Yes."

"And you, Trace? Of your own free will and in front of these two witnesses, are you willing to take Cassandra to be your lawfully wedded wife, to assume this solemn responsibility of caring for her all the days of your life? Are you willing to put her before all others, emotionally, mentally and physically?"

Cassie thought his hand tightened around hers. "Yes," came the grave reply.

"If you have rings to exchange, now is the time. You first, Cassandra."

Cassie had been wearing the simple gold band she'd bought for Trace on her middle finger so she wouldn't lose it. She quickly removed it and slid it on Trace's ring finger. The fit was perfect, and he gave her a private smile that unaccountably stirred her senses.

"Now you, Trace."

Cassie held out her left hand so Trace could nestle

the white-gold wedding band next to the beautiful emerald engagement ring he'd given her on the plane as they'd flown to Phoenix. His movements were sure and steady.

"That's fine." The officiant smiled once more. "Now, by the power invested in me by the state of Arizona, I pronounce you husband and wife. It's not part of the official ceremony to kiss the bride, but..."

Before the man had even finished speaking, Trace's head descended and his mouth swiftly covered Cassie's as he pulled her close, sending a voluptuous warmth through her body. Cassie hadn't expected more than a chaste kiss on the lips. She wasn't prepared for the heady sensation that left her clinging to the lapels of his suit.

"Ma-Ma! Ma-ma!" Jason's and Justin's cries slowly penetrated her consciousness. Cassie moaned in shock and embarrassment, and broke the kiss Trace seemed reluctant to end. In that split second before she turned her burning face away, she thought she saw a smoldering look in his eyes. But by the time he lifted his head, it was gone. She decided she'd imagined it.

Moving out of her husband's arms, she shook the officiant's outstretched hand and thanked him, then hurried over to Nattie. Still holding Jason, the older woman gave her an awkward hug and murmured her congratulations. She handed the uncontrollable child to Cassie with a wry smile of relief.

He calmed down at once and started pulling orange blossoms out of her corsage. Trace was equally busy trying to pacify Justin, while Mike continued to take pictures. Cassie took one look at the flush on Justin's fair skin and said, "Trace, I think we'd better leave for the hotel. Justin should be in bed. He needs something to bring down his fever."

Within a few minutes the children were strapped into their seats in the back of Trace's sedan. Cassie hugged Mike and Nattie and thanked them again for everything, then at Trace's urging got into the car and they drove off.

The resort hotel, a few miles away in Scottsdale, had sent a basket of fruit and a congratulatory bottle of champagne to their suite. There were also two cribs; amused, Cassie wondered what the management thought about that as she busied herself putting the boys to bed, while Trace dealt with all the baby bags and luggage.

The hotel offered baby-sitting services, but Cassie didn't feel comfortable about leaving Jason and Justin with a stranger just yet. She urged Trace to go for a swim in the pool and relax. But he insisted on staying to help her settle the children, after he'd ordered lunch to be served in the room where he'd put his bags.

By the time both boys had fallen into an uneasy—and, as it turned out, short-lived—sleep, their lunch was more or less ruined. The pasta with its cream sauce had grown cold, the salad was soggy, the chilled white wine room-temperature. Cassie was too tired and anxious to care. All her attention was focused not on her new husband but on the two miserable little boys. Trace seemed equally distracted.

What should have been a fun three-day holiday, a chance for the four of them to really get to know each other, lasted exactly one sleepless night. Justin couldn't keep anything in his stomach; he was content only when Cassie or Trace held him. And as soon as Jason saw that Cassie's attention was diverted from him, he wailed loudly, and not even Trace could settle him down for long.

At eight the next morning, they packed up the car and drove home, frustrated and completely exhausted. It had become apparent that they would have to take Justin to his pediatrician as soon as they got home; in fact, Trace had called ahead from the hotel. Leaving Jason with Nattie, the three of them went to the clinic. Cassie was anxious to meet the man who'd been taking care of Justin, because he would automatically become Jason's doctor, as well.

Although Justin didn't have anything seriously wrong, several days went by before he was restored to his normal sweet disposition. Several weary, emotionally draining days, especially for Cassie. She'd spent all her time with the children since Trace had returned to his office to deal with some very delicate negotiations in his planned buy-out of a small Southwest banking chain.

Then, on Friday morning Trace shocked her by announcing that he'd invited everyone in his family to an informal garden party that evening to meet his new wife and son. Understandably enough, they were consumed with curiosity about his unexpected marriage. Gathering all the relatives under one roof, he told

Cassie, would provide the perfect opportunity to reveal the switch and to explain their subsequent decision to marry for the boys' sake.

Intellectually, Cassie saw the wisdom in getting it over with as soon as possible. Emotionally, she was numb.

Alone with Trace and the boys, she could relax as she performed the normal duties of a busy mother without worrying about others' reactions to their platonic union. Tonight, however, she would be on trial in front of a roomful of Trace's relatives—people who would draw their own conclusions about her motives for marrying a man who wasn't in love with her.

She couldn't blame them if they believed her to be a mercenary person attracted to his money and social prominence, someone willing to be bought in exchange for mothering his sons.

None of them would understand her bond with Jason or the happiness it brought her to raise him as her own son. Only Trace knew.

Cassie dressed in the same outfit she'd worn to her wedding and put on a fresh spray of orange blossoms Trace had thoughtfully sent her. Needing her husband's support as never before, she took a deep calming breath as she prepared to meet his family. She clutched Jason in her arms, hugging him tight, then mustered her courage and walked slowly downstairs.

From the landing she searched for Trace's dark hair among the group assembled on the patio. But she soon realized black hair dominated the family scene; there was only a sprinkling of sandy-brown and russet hair. She gazed down at the group, panicking just a little as she realized that the adults and children chatting with one another numbered at least forty.

Justin sat contentedly on his grandmother's lap, examining her pearl necklace—real pearls, Cassie was sure. His hair gleamed a pale gold in contrast to her coal-black tresses, swept back in an elegant chignon. His complexion was pale against her darker skin. Somewhere in her ancestry there must have been Indian blood. Even at seventy, Trace's mother was the most beautiful woman Cassie had ever seen. In fact, the whole family had more than its fair share of tall, good-looking people.

There was a sudden hush as Cassie walked out on the patio. Rolfe had often called her his "pocket Venus." And right now she was more aware than ever of her full curves and diminutive height. She felt even more conspicuous being the only person, aside from Justin, with a head of golden blond curls.

To her relief, Trace broke off his conversation with a man she guessed to be one of his brothers and strode toward her. In a light tan suit with an off-white Italian silk shirt open at the neck, he looked so incredibly handsome Cassie purposely glanced elsewhere to prevent herself from staring.

She thought he would reach for Jason. Instead, he slid a possessive arm around her waist and held her tightly against him. In confusion she gazed up at him, only to discover his eyes wandering over her face with unmistakable admiration.

At breakfast he had told her she would have nothing to worry about at the party. All she had to do was behave naturally and follow his lead. The trouble was, his act was too convincing, and she was distressed to find herself wondering how it would feel to be truly loved by this man. This complex man who presented a formidable, dynamic front to the public, yet could reduce her to tears with his sweetness when he kissed his sons good-night.

He turned to his family. "I know it came as a shock to hear that Cassie and I were married over the weekend. But what was I to do? My charming bride burst into my office a couple of months ago with an astonishing story—that Justin was really her nephew and that this little tiger was my natural son."

He reached for Jason, who'd been trying to wriggle out of Cassie's arms to get to his father. "It seems the babies were switched at birth." He paused dramatically at the incredulous murmurs around him. "We have subsequently found out that because of a disaster that stretched hospital resources to the limit, the infant intensive-care unit ran out of wrist tape. One of the nurses sent an orderly for more. When he returned, the identification bracelets were inadvertently put on the wrong babies."

The family's stunned reaction proved to be even greater than Cassie had imagined. For five minutes pandemonium reigned. It took another five before everybody settled down enough so that Trace could continue with the details. He briefly described the background—Ted's accidental death and Susan's unsuccessful struggle to throw off pneumonia, Susan's belief that Jason wasn't her son and Cassie's taking on the responsibility not only of raising her nephew but of uncovering the truth.

He kissed the top of Jason's curly head and unexpectedly smoothed a wayward lock of hair from Cassie's brow. Then, with a smile lighting his eyes, he said, "To make a long story short, the four of us got along so famously, we didn't want the fun to stop. So we decided to become a family." The sudden tremor in his voice added the perfect touch, almost convincing Cassie it wasn't an act. "Cassie, please meet my mother, Olivia Ramsey."

He turned to face the older woman. "Mother, may I present my wife, Cassandra Arnold Ramsey, and my son, Jason?"

"Trace!" Her cry held the joy Cassie had hoped to hear, dispelling her anxiety that Trace's mother wouldn't accept her new grandson—or her daughter-in-law.

While one of the wives relieved the older woman of Justin, Trace helped her to her feet. Dressed in deep-rose silk, she walked toward Cassie with the dignity of a queen.

"Welcome to the family, darling." She embraced Cassie warmly, then stood back, holding her lightly by the upper arms. Her deep-set, clear gray eyes searched Cassie's as if she were gazing into her very soul.

"I can't tell you how happy, how thrilled, I am by this news. Trace is my baby and he's always been my greatest worry. To see him settled at last, with a beautiful wife and two lovely children, has given me a whole new lease on life."

"Thank you, Mrs. Ramsey." Cassie could hardly form the words after the older woman's loving reception. That Trace's mother adored her youngest son was obvious. Cassie felt a sudden surge of guilt; she hated deceiving anyone, particularly this welcoming and truly gracious woman.

"Cassie, please feel free to call me Olivia, like my other daughters-in-law. 'Mrs. Ramsey' is so formal, isn't it?"

Cassie nodded, not trusting herself to speak as she blinked back tears.

"Mother?" Trace gently interrupted. "How about saying hello to my son. Jason?" He turned the baby around. "This is Nana. Na-na."

"Oh, Trace!" she cried, reaching for Jason, who showed all the signs of bursting into tears at the sight of so many strangers. "I can't believe I'm not thirty-three years old and holding you in my arms again. He's identical to you. Look, everybody! Another heartbreaker!"

*Heartbreaker is right,* Cassie thought, allowing herself a covert glance at her husband. He had probably been attracting the attention of the opposite sex since he'd been old enough to crawl!

But before she could dwell on that curiously disheartening fact, she and the baby were suddenly besieged with hugs and kisses. Such spontaneous warmth and affection made Cassie feel worse than ever about the pretense. All the cheerful joking from

James and Norman, who'd introduced themselves as Trace's brothers, told her the family assumed Trace was in love. And everything he said and did tended to verify their assumptions.

But the excitement proved to be too much for the babies. Once Jason started crying, Justin quickly followed suit. Cassie extricated herself from a group of nieces who were fighting over who got to hold Jason and hurried to retrieve Justin, who was clearly unhappy being tended by one of his aunts.

The second he saw Cassie his tears stopped and a smile appeared. It was clear that during his brief illness, a bonding had taken place between them. He reached eagerly for her and wrapped his arms around her neck. Together they wandered over to the banquet table the caterers had laden with everything from luscious fresh pineapple slices to salads and salvers of prime rib. Catering staff brought flutes of champagne and glasses of sparkling juice for the children.

As she handed Justin a piece of banana, Cassie caught sight of a group of latecomers walking out on the patio. She saw Trace, still carrying Jason, break away from the others and move toward a slender, auburn-haired woman.

Lena. Cassie could tell by the tender expression on her husband's face that he had a soft spot for his only sister. From what he had told Cassie, Lena resembled their father, Grant Ramsey, who had died of a stroke a few years earlier, leaving his children to carry on and expand the family business.

From the distance, Cassie watched in fascination as

Trace bent his head and filled Lena in on the details. Eventually Lena held out her arms to Jason, who refused to go anywhere and clung to his father. While everyone chuckled, Trace looked around until he spotted Cassie with Justin, then pointed her out to his sister. Lena left the group and hurried toward them.

Her hair had been drawn into a braid and hung over one shoulder. In comparison to Cassie's curves, Lena's build was thin and wiry. Except for the same proud chin, Cassie saw very little of Trace in his sister, whose pert nose and dark gray eyes made her face gamin rather than beautiful.

She leaned over to give Justin a kiss on the cheek, but he began to cry and tightened his hold on Cassie. Lena shrugged good-naturedly, then turned her attention to Cassie, eyeing her the way she might size up a scene she wanted to paint. "I'm Lena Haroldson, Trace's sister, and I have to tell you I'm speechless at the news. You have to be the reason Trace looks ten years younger tonight. If you can keep him this happy, I'll love you forever." She smiled warmly, then added, "Welcome to the family, Cassie."

Though the words were meant to be complimentary, Cassie's heart plummeted to her feet. It was obvious that Lena adored Trace and guarded his happiness jealously. And it was equally obvious that she was the one Ramsey Cassie would never be able to fool.

"Thank you, Lena. I—I'm going to try to make our home a happy one." At least that was the truth.

A mischievous smile lifted the corner of Lena's

mouth. "I'd say uniting Trace with Jason is a giant step in the right direction. I want to hear all about it from start to finish, but tonight's not the right time. I suspect Justin needs to go to bed. How about lunch next week when you're settled in? I'll take you to my favorite restaurant."

"I'd love it." Lena would never know how much her friendliness meant to Cassie. "In fact, I've wanted to meet you ever since I first saw your watercolors in Trace's office. They're good—very good."

Lena shook her head, but by the way her eyes lighted up, Cassie could tell she was pleased. "Trace told you to say that, didn't he?"

"No," Cassie declared baldly. "He was too busy trying to haul me off to jail on a kidnapping-extortion charge."

"What?" Lena gasped. "That doesn't sound like Trace. I know he's got a tough reputation when it comes to business, but he wouldn't dare do such a thing to you!"

"I'm afraid I would and almost did," a deep voice interjected. "But in the nick of time this little fellow saved his mother from the long arm of the law, didn't you, Tiger?"

Surprised, both women turned to Trace who had approached them unnoticed. Apparently Jason had had enough partying for one night. His pale blue outfit was crumpled and stained with what looked like fresh strawberry. In spite of Cassie's precautions in double-tying his shoes, he had managed to kick one off, which Trace held in his free hand.

"Mama!" Always vigorous, Jason practically propelled himself out of his father's arms to reach Cassie. If it hadn't been for Trace's lightning reflexes, he would have landed on the floor. By now, Justin was being just as impossible and refused to allow Trace to hold him.

"Well, well, little brother." Lena grinned at Trace. "It looks like you've got competition."

Trace sent Cassie an enigmatic look that for some reason gave her an uneasy feeling. "I don't mind, Lena," he muttered. "Now if you'll excuse us, we'll put the children to bed. Be a sweetheart and hold down the fort till we come back." He bussed his sister's cheek, then slid one arm along Cassie's shoulders.

As they made their way inside, everyone crowded around to say good-night to the boys. Cassie smiled and laughed, though it all felt a bit forced. Trace was making her unaccountably nervous.

"You didn't have to help me," Cassie murmured as they entered the nursery together. "Please feel free to go downstairs. It isn't very nice for both of us to disappear."

"You sound like you're trying to get rid of me," he said softly, but there was no amusement in his tone. "If I leave you on your own, you'll probably stay up here the rest of the night."

Perhaps he hadn't meant to sound critical, but his remark stung, increasing the tension she could feel building between them. She put a fresh diaper on Justin and eased him into his sleeper while Trace did the same for Jason. "Your family's wonderful. I wouldn't dream of offending them."

"Be that as it may, you seem to have no qualms about offending me." He paused, not looking at her. "Do me a favor. When we go back downstairs, pretend to like me a little bit."

His words produced a wave of heat that scorched her neck and cheeks. "I—I had no idea I had done anything else. I'm sorry, Trace."

After a slight pause he said, "It's not conscious on your part. You always treat me as if I wasn't there. I've never felt invisible before and don't particularly like the sensation. I thought we could at least be friends."

"We are." Her voice quailed despite herself.

"You have an odd way of showing it. Friends normally look at each other and smile once in a while, enjoy a private joke. You, on the other hand, reserve your affection strictly for the children. But you can't use them as a shield all the time."

She wheeled around, baffled by the total change in him. "A shield?" she cried, forgetting for the moment that their voices would keep the babies awake.

The dangerous glint in his eye unnerved her. "I don't know what else you'd call it. There aren't very many newlyweds who'd take two babies on their honeymoon."

*Honeymoon?* Cassie was aghast and looked away quickly. "After the chaos of Christmas and the move from San Francisco, I thought we agreed a little vacation with the children was exactly what we needed...so all of us could get acquainted away from the pressures of work and other people."

"If you recall, you were the one who suggested the idea. I simply went along with it, because I assumed you'd allow the hotel baby-sitters to take over once in a while to give us some time alone."

"I was afraid to trust them, particularly when Justin was running a temperature."

His jaw hardened. "That particular hotel has an impeccable reputation, with licensed sitters, a full-time registered nurse and a doctor always on call. If Justin had shown the slightest sign of any complication, we would have had the best care available at a moment's notice."

Her hands tightened on the bars of the crib. "I had no idea you weren't agreeable to the idea. You should have told me."

"I did, repeatedly, but you chose to ignore my hints and continued to cling to the children. Justin has become impossible. He knows all he has to do is look at you and you're right there to cater to his every whim. There *is* such a thing as a surfeit of attention."

*Had* she been spoiling Justin? Was Trace afraid she'd supplanted *him* in Justin's affections?

"I—I'm sure you're right. I've probably gone overboard in an effort to make up for lost time."

Her words didn't seem to mollify him. "You may not be sleeping in my bed, but in all other ways you're my wife, and there are things I expect of you besides being a mother to the boys."

*What things?* She had no idea all this had been seething inside him. "I'm not sure I understand you."

"How could you? We haven't had a moment to ourselves since we met!" He paused. "As chairman of the board, I attend a variety of social functions, and I do a certain amount of entertaining myself. Now that I'm married, it would create unnecessary and possibly damaging speculation if you didn't accompany me and fulfill your role as hostess when we're dining at home with friends and business acquaintances. Naturally the children won't be invited to those events," he added sarcastically. "Did you think you were being hired as a nanny when you accepted my proposal?"

"Not in so many words," she admitted, so confused by his anger that she didn't know what to believe. "But when you came to San Francisco, I was caught up in my feelings and concerns for the children—to the point that I wasn't capable of looking beyond their needs."

"That was almost two months ago, Cassie. It's time we talked about *our* needs."

His remarks caught her completely off guard. "Trace," she whispered, "your family is waiting for us. I don't think this is the time for the kind of discussion you seem to have in mind." She rubbed her palms agitatedly against her hips, noting that his eyes followed her movements with disturbing intensity.

There was a beat of silence, then, "For once you're right." He kept his voice low. "But be aware that I intend to pursue this after we say good-night to the family. In the meantime I would appreciate it if you'd join me in creating a united front. Mother would never admit it to you, but she's not as well as she pretends."

Unconsciously Cassie's hand went to her throat. "What's wrong with her?"

"She had a heart attack recently. The doctors have warned her to slow down and take life easier. Since our marriage seems to have brought her so much pleasure, the last thing I want to do is upset her. She happens to believe that the greatest happiness in life is achieved through a good marriage. My divorce, I'm sorry to say, hurt her deeply, and ever since the attack she's been worried she might die before she sees me settled with a wife and family of my own."

Inexplicably Cassie felt a strange, searing pain. Was *that* his underlying motive for asking her to marry him? The marriage would guarantee his mother's peace of mind and explain her reaction when they were introduced earlier in the evening. It was yet another example of Trace's unswerving devotion and loyalty to those he loved.

She took a deep, shuddering breath. "You know I wouldn't deliberately do anything to hurt her."

His hands curled into fists, then relaxed, as if he had come to the end of his patience. "All I'm asking is that you try to act more natural and comfortable with me—even when the children aren't around." He sighed. "I don't understand you, Cassie. I can't figure out if you're still in love with your ex-fiancé, or if he did something to put you off men for good."

# CHAPTER FIVE

TRACE GAVE HER no chance to respond. He grasped her hand and started for the hallway; she didn't try to resist. It shouldn't have come as any surprise that while they mingled with the family for the rest of the evening, he kept his arm firmly around her shoulders. It was a deceptively casual gesture, but Cassie knew that if she tried to pull away, she'd feel the bite of his fingers against her skin.

Shortly before the end of the party, as people were preparing to leave, he lowered his head to Cassie's ear. She couldn't tell if the caress of his mouth against her hot cheek was intentional or not, but his touch shot through her body like a spurt of adrenaline. "It's exceptionally warm tonight," he whispered. "Join me for a swim after everyone leaves...and we'll continue what we started upstairs."

She bit the soft underside of her lip. The thought of being alone with Trace in the swimming pool made her panic. Since the kiss he'd given her at their wedding, she'd become physically, sensually, aware of him—something that had never happened with Rolfe in all the years they'd spent together.

She found herself remembering things Susan used

to say about Ted. "I never want to say good-night to him, Cassie. One kiss isn't enough. All he has to do is touch me and I go up in smoke. Everything about him fascinates me, even the way he chews his toast. If we don't get married soon, I don't think either of us can hold out any longer."

Frightened that he could feel her trembling, Cassie eased herself away from Trace's hold. "First I'll have to help Nattie clean up."

"Nattie's job is to supervise the caterers, who were hired for that express purpose, and Mike has a whole retinue of gardeners to put the grounds in order. In case you're about to offer any other excuses, you can forget them. Tonight I need to be with my wife. Is a midnight swim and a little honest conversation too much to ask?"

His question whirled around in her brain as she said good-night to Trace's family and escaped to her bedroom. Out of breath from an attack of nerves and a heart that was pounding out of rhythm, she leaned against the closed door. That was when she spied a gaily wrapped package sitting in the middle of her bed.

There had been so many gifts since her arrival in Phoenix, she certainly hadn't expected any more. Curious, she walked over to pick it up, wondering if someone in the family—Lena?—had thought to welcome her with something a little more personal. Quickly she unwrapped the box and lifted the lid. A handwritten card had been placed on the layers of tissue.

"It occurred to me," the card read, "that Justin's cold wasn't the only reason you wouldn't swim with me in Scottsdale. In case you didn't have a decent suit and hadn't found the time to shop for one, I took the liberty of picking something out for you. The green matches your eyes. I couldn't resist. Trace."

Carefully she moved aside the tissue paper and eased out a two-piece swimsuit. It was more modest than some of the bikinis she'd seen on the beach, but the fact remained that she'd never worn a two-piece before. Though slender, Cassie took after her mother in the full-bodied-figure department.

She'd always felt more comfortable in a one-piece outfit, but she wouldn't have been caught dead in the only suit she owned. It was so old and faded that she was planning to throw it out. Trace had probably guessed as much.

She flushed at the thought. It seemed he knew her better than she knew herself and refused to take the chance that she would use the lack of a proper swimsuit as an excuse for not meeting him at the pool.

Suddenly there was a rap on the door. "Cassie? I'm giving you five minutes. If you're not downstairs by then, I'll be back up to get you, and a locked door won't stop me. It would be a shame to ruin that lovely dress you're wearing, but I won't hesitate to throw you in, emeralds and all."

His threat galvanized her into action. In three minutes, her clothes lay everywhere and she'd put on her new swimsuit. She ran for her terry-cloth bathrobe, then dashed barefoot down the stairs.

The caterers must have cleared the tables in record time. When Cassie arrived on the patio, everything was quiet and only the lights from the swimming pool had been left on. The warm night air, sweet with the scent of sage blowing off the desert floor, felt like velvet against her heated skin. She'd never seen a more romantic setting in her life.

When she and Susan were little girls, they'd often played house on long Saturday afternoons. They always pretended they were married with families, living in far-off exotic places. But never in Cassie's wildest dreams had she imagined a setting like this, with a husband who looked like Trace, and children as adorable as Justin and Jason. If Susan could see her now...

"How nice to find my bride waiting for me." His deep, mocking voice startled her.

*His bride?* She whirled around in time to see Trace dive into the water and swim to the opposite end of the pool in a fast-paced crawl. Halfway back he stopped, treading water, and shook his head. In the near darkness she could just make out his dazzling white smile.

"Come on in. The water's perfect."

Even though he was some distance away, Cassie felt self-conscious as she removed her robe. "I love to swim, but I'm not very good at it."

"I usually swim early in the morning and again at night before I go to bed. Now we're married, we can work out together." Shivers raced over her body, because something in his tone implied that he expected her to join him on a regular basis and wouldn't take no for an answer. She couldn't understand why it mattered to him, since they'd be alone and there'd be no need to keep up the pretense. "It helps me unwind more than any sport I can think of." He looked at her a moment. "Are you about ready to jump in?"

She had just put a cautious toe in the water, bracing herself for the shock. But the temperature was so different from the chilly Pacific Ocean at Carmel, where she'd occasionally swum with Rolfe, it was as though she'd stepped into a bathtub. "I don't even have to get used to it!" she cried out in delight. "Gaugin was wrong. Paradise is right here!"

She heard Trace's deep-throated chuckle as she pushed off from the bottom step and swam to the other side, making sure she didn't get too close to him. On her third lap across, she felt a pair of hands grasp her around the waist and flip her onto her back.

"Trace!" she gasped, not only from the unexpected contact, but because he had taken her beyond the patio overhang and she found herself looking up into a blue-black sky dotted with brilliant stars.

"I'm not going to let you drown," he reassured her. "Lie there and relax, kick your feet. You're more rigid than Justin at his worst."

Only once did she venture a glance at his face. His skin was beaded with moisture and his black hair lay sleek against his head. She quickly closed her eyes again. She felt helpless and exposed with his gaze free to wander over her semiclad body.

It took all her control not to examine his hard-muscled physique with the same concentrated thoroughness. If she tried to move, her arm rubbed against his hair-roughened chest, reminding her how utterly male he was. Everything about him excited her. His size, his masculinity, his firmly carved mouth.

She came to the stunning realization that the bittersweet ache that seemed to be part pain, part ecstasy, was *desire!*

Susan had once tried to explain the sensation to her and had finally given up. But she'd insisted that Cassie would recognize it the moment she experienced it. She hadn't—until now.

Was this the way Rolfe had felt throughout their long courtship? If so, she had to admire his self-control. No wonder he grew more upset and moody each time she put off the wedding.

Without even trying, Trace had brought her alarmingly alive. From the first, he had accomplished what Rolfe had never been able to do. If she'd desired Rolfe like this, wouldn't she have wanted to get married as soon as possible?

Right now, she quivered with anticipation. She could hear every breath Trace took and feel the heat from his body sending a languorous warmth through hers. The longing to mold her soft curves against his solid strength was fast becoming a driving need.

Terrified that he could sense her desire and see the pulse throbbing in the hollow of her throat, she challenged him to a race. Without waiting for a response she catapulted out of his arms.

Of course he won. He waited for her at the far end

of the pool with a rakish smile on his face. She touched the edge at least ten seconds after he did and drank in gulps of fresh air before bursting into laughter at her inelegant performance.

He studied her mouth intently, a gentle yet ironic smile curving his own lips. "Do you know that's the first time you've laughed with me when we've been alone? I like it."

Oddly embarrassed, Cassie sank down against the side of the pool until the water reached her neck. "As you've witnessed, I've got a long way to go to keep up with you."

His expression sobered. "I don't see our marriage as a competition, Cassie. What I'm hoping is that we'll share each other's lives. The children will grow up happier and healthier emotionally if they sense our marriage is a stable one. No one has to know what goes on—or doesn't—behind our bedroom doors except the two of us. Is that too much to ask? You don't dislike being with me, do you?"

Cassie was beginning to feel slightly hysterical. If he had any idea how much she didn't dislike being with him, he would run as far as he could in the opposite direction! Striving for composure, she smoothed several wet tendrils out of her eyes.

She didn't doubt his sincerity where the children's welfare was concerned. But now Cassie understood that his mother's fragile health had prompted him to enlist her cooperation in presenting a normal picture of married life to the rest of his family.

Her greatest problem would be to carry on a friendship, day after day, without ever betraying the physical side of her attraction for him. She finally said, "I admit it would be better for the children if they see us relating to each other as friends and companions."

Maybe she was mistaken, but she thought some of the tension eased out of him. "I'm glad you agree, because in two weeks the family's going on our annual skiing vacation to Snowbird, Utah, and I wanted to give you plenty of time to prepare for it."

She had that suffocating feeling in her chest again. "What about the children?"

"Nattie will take care of them."

"I see. How long will we be gone?"

"A week."

*A week with Trace? Alone in the same room?* She swallowed hard.

"Snowbird isn't the end of the earth, you know," he said harshly, his brows drawing together in displeasure. "You can phone the house every day to assure yourself the children are all right. If anything of a serious nature developed, we could be home in a matter of hours."

Cassie decided to let him go on believing that the children were her only concern. "You may as well know I've only been on skis twice in my life. I'm afraid I'd embarrass you on the slopes. Why don't I stay home with the boys and you go with your family? In fact, it might be a good time for Nattie to have a vacation, as well. She—"

"Either we go together, or we don't go at all!" he broke in angrily. Like quicksilver, his mood had changed. He suddenly shoved off for the opposite end of the pool, moving with tremendous speed. He was out of the water before she could call him back.

"Wait!" she cried out and swam after him, afraid she'd really alienated him this time. Unfortunately, she couldn't make it to the other end of the pool without stopping several times to catch her breath. She was terrified he would disappear into his own rooms, leaving her with everything still unresolved. "Trace," she gasped as her hand gripped the edge, "I was only trying to spare you. I ski like I swim."

He was toweling himself dry and slanted her a hostile look. "Do you honestly think I give a damn *how* you ski? Or even *if* you ski? I don't care if you lie around in the hotel bed all day watching television! From what I gather, for the last five years your life hasn't exactly been easy.

"Between Susan's and Ted's deaths, not to mention your mother's, a broken engagement and caring for Jason, you've had more to deal with than most people I know. And at the same time, you've been working all hours to earn a living. You don't seem to understand that I'd like to give you a chance to relax and play for a change, away from your work and the constant demands of the babies."

Her legs almost buckled at his unexpected explanation. Whenever she thought she had him figured out, he said or did something that increased her respect and made her care for him that much more.

A new ache passed through her body. She didn't *want* to care about him. She didn't want to worry about him—or think about him all the time. Lately she'd started fantasizing about what it would be like if he made love to her. Much more of this, and she'd end up an emotional wreck.

Her green eyes, wide with urgency, beseeched him to listen. "If I sounded ungrateful, I'm sorry. I suppose it's a combination of worrying about being away from the children for the first time and fear that you'll regret taking me along."

The expression on his face altered slightly as he held out her robe in invitation, but his eyes were still wary. As fast as she could manage, she clambered out of the pool and slipped her arms into the sleeves. His hands remained on her shoulders while she cinched the belt around her waist.

"You're an independent little thing," he whispered, kneading the taut muscles in her shoulders and neck. "It's time someone took care of you for a change."

She could feel the heat of his hands through the damp fabric. If he continued this, she was afraid of what she might do, afraid she'd embarrass them both. "You've spoiled me and Jason, and you know it, Trace. But I worry you've taken off too much time from your responsibilities at the bank, helping us move here and settle in. I wish there was something I could do for you in return."

His hands stilled for a moment. "There is," he muttered before removing them completely. Part of her was relieved he had broken contact, but another part craved his touch. Not trusting herself, she walked to the nearest lounge chair and sat down, making sure the robe covered her knees. This far from the pool, he was almost a silhouette in the near darkness.

"Tell me what's on your mind," she urged him.

He stood there holding both ends of the towel he'd slung around his neck. "You may not be an expert swimmer or skier, but your genius with needle and thread is nothing short of phenomenal. When I walked into your apartment with Jason that morning, I was overwhelmed by your talent and creativity."

A compliment from Trace meant more to her than the adulation of anyone else in the world. "Lots of women do what I do."

"Perhaps. But the finished product isn't always a masterpiece. I hope you won't be angry when I tell you I went through your apartment rather thoroughly, examining the goods, so to speak. Nothing bought for Justin in any store, anywhere, compares to the quality and originality I saw displayed in your apartment. I stand in awe of your accomplishments, Cassie."

"Thank you," she murmured shakily.

"I also felt like a fool for the callous way I suggested you move to Phoenix when I had no idea of the complexities involved in earning your livelihood." There was a slight pause. "Tell me something honestly. Is your work a labor of love?"

She couldn't help but wonder what he was getting at. "Long before I made any money at it, I loved creating an idea and seeing it through to completion. It's...something I have to do. When they find me dead, I'll probably be buried in batting, slumped over my sewing machine with a bunch of pins in my mouth."

"Somehow I knew you'd say that." He chuckled. "You and Lena are kindred spirits."

"I liked her very much, even after only one meeting."

"Maybe you're the person who'll make the difference." The cryptic remark intrigued her.

"What do you mean?"

"You're both artists. You live in that elite world reserved for those who were born gifted."

Cassie made a noise of dissent. "You can't seriously compare what *I* do to her talent!"

"I already have." His firm tone told her that to argue the point would be futile. "You make a child's world the most exciting, magical place on earth, just as it should be. Lena makes it possible for those of us who shove paper around to enjoy the breathtaking beauty of the desert without ever leaving our air-conditioned offices."

"There's a certain genius in shoving paper around. Particularly *your* paper," she quipped. "Give me three days in your office and your entire family would find themselves without a business and no roof over their heads."

The patio rang with his uninhibited laughter. "Well, since you brought up the bank, I have a proposition for you." Cassie sat forward, instantly alert.

"We lease properties, both residential and commercial. Right now, there's a studio vacant in Crossroads Square, an area of Phoenix that attracts tourists, as well as locals. By most standards it's not large, but it has four separate rooms with a cottage kind of feel, like you might see at a beach resort in Laguna or Balboa. It would be the perfect place to display your handicrafts. You need a showroom."

She had been concentrating on the sound of his voice, and it took a minute before she actually heard his words. She jumped immediately to her feet. "There's nothing I'd love more. It would be a dream come true, but I could never afford the rent, because I looked into the possibility in San Francisco and—"

"Don't jump to conclusions until you've heard me out," he cautioned before she could say another word. "How much do you have saved from your Christmas sales after taxes?"

"About eight thousand dollars."

"With that much money, you could sign a six-month lease."

"But six months wouldn't give me enough time to fill it with inventory, and then I'd have no money to reinvest in materials and—"

She heard him make a sound of exasperation. "Cassie, you said you wouldn't interrupt until I'm finished. Sit down before you wear out my patio with your pacing."

"I'm sorry." With so much nervous energy to expend, she needed some form of movement. She found a spot at the edge of the pool and dangled her feet in the water, splashing gently. He wandered over to her and it was then that she noticed his right foot. Without thinking, she bent closer and touched it with her index finger. *"You have webbed toes, just like Jason!"* Her astonished cry rang out and she clapped a hand over her mouth at its loudness.

"A legacy from the Ellingsworth side of the family," he drawled in amusement. "Both of Mother's feet are similarly...afflicted."

"I wouldn't call it an affliction," Cassie argued. "When I first saw Jason's foot, I thought it was rather sweet. Susan and I investigated the medical records available in both Ted's and our family, but we couldn't find any mention of webbed feet. I guess that's when I started to take Susan's suspicions seriously."

"And your odd little duck turned out to be mine," he said, causing both of them to chuckle.

"Is that what convinced you he was your son?" She could still picture the expression on his face when he reached for Jason's tiny foot that first day in his office.

"No. I took one look at the shape of his body and his complexion. He had to be my son. The Ellingsworth webbed toes were just the final proof."

"And all the time I thought he was a Ramsey."

"Oh, I'm sure a little Ramsey is in there somewhere. But what's most important, he has you for a mother. You're a natural, did you know that?"

"Except I've been spoiling Justin, as you pointed out yourself."

"True, but no more than I've spoiled Jason," he replied with surprising honesty. "I admit I was somewhat hasty in judging you, especially since I've been equally guilty. However, I imagine time will remedy the urgency we both feel to make up for those lost months. And returning to your crafts work will put a balance back in your life. You've been missing that since you agreed to marry me."

Again his perception and honesty surprised her. She'd been so preoccupied by her new responsibilities and her growing attraction to Trace, she hadn't yet found a moment to give serious thought to her business. "Maybe a few years down the road I'll have enough money to look into the idea of opening a shop."

"But that might be too late for Lena."

Lena again.

"She needs someone outside the family who believes in her work and will encourage her to see it as a viable career. Someone who has validity in her eyes. I think you could be that person. You could infect her with your own interest. Your joy in what you're doing."

What was he getting at? "You mean like going into business with her? Opening a gallery with her art and my crafts?"

He nodded. "Maybe you could call it something like The Mix and Match Gallery—in honor of the unusual way we met and became a family." There was a perceptible pause, then he asked, "Does the idea appeal to you?" She noticed the tiniest hint of anxiety in his question, as if her answer was important to him.

"*Appeal?*" She jumped to her feet and gazed into

his face, giving him a full, unguarded smile. "It's a fantastic idea! In fact, why don't we call it Mix and Match Southwest, since we'll be mixing and matching her art and my crafts and everything will have a southwestern theme?" Her thoughts were tumbling excitedly over each other. "We could have a logo with a cactus and maybe a setting sun or a coyote, and...oh, it'll be wonderful!"

His eyes kindled. "You mean it? You wouldn't mind sharing space with her, provided she was willing? It would be predominantly your shop of course—at this stage, anyway. If necessary, I'll pay the rent for the second six months, only that would have to remain our secret. It seems to me that between the two of you, there should be enough profit to stay in business another year." He paused again. "Would it make *you* happy, Cassie?"

When they'd begun this conversation, she thought he'd brought up the idea of a gallery solely for Lena's benefit. But the concern in his voice just now led Cassie to believe he was trying to please her, too, and that belief filled her with an all-consuming warmth. "You know it would," she answered in an unsteady voice. "Do you recall that watercolor at the top of the stairs? The one with the little Hopi girl standing next to those rocks at sunrise?"

He nodded. "It's one of my favorites."

"Every time I pass it, I itch to get out my sketch pad and design dolls and wall hangings based on that lovely child. In fact, living in this house has inspired me with the flavor of the Arizona desert. I've already planned out an area rug for my room, and the watercolor of the flowering cactus hanging in your office would look perfect next to it. Trace, for the opening I could use a Southwest theme with Lena's watercolors as the focal point!"

Before she could say anything else, he lowered his head and pressed his lips to her forehead. "You have a generous nature, Cassie. I'm counting on you to win Lena over to the idea."

Her heart hammered in reaction to his touch—and yearned for more. "Maybe I could work up some items before we go to lunch next week and invite her back to the house. If she saw them arranged around the watercolors, it might excite her."

"I'm sure it will, but getting her to make a commitment is something else again." A troubled look entered his eyes. "In college she fell in love with her art teacher. They had an affair that ended when she walked into his apartment and found him in bed with another student."

Cassie cringed at the all-too-common scenario.

"Considering that she thought they were getting married, that alone would have been devastating enough. But not satisfied with betraying her, he attacked her art and told her she was wasting her time. His final insult pretty well destroyed her confidence. He told her she'd never be more than a mediocre painter at best."

"But anyone with eyes can see how brilliant her work is!" Cassie insisted. "When did this happen?"

"Twelve years ago. She hasn't done any painting since."

"You mean the watercolors in your office and here at the house were all done while she was still in college? She was that good, even back then?"

"That's right," he said, tight-lipped.

"Her teacher probably recognized her talent and couldn't bear the competition. No doubt her work surpassed his. I've seen the same situation in the music department at the university where I studied piano theory. To think she let his rejection prevent her from working at her art all these years. It's tragic."

He nodded gravely. "Her husband, Allen, knows she'll never be completely fulfilled unless she gets back to her painting. He's done everything possible to encourage her but she refuses to even talk about it."

"The hurt must have gone very deep."

"It did. And to complicate matters, she feels insignificant around the family, overpowered by us. She's not like you, Cassie. She would never have fought me for Jason the way you did. You live by the strength of your convictions and don't let anything defeat you. You're practical and resilient—a survivor. You'd stand alone if you had to. If some of your confidence could rub off on Lena, it might change her life."

"I'm glad you told me about her," she said in a small voice. "I'll do what I can. Now if you don't mind, I'm very tired and I need to go to bed. Good night, Trace."

His whispered good-night followed her across the patio and up the stairs.

Though he obviously meant his remarks as a compliment, her spirits plummeted. Apparently she and his ex-wife, Gloria, had something in common, after all. They were both the antithesis of the fragile, helpless woman who aroused a man's undying love and brought out his instinctive need to protect and cherish.

The Joan of Arcs of this world would always be admired, but they would remain on their pedestals *alone*....

# CHAPTER SIX

EXCEPT FOR A VISIT to the vacant shop in Crossroads Square and the subsequent signing of a year's lease, Cassie saw Trace only in passing during the next week. He explained that he had a backlog of work; as a result, he stayed at the office through the dinner hour every night so he could catch up before they left on their ski trip.

Cassie told herself she was glad his banking responsibilities kept him away from the house. Without his disturbing presence, she could simply relax with the children and sew at her own pace. Trace had helped convert the middle guest bedroom into a workroom. The light was perfect. Best of all, she was close to the children and could hear them when they woke up from their naps.

But to her dismay, Trace was continually on her mind. His energy and vitality, his handsome face and powerful body, made it impossible for her to concentrate fully on anything else. And when he was home, even if he was locked in his study or playing with the children, she was aware of him. No matter the hour, her pulse raced when she heard his car in the driveway. But what alarmed her even more was the disappointment she felt when he drove off to work each morning.

After five whole weeks of his attention and companionship, she discovered life wasn't nearly as exciting without him around. Always before, she'd been able to immerse herself happily in her work, unconscious of time passing. Now while she bathed and fed the children or cut out patterns, she often glanced at the clock, estimating how many hours it would be before he came home.

Lena called early in the week to make a date for lunch. Cassie put her off until Friday so she'd have enough time to work up several pieces that drew their inspiration from three of Lena's paintings. Trace brought home one she'd requested from his office. She used another two from the group hanging on the wall along the staircase.

In order to make the impact as striking as possible, she enlisted Nattie's help in converting the dining room into a sort of gallery. The effect was even more stunning than Cassie had imagined, because the room, with its arboretum of exotic desert plants, lent itself perfectly to the Southwest theme.

Though she kept her thoughts to herself, Cassie felt that something out of the ordinary had been achieved. She could hardly sit still through lunch with Lena, waiting for the moment they would go home.

If Trace's sister sensed Cassie's suppressed excitement, she hid it well. She asked dozens of questions and insisted on knowing all the details of Cassie's life and the events that eventually led her to Trace's office. Several hours later, when Cassie invited Lena back to the house to see the children, Lena was still chuckling over Trace's initial plan to have Cassie arrested. But her laughter subsided when she caught sight of her own watercolors displayed with Cassie's creations in plain view of anyone standing in the living room.

Like a person walking through water, Lena moved into the dining room. Cassie followed a few steps behind, uncertain of Lena's reaction and almost afraid to breathe. Those paintings were associated with a painful time in Lena's life. At this early stage in their friendship, the last thing Cassie wanted to do was open old wounds or create a rift between them. It was because she had Trace's blessing that she dared to involve Lena at all.

Lena studied the arrangement in silence for a long time. "Do you mean to tell me you've made all these since you came to Phoenix?" she finally asked.

"Yes, except that they aren't completely finished."

"They're fabulous."

"Your paintings inspired them, Lena. I took one look at your little Hopi girl and I could visualize her adorable face on dolls and wall hangings and all sorts of things. Every one of your paintings has given me a dozen new ideas. I can't work fast enough to keep up with them."

"Trace told me you were a genius with fabric."

"And I told him that whoever painted those scenes in his office has incredible talent. Your work excites me and makes me reach out for things I didn't know were in me. You know what I mean?"

Lena turned around and stared at Cassie. "You really meant what you said the other night, didn't you?"

Taking a deep breath, Cassie answered, "You already know the answer to that. Have I made you angry, using your paintings for inspiration without telling you?"

"Angry?" Lena's gray eyes widened in surprise. "I've never been so flattered in my life."

Cassie's body went limp with relief. "As you know, I've only ever sold out of my own home. At first I started making up dolls and stuffed figures from fairy tales and cartoons to help bring in a little more money. Pretty soon I was flooded with orders. I've sewn everything from frogs to princes. But I've never had a theme for my work or even considered it until I saw your paintings."

Lena fingered her long braid absently. "You obviously went to all this trouble—arranging everything so beautifully—for my benefit. Why?"

"Before I met Trace, I planned to open my own boutique in San Francisco as a showcase for my work. But everything changed when he asked me to marry him. Now that we're settled, I've used the profits from my Christmas sales to sign a lease on some space in Crossroads Square."

"Crossroads Square?" Lena mouthed the word wistfully, sounding very faraway. "That's a perfect place if you want to attract the tourist trade." She stared at Cassie in puzzlement. "Does Trace know about this? I-I thought you were going to stay home with the children."

"I do stay home. Every day. And I manage to enjoy the children and sew at the same time. How else do you think I could turn out so much work?" Cassie smiled mischievously. "But if I don't have a place to display and sell it, pretty soon Trace will have to build me a warehouse."

Lena burst into laughter. "You're a complete surprise, Cassie Ramsey."

"No." Cassie shook her head, liking the sound of her new name. "Just driven by a compulsion stronger than I am."

A shadow crossed Lena's face; she started to say something, then apparently changed her mind.

Cassie hesitated a moment, then decided to plunge ahead. "Lena, I have to admit I had ulterior motives in inviting you back to the house today. You see, I'm holding my grand opening in a month, and I need your permission to display the things I've already made. The fact is, I've copied your work and I really have no right to sell any of this." She gestured around the room. "Believe me, I'll understand if your answer is no. But as time is of the essence, I need to know how you feel...in case I have to get started on another theme entirely."

Picking up one of the dolls, Lena studied it carefully, then looked at Cassie, eyes brimming. "How could I possibly turn you down when you've done such exquisite work? It would be on my conscience forever."

Impulsively Cassie threw her arms around Lena in an exuberant hug. "I was praying you'd say that, because I can't think of another theme that could possibly work as well as this one. To be honest, I knew my opening would have to be unique in order to generate business. And when I saw your art, I was immediately drawn to it. I think other people would feel the same way."

In the heavy silence that followed her remarks, Cassie removed the paintings from the groupings of crafts, then leaned them against the far wall. Lena gazed at her uncomprehendingly, and Cassie had to bite hard on her lower lip to keep from smiling.

"Take a good look at everything without your paintings to show them off, Lena. The things I've made are nice in and of themselves, but the display falls flat, don't you think? Be honest now."

After another quiet interim, Lena nodded.

Crossing her fingers behind her back, Cassie ventured, "Would you allow me to use your paintings the way I've done here to open the show?" Without giving Lena a chance to respond, she rushed on. "I have to admit I've sketched out ideas for dozens of fabric crafts based on another ten of your paintings. If I work night and day, I can have everything ready for the opening. But without your art as a foil, I won't be able to achieve the same impact."

While Lena hesitated, Cassie quickly put the paintings back in place among the crafts for her sister-in-law's benefit. "You see? I'm right, aren't I?"

After a minute of studying the display, Lena nodded, looking slightly bemused. "Everything works perfectly together."

"Then you'll let me use them?"

"I'd be cruel if I said no."

"Thank you, Lena." Cassie couldn't help giving her another hug. "It's one thing to sell things out of your own home, and another to display them in a shop. I've been terrified at my own audacity. But with your paintings, I know the opening will be an eye-catcher."

Conscious of taking a calculated risk, Cassie added, "I noticed you haven't signed your paintings."

"No," came the quiet admission.

"I'm afraid you'll have to if I'm going to show them. Otherwise clients will assume I painted them."

Lena was examining the Hopi girl canvas, frowning in concentration. "I need to finish the detail on her dress if you're going to use this." She finally stood up and faced Cassie. "I'll tell you what. Ask Trace to bring home the paintings from the office you're planning to use. Next week I'll go to the art store for supplies and come over to sign them all."

"Don't you have materials at home?" Cassie asked, striving to remain unemotional when inside she was bursting with excitement.

"Heavens, no." She let out a bitter laugh. "I'm afraid my art career was very short-lived and I tossed everything out. In fact, I haven't touched a brush to canvas in years. When I worked on these paintings, I never dreamed anyone else would ever see them. I would have thrown them away, but Trace said he wanted them and offered me money to take them off my hands. Of course I wouldn't have let him pay me for junk." She sighed, shaking her head. "My brother..."

"He believes in your work."

Lena's gaze slid away. "Well, now that I've committed myself, I'd better look over everything you plan to use. I might find other details that were left undone."

"Lena, I can't thank you enough. To be frank, I've been frightened to tell you what I've been up to—particularly since I'm calling the shop Mix and Match Southwest. If you hadn't given your permission, I don't know where I would have turned for inspiration. Trace seems to believe in my work, as well. I—I want him to be proud of me."

"In case you hadn't noticed, he already is," Lena said wryly. "Of all my brothers, I feel closest to him, and I can tell you honestly that when Allen and I arrived at the party, Trace's eyes had a glow I've never seen before. Only you could have put it there."

"That's because he's so crazy about Jason." She fought to keep the tremor out of her voice.

Lena eyed her shrewdly. "Of course he is, but I saw the way Trace looked at you, the way he held on to you all evening. I've never seen him behave like that with any other woman."

"Not even Gloria?"

"Especially not Gloria."

Cassie wanted to ask more questions about Trace's former wife, but restrained herself; this wasn't the right time. "Trace's attention to me was solely for your mother's benefit."

"What does Mom have to do with how my brother treats you?" Lena asked in a perplexed voice.

"It's because of her heart condition. He wants her to believe our marriage is a love match."

"And it's not?" Lena burst out.

Cassie sucked in her breath. "Trace is grateful to me for uniting him with his son. But you might as well know he asked me to marry him and I accepted so neither of us would have to be separated from the children. I couldn't bear to lose them," she whispered.

*"What?"*

"Trace isn't in love with me, Lena. Ours is what people used to call a marriage of convenience. I can't go on pretending something that doesn't exist. At least not to you, because...because I want us to be friends."

"I do, too," Lena murmured, "but if you're telling me you're not in love with my brother, I don't believe you."

Lena's directness caught Cassie off guard and she felt heat rising to her cheeks. "None of it really matters, because Trace isn't interested in me that way. In fact, one of the conditions he set for our marriage was that both of us could see other people, as long as we were discreet."

"My brother said *that?*"

"Lena, we've never slept together. He's only ever kissed me once, the day we were married." Her voice trailed off as she recalled the thrill of it. Before Lena could respond, Cassie blurted out, "I can hear noises from upstairs. The boys must have awakened. I'll get them ready and bring them down."

Without waiting for a response Cassie raced from the living room and dashed up the stairs, thankful the babies had interrupted her painful conversation with Lena.

As Cassie changed their diapers, Nattie poked her head into the nursery. "Do you need help?"

"No. Jason seems to be a little off color, but I'm sure it's nothing. Since Trace won't be home for dinner, I can fix a simple meal for myself and the boys. So why don't you and Mike take the rest of the day off? You deserve a rest."

Nattie's face lit up. "You're sure?"

"I'm positive. Lena's going to stay a while and keep us company."

"All right. Thank you, Cassie. It's a joy to work in the same house with you."

"The feeling's mutual, Nattie. Go and have a good time."

When Nattie had left, Cassie dressed the boys and carried them downstairs to see their aunt. To her relief, Lena made no mention of their prior conversation and enjoyed getting to know Jason better while Cassie encouraged Justin to take a few steps. It wouldn't be long before he was walking on his own.

Jason, on the other hand, could crawl everywhere and went after anything he wanted with an unswerving certainty that reminded both women of Trace and sent them into gales of laughter. But, unusual for Jason, he soon tired and cried to be held.

Cassie and Lena spent the rest of the afternoon exchanging anecdotes about the children, but as the dinner hour approached, Lena declared that she had to go home and feed her starving horde. Cassie was reluctant to see her leave, but was growing concerned about Jason, who'd become irritable and weepy, despite his long nap. His forehead definitely felt warm to the touch.

She put Justin in the playpen, then walked Lena to the front door, carrying Jason in her arms. "I'll phone you as soon as Trace brings the paintings home from his office."

The other woman nodded. "Cassie, will you do me a favor and not mention this to anyone else in the family?"

"You mean about using your art for my opening?"

"Yes. I'd like this to be our secret, if you don't mind."

"Of course I don't. I'll tell Trace not to say anything, either."

"Good. It's just that I stopped painting years ago and, well, I just don't want to deal with everyone's speculations..."

Cassie put a hand on Lena's arm. "If that's how you feel, I understand. You have my promise."

"Thanks." Lena kissed Jason's cheek, then Cassie's. "We'll talk again soon. We'll be able to spend some time together during our trip to Snowbird, too."

Lena's unexpected warmth pleased Cassie. "Thank you for your help, Lena. It means more than you know."

Cassie had a feeling that her sister-in-law wanted to say something further—perhaps about her marriage to Trace. But Lena seemed to think better of it. As soon as she drove off, Cassie headed for the kitchen to get Jason a bottle of juice. Then she gave him a sponge bath to bring down his slight fever and put him back to bed.

But while she was taking care of him, her mind was on Lena. Though Cassie had obtained her permission to use the watercolors, it didn't mean she'd automatically begin painting again. Trace was right; Lena still sounded far too bitter over her ex-lover's rejection. She'd lost all her self-confidence and, even worse, belief in her own talent.

But she hadn't turned Cassie down, and that meant she'd taken the first, necessary step. Cassie couldn't wait to tell Trace. She listened for him all evening as she fed Justin and bathed him, then put him in his crib. Jason fell asleep almost immediately.

After turning out the nursery light, she went downstairs to put the crafts and paintings away and restore order to the dining room while she waited for Trace. Around eight she heard a car pull into the drive. Moments later, the sound of the back door opening told her he was home.

Cassie rushed to the patio to meet him, anxious to

share her news about Lena. "I thought you'd never get here, and I have so much to tell you! Lena and I—"

His eyes looked warm and expectant, but the ringing of the telephone prevented further conversation. He reached for it, and Cassie sat down at the small table, silently admiring the blackness of his hair, the laugh lines around his eyes and mouth, the deepness of his voice.

By his clipped response she could tell the call had to do with bank business; she hoped it wouldn't detain him for the rest of the evening. He pulled out his pocketbook and jotted down some notes, then finally hung up. She was bursting to tell him her good news, but swallowed her words when she saw his dark expression. One phone call had transformed him into a remote facsimile of himself. He turned his head to stare at her broodingly.

"What's wrong, Trace?" she asked in alarm.

"That was Western Union with a cablegram for you from a Mr. Rolfe Timpson in Brussels. I told the operator to go ahead and read it." He tore the page from his pocketbook and handed it to her.

The hostility emanating from him troubled Cassie a great deal more than the paper in her hand. Her gaze was drawn to Trace's crisp handwriting. "Dearest Cass," it read, "I got your letter and I strongly feel we have to talk. We've loved for a lifetime and I don't ever see that changing. I'm coming back to the States next month to see you. I'll call you as soon as I arrive in Phoenix. My deepest love, Rolfe."

After all this time, Rolfe was coming to see her. She would always love him in a special way. But her response to Trace in the pool had revealed a truth that changed everything where Rolfe was concerned.

What was it Susan had said? That Cassie and Rolfe had never been apart and needed the separation to make things clear, one way or the other....

They were clear, all right.

Her eyes shifted from the paper to the man who'd taken her heart by storm and brought her body to glorious life. *Oh, Trace, if you only knew...*

"He wants you back," he said in a harsh tone, "but that's just too damn bad because you're married to me now, Cassie, and that's the way it's going to stay."

If she didn't know why he'd asked her to marry him, his angry pronouncement would have led her to believe he was starting to care for her.

"Whatever Rolfe has to say, I'd never leave you and the children," she said honestly.

"Don't take me for a fool, Cassie. Do you think I don't know the bond that exists between the two of you? The years invested? The intimacy you shared?"

"We weren't intimate in the way you mean," she confessed in a quiet voice.

His eyes blazed. "If you're trying to tell me you never slept together in all those years, I don't believe you."

"Nevertheless it's true. Mother had very conservative beliefs and raised Susan and me to save ourselves for marriage. She challenged us to be the only girls in the neighborhood who didn't know all there was to know about what goes on between a man and a woman. She promised us it would be a lot more fun and exciting to learn along with our husbands."

He stared at her as if she was speaking a foreign language. "What went wrong between you and Rolfe?"

She wanted to blurt out that she wasn't in love with Rolfe. That was what had kept her from marrying him. But she hadn't known it, not until she met Trace. And fell in love with him.

"We were engaged a long time. When he pushed me to set a wedding date, I couldn't, because I was still grieving over my mother. After Ted was killed, he pressed me again, but I was so worried about Susan I couldn't even consider marriage just then, even though I loved him very much. I don't blame him for finally getting fed up and breaking our engagement."

"Is that when he left for Europe?"

"Yes. But none of it matters anymore. Trace," she began in an excited voice, "I wanted to tell you about Lena. She—"

"Not now, Cassie," he interrupted tersely. "I'm in the middle of a hellish merger and I'll be spending most of the night in my study."

Not since that first day in his office had he ever been intentionally rude to her. Here she'd done everything in her power to show him the past was dead for her and he treated her like this! Even if things had been different and she'd wanted to see Rolfe again, did Trace honestly believe she'd walk out on him and the children? He would have to divorce her before she'd leave!

He turned abruptly and took the patio stairs two at a time. Cassie felt like throwing something at him. After he'd disappeared from view, she stood there for a few minutes to get her temper under control, then went upstairs herself. When she heard Jason crying she made a detour to the nursery. The minute she picked him up she realized why he'd awakened in such distress. He was burning with fever. One look at the rash covering his chest and neck dispersed all thoughts of the tense scene on the patio.

She quickly undressed him and headed for the bathroom, knowing she had to get his temperature down as fast as possible. The rash covering his chest was a brilliant pink, and she could actually feel the heat radiating from his body. She filled the tub with cool water and lowered him in. He began to scream uncontrollably. All of a sudden she heard Justin, who'd been awakened from a sound sleep, bellowing at the top of his lungs, too.

"Cassie? What can I do to help?" came Trace's voice over all the commotion.

Relieved he was there, she turned to him eagerly. "Jason's fever is so high he has a rash. There's a new bottle of infant's pain reliever in the other bathroom. Would you mind getting it?"

"I'll be right back. And Cassie, don't worry too much. Justin once had the same thing. It looks like roseola to me. A virus—extremely uncomfortable for them but usually no serious effects."

Cassie nodded her relief but begged him to hurry. She was finding it difficult to calm Jason, who hated the cool water and fought her in earnest. Soon Trace returned, crouching beside her as he unsealed the brand-new bottle of pain reliever and removed the dropper.

He'd rolled his sleeves to the elbow, exposing his tanned hands and arms with their smattering of dark hair. "You continue to sponge him and I'll get this stuff down his throat. It should reduce his fever within half an hour and make him feel a lot better."

She couldn't figure out how Trace could remain so composed when she was practically falling apart with anxiety. After several attempts, Trace finally managed the impossible.

The sight of him bent over the tub ministering to Jason's needs filled her with an indescribable tenderness, and her earlier anger evaporated completely. But Jason seemed to be furious with her, and although it wasn't really rational, she couldn't help fearing that he'd never forgive her for this.

"Don't look so worried, Cassie," Trace said. "Jason's going to be fine, and in two days he'll have forgotten all about tonight. He already seems better, don't you think?"

Cassie reached out to touch Jason's cheeks and forehead. Trace was right. He wasn't as hot and had quieted down considerably.

"You're going to get better. Mommy and Daddy are right here. You poor little darling. You're freezing!"

"That's the idea," Trace murmured, continuing to scoop the cool water over Jason's blotchy red neck and chest.

"Mama. Dada." Jason called both their names clearly, and Trace flashed her a look of such sweetness, her breath caught in her throat.

With her upper arm she brushed the tears from her cheeks and grasped one of the child's hands. "Just a few more minutes and Daddy will take you out of the tub, darling. It'll be over soon."

Jason began to cry again and tried to sit up. It seemed like an eternity before his father finally said, "I think this little guy has had enough for now."

As soon as Trace lifted him from the water, Cassie had a towel ready and wrapped him in it. Jason clung to Trace as they left the bathroom. Cassie thought he'd take the baby to the nursery, but instead he headed down the hall for the master bedroom. Over his shoulder he asked, "Cassie, will you please bring me the juice I saw in his crib? If I hold him on my bed for a while, maybe I can get him to drink it."

Cassie hurried into the nursery for Jason's bottle, as well as a fresh diaper and a light cotton quilt. Justin was standing up in his crib, crying hoarsely. "Just a minute, Justin. Here, darling." She handed him a stuffed pig. "Mommy'll be right back."

The only time Cassie had been in Trace's bedroom was once with Nattie, when they'd put some clothes away in his drawers. She'd certainly never entered it when he was home. But right now she didn't think of that. She swept inside and dashed over to the side of the bed where he lay sprawled out full-length, his tie off and his shirt unbuttoned halfway down his chest. Jason lay in the crook of his arm staring up at his father, still whimpering a little but obviously content.

Trace took the bottle and offered it to Jason while Cassie changed his diaper and replaced the damp towel with the quilt. She and Trace exchanged relieved glances, as Jason drank thirstily, even holding the bottle by himself.

Unfortunately, Justin was still howling mournfully. Trace sent Cassie a humorous smile, and something in his expression made her feel they really were husband and wife, in every sense of the words. She had to fight the impulse to lean down a little farther and kiss his mouth.

"I'm going," she whispered. "I'll be in the other room if you need me."

"Not yet," he said softly. He lifted his free hand to her face, shaping the palm to the contour of her cheek. "I was inexcusably rude to you earlier. Tell me what happened with Lena. Did you get anywhere with her?"

"Yes. She's willing to let me use her paintings for the opening."

There was a brief pause. "You made a better start than I'd hoped for," he said. "When we get to Snowbird, I intend to show you my appreciation. With no worries and no children, I'll be able to concentrate on you for a whole week."

Excitement coursed through her veins. For the first

time since their wedding, they were going to be alone together, and Trace sounded as if he was really looking forward to it. Of course, she knew he was motivated by concern for his sister and by gratitude for Cassie's help, but she hoped he was beginning to be aware of her as a desirable woman.

"It sounds wonderful." She purposely kept her voice low and steady for fear she'd reveal too much. She left the room immediately afterward.

With her skin still tingling from Trace's touch, she quieted Justin by picking him up and carrying him downstairs for a snack. Happy to be cuddled, he ate a graham cracker and gulped down some warm milk. A half hour later he was ready for bed.

After she'd settled him for the night, she went directly to Trace's room and tiptoed inside. As she took in the sight of Jason lying on his father's chest, her eyes moistened. Father and son were sound asleep.

Careful not to disturb them, she felt Jason's forehead; his temperature had gone down, just as Trace had predicted.

Unable to help herself, she let her gaze wander back to her husband, whose disheveled black hair made him look uncharacteristically boyish. For a few minutes she studied the lines of his strong, straight nose and mobile mouth, the way his dark lashes fanned out against bronzed cheeks. She stared at his arm, still protectively circling his son.

*I love him,* she thought. *I love him so much I can hardly bear it.*

Before she could do something foolish—like lie

down next to him—she crept out the door and flew to her bedroom, where she could give way to her emotions in private. Trace would never know how excited she was to be going on this trip with him, how desperately she wanted to spend time with him alone. But she'd have to be very careful never to let him know how much she craved his touch. How much she craved not just gratitude and respect, but love.

Unable to sleep, Cassie pulled on a nightgown and robe and went to her workroom, where she could unleash her energy on an idea that had been unfolding in her mind.

Going to her files, she found the pattern she wanted and began cutting out fabric. Four hours later, a stuffed, six-foot alligator with black hair and calculating blue eyes lay on the floor watching her with a wicked grin. Across the tail she had stitched the word "Daddy."

When it was finished she opened the closet door and stood the alligator on end in the far corner. To make sure it remained hidden, she draped it with a swath of white canvas, then shut the door.

If Trace ever saw it, he'd know the truth. He'd know she was in love with him. Cassie couldn't imagine anything worse—because he wasn't in love with her. He'd feel only pity, and Cassie didn't think she could stand that.

## CHAPTER SEVEN

"I'VE NEVER SEEN so much snow," Cassie gasped as the large airport limousine carrying the Ramsey clan approached the lodge at Snowbird. She was pressed between Norman and Trace, who kept his arm constantly around her; her joy was diminished, since she realized it was a show of affection for his family's benefit.

"Actually Utah's had a mild winter this year," Trace said in a low voice near her ear. "I can remember coming up here several times when there were literally walls of ice. The state's in a drought cycle right now."

She surveyed the towering white mountain peaks knifing through the thin, freezing cold air. "You'd never know it." She tried desperately to appear unaffected by his nearness, but her heart was hammering out of control. She didn't know if her disorientation was due to the altitude or to the fact that she'd be sharing a bedroom with Trace in a few minutes.

"I can't wait to hit the powder!" James announced as the limo pulled to a stop. "Last one out brings the skis for everybody."

"Oh, brother!" This came from his wife, Dorothy,

who sat across from Jane, Norman's wife. Lena and Allen shared the front seat with the chauffeur.

A great deal of good-natured bantering went on as they proceeded to find their bags and carry in their ski equipment.

The heat generated by a roaring blaze in the giant hearth off the lobby welcomed new arrivals. Cassie wandered over to it while Trace dealt with registration. A jaunty-looking Lena gravitated to the fire with Cassie, sporting an all-navy ski outfit that suited her trim figure perfectly. Cassie, on the other hand, felt conspicuous, dressed in brand-new fluorescent-green ski bib and white, green and blue matching parka.

Several days after Jason had fully recovered from his roseola, Trace had purchased the outfit, along with skis and boots, and had brought everything home giftwrapped. He made her open the packages the second he bounded in the house from work.

A card lying on top of the tissue had caught her eye. Gingerly Cassie picked it up and read: "You have my undying gratitude for being such a wonderful, caring mother to our sons. I hope this gift will convey in some small measure my appreciation for the way you've turned this house into a haven I love to come home to. You've more than kept your side of our bargain, Cassie. I hope to show my appreciation when we go to Snowbird. We'll have a week to ourselves—a chance for Cassandra Ramsey to feel a little indulged for a change! Trace."

The sincere sentiment had moved her. But his note didn't contain the words she wanted to read, to hear, above all others. The realization that Trace might never fall in love with her filled her with a sudden deep despair. She fought to keep a smile on her face as she thanked him for the presents. But knowing she couldn't keep up the pretense for long, she'd made an excuse to leave the room, claiming she wanted to phone Lena.

As she called her sister-in-law, she felt Trace's probing gaze and sensed a strange undercurrent that she found more than a little troubling. To her vast relief, Lena was home and Cassie launched into conversation about their ski trip with feigned enthusiasm.

Even when Trace left the room, she could still feel his strained reaction and wondered what had caused it. Maybe she hadn't sounded grateful enough. Or maybe he resented her talking on the phone the minute he came home from work.

Whatever the problem, for the next week Cassie had taken great pains to make their home the haven he'd mentioned in his note. In between her sewing activities, she went on a cooking spree and fixed delicious meals, preparing some of his favorite Southwestern dishes. But if anything, her actions seemed to increase the tension between them. The more she tried to please him, the more polite and remote he became. It reached the point that she'd actually dreaded their trip.

At least around the house, the children acted as a buffer. But now she'd be alone with a difficult husband for six whole days and nights. She wondered how she'd survive their vacation, or even *if* she'd survive.

"Well, well. Where did you come from?" a friendly male voice said directly behind her. Cassie turned around to confront what she considered the classic male ski enthusiast. He was athletically built, with light brown hair bleached by the sun and a tan that resembled leather. A confident smile revealed a splendid set of white teeth. The man simply exuded self-satisfaction.

"We're from Timbuktu," Lena unexpectedly blurted out in a brash tone meant to send him packing. But his confident smile didn't crack, and he continued to stare admiringly at Cassie.

"If you want some help with your technique, I'm your man. Name's Hank. You'll find me by the lift every morning. I give group and private lessons."

Cassie tried hard not to laugh out loud at the man's aggression, but she would never have responded as rudely as Lena had. She merely gave him a bland smile. "Thanks for the tip. If I decide I need instruction, I'll look you up."

"Great! In that terrific outfit, you'll be easy to spot."

"Our room is ready." Trace had found her and was looking every bit as disgusted as his sister with the other man's attention. Cassie hadn't heard that icy tone since the first day in his office, when he'd almost succeeded in having her carted off to jail.

An impish mischief made her green eyes sparkle as she said, "Trace, this is Hank, one of the ski instructors for the lodge. Hank, this is my husband, Trace, and his sister, Lena."

"How do you do?" Hank put out a hand, which Trace was forced to shake. "Your sister says you're from Timbuktu. As I understand it, you don't get a lot of snow in that part of Africa."

Hank had a sense of humor, she'd give him that. There was a protracted silence. "That's right," Trace finally muttered, stone-faced. He glared at Cassie. "Are you ready?"

Swallowing hard, she said, "Whenever you are."

"Then let's go."

In the uncomfortable silence that followed, she turned to Hank. "It was nice to meet you."

Hank grinned. "I always enjoy meeting people from foreign places. See you around."

Suddenly Trace was ushering her from the foyer, his grip on her arm firm. Lena found her husband, and the four of them rode the elevator together.

"Hey, why so serious?" Allen questioned his wife. "Can you believe six whole days without the kids?" He swooped down and kissed the end of her cold nose. "Brrr," he joked, causing Lena to laugh, bringing her out of herself. "It looks like you need warming up."

Cassie averted her eyes, envious of their easy relationship and their intimacy. When the doors opened to the fourth floor, she couldn't get out of the elevator fast enough and, apparently, neither could Trace.

"See you at dinner," they called out before the doors closed again.

Trace led the way to their room, which overlooked the snowy Wasatch Mountains where they'd be skiing. The afternoon sun glistened off the dazzling white peaks, making her eyes sting.

"I can't believe we're here. Only this morning I was looking out at the desert from the nursery window."

"And wishing you didn't have to come?" he asked grimly.

Cassie whirled around in surprise. "Why do you say that?"

"I'm not blind, Cassie. I saw the way you clung to the children this morning. Anyone would've thought I was dragging you off to—" he paused "—Timbuktu for a year, instead of a short holiday. Since I know you're dying to find out if they're still alive, I'll go downstairs and bring up the rest of our things while you phone home for a report."

He left the room before she could refute his words. But in all honesty, what was there to say? She *had* been dreading this trip, but not for the reasons he imagined. Snowbird had to be one of the most romantic places on earth—and it served as a painful reminder of the mockery of a marriage to a man who didn't love her.

Her gaze strayed to the two queen-size beds. She felt a wave of humiliation. Trace couldn't possibly feel any desire for her or he wouldn't have arranged for a room with two beds. Who in the family, except Lena, could guess that for the next week, Trace and his wife would be roommates, nothing more?

Hot tears spilled down her cheeks, but she quickly dashed them away with her hands. At home, when she grew frustrated over her futile love for Trace, she could escape to her sewing room or the nursery. But now that they'd arrived at the lodge, she had to make the best of an almost intolerable situation. She could think of only one thing to do. Ski!

Perhaps in six days she could learn the basics of a sport Trace loved. But she'd need lessons from one of the instructors—and judging by Trace's reaction, it had better not be Hank. Cassie disliked that type of obsessively flirtatious man, anyway. Perhaps there was another instructor available, one more interested in skiing than in the female skiers!

With an actual plan, Cassie felt a little better. She phoned the house in Phoenix, and Nattie put her mind at rest, assuring her the children were fine. She urged Cassie to forget everything and concentrate on Trace.

When she replaced the receiver, Cassie found herself wondering if Nattie's last comment was meant to be taken as a piece of womanly advice. The housekeeper knew Cassie and Trace slept in separate bedrooms. She probably found their relationship unnatural. *Well, so did Cassie!* But there didn't seem to be a thing she could do about it.

"Are they still breathing?"

Trace's biting sarcasm jolted her out of her reverie. She turned around, counting slowly to ten before answering. Somehow she had to salvage this trip; she had to get on better terms with her husband—who at the moment looked far too attractive for her peace of mind. The gray-and-black-striped ski sweater complimented his dark good looks and emphasized his trim, powerful build.

"The children are fine, and you're right. I've doted on them to the exclusion of too many other things. Maybe it's because I'm not their natural mother, so I've taken on a greater sense of responsibility than is warranted. Please believe me when I say I'm happy to be here."

At her words, the stiffness seemed to leave his taut frame and he moved closer. His eyes searched her face for endless minutes. "Cassie, I realize you led a completely different life until you married me, and I've expected far too much, too soon. Chalk it up to my boardroom tactics." With a slow smile that made her heart turn over, he put his hands on her upper arms. "For the rest of this week, could we pretend there's just the two of us and enjoy a vacation we both badly need?"

"I'd love it."

"Good," he whispered, then leaned forward to kiss the top of her head. Maybe it was her imagination, but she thought he buried his face in her hair an extra-long moment before lifting his head. Her body seemed to dissolve with desire. The slightest contact triggered a physical response she couldn't control, and she wondered if he could tell what his nearness did to her. "Are you hungry?" he asked as he stepped back, releasing her arms.

"Starving.

"Let's grab a hamburger. Then I'll take you out on

the bunny hill and teach you a few fundamentals. In a day or two, you'll be ready to go up on the lift.''

Cassie would willingly have gone anywhere with him. And since he'd offered to give up his own skiing time to teach her, she could hardly refuse.

The rest of the day Cassie reveled in his company. She alternated between fits of laughter and spills in the snow—with the occasional success—as she tried to master the snowplow and the art of falling down safely. If Trace thought her a lost cause, he didn't say so. But she'd never seen him smile so much, which gave her more pleasure than she dared to admit, even to herself.

As the sun started to go down, he grew more playful and began tossing snowballs at her. She tried to escape, but her skis crossed and she fell headlong into the snow. When he saw her predicament, he took off his own skis and scooped up a fresh handful of snow. She struggled onto her side and giggled as he started toward her with a predatory gleam in his eye.

"No, Trace!" she screamed through her laughter, trying to shield her face. With one gloved hand he easily caught her wrists and pinned them in the snow above her head, leaving the other free to begin his torture.

"Be kind," she pleaded on a shallow breath, her eyes half dancing, half fearful, as she met his gaze, which darkened in intensity the longer they stared at each other.

"My words exactly."

A moan trembled on her lips at the passion in his

husky voice. The blood surged through her veins as he lowered his head and found her mouth with his own, creating an aura of scorching heat despite the near-zero temperature of the air. Each kiss grew deeper, hungrier. Cassie could no longer contain her own frantic response. When he wrapped her in his arms and pulled her against him, she feverishly kissed him back, losing all sense of time and place.

"Good grief, Trace. You've got a perfectly good room at the lodge for that sort of thing. I think you'd better take a run with us and cool off, little brother."

Norman's teasing voice penetrated Cassie's rapture, and she pulled sharply away from her husband. Not only was she more embarrassed than she'd ever been in her life, but to be so rudely transported back to reality made her want to weep with frustration.

With enviable aplomb, Trace got to his feet, then helped her up and handed her the ski poles she'd dropped. Cassie couldn't recover her own composure as quickly. She had to support herself with her poles so she could stand upright while she faced Trace's two brothers, who stood there unashamedly grinning at her. She didn't dare look at Trace. At this point he could be in no doubt that his wife more than welcomed his lovemaking.

She heard him ask, "Hasn't the lift closed yet?" When James said there was time for one more run, Trace turned to her. "If you don't mind, Cassie, I'll go with James and Norman and meet you back at the lodge for dinner."

*What was going on?* He seemed to be relieved that

his brothers had interrupted their lovemaking; he'd leapt at the chance to join them. Yet Cassie could have sworn he was as shaken as she was by the passion they'd just shared. She'd thought he would tell his brothers to ski without him, that he and Cassie had other plans.

What a fool she was!

Trace was a man of experience and he'd simply been having a little fun in the snow. He hadn't meant anything serious. Most likely he was already regretting their interlude, because he hadn't expected her to respond the way she had. Well, she'd make sure he wouldn't worry that she'd gotten the wrong idea!

Lifting her head, she smiled brightly at the three of them. "To be honest, I was hoping someone else would come along to entertain Trace. For the last while, I've been dying to take my poor aching body back to the room and have a long hot soak in the tub. The altitude has made me so tired, I think I'll have a quick sandwich and go to bed. By the time you return, I'll probably be out like a light until morning."

"You sound like Dorothy," Norman moaned.

Trace's expression became shuttered, as if her answer displeased him. She couldn't figure him out. "I'll see you later then," he murmured, turning abruptly to get his skis.

With an aching heart Cassie watched until the three of them disappeared over the crest of the beginners' hill. He didn't once look back or wave.

What did he want? Should she have begged him in front of his brothers? Begged him to stay, to keep up the pretense that they had a normal marriage? If he hadn't regretted those intimate moments in her arms, then why had he left her?

Cassie didn't know what to make of his erratic behavior. Vowing never to get into such a vulnerable situation again, she trudged back to the lodge, ate another hamburger and went up to their room. An hour later, she climbed out of the tub, almost overcome with lethargy. She searched for the red flannel nightgown she'd made especially for the trip and fell into bed, exhausted. Once under the covers, she let out a deep sigh and was aware of nothing more until she wakened early the next morning, suffering from hunger pangs and sore muscles.

She glanced at her watch, surprised she'd slept so long. Trace was in the other bed, still asleep. When had he come to bed? She could hear his deep even breathing and noticed a tanned arm and shoulder above the blankets.

Carefully she turned on her side to watch him. Everything about him enthralled her. If he only loved her and she could be sure of his welcome, she'd climb in beside him right now and kiss him awake. The longer she gazed at him, the deeper her yearning.

When she couldn't bear it any longer, she slipped out of bed and hurried into the bathroom to dress. Now was as good a time as any to start ski lessons. Maybe later in the day Trace would join her again and she'd be able to show some improvement.

As quietly as she could, Cassie left the room and went down to the lobby to eat breakfast and arrange for lessons. Fortunately there was a woman on the ski patrol who taught group lessons in the morning before the lift opened, and Cassie signed up with her.

The class contained both children and adults at various stages of proficiency. Cassie discovered that Trace had taught her well, because she could keep up with the best of them. When the lesson was over, she hurried back to the room to tell him, but he'd already gone.

The rest of the day brought little pleasure. The flirtatious instructor, Hank, saw her on the hill later in the morning and wanted to ski with her, but she refused. Then it was time for lunch. She joined Dorothy, Jane and Lena, who all declared they'd had enough skiing for one day. Apparently the men had gone off together, so the women decided to play cards in front of the fire. Trace didn't make an appearance until everyone gathered for dinner in the main dining room that evening.

He greeted Cassie with a kiss on the cheek as if nothing was wrong, and laughed and joked with the others. Everyone described the day's events; inevitably, one of the women brought up the fact that Cassie had had a ski lesson. Trace murmured something appropriate and said that when she felt ready, they would take a run together. On the surface his behavior appeared perfectly normal. But Cassie sensed his withdrawal.

As the evening wore on, the family stayed downstairs for the musical entertainment. Cassie couldn't enjoy it because, although Trace always acted the part of a polite, concerned husband, he had distanced himself from her. This, more than anything, convinced her he wanted to forget what had happened on their first day in the snow.

Pleading fatigue, one by one each couple headed up to bed, until finally Cassie was left alone with Trace. "You seem tired," he said in that same polite voice. "Why don't you go up to bed? I'm going to have a drink in the bar."

Nothing could be plainer than that! Cassie murmured a good-night and barely made it to the room before she broke down sobbing. She couldn't take it much longer.

The next day started out like a repeat of the previous one, with Trace still sleeping soundly in the other bed as she left for her lesson. She was still agonizing over Trace when she entered the lobby afterward. Lena was waiting for her and asked if she'd like to take a shuttle bus down to Salt Lake City to do some shopping. Allen's birthday was the next weekend and Lena wanted to get him something special. Cassie didn't have to think twice about accepting her invitation. She wasn't an enthusiastic shopper, but anything was better than spending the rest of the day on the slopes hoping she'd run into Trace, or worse, praying in vain that he'd come to find her.

Lena wanted to keep their expedition a secret, so Cassie left Trace a note saying only that she was going down the canyon. They left the lodge with a group of other people to do a full day's shopping and sightseeing. The first thing Cassie bought was postcards, and while she and Lena ate Mexican food at Chef Trujillo's, she wrote short notes to some of her friends in San Francisco, including Beulah.

They spent the afternoon trailing in and out of shops. Cassie found hand-knit toques and mittens for the boys, some gourmet preserves for Nattie, and a small bottle of Canadian rye for Mike.

She managed to buy a gift for Trace, too. Quite by chance she'd seen a framed photograph of the mountains around Snowbird in a tourist shop, where Lena had already found another snow scene for Allen's gift. The shot was quite spectacular, with the early-morning rays tinting the snow-covered peaks. Luckily it didn't cost a great deal and was something she could buy with her own money, but she thought he'd like it.

By the time their bus pulled up to the lodge in the evening, the family had eaten and gone their separate ways. Cassie hurried upstairs with her packages, anxious to give Trace his present. But he wasn't in the room. If he'd gone to the bar, presumably he wanted to be alone, and she had no intention of disturbing him. If he was visiting with one of his brothers, she was equally unwilling to intrude. Dejected, she took a shower, put on her flannel nightgown and climbed into bed with a recent mystery novel she'd bought that afternoon.

Trace walked in half an hour later. Slowly Cassie's gaze lifted to his above the pages of the book. As always, she was achingly aware of him. He was dressed in sweats, with a deep tan that attested to a day's skiing—she noticed that instantly but she also noticed the tension in his posture and expression. "Hello," she said in an unsteady voice.

"So you're back." Grimacing, he tossed the room key on the table. "Did you have a good time?"

Cassie sat up straight, anxious to tell him about her day, to hear about his. "Yes. And I bought something for you. It's there on the bed."

He moved slowly to the bed and unwrapped the gift. "It's beautiful, Cassie—but you don't have to bribe me into going home. I know you never wanted to come to Snowbird in the first place."

The book fell out of her hands. "I don't want to leave. I'm having a good time."

His expression grew bleak. "Well, I'm not. I brought you here to spend time with you. But every time I turn around, you're missing. The family is beginning to wonder what's going on."

Anger made her face feel hot. "I thought the purpose of this trip was to be by ourselves and do what we wanted. If you remember, *you're* the one who took off with your brothers the first night we were here." She could have bitten her tongue for referring to that evening, but it was too late now.

Trace's mouth hardened, as if he didn't like being reminded of the incident. "Did you go to Salt Lake City alone?"

Cassie averted her eyes. His unexpected question had conveniently changed the subject. "No."

"I didn't think so."

Throwing back the covers, she got out of bed to

face him. To her dismay, his eyes traveled unhurriedly over her curves, which weren't hidden by the red fabric, then finally lifted to her flushed face. It was almost enough to make her forget what they were arguing about.

"In case you're thinking I was with that ski instructor," she said calmly, "then you couldn't be more wrong. For your information, I went to Salt Lake City with Lena—at her request. I thought you'd realize she and I were together. She wanted to buy something special for Allen's birthday and didn't want him to know about it."

"Be that as it may, your disappearances have pretty well let the family know that your interests lie outside your marriage."

"That's unfair!" she cried. "How can you say such a thing? Except for the first day, have you ever asked me to ski with you? Have you invited me out to dinner? Did you ask me to stay with you in the bar and dance?"

His expression was tight with fury. "After hearing you tell my brothers you were hoping someone else would come along to entertain me, I had doubts that any invitation of mine would be welcome."

Cassie's eyes closed tightly. "I only said that so you wouldn't feel obliged to stay with me. I know how much you love to ski with them."

They stood facing each other in silence, like adversaries. Finally he said, "Whatever the reasons for our misunderstandings, this trip isn't working out. Be packed and ready to go in the morning."

He placed the photograph and its crumpled wrappings on his night-table with a deliberate care that confused her. Then he disappeared out the door, leaving Cassie furious—and heartsick.

# CHAPTER EIGHT

AFTER EATING a bit of the chicken salad a surprised Nattie had left for her, Cassie started up the stairs to check on the children, whom she'd put to bed earlier. As she reached the first landing, she heard the phone ring. She fervently hoped it was Trace. He'd left for the office after they'd returned from Snowbird that afternoon and hadn't bothered to come home for dinner. She dashed into his study, picked up the receiver and said a nervous hello.

"Cassie? It's Lena!"

"Lena? What are you doing calling me from Snowbird?"

"More to the point, what are you and Trace doing back in Phoenix? Allen and I decided to sleep in this morning. When we got up, James told us you and Trace had left the lodge to go home. Something about a problem with one of the boys. I think everyone else believed it, but I don't. Can you talk, or is Trace around?"

"He went to the bank to see if there was anything pressing. I put the children to bed an hour ago and just had some supper."

"Then you can talk. What's wrong? You know I'd do anything for you and Trace."

"You shouldn't have said that." Cassie swallowed back a sob. "Trace and I have had one misunderstanding after another," she said hopelessly.

"Which one of you called off the rest of your vacation, or am I being too nosy?"

"Of course not. If you want the truth, I think he's tired of having to pretend everything's perfect with us when we're around the family. I never seem to be able to say the right thing. We do much better alone at the house, with just the children. Our marriage won't survive another vacation."

"I'm sorry, Cassie. This must be so hard for you. I was once in love with someone and I thought he loved me, until I learned the truth the hard way. It took me a long time to get over him, so I can just imagine what you're going through right now. I wish there was something I could do to help."

"I appreciate your support and friendship. Unfortunately no one can make Trace fall in love with me," Cassie said in a voice that quavered despite her effort to sound matter-of-fact. "If it hasn't happened by now, it never will. That's the reality and I'm going to have to live with it. Don't forget, I went into this marriage for the children's sake."

"But the children will never be enough now."

"I hope you're wrong," she said softly, then broke off when she heard footsteps on the stairs. "Lena, I'll have to hang up. I think Trace is home."

"All right. I'll call you as soon as we get back."

"Thanks for everything." Cassie put down the receiver as the study door flew open and Trace stood there, silhouetted in the light from a hallway lamp. Cassie muttered a greeting, but something in his stance made her unaccountably nervous.

"You're upset. Did something go wrong with the merger while we were on our trip?" she asked.

"If you weren't so preoccupied with your phone call, you would have been able to hear the boys crying. Who has such a claim on your time you've been neglecting them?"

His unfair accusation stung Cassie to retaliation. "How dare you say that to me when you didn't bother to come home for dinner to be with them—or even call to let me know you'd be late!" she demanded, her chest heaving with indignation.

His hands curled into fists, and without volition, her eyes took in the strength of his body, the powerful thighs in tight-fitting jeans, the black knit shirt that clung to his chest like a second skin. They were close enough that she could feel the warmth of his body and smell the soap he'd used in the shower. Right now she couldn't think or move as desire for him engulfed her like a sudden burst of flame.

"I dare because I'm your husband." A hand shot out and grasped her wrist, bringing her closer and making her far too conscious of his body. "You still haven't answered my question."

She could have told him the truth—that it was Lena on the phone—but she didn't. She was too angry, because he didn't seem to trust her. And at the same time she needed to put distance between them before she lost complete control.

"As I recall," she said coldly, "*you* were the one who said what we did with our private lives was our own affair, as long as it didn't hurt the children. I never question the unorthodox hours you keep, and I'm not doing anything you haven't done since the day we were married." She tried to pull away, but he held her fast.

"And just what is it you think I've been doing?" he whispered. "Making secret assignations behind your back? Why should I do that when I have a wife who seems perfectly capable of filling everyone's needs—but mine? I think it's time you took care of them."

In the next instant he drew her into his arms and found her mouth with a savagery that made nonsense of her efforts to resist. For so long she'd wanted him, but not like this, not angry and suspicious of her motives. Yet she wasn't prepared for the intimate caress of his hands against the skin of her back, where her blouse had separated from her jeans. His touch softened and Cassie melted against every line and angle of his hard body, helplessly yielding to the seductive pressure of his mouth, his hands.

Cassie hadn't ever known this kind of ecstasy before, and she didn't want Trace to stop. Her arms slid around his neck so she could get even closer. She wanted to give, and go on giving until he knew in every single cell of his body that she loved him. That she always would.

Perhaps it was her moan of pleasure that caused a shudder to pass through his body. The next thing she knew, he had thrust her away from him. She cried out in surprise and clung to his desk to prevent herself from falling.

The faint light made it impossible for her to see his expression clearly. But if his shallow breathing and the tautness of his body were any indication, he'd been equally disturbed by their passionate embrace.

Then she heard a muttered curse before he blurted out, "I had no right to lay a finger on you, Cassie, let alone demand an accounting. Whatever you do with your free time is none of my damn business. I'm the one who's broken the rules of our contract and I swear it won't happen again. Why don't you go on up to bed. I know you're under a lot of pressure, getting ready for your opening. I'll lock up and take a look at the boys before I turn in."

She watched him leave the study and ached to call him back. But without knowing how he really felt about her, what he really wanted from her, she didn't dare. Living in the same house day after day had made them aware of each other to the point of physical need. She'd felt Trace's desire for her. But that didn't mean he was in love with her.

Drained from the explosive emotions, Cassie followed his suggestion and went to bed. But she was plagued with insomnia. Trace had set her on fire, exposing the primitive, womanly side of her nature, changing her preconceived notions about physical love for all time.

By two o'clock, her body was still reliving the taste and feel of his mouth and she couldn't fall asleep.

Disgusted with herself, she went to her sewing room, where she immersed herself in work and didn't come out until seven in the morning.

When she went downstairs to start breakfast, she discovered that Trace's car wasn't in the driveway. He'd deliberately left the house early; when she realized this, her hurt intensified. She went through the motions of her morning routine, which included bathing and feeding the children. At noon Nattie took over so she could leave the house and drive to the gallery with as many things as she could load into the station wagon. This set the pattern for the next few days.

Besides all the new crafts she'd been making, she decided to sell all the stock items from her inventory, too. There was a second display room, which would be perfect. But even with Mike's help, it took several days to move everything from the house to the shop. During that time, she saw next to nothing of Trace, who came home too late to do more than kiss the boys good-night and disappear into his study.

On Friday, as Cassie was unpacking another set of freestanding shelves at the shop and trying not to think about the impossible state of affairs between her and Trace, Lena walked in, carrying some paintings.

Cassie stared at her sister-in-law. "I'm so glad you're back."

"I bet you thought I'd deserted you, staying so long at Snowbird, but Allen and I had to be alone. I've tried to make up for lost time today by signing the rest of the paintings. As you know, my car won't hold more than two at a time, so I'll have to make several trips."

Shaking her head, Cassie said, "We'll go back to the house in the station wagon and get the rest. Now that you've finished them, I'm going to stay here all evening and set up as much as I can to view the full effect." She glanced around. "I think I'm going to have to buy some more plants, though."

Lena scrutinized everything with her artist's eye. "I'll tell you what. I want to be home with the children for dinner. Then I'll come back here to help, but it'll have to remain our secret. Allen can think I've gone to a PTA meeting."

"Are you sure?" Cassie cried out excitedly. Trace would be overjoyed if he knew how involved Lena had become with Mix and Match.

"You're a remarkable woman, Cassie, but even I can see how much work still has to be done."

"The opening's coming up much too soon," Cassie agreed, "and there aren't enough hours in the day to accomplish everything. Now let's go home and get the rest of the paintings."

She didn't particularly relish the prospect of being at the shop alone at night and would be thankful for Lena's presence. Although she wasn't entirely comfortable with her sister-in-law's apparent penchant for secrecy, she could understand it, too. Lena was so terribly unsure of herself and of her talent.

As it turned out, Lena and Cassie worked side by side for the next two nights, attempting to set up the most appealing displays possible. And they shared more confidences. Cassie marveled at her sister-in-law's decorating sense and thanked her repeatedly before they parted company Saturday night.

"Don't forget Allen's surprise birthday dinner at seven tomorrow. I phoned Trace earlier and invited him, so he knows you're both expected."

*And probably dreading another evening with me in front of his family,* Cassie mused painfully. "Will everyone be there?"

"No. It's just going to be the four of us," Lena explained, lessening Cassie's anxiety somewhat.

The next morning didn't begin well. Nattie informed Cassie that Trace had left to keep a golf date with a business acquaintance. When he did come home, he spent some time with the children, and she didn't see him until they were ready to go to Lena's.

They behaved civilly to each other, but during dinner Trace couldn't have been more distant with Cassie, more removed from her emotionally—a fact Lena was quick to observe. While they cleared the table, she flashed Cassie a look of commiseration.

Cassie was grateful for Allen, whose conversation as he opened his presents provided the only comic relief. His eyes met his wife's as he unwrapped the framed photograph she'd bought him in Utah and he sent her a message of love so fervent that Cassie lowered her own eyes. She knew he must be remembering the private time he and Lena had spent at Snowbird. But the moment was brief and he quickly moved on to the other gifts, ending with Cassie's. Lena had told her that Allen loved to barbecue, so Cassie had made him a chef's apron embroidered with French cooking terms.

"So tell me, you lucky cuss." Allen poked Trace in the ribs. "How did you manage to end up with Cassie? She can cook, sew, she's a great mother and her skiing's coming along nicely. She's a looker, too."

Normally Cassie would have been amused by Allen's remarks. But she was too sensitive to Trace's mood just now. She found herself waiting uncomfortably for one of his carefully worded responses while she pretended interest in the birthday cake.

"You left out the part about her being a savvy business woman," Lena interjected on cue, saving Trace from having to utter a word.

"That's right," Allen murmured. "How's the shop coming?"

His question was directed at Cassie, but it was Trace who answered. "Judging by the nights she's stayed up sewing, I'd say she probably has more than enough things to fill several shops." Although his comment sounded innocent, Cassie wasn't deceived. She lowered her head, but not before Lena had sent her a sympathetic glance.

"When's the opening?" Allen asked, seemingly ignorant of the undercurrents. "Lena and I plan to be there."

"Next Saturday," Cassie said faintly. The tension emanating from Trace left her so nervous, she was finding it more and more difficult to speak.

Suddenly Lena cleared her throat and looked nervously at her husband. "Darling, I think it's time I made a confession." There was an air of expectancy after her announcement.

"We're not pregnant again, are we?" he teased, but Cassie could see the love shining in his eyes.

"No." Lena laughed. "When I told you I had meetings the last two nights, I was lying." Allen's smile slowly faded. "Actually, I've been helping Cassie at the gallery."

Allen blinked. "That's great. But why didn't you just say so?"

"Because...Cassie's using some of my old paintings as part of her display. At first I didn't want you to know about it because..."

He stopped eating his cake and gazed at his wife solemnly. "Does this mean what I think it means?"

She took a deep breath. "It means that I've been a fool to be so sensitive about the past."

"Honey..." Allen's hand grasped hers.

Something was going on here that Cassie didn't quite understand. Allen seemed overwhelmed with emotion. She automatically glanced at Trace and discovered his eyes focused on her, sending her a private message of gratitude. Even if the warmth in his regard had everything to do with her influence on Lena, Cassie basked in his approval. She had no pride anymore. She loved him too much.

In the background she could hear the phone ringing and then Becky, Lena's daughter, poked her head around the dining-room door. "Aunt Cassie? Uncle

Trace? Nattie says you'd better come home. Jason woke up croupy."

The twelve hours following Lena's dinner party would have been a nightmare for Cassie if Trace hadn't been there to help nurse Jason through the night. First roseola, now a croupy cough that kept them all awake. By noon the next day, however, he seemed much better and Cassie finally relaxed.

She couldn't say the same for Trace. Fatigue lines etched his face from hour after hour of walking the floor with Jason. Cassie urged him to call Mrs. Blakesley and cancel any appointments for the day so he could go to bed. But Trace insisted he had to be at the bank for an important afternoon meeting and left the house at a run.

Once again she found herself marveling at the extraordinary strength of the man she'd married. Trace was unfailingly responsible, always dependable. The longer she lived with him, the more Cassie realized how much she, as well as others, particularly his family, relied on him. Though the youngest Ramsey, it was no accident that his brothers had made him chairman of the board. His confidence and his abilities made people put their trust in him.

Because he worked so hard, Cassie was concerned about his not getting enough rest, and she spent the remainder of the afternoon and evening worrying about her husband instead of Jason, who was starting to behave more like himself again.

Cassie had been asleep for some time when she heard a knock on her door. Alarmed, she glanced at the bedside clock, which said it was after midnight. The knock sounded again.

"Nattie?" she called anxiously and sat up in bed.

"It's Trace, Cassie. I need to talk to you. May I come in?"

"Yes. Of course." Her voice shook as she turned on the lamp and pulled the covers to her chin. "Is Jason bad again?" she asked as he entered her bedroom wearing his bathrobe. He must have come from the shower because the clean scent of soap wafted in the air.

Trace closed the door behind him and approached her bed. "No. I just checked on him. He's fine. So's Justin."

She swallowed hard. "When did you come home? I held dinner until nine, then put yours in the fridge."

"I'm sorry I was late again. I only just got home." The lines in his face were more pronounced than ever.

"You should have been in bed hours ago, Trace. You look exhausted. How did your meeting go?" Cassie had the hysterical urge to laugh because he'd never been in her bedroom this late at night before, and here were the two of them talking like a comfortably married couple.

"Very well, as a matter of fact, but I didn't waken you to talk about bank business. I have something much more serious on my mind."

"Is it about Lena and Allen?"

Her question seemed to baffle him. "No. Why would it be when things have never been better between them?"

"I meant to ask you about that. Why was Allen so overcome by what she said?"

"Because for all the years they've been married, Allen had a secret fear that Lena couldn't talk about her painting or even admit she was once an artist because she was still in love with her ex-lover. Allen hasn't always been the comedian he pretends to be. His jovial behavior has been a front for insecurity, even pain."

"But that's crazy!" Cassie cried. "Lena adores Allen. She's confided everything to me, and I promise you, she got over that affair years ago. She asked Allen if they could stay on in Snowbird after everyone left because she wanted to have a second honeymoon with him."

The pulse at the corner of his mouth throbbed. "Every man should be so lucky. After her unprompted confession last night, I think he's beginning to believe she loves him wholeheartedly—thanks to you."

Cassie shook her head. "Not me, Trace. You. It was your suggestion that prompted me to talk to Lena in the first place. Somehow you have a gift for making everything right for everybody. The boys are very lucky to have a father like you," she said with a catch in her voice.

"I wonder if this gift you credit me with can fix something a little closer to home."

Her heart thudded painfully at his sober tone. "What is it? What's wrong?"

A grimace marred his handsome features. "When

I asked you to marry me, we agreed that if there ever came a time when we didn't like the arrangement, we'd face that problem when it arose.''

It was a good thing Cassie was already in bed or she might have fainted. "I remember," she whispered, hardly able to get the words out. "I've been aware for some time that you haven't been happy. Actually I've wanted to talk to you about it, but the opportunity never seemed to present itself."

After a long pause, he said, "That's my fault. I realize I've been impossible to live with. Cassie, I can't go on this way any longer."

A numbing sickness slowly crept through her body. "You don't need to say any more. I'll move out."

To her astonishment his head reared back. "What in the hell are you talking about? I came in here tonight to tell you I hate the rules of our marriage contract and I'm asking you to start sleeping with me in my bed."

When his words sank in, Cassie felt herself go feverishly hot, then cold. She raised her eyes to him in disbelief. He muttered something unintelligible and shook his head when he saw her stunned expression.

"Living in the same house with you and not being able to make love to you has almost driven me out of my mind. Surely after the other night you can be in no doubt about how much I want you. I almost couldn't let you go."

His admission opened a floodgate of emotions in Cassie. There was no mistaking the look of desire in his eyes as he sat down on the bed next to her and traced the outline of her flushed face with his fingers. "I'm aching to touch you and hold you all night long. You're in my blood, Cassie—and I know of only one way to solve that particular problem."

In the next instant his mouth covered hers, forcing her head back against the pillow. For a little while Cassie refused to listen to her heart, which told her there was all the difference in the world between a man's desire for a woman and his love. The sensations his lips aroused against the tender skin of her neck and throat were so addictive she never wanted him to stop. She could no longer think coherently.

But when he lifted the covers to slide into bed beside her she couldn't help remembering that this was how his son's conception had begun. By Trace's own admission, he'd never have married Gloria if he hadn't made her pregnant. Their passion had resulted in a baby, but Jason wasn't the product of two people deeply in love who needed to express those feelings in the age-old way. They had divorced soon after the birth.

Cassie loved Trace with a fierceness he hadn't even guessed at. As for his feelings, she wasn't so naive that she didn't know this would be simply another night of physical passion for him. Sexual gratification, without the heart-deep commitment she desperately needed. Cassie had no way of determining how many times he'd experienced this same desire for the latest woman in his life. *Because that was all she was— and she happened to be available!* The word "love" hadn't even been mentioned. When he tired of her, they'd go back to being housemates again.

Unable to tolerate that possibility, she pushed herself away from him and got to her feet. When he stood up, they faced each other from opposite sides of the narrow bed. Trace ran a hand through his already disheveled black hair, a gesture so sensual she had to close her eyes against its appeal. He would never know what denying herself his lovemaking was costing her.

"The desire seems to be all on my part."

She swallowed hard. "When two people aren't in love, then it's wrong."

The silence seemed to stretch endlessly before he said, "It's inconceivable to me that a woman as warm and beautiful and desirable as you would be willing to go through her whole life without ever experiencing sexual intimacy. I was wrong in asking you to enter this farcical arrangement."

With those words Cassie lost every vestige of hope that he might come to love her. "So far, I—I've been...happy with it," she stammered. "I'm sorry if it hasn't worked out for you, since you've had ample opportunity to spend your free time with anyone you wanted, no questions asked."

His features could have been cast in stone. "You're right. I have," he retorted.

"I'll move out after the opening if that's what you want."

"It's not!" he fired back, sounding more intense than she'd ever heard him before. "The boys adore you and I have living proof that they're your whole raison d'être. Any problems we have are mine and mine alone." He strode from the room without a backward glance.

Since she couldn't imagine a life without him, she should have been overjoyed that he hadn't taken her up on her offer to leave. But once he'd gone, Cassie flung herself on the bed and buried her face in the pillow to stifle her sobs.

Contrary to her expectations, for the rest of the week Trace was surprisingly kind and considerate, and never once alluded to the ugly scene in her bedroom. He came home early every night to help with the children so Cassie would be free to prepare for the opening. It reminded her of the first few weeks of their marriage, when they'd enjoyed an easy camaraderie and shared the joys of caring for the children.

But in those early days she'd still retained the hope that Trace would fall in love with her and make their marriage a real one. All she could do now was shower her affection on the children and concentrate on her business in an effort to ignore the aching void only Trace could fill.

Late Friday afternoon, before the grand opening on Saturday, Cassie was at the gallery finishing up some last-minute details when she heard a familiar voice call her name.

She spun around to face the tall, rangy man with dark brown hair and eyes who'd been watching her. "Rolfe!" Somehow in the rush of things she'd completely forgotten about his coming to Phoenix.

"You look wonderful, Cass." He held out his arms and she ran into them, hugging him tightly. "I've missed you," he murmured into her hair.

"I've missed you, too." But the way he was holding her made her realize he was about to kiss her and she quickly pulled out of his arms. "I had no idea you were in town."

"I flew in an hour ago and phoned the number Mother gave me. Your housekeeper said you were down here, so I thought I'd come and surprise you."

"You certainly did that." She smiled, then asked deliberately, "Did you bring your fiancée back with you?"

He frowned. "I thought you'd be able to tell from the telegram that I'm no longer engaged."

"And you thought you'd come back into Cassie's life and pick up where you left off?"

Cassie's eyes widened in astonishment to discover that Trace had come into the shop and was strolling toward them, still dressed in the suit he'd worn to work. He carried a sack of take-out fried chicken. She was so surprised to see him and so thrilled that he'd been thoughtful enough to bring dinner she wished Rolfe a thousand miles away.

"Trace, this is Rolfe Timpson. Rolfe, I'd like you to meet my husband, Trace Ramsey."

The two men took each other's measure, and Trace nodded, but neither put out a hand.

"What is it you're after, Timpson? My wife is busy getting ready for her opening. This isn't the best time to come calling."

Rolfe's gaze slid to Cassie's. "She knows why I'm here. Cassie and I have always belonged together. I made a mistake when I broke our engagement. I was too impatient, but I've learned my lesson and I want her back, no matter how long it takes."

"It's too late," Trace interjected before she could say anything. "Cassie's my wife now."

Undaunted, Rolfe continued to stare at her. "But I know how she really feels, and I have a letter to prove it. She married you to be close to Susan's baby, nothing more."

*Dear Lord. The letter.* Cassie had forgotten all about it. But that was before she'd married Trace and fallen in love with him.

Trace's body tautened. "That's right, Timpson. Now she's the mother of both my children, and that's the way it's going to stay. Have a good trip back to San Francisco." Trace put the food on the counter and darted her a mysterious glance. "I presume I'll be seeing you at home soon? Early enough to help put the boys to bed?"

"Yes," she called after him softly. "I was just closing up. Thank you for dinner." She would have kissed his cheek, but he'd already turned on his heel and walked out of the shop.

Rolfe studied her, and the silence stretched between them. "Did I misunderstand your letter, Cassie?"

She shook her head. "No. But I wrote it before I married Trace."

Again there was a long period of quiet. "You're in love with him, aren't you?"

"Yes."

He took a fortifying breath. "You were never in love with me, but I didn't want to believe it."

Cassie's eyes clouded over. "I'll always love you, Rolfe—like a brother. You're the most wonderful man I know, next to Trace."

"I threw it all away when I broke our engagement."

"No. Don't you see? If you'd really loved me the way I love Trace, you wouldn't have left. But you did because you sensed it wasn't right between us. And even if your engagement to the woman you met in Belgium didn't last, it proves you were ready for another relationship."

"I'll never forget you, Cass."

She smiled. "And I'll always remember you, because you were my first love."

# CHAPTER NINE

CASSIE COULD HARDLY WAIT to get home to Trace. Maybe he wasn't in love with her, but he'd let Rolfe know in no uncertain terms that he wanted Cassie to remain his wife. It was a beginning, and she was determined that in time their marriage would become a proper one.

The minute Rolfe left the store, she closed up and sped home, snatching bites of the delicious chicken he'd brought her every time she stopped for a light.

The absence of his car in the drive sent her spirits plummeting as she pulled up to the house. And Nattie's explanation that he hadn't come home yet filled her with dread. She'd expected him to be here, playing with the children. Waiting for her.

When eleven o'clock arrived, he still hadn't come home. Cassie finally gave up her vigil and went to bed, needing sleep before her opening the next day. But it was fitful and she awakened restless and out of sorts.

The next morning after her shower, she put on a smart navy silk suit she'd purchased a few days earlier. The tailoring and sophistication bolstered her waning confidence.

Lena planned to meet her at Mix and Match at eight. Cassie went in to kiss the children goodbye before leaving for the gallery, skipping breakfast altogether. If Trace was up, she didn't see a sign of him, and she drove away from the house in tears.

"You look beautiful," Lena told her when Cassie arrived at the back entrance to the shop. "But you've been crying. What's wrong?"

"Let's go in and I'll tell you."

While they got the shop ready, Cassie explained what had happened the night before. "I don't understand him, Lena. He's like a wind that blows hot, then cold. I can't live the rest of my life this way."

"I don't like the sound of that. What are you planning to do?"

"I—I'm not sure. I have to get through today before I can make any serious decisions."

"Cassie, a word of advice. Don't act hastily. Give everything more time."

"Time seems to be making things worse."

She wasn't destined to hear Lena's response because a young man appeared at the door holding an enormous spray of the most exquisite yellow roses Cassie had ever seen. There had to be five or six dozen, at least. "I have a delivery for Cassie Ramsey."

"Oh, they're gorgeous!" Lena exclaimed. "And I have a pretty good idea who sent them."

Cassie signed for them, and when the delivery man had gone she hunted for the card tucked among the sprays of fern. "A woman like you makes her own luck, but you have all my best wishes just the same. Trace." The words reminded her forcefully of another time when he'd complimented her for being able to stand on her own two feet. *Alone.*

Crushing the card in her hand, she whispered to Lena, "Would you find a good spot for these so Trace will see them when he comes by later?"

Lena took the flowers from her. "Heavens, Cassie. You look so pale. What's wrong?"

"Nothing. Just more of Trace's...kindness. If you'll open the machine, I'll get busy putting out the rest of the door prizes in case we have an overflow. I'm being optimistic, aren't I?" She laughed nervously.

Lena slid a comforting arm around Cassie's waist before they both went to work. At five to ten, there were people milling around the store entrance. Her thoughts went back to a time in San Francisco when she hadn't a prayer of realizing her dream of opening a boutique. Again she had to remind herself how lucky she was. But at what price?

The next hour flew by in a blur of activity. Besides curious shoppers who lingered and raved over the displays, unable to make up their minds about what they wanted to buy, there must have been half a dozen more florist deliveries from every member of Trace's family, as well as the manager of Crossroads Square.

At eleven o'clock, another flower arrangement arrived, from Beulah no less. And right after that, three men brought in an enormous flowering cactus. A banner that wished Cassie and Lena good luck was signed, "Compliments of the Greater Phoenix Banking Corporation."

The noon hour brought in more traffic, and suddenly everyone seemed ready to make purchases. At one point, Cassie looked up and noted to her astonishment that the shop was slowly being denuded of its inventory. She couldn't believe it.

"Mrs. Ramsey?" someone called to her.

She turned her head and thought she recognized the manager of a well-known restaurant down the street from Crossroads Square. "I know we've met, but I'm embarrassed to say I don't remember your name."

"Hal Sykes." He grinned. "Welcome to the block. I saw your ad in the paper and decided to drop in. I'm very glad I did. There are three paintings I'm interested in purchasing, but I don't see a price on any of them. Does that mean they've already sold?"

Cassie grinned widely as she looked at Lena, madly ringing up one sale after another. "I'll tell you what," she murmured. "You can talk to the artist, Mrs. Haroldson, and see what she says. Just a minute."

With her adrenaline pumping, Cassie worked her way through the crowd to the counter. "Lena, I'll take over here. There's a Mr. Sykes standing by the cactus who wants help. He's in the pink shirt."

Lena darted him a glance. "His face looks familiar."

"That's because we ate in his restaurant the other day."

"I remember. Okay. I'll be right back."

Cassie chuckled to herself in glee when yet another

customer inquired about one of the paintings and left her card. Lena didn't return until a half hour later, looking positively dazed. "What did Mr. Sykes want?" Cassie asked between sales.

Lena blinked. "He offered me five thousand dollars for the three paintings over there. He's remodeling part of his restaurant and says they'd be perfect for the decor."

Keeping a poker face, Cassie said, "I hope you told him ten thousand or nothing."

"*Cassie!*"

"Well?"

"I—I told him they weren't for sale, but he wrote out a check, anyway, and said he'd be back before we closed at seven, in case I changed my mind." She handed Cassie the check, made out to Mix and Match Southwest.

"I could use money like that to replenish my inventory," Cassie said matter-of-factly and put the check in the till. "Before you turn him down flat, why don't we talk about it? Say fifteen percent for every painting sold out of the store, and the rest for you?"

"Be serious," Lena said in a trembling voice.

"I am," Cassie came back. "A few minutes ago a woman told me she was interested in your sunset painting, the one with all the pinks and oranges. She's a New Yorker who wanted to take home a souvenir of Arizona. She's also an art dealer and offered four thousand for it. Here's her card. You're supposed to get in touch with her at that number next week."

"Hi, honey. How's it going?" a familiar voice broke in on their conversation.

Lena whirled around, her gray eyes luminous. "Allen!"

"I'm glad you're here." Cassie beamed at her brother-in-law. "Business is booming and we both need a break. Why don't you take your wife out for a quick lunch? When she returns, I'll grab a bite."

"Are you sure?" They both spoke at once.

"It's not quite as busy as it was earlier. But don't forget to come back. I can't run this place without you."

"A half hour," Lena promised. "No longer."

"Be sure and tell Allen about the nine thousand offered for your paintings already. And the day's only half over!"

In front of any number of interested customers, Allen let out a whoop of joy and swung Lena around before hustling her out of the shop.

Trace's clever scheme to help his sister looked as if it had succeeded, and Cassie couldn't help but take personal delight in the knowledge that she'd played a part. But with the steady stream of customers waiting to pay for their purchases, Cassie didn't have time to dwell on anything. Including the bleakness of her own future after she left Trace....

There had hardly been a lull since the doors opened. Naturally the opening would attract more shoppers than Cassie could expect on a regular business day. Still, she had to admit the large turnout was gratifying, and she prayed it augured well for future sales, since she wouldn't be depending on Trace's support any longer.

While she chatted with customers and took orders for items already sold out, she was making plans to search for a small apartment in Phoenix. She could live there and still have regular access to the children. She and Trace wouldn't have to see each other; Nattie and Mike could help make visitations smooth and pleasant.

Even if Cassie felt like the boys' mother, the fact remained that she was Justin's aunt and had no blood ties to Jason whatsoever. Under the circumstances, it would be wisest to move out of Trace's home now and establish herself in the community where she could earn her living. She'd see the boys whenever possible. As long as they wanted a relationship, she would be there for them in the capacity of aunt and friend.

No matter what Trace said, in time he'd fall in love and want to marry for all the right reasons, ultimately providing the boys with a stepmother. Painful as that would be to face, Cassie knew what she had to do for the welfare of all concerned.

"Look who I brought back with me." Lena's happy voice broke in on Cassie's thoughts as she was straightening the counter. She glanced up in time to see most of Trace's family enter the shop. The Ramseys' striking looks caused heads to turn. One by one they came over to give Cassie a hug while she thanked them for the flowers.

"I'm so proud of you, dear." Olivia patted Cassie's cheek. Then nodding toward Lena, who'd taken over at the cash register, the older woman whispered, "Bless you, Cassie."

"It's Trace's doing. You know that," Cassie whispered back.

"I know a lot more than you think."

Cassie barely had time to ponder her mother-in-law's mysterious reply, because there was a commotion at the door. As she turned her head, she caught sight of a tanned, relaxed-looking Trace, wheeling in the children seated in their two-seater stroller. Their entry caused delighted outbursts from his family, as well as other shoppers who crowded round.

Trace wore chinos and a navy sports shirt, open at the neck. The boys were dressed in identical navy sailor suits she'd made for them. On their feet were spanking white shoes and socks. They looked so marvelous Cassie forgot where she was and could do nothing more than lean against the glass countertop for support, feasting her eyes. There they were, not ten feet away. The three people in the world she loved more than life itself.

At that moment she experienced a pain so staggering she thought she might faint. Since the children hadn't yet seen her, she said, "Lena, excuse me for a minute." Without waiting to hear her sister-in-law's reply, Cassie hurried to the back room, which served as a supply area with an adjoining bathroom.

She waited until the wave of sickness had passed, then applied fresh lipstick before going back out. Trace was waiting for her on the other side of the door, his face alarmed. He put a hand to her forehead. "I saw you dash in here. You're white as parchment. Are you sick?"

Cassie took a deep breath. "No. It's probably a combination of nerves and the fact that we've been so busy all day I haven't had a chance to eat yet."

A pulse throbbed at his temple as he ushered her to a utility chair and forced her to sit down. "Then let's get you something right now. Lena said she'd be fine and Mother's watching the children."

"Actually, I don't feel like going anyplace, but a drink would be wonderful. There's a grocery farther down in the mall."

"Stay here and I'll get it." He was gone in a flash and returned not only with a carton of milk but an apple. Cassie thanked him and proceeded to enjoy both.

"The color's returned to your cheeks," he murmured after she'd finished the milk.

"I feel fine now, and a bit of a fool. Thank you for coming to my rescue. I should've packed a lunch and brought it with me, but I never dreamed there'd be so many customers."

He studied her face for a long moment. "I told the boys their mother's shop would be a raving success. They wanted to see for themselves, and so did I." He paused, still watching her closely. "I hope you don't mind."

Cassie jumped up from the chair and averted her eyes to hide the turmoil going on inside her. Did he mean what he was implying, or was this another ploy to convince the family they were a happily married couple?

"Of course I don't mind. I'm thrilled to see them. They look adorable in those outfits, don't they? Let's go find them."

Trace put a detaining hand on her arm. "Are you sure you're feeling all right?"

"Of course. I just needed a pick-me-up. Thank you."

Too affected by his nearness, Cassie hurried out front with Trace at her heels and discovered the boys being held by James and Norman. The minute the children saw Cassie they squealed in excitement and wriggled in their uncles' arms, trying to reach her.

With patrons in the store to wait on, she couldn't do more than kiss the children. They started crying when she left them to walk behind the counter.

"I'll get them out of here before we disrupt things any more," Trace offered.

"The flowers are beautiful. Thank you for making all this possible. And for coming."

She heard his quick intake of breath. "I'm your husband, for heaven's sake. Why wouldn't I be here?" he muttered angrily. She dared a brief glance at him and thought she detected a flash of pain in the blue eyes that bore into hers. He fairly bristled with emotion as he turned swiftly to gather the children. Cassie wanted to call him back, but now was not the time.

For the rest of the day she was haunted by the look in Trace's eyes, and she simply went through the motions as she greeted customers and rang up sales. By six-thirty the crowds had diminished; for the first time all day Cassie and Lena were able to straighten the remaining merchandise and start ringing out the cash register.

"All the Southwest pieces sold," Cassie commented in surprise. Automatically her eyes sought out the painting that had first inspired them, but it wasn't there. She frowned. "Lena? Where's your Hopi girl painting?"

Her sister-in-law blushed. "Would you believe Allen bought it and took it home with him? He left a check in the register."

"Good for him," she murmured. "Trace thinks it's your best painting and I agree with him. Lena, would you mind very much closing up for me tonight? I have something I need to do."

"I might as well start now, since I'm going to need the practice." Cassie's head lifted in query. "You might as well know. I've been painting again and I've been having the time of my life. Allen and I talked about it over lunch. If your offer is still open, I'd like to be the other half of this business venture."

Wordlessly Cassie flung her arms around Lena's slender shoulders and hugged her.

"Allen's coming any minute and we'll take care of everything. Go home to Trace," Lena urged.

"That's what I'm going to do. I love him and I'm going to tell him exactly how I feel. No matter what his response is, I can't hide my emotions any longer."

But when she returned to the house, it was still and

dark. The children were gone. Not even Nattie and Mike were around. In a state of panic, Cassie phoned the shop and cried out in relief when Lena answered.

"Lena, it's Cassie. There's no one home, not even the children. Do you have any idea where Trace might have gone with them?"

"I think I heard Mom offer to take the boys overnight."

"Thanks. I'll call over there." Sure enough, Olivia Ramsey was baby-sitting and told Cassie that Trace had said something about working late at the office. Cassie thanked her and hung up the phone, a plan already forming in her mind.

She ran to her workroom closet and retrieved the six-foot alligator hidden behind the material. After stuffing it into the car, she sped along the highway toward the heart of Phoenix. Nighttime traffic was moderate, so she made it downtown within half an hour. Fortunately, the parking lot, almost empty now, stayed lighted all night long. As she drove in, she immediately saw Trace's black Mercedes, and she pulled up next to it, her heart hammering almost painfully.

The alligator made an awkward burden but she managed to half-carry, half-drag it to the security guard's cubicle. He had no idea who she was, since she'd been in the bank only once before. It seemed a century ago to Cassie.

He stared at the alligator, then at her, his eyes narrowing suspiciously. "Can I help you, ma'am?"

"My husband is here working late. I decided to surprise him."

He looped his thumbs over his belt, drawing her attention to his hip holster. "The only person in the building is Mr. Ramsey."

"I'm Mrs. Ramsey. We've never met." She put out her hand but he didn't shake it. Cassie's mood bordered on hysteria—why was she barred from seeing her own husband?

"I'll have to call and let him know you're down here."

"But that would spoil my surprise." She tried to appear friendly as she said it, hoping to win him over. But the man remained adamant.

"Sorry. I can't let you in without his okay."

She bit her lip in frustration and searched in her handbag for her wallet. "Here." She thrust her credit cards and driver's license at him.

He glanced at them, then shook his head.

She sighed angrily. "Then you leave me no choice. Will you please let him know Cassie would like to see him?"

The sandy-haired man nodded and picked up the phone. "Mr. Ramsey? There's a woman down here who claims to be your wife. She says her name's Cassie and she has ID to that effect—but you never know…"

Cassie tapped her foot impatiently as the guard gave her the once-over.

"She's about five two or three, blond, green-eyed. She's also good looking—and, uh, built, if you know what I mean," he murmured in a lowered voice, but Cassie heard him and felt heat rush to her face. "The thing is, she's carrying this stuffed animal around that's bigger than she is," he confided. "Yes, sir." He nodded, then turned to Cassie. "Can I see that thing, ma'am?" he asked unexpectedly.

"Be my guest," she muttered, wishing she could throw it at him.

Putting down the phone, he grabbed the alligator and looked it up and down, then examined it front and back, before picking up the receiver again. "It's a green 'gator about six feet in length with black hair, blue eyes and a wicked grin. It says 'Daddy' on the tail." He laughed as he spoke. After another moment, he said, "Yes, *sir!*" and hung up. All signs of mirth had vanished.

"*Now* do I have your permission to go up?" she asked in her iciest tone. Enough was enough!

"Sorry, ma'am. I can't let you do that." After propping the alligator against the glass, he reached for his belt, and before she knew what had happened, he had fastened something metal around her wrist. She was so astonished she'd actually stood there and let him handcuff her to his wrist.

"Now, wait just a minute!" she raged, trying to pull away from him, thinking it had to be a trick. But she might as well have saved her energy.

"It seems a woman bearing your description barged into his office a few months ago with some outrageous story. He said if you were the one, you could be dangerous. He told me to detain you until he comes down and checks you out. I'm only doing my job, ma'am."

"Which you do admirably, Lewis."

Furious, Cassie turned in the direction of her husband's voice. He stepped out of the elevator, his black hair attractively mussed, still wearing the casual navy outfit he'd had on earlier. Without giving her as much as a glance, he reached for the alligator and studied it thoroughly.

"She's the one, Lewis. Unlock the handcuffs and I'll take her upstairs. I want an unofficial statement from her before she goes anywhere."

"Yes, sir!"

Firmly gripping her elbow with one hand and clutching the alligator under his other arm, he guided her into the elevator. "By the way, Lewis," Trace offered before the doors closed, "she *is* my wife, but don't let anyone else know she's been running around loose on the premises carrying this monster."

The elevator began its ascent. "And now, Mrs. Ramsey..." Trace backed her into a corner, trapping her with his powerful body and the green felt alligator. "You have exactly ten seconds to explain yourself. I'm counting."

He looked and sounded every bit as forbidding as he had that first day in his office. But this time, she wasn't planning to reason with him. Nor was she going to bait him.

"I'm in love with you," she admitted simply.

"Since when?" he retorted with lips tantalizingly

close to hers. The elevator doors opened and he urged her out, but she was barely aware of her surroundings.

"Since the moment you first accused me of being part of a kidnapping scheme, she whispered."

His left brow dipped in displeasure, just like Jason's always did. "Don't lie to me, Cassie."

"I'm not. I swear it!" she cried. "In spite of everything, I felt this overwhelming attraction to you and I knew from your reaction how much you adored Justin. I began to realize then that I'd met the man I wanted to live with for the rest of my life."

She felt his body tauten. "Why didn't you admit it when I took you to Snowbird, or the other night when I was begging you to sleep with me?"

"Because I didn't think you loved me! You never told me you did."

He groaned, shaking his head impatiently. "Because I didn't want to scare you off after that absurd marriage contract I'd made with you. Don't you know I fell in love with you the second you raced across the office to comfort my howling, black-haired son? I thought if I could ever get you to love *me* that fiercely, I'd be the happiest man alive."

"Trace..." She reached up to cover his mouth with her own, revealing the burning intensity of her need, realizing that this was what they'd both been hungering for from the very beginning. One day soon she'd tell him about her talk with Rolfe. But not right now.

Right now... She moaned in ecstasy at the way Trace was making her feel, the things he was doing to her with his hands and mouth.

"Do you have any idea the kind of hell I've been going through, waiting for Rolfe to show up, terrified you'd decide to go back to him?"

"I have an idea, yes," she said softly, pressing hot kisses against his eyes and lips. "All this time I've been afraid you wanted to make love to me because it was convenient, that eventually you'd grow tired of me and I'd end up being ex-wife number two."

"Never!" He kissed her long and hard. "I should have told you how I felt when I came to your apartment in San Francisco. But I was afraid to admit the truth—it seemed too soon to be feeling like that. We barely knew each other. And after that fiery scene at the airport, I couldn't risk losing you, so I had to come up with a foolproof plan to make you fall in love with me."

She traced his mouth with her fingertips. "And you succeeded. To be your wife, even if it was in name only, brought me more happiness than you can possibly imagine. I knew then that my feelings for Rolfe weren't the kind a woman has to have for the man she marries. I love you, darling. Only you. Forever."

"I've waited to hear those words for so long," he whispered against her lips. Then he started to kiss her with passionate urgency, bringing to life every nerve ending in her body. The world reeled away as Trace picked her up in his arms. Ignoring the alligator, he carried her into a room she hadn't seen before. It looked more like the interior of an elegant hotel.

"This isn't part of your office, is it?" she asked,

trying to catch her breath when she saw the photograph she'd given him hanging on the wall.

Trace favored her with a voluptuous smile. "We're about to begin our honeymoon in my penthouse suite."

Cassie blinked. "I didn't even know you had one. Is this where you stayed on the nights you weren't at the house?"

"That's right." He carried her to the big picture window, which looked out over the city of Phoenix. "I've spent hours standing here, gazing in the direction of our house, wondering if you ever lay awake nights wanting me, aching for me the way I did you."

Cassie pulled his head down and moved her lips sensuously against his. "Let's go to bed and I'll show you what it's been like for me."

She blushed at his appreciative chuckle and hid her face in his shoulder. "To think Jason brought me here...to this..."

"Cassie!" He tightened his arms around her. "What if you'd given up your search too soon?"

"But I didn't." She bit delicately on his earlobe, producing a groan that vibrated through her body. "Susan wanted Jason to be united with his real father, and I wanted that, too."

He pressed her closer still. "I love your sister for that. I love our sons, but above all, I love you, Cassie. I need you in all the ways a man needs his wife. Don't ever stop loving me."

His vulnerability was a revelation to her. "Why do you think I agreed to your scheme to open a shop for

Lena's sake? I planned to be so well and truly tied to you you'd never be able to get rid of me."

A deep, happy laugh came out of Trace as he moved them toward the bed. "My adorable wife, much as I love my sister, *you* were the real reason I thought up that scheme. I hoped it would fulfill you so much you'd never leave me. I threw in Lena's problems to win your sympathy, hoping but never dreaming she'd actually go along with it."

Cassie had never known this kind of joy before. She sought his mouth again and again, craving the feel and taste of him. "Then you got more than you bargained for, because tonight she informed me she wants half interest in the business. Apparently she's started painting again."

She felt his fingers tighten in her curls. "I know. Allen confided as much to me earlier today. He's anxious to talk to you and thank you for helping strengthen their marriage. But I told him he'd have a long wait because I had plans of my own where you were concerned."

"I'm glad you said that," she murmured. "You're right—Jason and Justin are entirely too spoiled. Another baby would be good for them—and for me. How about you?"

His smile slowly faded, to be replaced by a look of such burning sensuality she trembled in his arms. "I'm prepared to indulge your desires indefinitely, Mrs. Ramsey."

**Leigh Michaels** has always loved happy endings. Even when she was a child, if a book's conclusion didn't please her, she'd make up her own. And, though she always wanted to write fiction, she very sensibly planned to earn her living as a newspaper reporter. That career didn't work out, however, and she found herself writing for Mills & Boon® instead—in the kind of happy ending only a romance novelist could dream up!

Leigh likes to hear from readers; you can write to her at PO Box 935, Ottumwa, Iowa, 52501-0935, USA.

# *TEMPORARY MEASURES*
## by
## LEIGH MICHAELS

# CHAPTER ONE

CHICAGO'S MAGNIFICENT Mile—the mad bustle of pedestrians surging in waves down the pavements, the constant roar of traffic on North Michigan Avenue, the distant wail of a dozen sirens scurrying in all directions—she had missed it all.

Coming home to Chicago was by far the best part of her frequent business trips, Deborah Ainsley thought as she made her way with the ease of long practice through the rivers of people on the pavement until she reached the safe haven of a small sheltered entrance. She stopped just inside the glass door of the Ainsley Gallery and swung the canvas bag down from her shoulder, reaching into it for a pair of ultrafashionable high-heeled pumps to replace the running shoes that had smoothed her walk along the Magnificent Mile from her apartment not far from the lakeshore. She dropped the running shoes into the bag, straightened the Paisley scarf at her throat—the only bright accent against her cream-coloured dress—and stopped to admire a tiny oil painting that glowed like a jewel against a grey velvet drape on an easel near the entrance.

The gallery was quiet and peaceful, a haven that encouraged the art lover to browse and study and meditate as he would in a library or in a museum or in a church. It was almost dim, except where subtle spot-lighting emphasized a painting here and there, inviting the observer to look deeply and fall in love.

The Ainsley Gallery was not large, but in the three years since it opened, Deborah had carved out a niche among the hundreds of galleries in the Chicago metropolitan area; she had gained a reputation for handling the best new contemporary artists in the region. If a client wanted a Dali print or a Monet poster, the Ainsley Gallery politely suggested a competitor who specialised in those things. But for the Chicagoan who wanted to own an original piece of art instead of a mass-produced copy, but who couldn't afford the tremendous prices of already well-known artists, the Ainsley Gallery was the best place to go.

The art of tomorrow, Deborah called it. After all, as she had frequently been heard to say, a majority of the paintings hanging in the Art Institute of Chicago had not cost millions—they had been purchased originally by ordinary people, with ordinary pocket money, simply because they were attractive, and only in later years had the judgment of the art world made them valuable. And, she was fond of saying, it would inevitably happen again, with some of the very paintings her clients were buying now.

Already, several of the artists whose work Deborah had hung in her early shows had gained a national reputation. That was why she kept seeking out new ones whose work was still affordable to the secretary with a walk-up apartment, or to the couple furnishing their first house in the suburbs. That was why she had been in Michigan all week, and that was why she was so delighted to be home once more.

She ran a practised eye around the gallery, not even trying to look at each piece, but instead observing the symmetry and grace of how things were hung, how the placement of paintings and sculpture invited the client to wander and observe. Peggy deserved a compliment, she decided; she was by far the best assistant Deborah had ever had.

A classical melody rippled from the speakers concealed in the walls, playing so softly that it scarcely broke the surface of her conscious mind. It did not drown out the sound of the discreet doorbell, or of the low-voiced conversation at the back of the gallery, where Peggy was telling a client about the person who had created the luscious watercolor he was admiring.

Deborah turned with a professional smile, to greet the customer who had just come in. Then her expression warmed into a delighted glow, and she hurried towards the grey-haired man who had stopped to admire the same tiny oil that had caught her eye as she came in. She slipped a hand into the crook of his elbow. "It's wonderful, isn't it, Daddy? Peggy was absolutely right to put it there, where it catches everyone's eye—"

William Ainsley gave her a wry half smile. "Do you ever take your mind off art, Deborah?"

"Oh—I haven't seen you in two weeks, have I?" She darted a coquettish look up at him. "I *am* sorry not to have shown you how happy I am to see you. Of course, it's not my fault that you haven't changed an iota in ten years. When a man simply stays as handsome as you are—"

"Watch out," he warned. "You're sailing a bit close to the shoals."

Deborah grinned and leaned her head against his shoulder. Her long, glossy brown hair swung smoothly against his grey linen jacket. "You're right," she admitted. "The truth is, when a man stays as handsome as you are, everybody notices. I was just too bowled over for words when you walked in."

"Rubbish. How much are you asking for that painting, Deborah?"

She glanced at the discreet tag on the velvet next to the gold frame. "Nine hundred. But for you, Daddy, I could make a special deal."

"And sell it to me for a thousand, I suppose." He looked at it again. "I should stay out of here. You know my weaknesses too well when it comes to buying paintings." He turned his back on the easel with determination.

Deborah smothered a smile. "You're the one who dragged me to the museums every Saturday," she pointed out. "And to the galleries after school, and to the art fairs on Sundays."

"I should get a special deal, that's for sure," William Ainsley said a bit grumpily. "You'll inherit my entire collection and have it all back again some day, anyway."

"Not for a very long time, I hope."

He pretended to misunderstand. "Yes, and I suppose you'll make an even larger profit when you sell it the second time. Well, beware—if you do, I'll haunt the damned gallery."

"Oh, good," Deborah murmured. "My very own ghost. It'll be a marvellous advertising gimmick." She looked up at him through long black lashes.

"Humph." But there was a sparkle in his eyes, and she couldn't help laughing in response.

"So why are you here?" she asked. "I don't often see you on Wednesday mornings, you know."

"I thought perhaps we'd have dinner at my club tonight."

"Oh, I can't. Bristol's leaving town tomorrow on a business trip, and we're going to Coq au Vin tonight." She saw his face fall, and regretted having to refuse him; he'd been so lonely in the past few years since her mother died, and though she tried to spend time with him, she was so busy and out of town so much that it was difficult. He was also far too sensitive about intruding on her life, she thought, and sometimes when she had to refuse an invitation it was weeks before he asked again. "Why don't you join us?" she said.

"Oh, no. I'm sure Bristol will want you to himself."

She laughed. "He won't mind. Bristol's an adult, after all—too mature to be jealous."

"That's for certain."

It was only a murmur, almost under his breath, and for an instant Deborah wasn't quite sure she'd heard properly.

Then William sighed and said, "Your mother would probably be stepping on my toes by now to shut me up, I'm sure, but I feel I have to say it anyway. Deborah, I wish you weren't seeing quite so much of Bristol."

"I thought you liked him."

"I respect him," William corrected.

"Isn't that what I said? He's the foundation's attorney, after all. You hired him, and you introduced him to me—"

"I introduce you to nearly everybody who works for the foundation, Deborah, but that doesn't mean I want you to start dating them all. Dammit, honey, the man is old enough to be your father."

"I beg your pardon," Deborah said crisply, "but fourteen years' age difference does not exactly make him old enough to be my father!"

"Well, he certainly acts like an antique," William Ainsley muttered. "You aren't thinking of marrying him, are you?"

After a long moment Deborah said quietly, "I simply enjoy his company, Daddy. Shall we just leave it at that?"

William stared at his black wing tips and drew a pattern on the carpet with the toe of one of them. "I understand, of course. After the experience you had with that artist, the security that Bristol represents must look very—"

"Daddy, shall we leave it?" she repeated. It was very soft.

He stopped drawing lines on the carpet and looked at her with sad-puppy eyes. "You sound just like your mother," he said. "Vivien could have stopped an army division with that tone of voice."

Deborah's eyes misted. Her mother was never far from her mind, and the longing loneliness in William's voice could have melted glass. It turned Deborah's heart, always a bit soft where her father was concerned, into a soggy puddle.

"I'm sorry, darling," he said unsteadily. "Of course it's your business. But I'm so worried about you. All I want for you is what your mother and I had."

"Oh, is that all?" Deborah asked a bit wryly. "That's a tall order, Daddy." She hugged him tightly, her head buried against his shoulder, her nose tickled by the spicy scent of his after-shave lotion. "How about tomorrow?" she whispered. "I'll even buy your dinner."

He smiled. "It's a date, honey." He kissed her cheek and gently set her aside. "I suppose I should let you get to work, shouldn't I?"

"I'd better. After a week away, my desk probably doesn't bear thinking about." As he put a hand on the doorknob, she called, "Oh, Daddy..." He turned, and she added impishly, with a gesture towards the easel, "Shall I have the painting delivered?"

William Ainsley's eyebrows climbed. "Of course," he said, as if there had never been any doubt. "Why do you think I came in, anyway?" Then he winked and ducked out into the maelstrom of North Michigan Avenue before she could retort.

She was writing notes of thanks to the clients and artists she had visited in Michigan when Peggy came into their shared office and dropped into the chair beside Deborah's desk. "He bought the watercolour," she said. "Patience pays off again."

"I seem to remember telling you that if a person doesn't buy something on his first visit, it doesn't mean he won't ever make a purchase at all."

"I know. 'A client who does not buy is not a lost sale, but an opportunity,'" Peggy recited. "But he's been an opportunity three times a week for the past month, and I was starting to think he was only coming in to stare at my age spots."

Deborah didn't look up from the jade green envelope she was addressing. "They're freckles," she corrected mildly.

"Yes, but I'm sure he wouldn't agree. When one hits forty-five, you know..." Peggy reached into her top desk drawer for a tiny mirror and studied herself in it. "I'm so terribly average," she said dispassionately. "Not short, not tall. Not fat, but certainly not slender. My hair can't even make up its mind whether to be blond or brown. It's unfair that my sole distinguishing feature is freckles. I should have outgrown them in my teens." The doorbell chimed and she put away the mirror and went out to greet the new client. Then she leaned back into the office to say, "I forgot—it's in your messages, but I said I'd make sure to tell you anyway. Your cousin is awfully anxious to talk to you. Riley—is that his name?"

Deborah sealed the envelope and reached for another one. "That's his name, all right."

"He sounded like the sort of man who might appreciate freckles."

Deborah spread a sheet of engraved notepaper on her

blotter. "I should hope so," she said. "He certainly has plenty of them himself. But sounds can be deceiving. Especially when it's Riley who's making the noise."

She finished writing her notes and stacked them, stamped and ready to go, on the corner of her desk before she even bothered to look through the stack of messages. But her conscience had started to nag at her long before that. It was hardly fair to assume Riley was still behaving like the annoying teenager who had seemed to find his greatest pleasure in tormenting the life out of her. After all, she hadn't seen him in years. He must be thirty by now.

"Thirty-one," she muttered. "He's three years older than you, Deborah, and as much as you hate to admit it, you're going to be twenty-eight soon."

She found the pink message slip midway down in the pile. It was crammed with tiny, cramped writing, and on closer examination she discovered it wasn't a single lengthy message but a record of nearly a dozen calls made over the past three days. Peggy was right, she thought idly. Riley *was* awfully anxious to talk to her.

The number listed was a Chicago one, and she was mildly surprised when it was answered by the switchboard at the Englin Hotel, which efficiently put her through to Riley's room.

He must have come up for a few days of rest and recreation in the city, she thought, and he probably wants someone to take him to the zoo or something. Not a bad idea. He'd be right at home there with the rest of the animals....

"Yankee Stadium, home plate umpire speaking," said a voice in her ear.

She wanted to groan. Hadn't the man even started to

grow up? "Shall I call back after the game's over?" she asked tartly.

The voice warmed. "Debbie darling! I'm glad to see the natives didn't get restless in Michigan and do something nasty to you."

"Peggy actually told you that's where I was?"

"Only in self-defence, I assure you. She'd never have breathed a word if it hadn't been me asking."

"I certainly have no trouble in believing that," Deborah said drily. "What brings you to the Windy City, Riley?"

"Research," he said promptly.

And that, she thought helplessly, gave her precisely no information at all.

"And since I'm here, I thought I'd take you out to dinner and bring you up-to-date on all the family gossip."

"What now? Has Mary Beth run off with the mailman or something?"

"Of course not," he said with offended dignity, and then ruined the effect by adding candidly, "my esteemed sister has gained twenty pounds since her new baby came along—"

"Another baby? No one told me."

"Well, it's not exactly a *new* baby. I mean the one that's almost four now. At any rate, the mailman probably wouldn't have her. He's rather a handsome guy."

"Oh? Do you find yourself attracted to good-looking men these days?"

"Not at all." Riley sounded wounded. "I didn't notice it myself. Mom told me that he's one good-looking fellow. How's tonight? For dinner, I mean."

"I assumed that was what you meant." It was cool. "I can't. I have a dinner date."

He didn't seem offended. "Oh? Are you still dating the

thing with the beard that you brought to your Uncle Ralph's funeral?"

"Why do you want to know?" The tone was a little more crisp than Deborah had intended.

Riley didn't seem to notice. "So I can tell Mary Beth the gory details, of course."

"I didn't even know you were at Uncle Ralph's funeral."

"I came late and left early. You didn't exactly stay long in the bosom of the family yourself."

"Morgan didn't—" She stopped. It was certainly none of Riley's business.

"Morgan? What a name. How about tomorrow night?"

"No. I have a—"

"Dinner date. I'm amazed," Riley mused. "I didn't think that something like that would bother to comb the crumbs out of his facial fur in order to go out two days in a row."

Deborah was doing a slow simmer. "If you're finished, Riley—"

"Deb! Darling Debbie, don't hang up on me. I'm sorry I made noises about your fuzzy friend. Is that honestly his first name, or did he choose it as a protest statement? Never mind. I won't do it again, honest. I really do need to talk to you."

"Family gossip," she muttered. "I suppose next you're going to tell me Aunt Ida's fallen in love!"

"How did you guess?"

There was a long silence. Finally Deborah said, "You're not going to say any more, are you? Well, since etiquette obliges me not to be rude to family—"

"Wonderful thing, etiquette. I've always believed in it."

She didn't bother to counter that one. "I can arrange to be free the day after tomorrow."

"That's Friday." She could almost hear him shaking his head. "I have to go home Friday. How about breakfast tomorrow?"

"Civilised people don't eat breakfast, Riley. All right, all right. I have to admit I'm dying to find out what sort of tall tale you can concoct about Aunt Ida."

"No tall tales. I outgrew that years ago."

"Right," she said. "And I suppose you really are a home plate umpire at Yankee Stadium, too."

IF RILEY'S GOAL was to intrigue her, Deborah had to admit he'd succeeded; she didn't even remember eating her vichyssoise at Coq au Vin that night. In fact, as they were finishing their quail Normandy, Bristol said with heavy politeness, "Do pardon me if I'm boring you by talking about my business conference, Deborah."

"What? No, not at all. I've scarcely heard a word—" She choked back the rest of that sentence and said, "I'm sorry, Bristol. I was thinking about my cousin, you see."

Bristol Wellington waited until the wine steward had refilled his glass and then said punctiliously, "Your cousin? I thought neither of your parents had siblings."

"Oh, not my first cousin. He's...I'm not even sure what, it's so distant. My great-grandfather and his great-grandfather were brothers."

Bristol looked faintly interested. "Then the two of you are third cousins," he announced.

"Thank you," Deborah said politely. "I never could figure these things out. He's in town, and I'm going to have breakfast with him tomorrow."

"One should always maintain cordial relationships with one's family," Bristol murmured. "I, myself, correspond with—"

"That's easy to say. Of course, with Riley—"

"Riley?" Bristol sounded as if he'd bitten into something sour.

"Riley Lassiter," Deborah added helpfully. "He is from one branch of the Lassiter family, my mother was from the other. His branch got to keep the ancestral name, but her branch got most of the money. It always seemed like a fair trade to me. You see, what actually happened is that the original Lassiter brothers—the great-grandfathers I was telling you about—had a falling-out, and Riley's ancestor sold out to mine for a mere pittance, right before the patents they held became valuable."

"And I suppose he holds a grudge."

"Riley? I don't think he has a grudging bone in his body."

Bristol asked suspiciously, "He isn't a criminal element or the like, is he?"

"Who knows, with Riley." She sipped her wine. "You know, it's almost embarrassing, but I honestly don't know what Riley does. His parents had a farm near Summerset in southern Illinois, where the Lassiters all started out. Riley was just ready to begin law school when his father died. I know he dropped out of school, but I haven't any idea what he did instead, or what he's doing now."

"Raising pigs, probably," Bristol said. "Really, Deborah, must we—"

"It's a shame," she mused. "Mother always kept up with these things. I'll bet she even knew the names and birthdays of all of Mary Beth's kids...." There was a catch in her voice that surprised her.

Bristol sighed. He didn't ask who Mary Beth was.

"When I was a kid, I spent a lot of time down there, too," Deborah said. "I thought that Mother sent me down every summer just to get rid of me. Now I'm sure it was because she wanted me to have a close relationship with the little family that's left, Aunt Ida and Uncle Ralph and Riley's parents. Actually, it's too bad that it didn't work out that way." She stopped abruptly. "I'm sorry, Bristol. I didn't mean to bore you to extinction."

He bowed his head. "You could never do that, Deborah. I must confess, however, that I fail to see why—"

"Why I'm fixed on Riley tonight?" She stopped. She hadn't exactly thought about it herself till right now. "I suppose it's just that the whole thing is rather strange...his calling me," she said slowly. "I mean, he must have been in Chicago now and then, but I've never heard a word from him before. Now, suddenly..."

*Aunt Ida's fallen in love,* she had said. And Riley had answered, *How did you guess?*

No, she thought uneasily. He couldn't possibly be serious. Riley never was.

HE HAD ASKED HER to meet him in the hotel lobby. She was still yawning as she paid off her cab and stepped through gleaming brass revolving doors into the huge reception hall of the Englin Hotel, one of the city's grandest and oldest. But her sleepiness disappeared with a bang as she stopped short under a silver and crystal chandelier that was the size of the average automobile. "Damn," she muttered under her breath. "I forgot this place has about fifteen lobbies." Where, she wondered, was Riley likely to be waiting?

"Right here," a voice murmured behind her, as if he'd read her mind, and she wheeled around to face...Riley? she thought in disbelief. *This* was the same person as the gangly teenager with the red hair and the freckles and the ears that seemed too large for his head?

He smiled, and she relaxed a little. Yes, this was Riley, all right. Riley of the dancing hazel eyes and the perpetually mischievous grin. But what had happened to the rest of him?

Well, the hair still had a reddish cast; it was actually a rather wonderful shade of burnished auburn now. But the freckles were gone, and the gangly body was now well-knit and very athletic looking in a trimly tailored pin-striped shirt and dark trousers. No tie, no jacket, but then what had she expected of Riley?

"You finally grew into your ears," she said.

He kissed her cheek lightly. "And you're looking very well, too, Debbie darling," he murmured. "Much better than you did at Ralph's funeral. You were so pale then that I wondered for a while which one of you was the corpse."

Deborah sighed. "I knew it was too good to last."

"You're the one who brought up ears," he chided.

"I'll remember that it's a sensitive spot." She reached up and tugged gently at his earlobe. "It is good to see you, Riley."

He tucked her hand into the crook of his elbow and took her across the lobby to the Captain's Table, where a smiling waiter showed them to a table and poured their coffee.

"Honestly, you didn't have to make up tales about Aunt Ida to get me to come to breakfast, you know," Deborah went on. "I don't hold it against you any more that you were a terror when you were a kid."

His eyes started to sparkle. "Remember the time out on the farm when you were having a tea party for your dolls and I put the frog in the teapot?"

"Do I remember! When I lifted the lid and he leaped out at me—"

"I haven't heard such a shriek since. It's a good thing it was only pretend tea," Riley mused. "If you'd managed the real thing, we would all have been in hot water."

Deborah groaned. "Especially the poor frog."

"And you've forgiven me for all that?" He looked somber and serious; Deborah was morally certain that it was only a momentary lapse.

"Certainly. Besides," she added gently, "you can't possibly put a frog in my cup at breakfast. This is the Englin Hotel, after all."

"Do you honestly think that would stop me?" It was very soft.

She looked at her cup, suddenly suspicious.

He laughed. "No, Debbie, I've outgrown that sort of thing long ago."

"I suppose I'll have to take your word for it. How is your mother, by the way?"

"Happy as a clam. She's remarried, you know. Or didn't you?"

Deborah's forehead furrowed. "I think Daddy mentioned it, yes. She must have sent him a Christmas card or something."

"She and her new husband have turned the farm into a gigantic truck garden—everything from cabbages to kings, you might say."

"You're not still on the farm yourself then?" The waiter brought their plates. She eyed Riley's platter-size Denver omelette with a jaundiced expression. "Someone ought to tell you about cholesterol," she murmured, as she broke an oatmeal muffin in half.

He cut into the omelette and gave her a soulful look. "Deb darling, I didn't know you cared."

The nickname was beginning to grate a bit, but she had no trouble remembering what had happened the last time she had instructed him that her name was Deborah. She'd been almost eleven then and very serious about the fact that she was not Deb or Debbie. Riley had listened, patiently and perfectly straight-faced, and from then on he had called her Deborah, as she had requested. The problem was that he put the accent on the second syllable, and slurred it a little, until it sounded like a native of Brooklyn referring to a tiresome pest—da bore.

*Deb darling,* she concluded, however insincere it might be, was certainly an improvement over that!

"Besides," Riley said without looking up, "I know all about cholesterol. I'm running a restaurant now."

The statement was blithe, but underneath it she heard...what? Resentment? Self-pity? A sense of shame that the promising law student had come down to this?

She put down her muffin. "Oh, Riley—I'm so sorry," she said, and then wanted to bite her tongue off. As if he wanted her sympathy...as if it could do anything but make him feel worse!

He darted a curious glance at her; Deborah knew it, even though she was studying the china pattern, too embarrassed to look at him. "I'm—I shouldn't have said that," she muttered.

"Well, we can't all be dashing over the countryside discovering artists, can we?" he said reasonably. "Some of us wouldn't know one if we tripped over him. Me, for instance. As soon as I saw that bearded creature you had on a leash at Ralph's funeral, I said, there's an artist if I ever saw one. But for all I know he really spends his nights as a guard at the hospital for the criminally insane."

"He was an artist," she said reluctantly.

"*Was?* Does that mean he's stopped, or that he doesn't figure large in your life these days?"

Deborah's temper snapped. "Uncle Ralph's been dead for three years, Riley. For all you know, I could be working my way through every man in the Chicago telephone directory by now. So what business is it of yours whether I'm still seeing Morgan?''

He looked very innocent. ''None at all,'' he said gently. ''But if you'd like to talk about this sexual compulsion of yours, Deb—''

She bit her lip, knowing that once more she had reacted precisely as he had hoped she would.

He relented. ''Sorry,'' he said briskly. ''I don't see you as a nymphomaniac, actually, but I couldn't resist the impulse to see your expression. You really must learn to control that tendency of yours to make grandstand statements, you know.''

''The only thing I need to control,'' Deborah said with commendable restraint, ''is the amount of time I spend with you. And that will be very easy to do.''

He shook his head. ''I hope you'll think it over very seriously before you walk out of here, Deb.''

''Why on earth should I?''

''Because we haven't even gotten to the problem of Aunt Ida yet.''

''And her supposed lover? Oh, for heaven's sake, Riley, Ida's eighty if she's a day and she's been a spinster all her life.''

''That's partly why I'm so worried.'' He actually sounded serious. ''She must be infatuated or she wouldn't be acting like such an idiot.''

Deborah stared at him for a long moment. ''I suppose you're going to tell me she's acquired a gigolo! You can't expect me to take that notion seriously.''

He was shaking his head. ''Not a gigolo, exactly. He acts more like a tame python. Actually, he's a venture-capital specialist who wants to revive Paradise Valley.''

''The bankrupt resort complex? It's been sitting there rotting for ten years. I can't believe Ida would give him a minute, much less any money...." Her voice wavered. "She hasn't, has she?"

"Ida is in it up to the crook of her Roman nose," Riley said. "For one thing, her suave new investment counsellor is living at Lassiter House these days. And she's seriously considering investing not only her own money in his scam, but the trust's as well."

"The trust?" Deborah said weakly.

He nodded. "The trust. The unbreakable one that your great-grandfather wrote to protect his assets for his descendants—which is to say, you—yea, verily and unto the umpteenth generation. *That* trust."

"But what—"

"You see, he overlooked one weak spot. He put his kids in charge of the money—a sort of balance-of-power arrangement—but after Ralph died, your Aunt Ida was left as the sole trustee." He set down his cup with a firm click. "And now, Debbie darling, Ida can do any damned thing she wants with the cash."

## CHAPTER TWO

"AND DON'T YOU DARE tell me it's only money," Riley went on. "I don't know anyone who's noble enough to whistle away the income on a few million dollars."

"Daddy does every year," she said only half-consciously.

"That's different. It's not his own cash, it belongs to the foundation, and it all goes to charmingly worthy causes. It's not the same thing at all when it's going to support a con man in the style to which he'd like to become accustomed."

"You're quite sure it's a scam?"

"Paradise Valley?" It was almost a shriek. "It isn't honestly a lake in the middle of that resort at all, you know. It's an industrial-size sink, Deb, and it has sucked more money down the drain..."

"You sound like a person who's lost a little cash in it yourself."

"Not me, but my father took a flier on it the first time around." He sounded grim. "Mother just finished paying off *that* mortgage on the farm last year."

"Oh. I see."

"No, I don't think you do. I forgot that you haven't been around Summerset for years, so of course you don't understand what's going on. Let me tell you, Paradise Valley will never be a successful vacation resort, because not enough people want to spend their time and money in

Summerset. It's not exactly the entertainment centre of the world, you know. To draw the kind of crowd you'd need to make it pay would require a fantastic investment in a year-round amusement park, ski slopes and snowmobile trails as well as golf courses and tennis courts and beaches. To say nothing of the facilities to house all of them. It quickly reaches a point of diminishing returns—the more money you spend, the more people you have to accommodate, in a limited space, to earn it all back. The fact is, it can't be done."

"All right, so it's a bad investment."

He stared at her for a long moment. "That's a minimal way of putting it," he said finally. "Not that it matters, I suppose, whether it's a con or simply a bad investment—all the money will be gone anyway. But as it happens, I've met the oily snake who's selling it this time around, and I'm convinced it's a lot more than just a bad investment."

"So what do you expect me to do about it?" Deborah asked coolly. "And as far as that goes, why do you care? It isn't going to matter a snap to you if Ida throws away the family fortune."

"No. But I hate to see people taken for rides—especially when they didn't buy the tickets themselves. If Ida wants to fling away her own cash, that's one thing, every human being has the right to be a damn fool. But as trustee of the Lassiter Brothers money, she ought to be a little more careful."

"I'm charmed by your concern. Still…"

Riley sighed. "All right, I'll admit it, I do have a stake in it. The existing border of the Paradise Valley complex is just across the road from Mom's farm."

"I thought it was," Deborah murmured.

"And the oily snake is trying to buy the place from her."

"With Ida's cash? I don't see—"

"With no cash. He wants to give her stock in the corporation instead. Pretty little gold-edged certificates full of fancy writing."

"She can't just say no?"

"Of course she can. But she's not the only one whose land he's trying to buy, and other people, I'm afraid, aren't quite as farsighted as my mother is."

"Why so much land? I always thought Paradise Valley was a huge development."

"It is. But he wants to make it even bigger—private airstrip and parachute range and ski slopes."

"I thought you were kidding about the ski slopes. There aren't any hills on your farm."

"He's going to build some. At least he says he is."

"He's a big thinker."

"That, I believe, is what convinced Ida. It's all such a grand idea, and it would be delightful for Summerset if it actually ever got off the ground. It's hard not to be a believer when it all sounds so painless for the locals. After all—" there was an ironic twist to his voice "—he's got most of the money already, or at least he says he does, from big nameless investors on the East Coast. He's just offering the people of Summerset a chance to invest in themselves."

Deborah finished off her third muffin and absently reached for the last strip of bacon on Riley's plate. "I imagine you're looked on as something of a renegade, if you've been voicing these opinions."

He looked heavenward. "You might say. I'm a bit handicapped about speaking my mind, too."

"Why? Is business falling off at your restaurant?"

"I haven't noticed it. But the resort plans call for a

rather large restaurant complex to be built in order to feed all those people, so..."

"So all of the resort's supporters think you're just screaming because you don't want the competition?" Deborah nodded wisely. "Now I see. No wonder you want me to tackle it. They aren't as likely to ride me out of town on a rail."

"Something like that." He reached across the table and let his long brown fingers brush the back of her hand. "If you'd just talk to Ida and get this thing stopped."

Deborah shook her head. "I don't see how that would do much good. Oh, it might save the Lassiter trust fund, but if he's already got money committed for the project..."

"Personally, I think the big investors are remaining nameless because they don't really exist. I think he's planning to gather up all the cash he can around Summerset and then disappear."

"Why buy all the land, then?"

"To increase his borrowing power, of course, by making his investors think he's rock solid. It certainly isn't costing him anything, and a list of those investors certainly looks appealing to others who might be wavering about handing over their life savings. The truth is, if Ida withdrew her support, the whole thing would collapse like the house of cards it is."

Deborah chewed thoughtfully at her lower lip. "Well, it's worth a try, I suppose."

"Good. Come down to Summerset and stay a couple of weeks, and see for yourself what's really going on. You can talk to her, you can meet the snake. As a matter of fact, it would be difficult for you to avoid meeting the snake, since he's moved into Ida's house."

"Riley, be realistic. I haven't seen Ida in three years,

and even then it took her brother's funeral to get me there. I can't just come wheeling down there now out of the blue. She's not a fool, she'll know why I'm there, and all the barricades will go up. I'll never get a word out of her."

He shrugged. "It's simple. You're searching for artists."

"Is there an art exhibition in the town square this weekend?"

"Not that I've heard of, but—"

"Then be serious. For the first time in my years in business, I'm coming to Summerset on a whim to search for artists, and I just happen to choose the week after you've been in Chicago?" She nodded approvingly at his stricken look. "I see you've finally remembered that everyone in the whole town must know where you are."

"That is a problem," he conceded.

"I suppose I could pop up at the front door and scream, *Surprise!* but I think a better story would be useful." She caught a glimpse of his wristwatch. "Good heavens, I've got to get to work. I've got important things to do this morning. Let's finish this over dinner tonight."

"I thought you had a date."

"I do, with my father. Maybe he can help us figure it out."

"I don't think that's such a good—"

But she was gone, with a casual wave and a swirl of her tomato red skirt.

Riley sighed and reached for the bill and his wallet. "Important things," the waiter heard him say under his breath. "And this isn't?"

"I STILL DON'T THINK this is such a terrific idea," Riley said from the living room of Deborah's high-rise apartment, where he was coping with the cork in a bottle of white wine.

"I can't hear you," she called from the kitchen. "And I can't leave my béarnaise sauce just now."

He didn't answer, but he raised his voice. "Ida and your father never got along. She didn't think he was good enough for Vivien, you know."

"Is that what was going on? I wondered why he never seemed to be free when it was time for me to visit Aunt Ida."

"She also thought he was a hanger-on and a fortune hunter."

"Daddy? Surely you're joking."

"She would not be likely to take his advice on the subject of money."

The sauce was momentarily forgotten. Deborah leaned around the door to look at him in astonishment. "And you honestly think she'll take mine?"

"Not exactly. But she might be more careful about making sure there is some money left to leave to you. If it was only William, she'd probably spend it just for spite. The problem is, if you bring your father into it he may not be able to resist the temptation to call her up and scold her, or tell her what to do."

Deborah licked her tasting spoon thoughtfully. "And that would make her do the opposite?"

"I believe so, yes."

"Well, I think you're underestimating Daddy. He's developed into quite a diplomat since he went to work for the foundation." She waved a hand at the front door; the chimes were sounding. "In any case, he's arrived, so it's a bit late to dis-invite him, isn't it? My fingers are sticky...would you let him in?"

She retreated to the kitchen, catching her béarnaise

sauce just as it started to curdle. A couple of minutes later William joined her, a glass of sherry in his hand. "You're cooking, Deborah?"

"Well, I did promise you dinner. Would you be happier if I told you most of it came from the deli?"

"That's a relief. I thought you were trying to impress Riley. What's he doing here, anyway?"

She looked thoughtful. "Is that a trick question, like 'what did the bishop say to the actress?'"

"No, in fact, I'm delighted to see him. It's just that I seem to remember you saying when you were about fifteen that you'd never be caught dead in the same town with him again."

She stared into the distance, frowning. Then her brow cleared and she said, just as Riley came into the kitchen, "Oh, I remember. That was the summer I was in love with the lifeguard."

Riley handed her a glass of sherry. "You should see him now. You'd thank me for breaking it up."

"Don't take too much credit," Deborah ordered. "All you meant to do was embarrass me."

Riley grinned. "Well, you have to admit I succeeded in breaking it up. Whether I intended to or not isn't the point."

William shook his head. "This is not my idea of a usual family reunion," he said to no one in particular.

"And that's not the half of it," Deborah said. "Let me put the chicken on the grill and we'll sit down and talk about it."

William listened in almost utter silence throughout dinner. Deborah wondered about his unusual lack of comment, until she realised that the poor man couldn't get a word in over the dual explanation, and the accompanying bickering, to which he was being subjected. Finally, as she removed the men's gratifyingly empty plates and brought out a platter of fruit and cheese, William said simply, "I'm worried."

"Then she honestly can do it?" Deborah asked. "There aren't any safeguards?"

"Not any more. Since Ralph died, Ida's been the boss."

"I told you," Riley said under his breath. "But you never would take my word for anything, Deb."

"And why on earth should I?" Deborah muttered. "You're the one who told me that if a woman swallows a whole shrimp it grows into a baby."

"You asked," he reminded. "I certainly wasn't the one who brought up the subject of where babies come from."

"I still don't like shrimp. Childhood prejudices can be very deep-seated, you know."

Riley appealed to her father. "She was six years old. What was I supposed to tell her? The truth?"

William went on, unheeding. "But Ida has always taken advice before, from her attorney and from her banker."

Riley shrugged. "And now she's taking advice from her investment counsellor," he said. "She doesn't see that there's a difference, and she won't until it's too late and the Lassiter money has gone to Costa Rica, or wherever the crooks are hiding out these days."

Deborah stared into her wineglass, only half-listening. It was the first time she had really allowed herself to think about the consequences if Riley was right. The income supplied by the Lassiter trust wasn't as large as he supposed, but it was steady. And while the gallery was doing very well for a relatively new business, the overhead expenses of a location of Michigan Avenue were high, and every cent of profit went back into increased inventory. If she had to start paying her own living expenses from what the gallery brought in, she'd be in trouble all the way around.

"I may have to rely on those paintings you've been collecting to support my life-style after all, Daddy," she said morosely.

William didn't seem to be listening. "I wish I could remember the details," he mused. "I've got a copy of the entire trust document somewhere, but I'll be honest, I've always let the attorneys deal with the fine print rather than tangle with Ida. The income was always adequate, and so we didn't try to invoke the provisions for taking principal out."

"You can do that?" Riley sounded astonished. "That's the answer, then. You just get Ida to hand it over in lump chunks before she has a chance to throw it away."

William sighed. "It's not that easy, I'm afraid. The conditions for getting cash are strenuous. Old Jacob was determined to preserve what he'd gathered. I remember one, though." He smiled a little. "Vivien got a considerable sum when we were married."

"A marriage settlement?" Riley asked. "That makes sense. I always did think dowries were a civilised custom."

"That's not exactly what it was. It was to pay for the wedding, and for that purpose alone. And she even had to produce the bills to get the cash, at that. It seems old Jacob wanted the girls in the family to have wonderful weddings."

"Well, in his day marriage was the only profession women were allowed," Deborah pointed out.

"I don't think he even called it marriage, actually. The trust says something about dynastic alliances, I believe."

"Can we move on?" Deborah asked glumly. "This avenue is certainly getting us nowhere."

"Oh?" Riley asked. "You're not planning a large and elaborate wedding any time soon? Though I don't suppose your friend with the fleecy face would go for—"

"Fleecy face?" William asked.

"He means Morgan," Deborah explained. "He's behind the times, but that never bothered Riley. More wine, anyone?"

Riley held up his glass. "I suppose you could talk to Ida's banker and her attorney," he said halfheartedly. "I didn't feel I could barge into their offices and start asking nosy questions myself."

"It would be a source of information, perhaps," William said. "But I'm sure they're powerless to do anything."

"And probably just as frustrated as we are," Deborah mused. "And may I remind you that I still don't have a valid excuse for showing up in Summerset and starting to ask questions. I wonder...Ida's memory wouldn't happen to be slipping, would it?"

Riley snorted. "We should all be so alert at eighty. She plays bridge twice a week, she walks a mile every day, and she still chairs the hospital fund-raising drive."

"It was worth a try," she said.

"I'll look up that copy of the trust when I get home tonight," William said. "After all, Ida can't live forever. Surely Jacob considered the possibility."

Riley sounded a little disgusted. "If we don't concentrate on the problem at hand, it won't matter a damn whether Ida lives forever. Of course, Summerset might never be the same, but..."

"It's too bad we're all such law-abiding citizens," Deborah murmured. "If we weren't, we could just arrange for a hit-and-run on one of her long walks."

"Thank you," Riley said politely.

She stared at him. "I haven't any idea what you're talking about now."

"I'm touched that you've elevated me to the status of law-abiding citizen. I'll keep the memory of your kindness on the mantel among my trophies. Unless you thought I was going to volunteer to be the driver?"

She ignored him and started to clear the table.

"Well, I certainly didn't mean to imply anything of the kind," William said. He sounded hurt. "I would never set out to injure anyone. I've had my disagreements with Ida, but I've always shown her the respect due my wife's aunt."

"I'm sure you have," Riley said soothingly.

"And she always respected me as well, for Vivien's sake, if nothing else."

Deborah started to put the cheese plate away in the refrigerator. So things really had been bad between her father and Aunt Ida, she mused. If Ida had only put up with him for Vivien's sake...

Something seemed to stir in the back corner of her brain. *For Vivien's sake...*

She set the platter down very deliberately on the counter and went back into the dining room. "I've got it," she said.

Both of them looked up at her expectantly.

"I'm going to Summerset," she said.

"That's never been in doubt."

"Riley, would you shut up and listen? I'm not going to see Ida exactly, or at least not primarily to see her. I'm going down to introduce my intended husband and to talk to her about getting the trust to pay for my wedding."

William frowned.

"It's perfect, don't you see? That will force her to answer my questions about the trust."

"Great idea," Riley said enthusiastically. "Debbie darling, you might make a conspirator yet!"

"Deborah," her father said warily, "I don't think you've thought this through. I don't think that you and Bristol—"

"Bristol is out of town," she reminded him.

"Bristol?" said Riley. "Who the hell is Bristol? Never mind. Can you trust him not to spill the beans?"

"I won't have to. Bristol has nothing to do with this."

"Then who—"

She turned an expectant stare on Riley.

"Oh, Deborah," William began, "my dear girl—"

Riley said slowly, "If you're thinking of whom I think you're thinking of..."

"That's insane," William said uncertainly. "You can't pretend to be engaged to Riley."

"Why can't I? Do you already have a fiancée, Riley?"

"No. But—"

"Then acquiring one won't make any difference, will it?"

"But I don't want a fiancée!"

"Believe me, you won't have one for long. This is a very temporary measure. It was your mention of dynastic alliances that brought it to mind, Daddy. Reuniting the branches of a fractured family, restoring the family fortune, to say nothing of preserving the name to be carried on in generations to come. Ida will love it."

William said weakly, "But, Deborah..."

"It's a great idea, Daddy. And why shouldn't Riley make himself useful? He's already in the whole thing up to his—" She almost said ears, but thought better of it. "Neck. It even explains why he came to Chicago!"

Riley said faintly, "To see my long-lost love, I suppose you mean?"

"Absolutely." Deborah thought he sounded as if his collar were strangling him. Well, that was just too bad; he'd get used to the idea soon enough. It was such a satisfyingly symmetrical plot, after all.

And besides, she added, with a tiny secret smile, it was a world-class practical joke on Riley himself. Big enough to pay him back for every petty trick he'd pulled on her in all the years gone by....

AT FIRST she thought it was only Chicago traffic that was holding his attention so firmly, but long after they'd left the city behind and headed south for the tedious drive down the length of Illinois, Riley remained quiet, his eyes on the road, his hands steady on the wheel of her car.

She laid back her head against the leather upholstery and eyed him from behind her dark glasses. "I must say I always expected my fiancé would be a bit more excited than this on the day after our engagement became official."

Riley grinned. "Oh, but I am, Debbie darling. I'm having a wonderful day. It's the first time I ever drove a Jaguar, you know."

All right, she told herself, you got exactly what you asked for, Deborah Ainsley!

"It's going to take a bit of acting," she pointed out. "I think you're right that we don't dare take anyone in Summerset into our confidence, but we'll have to be very careful or no one will believe it at all."

"That we could actually be in love? I'll say."

"Let's not get personal, Riley. For one thing, we're going to have to curb the desire to grind each other into the dirt all the time."

His forehead furrowed. "No. I think we'd better just keep on acting normally, and simply give each other a longing look now and then, you know the sort of thing I mean.''

"In the hope that everyone will believe we're only teasing to hide the depth of our true feelings from the world?"

"Don't sound sarcastic. That's exactly what they'll think. Besides, I don't think we *could* stop scrapping, and the strain, if we tried, would be a dead giveaway."

She looked at him long and steadily, and said, "You're probably right. Now that I stop and think about it, Riley, I don't see you doing well in the role of Romeo."

"Heaven forbid! 'What light through yonder window breaks? It is the east, and Debbie is the sun—' Forget it. I couldn't pull it off because I'd be laughing too hard."

She decided not to bother answering that one.

"But longing looks I can handle," he added earnestly. "I'll just stare at you and think of a filet mignon with duchess potatoes."

"Thanks," Deborah said dryly. "And if I see you're getting into trouble I'll just whisper 'chocolate mousse' in your ear."

"That would be very thoughtful. Shall we practise?"

"What? The longing looks? You're driving, Riley."

"I could pull off the highway. That looks like a truck stop up ahead, and truck stops almost always have very nice homemade pies."

"Don't tell me, I already know. It's just research. Haven't you ever outgrown the need to eat every three hours?"

"No," he said simply. "That's probably why the restaurant opportunity looked so appealing. And speaking of appealing, that sauce last night was—" He took one hand off the wheel and kissed his fingertips in the best imitation of a comic-book French chef she'd ever seen. "What did you call it?"

"Béarnaise. And it was curdled, Riley."

"Oh? That must be why I didn't recognise it," he said airily. "We serve a lot of it."

"I'll bet. Does this restaurant of yours have a name?"

"Yes. But mostly the locals just call it Riley's Place."

"That sounds like Summerset," she said gloomily. "A week there and I'll be raving."

"A week? I thought you were planning to stay two."

"I can't take that long. Besides, Aunt Ida would smell a rat if I could suddenly leave the gallery for that long."

"Even to spend time with your one true love?"

He sounded injured; she ignored him. "And third, Bristol will be back in ten days, so that's my outside limit."

"Does he live with you?"

"Of course not! I just—"

"I know—you don't want to explain this to him. Perhaps you should tell me about Bristol."

"Why?"

"Well, there are things we'd be expected to know about each other."

"Come on, Riley, the man I date?"

"The man you *used* to date," he corrected. "Remember? You're engaged to me now."

She groaned. "I suppose I have to start living the part. His name is R. Bristol Wellington, and he's the attorney for—"

"R. Bristol *which*? That sounds as if it needs a number to be complete."

"It has one," she said reluctantly. "He's the fifth."

"Oh? I suppose his ancestors came over on the *Mayflower*?"

"No, he considers that crowd to be peasants. Did you

know you and I are third cousins, by the way? Bristol figured it out for me. He's very big on family."

"Yes, I can see that. Thoughtful of him. Who else?"

"That's about all, lately."

"I see. No wonder you didn't want to tell him about this."

"It's not that I wouldn't," Deborah defended herself. "In fact, I did tell him I was going to Summerset to see my aunt because talking to you again had prompted a wave of family feeling, and—"

The angle of Riley's eyebrows made her want to hit him. "I'll bet he liked that touch," he murmured. "It was probably a good idea to limit the details. He sounds like the humourless type."

"I didn't say he was anything of the sort. He would understand perfectly, but I…" She decided it was hopeless to try to explain to him that Bristol was serious and solid and dependable as the Rock of Gibraltar, and that she liked him just the way he was.

"What really did happen with you and the artist to make you settle down in this comfortable nonrelationship with Bristol?"

She wanted to groan. "You're not going to quit, are you? Just because I'm not living with the man. All right, I'll tell you. Morgan liked to keep his options open. He was like a man at a buffet dinner who takes a spoonful of everything because he doesn't want to miss out on something good."

Riley frowned. "I think I see. You mean that you wanted to settle down and he didn't?"

"Not only didn't he want to settle down," Deborah said dryly, "he seemed to think that women were like different varieties of macaroni salad, and he wanted to try them all."

He nodded thoughtfully. "That explains Bristol the fifth. No wonder he's so appealing to you."

She counted to ten and decided it was not necessary to give him a chance to explain that. "How about you, Riley? Any women in your life?"

"Oh, hundreds," he said airily.

"That's certainly helpful. Are there any I should watch out for in particular?"

His forehead wrinkled thoughtfully. "There are one or two who might consider poisoning your food, but I don't think they'll actually do it."

"What a comfort. I suppose the whole town is littered with your ex-girlfriends."

"Absolutely. By the way, that's quite a gallery you've got. Do you plan to sell it, or just close it down?"

She stared at him as if he'd suddenly grown antennae. "Sell it? Close it? Are you mad? I've worked myself to a thread for three years getting that gallery into shape. Why on earth would I give it up now that it's finally beginning to turn a profit?"

"You'll have to do something with it when you marry me and move to Summerset," he prompted gently. "Don't be a dunce, Debbie darling. You ought to expect to be asked that sort of question, you know."

"Not by you," she said a little sullenly. "When did you see the gallery, anyway?"

"I stopped on my way back to the hotel last night and peeked in the window. Good thing it was closed, too, window shopping is the only kind I could afford." He whistled.

She shook her head. "That's not true. I only buy originals, that's true, but there's a wide price range."

"The decorating scheme didn't look like it."

"Creating the look of success isn't cheap, Riley."

"So are you going to get out of the rat race and sell it?"

She shook her head. "Maybe you're the one who's going to move."

"To Chicago? Not me. Besides, if this is going to be your basic dynastic marriage, I have to stand firm, as the head of the household."

"Oh, for heaven's sake, Riley!"

"Pretend, darling. Practise saying it. 'When I marry Riley, I'm going to sell my gallery.'"

"Over my dead body. It's unique!"

He blinked. "The gallery, or the dead body? Never mind. Just repeat after me. 'And I'm probably going to have a dozen children....'"

Her practical joke was losing its flavour; it certainly seemed that Riley had adjusted himself to all the possibilities far better than she had managed to. "That's not funny," she muttered.

"You're the one who brought up passing on the name," he reminded.

"I always knew you were a chauvinist. You probably would expect your wife to stay home and raise the children."

"Stay home, no. Raise children, yes, I hope so."

"That's contradictory," Deborah complained. "Not that I expected anything else from you, but..."

"Why is it contradictory? I intend to change diapers, warm bottles at three in the morning, take out splinters—all the joys of parenthood—along with my regular job. Why shouldn't my wife have the same opportunity for a well-rounded life?"

She looked at him suspiciously. "That doesn't sound—"

"And stop trying to change the subject, anyway. I'm

sure Ida will be thrilled at the idea of our beautiful and charming children. What would they be to her, anyway?"

"Great-great-nieces and nephews," Deborah said almost automatically. "And they'd all be redheads, too, I have no doubt. My God, Riley, that's a nightmare!"

He didn't seem to hear. "On your side, yes, they'd be nieces and nephews. But what about mine? I'm some sort of cousin."

"Who counts that far?"

Riley snapped his fingers. "I know," he said cheerfully. "We can just call up R. Bristol the fifth. I'm sure he'd be happy to figure it out for us."

# CHAPTER THREE

AFTER THAT Deborah maintained a stern silence for almost twenty miles, until it became obvious that Riley didn't mind the sound of his own voice in the least, and if she wasn't going to talk to him he'd be quite happy to entertain himself. So she gave up the silent treatment, and the rest of the drive went by so quickly that she was startled when the car swept into the small city of Summerset, on the banks of the Summer River, and climbed steadily through the wide, uncrowded streets towards the highest point in town.

Lassiter House was by far the grandest private residence in Summerset; it rode the crest of the highest hill, reigning over the surrounding countryside. Now, in the midst of summer, it was hard to see it from a distance because of the trees that were far more numerous than people in Summerset, but in winter the house became a landmark that could be seen for miles.

Ostensibly, Jacob Lassiter had built his house atop the hill in order to catch the breezes from any direction, in the days when air-conditioning to battle the Midwest's relentless summer heat was still just a science-fiction dream. In actual fact, Deborah had always thought, he had liked the idea of sitting atop his hill like a feudal monarch on his throne, looking down upon his subjects. It had very nearly been a feudal town in Jacob's day, when half the workers in Summerset were employed by Lassiter Brothers, and the other half worked for the firms that provided food and clothing and services to them.

"You got awfully quiet all of a sudden," Riley said. "Are you mad at me again, or is it only nerves?"

"Neither. I was just thinking," she said. "I wonder if Jacob was ever happy up there, looking down on everyone."

"I imagine he sat up there with his binoculars and chortled while he watched the little ants scurry around, making his fortune grow."

"Do you really think so? I think perhaps he missed his brother, and regretted their quarrel."

Riley said shortly, "He had years to patch it up, if he regretted it. But he didn't bother."

She looked at him curiously. Had Bristol been right then? Did Riley nurse a grudge, and think that he and his family had been cheated?

Then he said, "What a romantic you are, Debbie darling."

She relaxed. "Perhaps. But I still think he must have missed the days when they lived side by side in the twin houses and walked to the factory together every day."

Riley made a sort of grunt. "I'm betting he didn't miss a thing. Well, there it is, in all its glory."

Lassiter House was a cross between a Swiss mountain chalet and a midsize cathedral. Or perhaps the architect had merely been working from Jacob Lassiter's mental image of those things, which he had never seen firsthand. It occupied almost the entire peak of the hill, and its three full storeys, under a steep slate roof, seemed to extend the hill into a man-made mountain. The house was solid and massive and bulky, with flying buttresses supporting the side walls and holding up the huge balcony that stretched the width of the front. A carved frieze of grape leaves and mature bunches of fruit nestled under the roofline and rimmed the balcony railing, while stone gargoyles, each one with a different face, decorated the innumerable corners of the house.

Deborah muttered, "I've always thought that the architect should have gotten an award for inventing an entirely new style. They could have called it Early Horrible."

"Thank heaven it didn't start a trend," Riley said.

As the Jaguar flashed through the tunnel of huge old oak trees that lined the avenue at the base of the hill, the alternating light and shadow were like a strobe against Deborah's retinas and made her head ache. Then the car turned away from the sun and began to growl up the long winding drive, and she relaxed a little.

Riley parked the Jaguar in the small space that had been precariously carved out of the hillside for guest parking and came around to open her door. "What did Ida say when you called her?" he asked. "She isn't expecting that I'll be hanging around for dinner, is she? I really need to get back to work."

"Oh, I'm sure that won't be any problem," Deborah said airily. She looked up at the wide steps—a hundred of them, at least—that led up to the imposing front door and sighed; the car park was little more than halfway up the hill. "I suppose it would have ruined the view if old Jacob had allowed his friends to park on the front lawn. But still…"

"He did it on purpose, you know," Riley muttered. "This way anyone who came to see him and complain about something was immediately at a disadvantage, exhausted and out of breath."

"I'd forgotten how steep it was," she said a little later, gasping, and stopped for a moment on one of the wide terraced landings. "I used to run up and down this slope as if it was nothing. It's terrible, the things that happen as one ages, isn't it?"

"I hadn't noticed."

Deborah thought resentfully that it was probably true; he wasn't even breathing hard. It was with a great sense of relief that she finally put her finger firmly on the ornate old doorbell button. The chimes seemed to echo inside.

Riley had turned his back to the door to survey the view of the city. "Now this is where the ski slope ought to go," he said. "It's a natural."

The door creaked a little as it opened, and Ida Lassiter's man of all work appeared in the opening, a spotless white apron over his dark trousers and pristine white shirt, and a perfectly knotted black necktie in place. Riley had told her once that Henry slept in his necktie; Deborah had half believed him for years.

"May I— Miss Deborah!" The leathery old face wrinkled even more. "And Mr. Lassiter. Welcome home, Miss Deborah!"

The door swung wide and Deborah stepped across the threshold into Lassiter House. The great hall was cool and dim, despite the heat of the afternoon sun outside. It took a moment for her eyes to adjust, but she didn't need to see the room to know that it had not changed at all; something about the smell of it told her that. It was the same old slightly musty aroma that she remembered from the first time she had been brought here to spend the summer, when she was almost four. In the far corner was the dull gleam of the same polished armour that had terrified her as a child, and along the floor was the same worn old runner on which she had played hopscotch in rainy weather. And, she thought, the same old man, wearing, probably, the same old tie. Perhaps he really did sleep in it.

"I'll tell Miss Lassiter you've arrived," Henry said. "Is she expecting you?"

"Yes," Riley said.

"Not exactly," Deborah murmured at the same moment.

The old man's beady eyes shifted from one of them to the other without comment, and then he shuffled off down the hall.

"Poor Henry," Deborah said. "I thought at first that he hadn't changed at all, but he walks like a crab these days."

"What the hell do you mean, not exactly?" Riley said. "You told me you called her."

"No, I didn't. Tell you that, I mean."

He glared at her. The silence stretched out for a long moment. "All right," he admitted. "What you said was, she wasn't planning on me staying to dinner."

She nodded.

"Because you didn't even call her. Dammit, Deb!"

"I thought it would be better to take her by surprise," Deborah said with a shrug, "and not give her too much of a chance to think about it before we got here."

"Take her by surprise? Debbie, you utter fool! How could you?" He stopped and sighed. "Well, at least you accomplished one thing. Ida will have no trouble believing that you've been hanging around with me, under my evil influence. You've lost all your manners."

"I am in love," Deborah said with dignity. "Remember? That excuses a lot of things. But you're probably right about Ida's reaction. You never had any manners to speak of."

"I resent that accusation. My mother taught me to always speak kindly to ladies."

Deborah gave a genteel little snort. "Oh? By telling them they're utter fools?"

"If you are unfamiliar with my technique," Riley pointed out, "you might want to consider the possibility that it's because you're not exactly a lady."

Deborah thought she heard a step coming along the upstairs hall, a heavy, deliberate step. Now that it was too late to call off this ridiculous farce, now that she was within a minute of having to face Aunt Ida and spin out this impossible story, she began to feel a sick sort of squeamishness in the pit of her stomach.

"Maybe you should just run along, Riley," she muttered, "and let me handle this end of it. If you can't act the part—"

"You have doubts?" It was a very soft, very gentle murmur.

To the end of her days, Deborah would never quite know how she ended up held so firmly in Riley's arms that she couldn't have broken free with a bazooka. And when she looked up with flame in her eyes, astounded at finding herself so trapped, and began to protest, he silenced her with his mouth on hers, kissing her slowly and deliberately and not at all as if it was the first time ever, taking advantage of her unwitting, paralysed co-operation to probe her mouth, his tongue exploring with infinite patience.

The sound of a throat being cleared, forcefully and loudly, brought her back to the edge of reality. Aunt Ida, she found herself thinking a bit vaguely, must be having an attack if she can't even say anything. Seeing this sort of thing going on in her own front hall will probably leave her permanently scarred.

Riley, who had his back to the stairs and who hadn't seemed to hear anything at all, just kept on kissing her. Deborah almost bit him, except that some tiny sane corner of her brain reminded her that however shocked Aunt Ida might already be, things could always be made worse. So she kept her eyes closed tightly and tried to pretend that she was somewhere else altogether.

The throat was cleared again, even more loudly this time.

Deborah opened one eye, tentatively. Over Riley's shoulder she could see Aunt Ida standing on the bottom step, seeming to loom over the great hall. Her angular body was as straight and spare as ever. Her hair was the same wiry iron grey that it had been for as long as Deborah could remember. And the pose, with her arms folded squarely across her chest—that was familiar too; Deborah remembered it well from various scoldings.

Finally Riley relinquished her mouth, very slowly, and turned his head a bit. "Ida," he said, almost as if he'd seen a ghost. "I'm so sorry. I got carried away, I'm afraid. You see, your niece has just promised to make me the happiest man in the world."

His words were ever so slightly slurred, as if passion had indeed gotten out of hand. It was a good performance, Deborah had to admit, as long as he didn't overdo it and end up sounding instead as if he'd had to too much to drink.

"She's planning to make you happy in private, I trust," said a familiar raspy voice, almost masculine in tone, "and not in my front hall. It would shock Henry."

Riley laughed sheepishly. "Didn't I make myself quite clear? I mean she's promised to marry me."

There was a half snort from the direction of the staircase. "These days, one never knows what a young woman might mean. So that's what brings you home to Summerset, young lady."

Deborah didn't answer. Obviously, she was thinking, I

overestimated the extent of Aunt Ida's shock. It doesn't seem to have bothered her at all. I wonder...

Riley pinched her. Deborah jerked back to reality, decided that stomping on his toes would not be appropriate, however inviting the temptation, and smiled at Aunt Ida. "I just couldn't wait to let you know how happy I am," she said in the most oozingly sweet voice she could muster. She thought the sound of it made Riley look a little ill.

"Speak up," Ida commanded. "Don't mumble so, Deborah."

Deborah sighed and said a little louder, "Of course I'm anxious to get the wedding plans under way, and I couldn't possibly do that without your advice. I can only spare a week right now, but I'm sure—"

"Well, come here," Aunt Ida ordered. "Surely you can leave your young man for long enough to give me a dutiful kiss."

It was only then that Deborah realised she was still firmly within the circle of Riley's arms, so closely nestled against his body that she seemed to have been glued there. It took physical effort to move away from the illusion of safety that he represented and take the few steps that brought her to Ida's side. The hug they shared was brief, stiff and a little awkward; Ida had not come down off her step, and her sharp chin dug uncomfortably into Deborah's scalp. It was a relief when the social amenity was fulfilled and Deborah could stand on her own again.

"You've had lunch, of course," Ida announced. It was not a question. "In any case, I couldn't invite you. Henry has far too much to do without being a short-order cook."

Deborah wanted to wince; the remark was so obviously an arrow aimed at Riley. Perhaps, she thought, she'd been wrong after all about Ida's reaction to dynastic alliances;

the woman hadn't seemed thrilled with the news. But she restrained the retort she'd have liked to make and said mildly, "Yes, we've had lunch."

"Then we'll let Riley go on about his business—I'm sure there are things needing his attention—while we have a chat," Ida said. She started down the long dim hall. "As for dinner, I'll have to tell Henry right away. An extra guest does complicate things for him, you know."

Riley winked at Deborah behind Ida's back and called after the old woman, "You needn't worry about feeding Debbie. She's having dinner with me tonight at the restaurant."

Deborah made a face at him.

"In fact," he went on, "I thought perhaps we'd celebrate with an impromptu engagement party, Ida—you, my mother, the two of us...."

Ida stopped but didn't turn around. "Yes, that would be very nice. But I'd hate to leave my guest alone, and it's just as hard on Henry to have to cook a meal for one as it is to have unexpected extras."

Riley smiled wryly at Deborah, who was wide-eyed with astonishment. "Bring him along," he said, and added under his breath, "After all, he's almost part of the family. Now do you see what I mean, Debbie, my dear?"

IT WASN'T A CHAT so much as it was a machine-gun firing of questions, with Ida not listening to—or perhaps not even hearing—the answers. The third time Deborah was ordered not to mumble, she found herself longing to ask Aunt Ida how long it had been since her hearing was checked, but she controlled the impulse and repeated the answer instead. She might as well not have bothered, however; by that time, Ida was off on another train of thought altogether.

"I assumed you'd marry some high-powered lawyer or stockbroker or something in Chicago," she said.

"Oh, I've dated a few people like that. But you see, Aunt Ida, there's just no one like Riley." And that, Deborah thought piously, is certainly the truth!

Ida did not seem sympathetic to the idea of young love. "I hope you both realise that the Lassiter trust isn't going to support you. The income you're already getting is all there will be."

I should be glad that she brought the subject up herself, Deborah thought, even though the way she did it makes me want to chew nails. "I assumed that," she said calmly. "But while we're talking about the trust, just what is the money intended for? I understand that there may be some funds to help pay for our wedding."

Ida's eyes narrowed. "William told you that, no doubt. I suppose that means he's used up his last dime and couldn't even afford to give you a ride to the church."

"Daddy's doing very well, thank you," Deborah said stiffly.

Ida snorted. "Well, I haven't time for an analysis of the situation just now. I have a bridge tournament this afternoon." She rose, straight and imposing. "We'll talk about it later."

Deborah retreated to the guest room at the head of the stairs with relief. It was going to take some time to readjust, that was all, she told herself. She simply wasn't used to Aunt Ida's abrasiveness.

As soon as she saw the vintage Rolls depart, with Ida sternly upright in the back seat and Henry hunched over the wheel, Deborah stopped unpacking, changed her cotton dress for brief shorts and a halter top and returned to the brick patio behind the house with a book and a glass of iced spring water, luxuriating in the knowledge that for the next three hours peace would reign over Lassiter House.

It actually lasted for a little less than three minutes.

The first indication of trouble was a bright red beach ball that sailed over the fence and landed with a soft splash at the edge of the swimming pool. Deborah looked up with a frown and studied the ball over the top of her sunglasses for a long moment, watching it bob gently in the water.

A couple of minutes later a head appeared over the brick wall that surrounded patio and pool. It was topped with a thatch of white-gold hair, and it was followed by a wiry body that scrambled over the top of the wall and landed with a small thud on the bricks. The boy was about seven or eight, she thought, and she watched quietly from her corner as he dusted off the seat of his shorts, kicked off his shoes and headed for the water.

Then she put down her book and tugged off her sunglasses. "Excuse me," she said.

He wheeled around to face her, with stark terror in his wide brown eyes; the freckles on his face stood out like tattooed dots.

"What on earth are you doing here?" Deborah asked. "This is private property."

The calmness of her question seemed, in an odd way, to reassure him. "I had to come and get my ball. It flew over the fence."

Deborah studied him for a long moment—the wiry body, the small, square face with a cleft in the chin. "Accidentally, I'm sure," she said. "While you were playing."

The boy nodded hopefully.

"But the question is, where were you playing? Unless you threw it all the way up here from the bottom of the hill, you must have been on Miss Lassiter's property."

He shuffled his bare feet on the bricks. "Well, how was I supposed to know you were here?" he asked reasonably. "You didn't even squeak when I threw the ball over the fence. If you had, I'd have been downtown before you ever saw me."

Deborah stifled her desire to giggle at this disarming honesty, but it took effort. "You've got quite a system figured out, haven't you? Have you lost a lot of beach balls that way?"

"Only a couple," he said modestly. "She goes off every Friday, and most Tuesdays, and sometimes on Thursdays, too."

Deborah shook her head. "I don't believe it," she said to no one in particular. "Under her very eyes..."

The boy gulped. "Are you going to turn me over to her? To the witch?"

She hid her smile. Ida Lassiter as the town witch...yes, she could see how that legend might have grown. "To be made into mincemeat pie or something? She's not that bad, you know, she's just not used to kids. She never was." It was true, she thought, with a hint of surprise; much of Ida's sternness, which had so terrified her as a child, could well have been uncertainty, instead, or a fear of embarrassing herself. Don't break your heart over it, she told herself abruptly. She's still acting the same way!

The French doors from the sun room opened, and a male voice said, "Ida? Have you someone here with you?" Then the man in the doorway saw Deborah on the chaise longue, and the voice warmed as he came quickly across the patio. "Well, you must be Deborah. Aren't you? I recognised you from the portrait in Ida's sitting room. I'm Preston Powell. I had no idea you were here. I am so pleased to meet you."

Preston Powell, she thought. The man Riley referred to as the oily snake.

He didn't look like a con man, she had to grant him that. He was older than she had expected, in his early forties, perhaps, with a distinguished touch of premature silver at his temples. His big blue eyes were wide and ingenuous and, at the moment, very admiring. His golf clothes were brightly coloured, but neat and well pressed—by Henry, she had no doubt. And he didn't look the slightest bit oily, or serpentine.

But then, Deborah told herself, no real con man looked like the movie stereotype, or he couldn't possibly make a living. The fact that the man looked like an older version of a Botticelli angel certainly didn't make him innocent.

His eyes fell on the child. "You again," he said. "You've been hanging around and annoying people long enough, and now I find you here. I ought to have charges filed against you."

The child's wide eyes turned to Deborah with a wordless appeal. He was actually terrified, she realised. "There's no need for that," she said mildly. "The young man is merely keeping me company this afternoon."

Preston Powell's eyes warmed again. "If I'd known you were here, and realised it was company you wanted..."

She put her glasses back in place on her nose and picked up her book. "I'm sure you're too busy developing Paradise Valley to spend the afternoon with me." Then she wanted to bite her tongue, because her words seemed to intrigue him.

"Has Ida told you about our plans, then?"

Deborah's heart sank. Riley was right; Ida *was* in it up to her Roman nose.

"I'd be happy to tell you all about it," he went on confidentially, "but right now I have a very important golf date. The whole future of the development may depend on it. If it wasn't so important, rest assured that I'd break my appointment just because you asked me to...."

She refrained, with an effort, from pointing out that she hadn't asked him to do anything of the kind, and reminded herself that she needed all the information she could get about Mr. Preston Powell, and if being polite to him was the best way to get it, then she'd just have to bite her tongue and be polite. "Some other time, then," she said. "I'll look forward to it."

She wouldn't have been surprised if he had kissed her hand before he finally got himself back into the house.

"Gee," the child began in a disgusted voice, "I don't think—"

Deborah silenced him with a finger across her lips, and pointed to the water in a wordless command. He frowned, but he plunged in, and a few minutes later, over the sound of splashing, she heard a car leave the garage and growl down the hill.

The child heard it, too, and he pulled himself up to the side of the pool. "He's gone," he announced.

"And not a bit too soon. What's your name?"

"Alec Chastain."

"And what did Mr. Powell mean about you hanging around?"

The child shrugged. "I offered to wash his car for a couple of dollars. But I wasn't on the property, honestly, I wasn't. I was down at the bottom of the hill. I don't know why he got mad about that."

Deborah could guess; that had sounded like a very high-performance engine. She wouldn't care to turn over her Jaguar to this infant for tender loving care, that was certain. And yet...

Alec climbed out of the water. "Thank you for not giving me away," he said politely. "My mom would kill me if I got in trouble. No, she wouldn't, exactly. She'd just look at me that way she has...." His voice trailed off. "Would you mind if I went out the gate? It's a little tricky climbing the wall when I'm wet."

Deborah didn't look at him. She turned a page and said casually, "If your mother objects, why do you do it?"

From the corner of her eye she could see him shrug his thin shoulders. "The town pool has a crack in it, and all the water leaks out as soon as they put it in, so it's been closed all year. And we can't afford to belong to the country club. So there's no place to swim, and I miss it a lot."

"And meanwhile this pool just sits here unused." She wondered why Ida had bothered to fill it this year. In this climate an open pool, surrounded by trees, was more nuisance than pleasure, and Ida was not a swimmer.

Alec nodded. "He uses it a lot." From the tone of his voice there was no doubt whom he meant. "It's a nice pool." With his bare toe, he traced the pattern of one of the ceramic tiles that lined the edge.

"It used to have pillars all around it, in a bad imitation of a Roman bath. I've been told it was the first swimming pool in town, and when it was built it had salt water in it."

Alec wrinkled his nose. "That sounds awful."

"Thus speaks a Midwestern child. It's just like swimming in the ocean."

"Is it? I've never seen an ocean." His voice was wistful.

Deborah looked quickly down at her book. Lots of kids haven't been to the ocean, she told herself. Don't get all sentimental about it!

"Thank you for letting me swim," Alec said. He retrieved his beach ball.

"I told Mr. Powell you were spending the afternoon

with me," Deborah said, without looking up. "So don't make a liar out of me. Back in the water, kid."

"I can? Honest?"

He'd have hugged her if she hadn't fended off his wet embrace. "I'm not promising anything in the future," she warned. "But for this afternoon, at least."

He spent most of the time in the water, but in the intervals he stretched out on the tiles beside her chair, and talked with the easy confidence of a longtime friend. Deborah heard all about school, and how glad he was that it was summer, and why he and his mother had come to Summerset after Alec's father died two years ago. In his voice Deborah could hear how tough the loss and the move had been on both of them. But he didn't seem to want sympathy; he stated the facts, and then skipped on to talk of Paradise Valley and how wonderful it would be when the resort was finished. Perhaps he could caddy at the golf course then, he said, and learn to water-ski on Paradise Lake.

Poor Alec, she thought. Despite his experience with Preston Powell, he seemed to see no contradiction between the promising plans and the anything but generous man who stood behind them. She wondered how many others in Summerset felt the same as Alec did. No wonder Riley was so concerned.

And when, she wondered, was she going to get a chance to talk to Riley again? Not at dinner, that was certain, with his mother and Ida and Preston Powell there, too.

Dinner, she thought with a sigh, and wondered if she should go raid Henry's refrigerator for a snack. Lunch had been bad enough; watching Riley eat a cheeseburger at a roadside truck stop where the closest thing to healthy food had been a fish of uncertain ancestry, pressed into a patty and deep-fried. She hated to even think about dinner.

Well, it was only a week, after all, and she'd be back in Chicago with Bristol, and she could have quail at Coq au Vin.

She could almost taste it.

PRESTON POWELL'S CAR turned out to be a Cadillac, pure white with a dark red leather interior. Deborah had to admit she wouldn't have turned it over to Alec for washing, either, but it didn't make her feel any more charitable towards Preston. And when he carefully ushered Ida into the front seat, but told Deborah with an expressive look that he wished it could have been her beside him instead, she wanted to bite something, or someone. Ida, perhaps, because she obviously had not told him of Deborah's supposed engagement.

Instead, she smiled sweetly and then settled back and pretended to watch with fascination as Summerset sped by. Still, she could see from the corner of her eye that he was spending more time looking at her in the driving mirror than he was watching the road. It wasn't her imagination, either; even Aunt Ida had a tart comment about it, and for a couple of minutes Preston seemed to concentrate very carefully on the traffic. But soon he was addressing Deborah again.

She began to wonder how far they could possibly be going, and she wished that she'd had the sense to ask Riley a few more questions about that blasted restaurant of his. He *had* said it was in Summerset, hadn't he?

No, she realised belatedly. He hadn't. Not exactly, at least.

The Cadillac slowed on the main avenue and turned down one of the city's original, narrow, brick-paved streets running towards the Summer River. Deborah frowned. There was nothing much down here except warehouses, which had been abandoned long ago when the riverboat trade dropped off.

But at least one of them was abandoned no longer; that was obvious from the number of cars that surrounded the tall, narrow old building. A discreet sign proclaimed that the place was now offering food and drink, and as the Cadillac drew up before the front door with a flourish, a young man in a dark green uniform sprang from the doorway and opened the passenger doors. He assisted Ida from the car, while Preston came around to help Deborah out. She stood on the pavement for a moment and stared at the building. This was what the natives called Riley's Place?

"Your car," she said automatically as Preston offered his other arm to Ida and started towards the door. But behind her the Cadillac's engine revved gently as the young man moved it away from the entrance.

Valet service, she thought helplessly. In a town like Summerset?

Inside the building it was invitingly dim, lit with the softness of candle glow. On the moss green walls of the foyer were old advertising signs, interspersed with a series of antique botanical prints that almost took Deborah's breath away.

A young blonde woman in a severe dark blue cocktail dress greeted them with a professional smile, which flickered as she recognised Ida and faltered altogether for an instant when she saw Deborah.

Ah, Deborah thought. This must be one of the young women who wouldn't mind poisoning my food. He's obviously broken the news to this one, at least.

The young woman led them past a cocktail lounge full of mirrors and crystal and stained glass, and through a dining room with tables draped in peach and moss green linen, to a smaller room at the far side of the building, with wide windows overlooking the river. A small group was already there: Riley's mother and a man with a shock of iron gray hair who Deborah decided must be her new husband. And, turning to greet them, Riley, in dinner clothes. The stern black and white, lightened with a moss green tie and cummerbund, made his hair look like burnished copper. He looked wonderful, Deborah thought. And also...comfortable, that was the word. As if he practically lived in dinner clothes.

She looked around the room. More botanical prints, more incredible antiques. Against one wall was a small table of hors d'oeuvres, their delicate fragrances filling the air. Nearby was a silver wine bucket, with a bottle already chilling.

This, she thought, was far from being the half café, half bar that she had expected. It wasn't even simply a restaurant. And Riley had given her no warning.

It's inevitable, Deborah thought. Sooner or later, I'm going to kill him. And at the rate he's going, it isn't likely to be later.

## CHAPTER FOUR

RILEY'S SMILE of greeting was slightly tinged with mischief, she thought, but then that was nothing new. And there was certainly nothing to criticise about the way he kissed her cheek—lightly, but just lingeringly enough to suggest that he wished he didn't have such a large audience—before he greeted Ida and Preston Powell.

Deborah crossed the room to Riley's mother with a combination of relief and genuine pleasure. During the long summers with Aunt Ida, Anna Maria Lassiter had sometimes been Deborah's salvation, and the big old white farmhouse had been a welcome change from the stiffness of Lassiter House—except, of course, for Riley's presence. Out on the farm, it had been possible to dig a hole halfway to China without repercussions, or to make a horrendous mess in the kitchen under the guise of hosting a tea party— things that, according to Ida, proper little girls didn't do. At least, not in her garden, or her kitchen.

So it was with genuine gladness that Deborah hugged Anna Maria, noted with a hint of sadness the lacy map of lines in the woman's face and was introduced to her new husband.

"Well, not *new,* exactly," Alan Holmes told her with a twinkle in his dark eyes. "Rather shopworn, I'm afraid, and my guarantee ran out long ago. I warned Anna Maria of that before she married me, but you know how women are. Once they make up their minds what they want, logic doesn't enter into it any more."

Deborah laughed and fluttered a hand towards Riley, in the far corner of the room. "I know," she murmured. "The same sort of thing has happened to me."

"Oh, it's not the same at all," Anna Maria said solemnly. "Riley comes with my personal guarantee—I promise that whatever happens, he'll do the unexpected."

"And in this case, I'm the unexpected," Deborah murmured.

Anna Maria smiled. "Yes, you are, though I didn't mean it to sound that way. The sparks you two used to strike off each other...who would have thought it would end up like this? But Deborah, I'm so glad!"

And she genuinely was, too, Deborah thought uneasily. No one could fake such sincerity, certainly not the forthright Anna Maria. There was going to be disappointment down the road....

Never mind, she told herself. If we manage to keep Preston Powell from putting the whole town in his pocket and walking off with it, any disappointment Anna Maria feels in the end will certainly be tempered with understanding.

A waitress in a dark green dress was scurrying around, bringing their before-dinner drinks. Deborah had asked for her favourite brand of sparkling water, a rather obscure imported variety, and she was not surprised when it appeared. Nothing much about this place would surprise her now, she thought.

She glanced at the table, set for six. "Isn't Mary Beth coming?" she asked.

Anna Maria shook her head. "She and Rod are giving a dinner party tonight. He's a partner now in his law firm.

She hated having to miss it, though. If Riley had only let her know—"

"It was my last-minute idea to come with him," Deborah interrupted. "I told him it was so he didn't have to cope with the commuter train, but the truth is, when it came right down to saying goodbye..." She tried to look girlishly shy.

Anna Maria smiled fondly.

And that's another one you owe me, Riley Lassiter, Deborah thought.

"Mary Beth is very eager to see you. I think she's dying to hear all about your wedding plans. Perhaps we can all get together at the farm tomorrow." She sounded almost diffident. "We've made a lot of changes out there, and I'd like you to see them. Of course if you don't have time..."

"Not have time to see the farm? I couldn't live with myself if I missed that." She listened for a moment to Ida's brusque, too loud voice. From all the way across the room she could hear something about resort financing. She sighed. "As long as I don't have to bring Aunt Ida and her sidekick with me."

Anna Maria smiled wryly. "You've heard, then, about the uproar? It's splitting the town, I'm afraid. Half the population are convinced they'll make their fortunes with Paradise Valley stock. The other half, well, no matter how it turns out it won't be pretty."

"Anna Maria, your prejudice is showing," her husband warned.

"I know, and this is not the place to discuss it."

"Certainly not with the sidekick coming this way," Deborah murmured.

"And why Riley included *him* in your engagement dinner is beyond me."

"You know Riley, always doing the unexpected." Deborah sipped her sparkling water.

Anna Maria broke into the brilliant smile that lit up her eyes and erased the lines from her face.

"Mrs. Holmes," Preston Powell exclaimed. He would have kissed her, Deborah thought, but Anna Maria's Manhattan glass was suddenly and inexplicably in the way, just where it could tip and dump its contents down the front of his bold plaid jacket if he wasn't careful. He settled for seizing her free hand and shaking it with gusto. "I've tried to get back to you in the past few days, but it's been so busy that I haven't had a chance."

"I hadn't given it a thought. I'm a bit busy myself these days, Mr. Powell."

"Oh, call me Preston, please. I've been thinking about our last talk, and I believe that perhaps I could do a little better on my offer for your land. After all, there is no sense in my pretending—it's a key piece of property." He put a hand on her arm and went on earnestly, "And of course, while we could do without it, it would make things much more difficult if we had to build the resort around you."

Anna Maria smiled. It was not her heart-stopping, genuine smile, but something cool and remote. "Good," she said sweetly.

For a split second Preston Powell looked confused. Then he laughed. "For a moment there, I thought you meant... We'll get together this week about my new offer."

Deborah wondered for a moment if the man was honestly so dense. No, she thought. He can't be. He knows quite well what Anna Maria means, he's just not going to go down without a fight.

"Shall we sit down?" Anna Maria led the way to the table and took her seat at the end of it.

Deborah found her hand caught in Riley's; he seated her

next to him, with a flourish. "What do you think, Debbie darling?" he murmured in her ear.

He couldn't have heard his mother's exchange with Preston Powell; he'd been too absorbed with Ida. So Deborah didn't pretend to misunderstand. "You know perfectly well what I think of your little restaurant." But she managed to smile sweetly as she said it, in case anyone was watching her. "You could have warned me, Lassiter."

"Admit it, Deb," he said as he pulled out his own chair. "You had this picture of me as a short-order cook in a greasy apron slopping out hash browns and eggs sunny-side up, didn't you?"

She looked meaningfully across the table at Aunt Ida, who was absorbed in her menu.

Riley didn't seem to notice. "It was too delicious an opportunity. I simply couldn't resist it. Anyway, you should take it as a compliment."

"A compliment?"

"Yes." It was a bare murmur. "I have so much trust in you now, after this afternoon, that I had no doubt that you could carry off a surprise with class. And I was right."

There was no answer to that, at least none that was safe considering the company they were keeping. So she smiled lovingly at him and jabbed his ankle with her spike heel instead.

He turned his gasp of pain into a cough.

"One surprise deserves another," she said pleasantly.

Aunt Ida looked up thoughtfully from the menu. "Do you have lobster tonight, Riley?"

"Certainly. They were flown in just this afternoon."

Ida leaned back in her chair expansively. "That's what I'm having, then. It's my favourite." She beckoned to the waitress. "Bring out a couple so I can choose. I like the liveliest ones, so don't bother to bring any that just lie there. Deborah, you've never tasted anything so wonderful as Riley's lobster."

Deborah shuddered a little. "I'll pass. I know it's silly, but I can't bear eating something that has actually looked at me."

"First it was shrimp," Riley murmured, "and now you're turning down lobster as well? And you wouldn't have a cheeseburger for lunch, either. My dear girl, you're missing out on the best things in life."

"What was that?" Aunt Ida asked. "Don't mumble, Riley. It's very rude."

Next to Ida, Alan Holmes raised his glass. "A toast to the new couple," he said. "To Deborah and Riley—may your life together be filled with happiness!"

Beside Deborah, Preston Powell frowned, but he raised his glass. "A new couple?" he said, over the clink of crystal. "That's hardly sporting, Deborah. You're not even wearing a ring."

Riley's eyebrows went up, but he merely said, "Thanks for reminding me, Powell. Debbie, bless her heart, hasn't even said a word about it."

Deborah thought, That's largely because Debbie-bless-her-heart forgot all about little things like engagement rings, and the fact that everyone will expect her to have one. Damn, I should have picked up something from my jewel box. Anything would have done. These days nearly any crazy thing can be an engagement ring.

Riley dug into his pocket. "And even though this doesn't have much monetary value, darling, I know you'll treasure it the same way I do—for the sentimental attachment it carries."

On his palm lay a dark maroon box, so worn along the edges that the nap was gone from the velvet covering.

Deborah looked at it with something that was almost dread.

Then she reached for the box and told herself firmly, No, he wouldn't have booby-trapped it.

But she held it for a moment anyway, assuring herself that it was safe to open. No tiny fake rattlesnake would leap out at her. No water would spray in her face. No horrible noise would greet the opening of this box. There was too much at stake here for Riley to indulge himself in a childish practical joke. Besides, he'd outgrown all that nonsense, hadn't he?

She held her breath and pressed the catch.

Inside the velvet box, on a bed of gold satin creased and cracked with age, lay a narrow gold band that held a single small diamond, hardly more than a chip. It was obviously antique; the style was that of a generation long gone. But the ring itself looked almost new. The gold was bright and unscratched, and the etched lines that formed the only decoration in the metal were deep and unworn.

Riley picked up her hand and slipped the ring onto her finger. It almost fitted, and it was so light that she hardly knew it was there. He looked into her eyes as if he'd like to drown himself in them.

With an unholy desire to giggle, she told herself, Remember, he's thinking of filet mignon.

"Thank you for waiting," he said, loud enough that even Aunt Ida could hear. He held her hand to his lips, and Deborah thought she saw his mother wipe away a clandestine tear.

Aunt Ida cleared her throat. "How very touching. I suppose this is going to be the splashiest wedding Chicago ever saw."

Deborah nodded.

At precisely the same instant, Riley shook his head.

She turned to glare at him, and he caught himself up short. "Not Chicago," he said smoothly. "We'll be married here in Summerset."

Deborah sighed inwardly. She supposed it was the best recovery he could have made, but still—

"Well, that will make it easier," Ida rasped. "All you have to do then is beat Mary Beth's record."

"We're not interested in competing, Aunt Ida," Deborah said in soothing tones. "Still, one's wedding day only comes once, and it's the most important day in a woman's life. It should be perfect. I've got my heart set on a big wedding—I must have ten friends who'll want to be bridesmaids."

Not at any wedding I'm participating in, Riley seemed to be thinking. At least, to Deborah's eyes, he looked a little sour.

She plunged on recklessly. "And a big reception, of course, and a dance..."

"Here at Riley's place." Ida gave a rusty laugh. "You've shown good sense there, girl. At least you won't need a caterer. Though you'd better be careful with the menu. If it gets too complicated, it might keep him from getting to the church at all, and you certainly wouldn't want that!"

ANNA MARIA AND ALAN were the first to go, pleading an early start to their days now that the vegetable harvest was in full swing. Ida and Preston followed. They seemed a little reluctant to leave Deborah behind, but Riley assured them that he would bring her home soon.

"With what?" Deborah asked suspiciously as soon as the older couples were gone. "I wouldn't put it past you to have a saddle horse tucked away somewhere. Or a donkey cart."

Riley laughed. "Nothing so mundane, I'm afraid. Just your Jaguar. Hadn't you noticed it wasn't up at Lassiter House?"

"You stole my car? Why, you—"

"Of course not. Surely you didn't expect me to walk all the way down here with my luggage. Just let me check on how things are going in the restaurant and we can slip off for a quiet chat. I think we need one, don't you? All this craziness about a wedding. It sounds more as if you're planning an average-size coronation!"

He was gone before she could protest. She sat down at the table again, tapping her fingers impatiently against the cloth.

The waitress returned with a cart and said, "Oh, I'm sorry. I thought everyone was gone."

"Don't let me hold up your work."

"If you're certain you don't mind..."

Deborah saw fine lines of fatigue around the woman's eyes. Quickly and competently she began to clear the dessert dishes, and without a word Deborah followed suit.

The waitress gave her a startled look, but not until all the dishes were on the cart and she was replacing the tablecloth with a fresh one did she speak. "Someone told me you run an art gallery in Chicago, Miss Ainsley."

Deborah decided she might as well get the worst over with. Riley had warned her there would be such questions, after all. "Yes," she said. "But not for long."

"Oh?"

"When Mr. Lassiter and I are married, I'll give it up, of course." And a good thing it is, she thought, that Mr. Lassiter and I aren't ever going to make it to the altar!

"Oh. Of course." The fresh tablecloth was precisely in place, and the waitress started to wheel the loaded cart toward the door. "I just wanted to tell you congratulations, Miss Ainsley. Riley is a wonderful man, you know."

Riley, Deborah thought. How democratic of him. Or, perhaps, was this another of the women who wouldn't mind poisoning Deborah's food? The waitress wasn't exactly a child, but she couldn't be past thirty, and she would be attractive if she didn't look so tired. Preston Powell had noticed, that was sure; he'd spent most of the evening flirting with her.

The waitress went on, "Riley is—"

"Back," he said gently from the doorway. "So please, no more applause. It will give me a big head. Thanks, Ruth, you did a wonderful job tonight."

The woman seemed to glow just a little. Deborah found it fascinating.

Riley led her to a wide stairway that stretched up into the dark recesses of the warehouse. At the second landing he stopped for a moment and tugged his tie loose, then unfastened the top button on his shirt with a sigh of relief.

"Where are we going?" she asked doubtfully.

He gave a villainous chuckle. "To my private lair."

"I can't wait, but do you suppose you could stop taking your clothes off till we actually get there? The contrasting styles of dress made dinner a bit uncomfortable, I'll admit, but you've gone quite far enough now to put me at ease—"

His fingertips touched the shoulder of her white cotton dress as if brushing a bit of lint away. "You were uncomfortable in this? It's a very pretty dress."

"But a bit casual, compared to your costume. I thought all the men in Summerset believed that formal dress meant wearing trousers and shoes instead of denim overalls and work boots."

His eyes lit appreciatively. "Most of us still do."

He turned an elaborately carved brass doorknob and ushered her into a large room lit only by moonlight pouring through huge windows that looked out over the river.

"And if you were uncomfortable because I didn't warn you about the restaurant," he went on reasonably, "you deserve it. You should have told me you hadn't bothered to call Ida."

That was true enough, she reflected. "Still, it could have been nasty if I hadn't kept my head."

"A minor fight between us now and then will add realism to the whole situation. If you had blown up, I'd have abased myself at your feet, and we'd have patched it back together. Then a few weeks from now when we call the whole thing off, everyone would say, 'Yes, we saw this coming when they had that fight the night of their engagement dinner.'"

Deborah frowned. "And they wouldn't think to ask whether we'd been telling the truth all along?"

"Something like that."

"Then you don't plan to tell them eventually that it was all a hoax?"

"Why should we? We'll have gained what we wanted, so why embarrass everybody who fell for the trick?"

"You'd actually rather have your friends think you were jilted than know the truth?"

In the moonlight and shadow, his smile gleamed. "But Debbie darling, who says I'm the one who's going to be jilted?" He snapped a couple of lamps into dim life, casting pools of soft light across the polished expanse of a wide oak plank floor. An overstuffed couch and two deep chairs were gathered in the centre of the room, on a geometrically printed rug. The rest of the huge space was practically empty. Some of the walls were the old, random brick of the original structure; others had been covered with stucco left its natural neutral shade. They were all bare.

"Obviously the person who decorated the restaurant has never been up here," Deborah murmured.

"Of course she has." He poured two glasses of cognac and waved a hand at the couch. "She keeps making noises about wallpaper. Personally I think I should decide where to put the walls, first."

"That does seem a good idea." She sipped her drink and looked around. "Don't put up too many."

"I'll keep it in mind. So far I've managed a bedroom, a bath, a kitchen and a lot of scraps of paper with possibilities for the rest."

She looked around the big shadowy room and shook her head in amazement. "I gathered you weren't on the farm, but I never imagined—"

"There comes a time, Debbie darling, when a man is too old to live with his mother." He sat down on the couch beside her, the cognac glass cupped in his palm. His other arm stretched across the back of the couch, and his hand rested gently on her shoulder, warming the soft cotton under his fingertips.

It was an almost automatic gesture, Deborah thought, as if he never sat down here at all without a female companion. Well, if what she'd seen just this evening was any indication, he had no lack of opportunities with his own employees.

"I still think we should tell your mother," she said.

"Why?"

"Because. Oh, I suppose it's because I don't care if Aunt Ida thinks I'm a blithering idiot when it comes to weddings, but I don't want to have your mother thinking I'm such a fool."

Riley frowned. His fingers began to toy with a long,

glossy strand of her hair. "Then why not just scale down the plans? Ten bridesmaids does sound a bit excessive."

"Don't you have any sense at all, Riley? The bigger the wedding the longer it will take to plan. Therefore the less suspicion there will be when we aren't making much progress on actually committing ourselves to things like a time and a date, much less a photographer and a florist and an orchestra—"

"Orchestra? As in symphony? A band isn't good enough?"

"You know what I mean. Besides, the more expensive the wedding, the more cash Ida is going to have to come up with from the trust to pay for it, and—"

His face cleared. "And therefore, the less she can spend on Paradise Valley."

"Congratulations!" Deborah said with heavy irony. "You may go to the head of the class!"

Instead, his fingertips moved to the nape of her neck and began to massage. "What did you and Ida find to talk about this afternoon?"

"What do you expect? You, of course. She started off by saying, 'So that's what's been taking Riley to Chicago so often. How many times has he been there lately?' and then she looked at me expectantly. And if you don't believe that called for some quick thinking, when I had no idea you'd been anywhere around! What *has* been bringing you to the big city, by the way?"

"I told you that a long time ago. Research."

Deborah groaned.

"So what did you tell her?"

"I fluttered my eyelashes, like this, and said, 'Not nearly often enough.'"

Riley laughed. "I knew my faith in my co-conspirator

was justified. But the eyelashes—" he shook his head "—need a little work."

"I'm gratified to know that. Batting my eyelashes is not my favourite pastime."

"Practice. You might learn to enjoy it. And as long as we're practicing things..." His hand dropped to her spine, just between her shoulder blades, and urged her towards him, very gently.

She didn't resist, but she couldn't help saying, "I thought you had faith in your co-conspirator."

"I do."

"Believe me, I already know how to conduct myself when I'm being kissed, Riley."

"I haven't a single doubt of that. Still, there are things I'd rather find out in private, like whether you enjoy being kissed on the nape of the neck, or if you slug anybody who tries."

His mouth was warm and invitingly soft against hers for a long moment, and then his lips stole softly across the hollow of her cheek to her temple.

"That is not the nape of my neck," she said, trying to sound firm.

"So I'll get around to it." It was only a husky whisper. "I think Ida could reasonably expect me to know these things, too."

She let a hint of laughter creep into her voice. "Ida probably thinks there isn't much you don't already know about me. All the time we've been together in Chicago, you know."

His mouth slipped down over her ear to the side of her neck, and then to the tiny hollow at the base of her throat, where he lingered, his tongue flicking softly at the pulse point there.

Her head had fallen back against the overstuffed couch.

After a long moment, he raised his head. "Does that mean she isn't expecting you to come home tonight?"

"Well, she didn't offer me a key." She opened her eyes with an effort. "And don't think I'm suggesting I stay here, because I'm not."

"Of course you aren't." It was soft and sultry. "You weren't invited."

She didn't mind having the nape of her neck kissed. She also didn't mind having her earlobe nibbled. And she positively enjoyed the brush of his long eyelashes against her cheek as he traced the line of her jaw with his tongue.

"You're right," he said finally. He stood up, shook his head a bit, started to refill their cognac glasses and then firmly set down the bottle as if something had changed his mind.

"What?" Deborah asked faintly.

"You do know how to conduct yourself in a kiss. R. Bristol the fifth should open a school. I think I'll call him up and suggest it."

"That's—" She bit her tongue.

Riley gave her a crooked grin. "Not a compliment? But I assure you, Debbie darling, I meant it to be one."

"I think it's time for me to go home," she said firmly.

"Before you get into trouble?"

"No. Before everybody at Lassiter House goes to bed. I'd hate to get Henry up to unlock the door. I'd never hear the last of it." You're babbling, Deborah, she told herself, but she went right on anyway. "Ida seems to think I only came to Summerset to be a nuisance to him, anyway. And if Preston was the one to answer the door instead..."

"I noticed that he seemed to find you irresistible."

"If you'd told me what sort he was, I wouldn't have bothered dragging you into this whole mess. I'd merely have gone after him."

"That would have been interesting—"

"Interesting is hardly the word."

"—watching him try to decide if he'd rather con the money from Ida or marry you for it."

Deborah gathered herself up and smoothed her skirt. "And what makes you think it's only the money he'd be after?"

Riley snorted. "Debbie, darling, do you think he's seriously interested in anything else?"

She gave him a sweet smile. "Perhaps he, too, likes the way I kiss!"

HER JAGUAR was tucked into the shadows behind the building, almost out of sight. She held out her hand for the keys, but instead Riley unlocked the passenger door and held it for her. She stood her ground. "I can get myself home, you know."

"But that would scarcely be gentlemanly of me, would it?"

She gave up and got into the car. "It's not my problem if you want to make trouble for yourself," she pointed out. "But the car stays at Lassiter House, so you're on your own when it's time to go home."

He looked up at the moon, riding high in the summer sky. "It's a lovely night for a walk," he murmured. "The moon and the clouds and the soft breeze, and the memory of the girl I love."

"Only one girl? You amaze me, Riley."

"Well, only one at a time," he amended with a smile.

"It would be only fair for you to tell me about the last few. Like the hostess at the restaurant. And the waitress."

"Ruth?" He sounded honestly amazed. "You must be joking."

A man's blind spots were uniquely interesting, Deborah

thought wryly. "Then I don't suppose you noticed that Preston Powell found her intriguing."

"No, I didn't," Riley said slowly.

"I'd be careful, Riley. He may steal her affections away from you."

"What have I got to worry about?" The teasing note was back in his voice. "I've got you!"

There was no getting ahead of him, so she stopped trying. "As long as we're talking of things we should know about each other..."

"Yes, Debbie darling?" he asked solicitously.

She bit her tongue. "This ring," she said. "I'm morally certain I ought to know where it came from, and I don't."

Riley shrugged. "There's no reason you should recognise it, actually. It was my grandmother's, but she hardly ever wore it. There was too much physical work on the farm, and she didn't like to take a chance of losing it."

In the glow of a streetlight as the Jaguar flashed by, the diamond chip sparkled faintly. "Owned by a little old lady who only wore it to church on Sundays," Deborah mused.

"That's about it. It even still has the engraving inside—her initials, and my grandfather's, and something suitably soupy and sentimental. Does it fit?"

"It's a little snug, but it will do for a few days."

"I can have it adjusted."

"Oh, no. I'll be less likely to lose it this way."

Riley shrugged. "Whatever you like."

"And in any case I wouldn't want to harm it." She turned her hand. It was such a tiny stone, in such a cheap little ring. And yet, to Riley's grandmother, it had obviously been very valuable, treasured and cherished and handed down to her only grandson for his bride. For a moment, Deborah was a bit surprised that he had trusted her with it, and then she realised that he could have done nothing else without causing family speculation. "I'll be very careful with it, Riley," she said. Her voice was a little husky.

He walked her to the front door of Lassiter House. "Just in case anyone's watching," he murmured, and kissed her good-night, long and lovingly. Deborah was too breathless from the walk up the hill to protest.

And she didn't realise until she was in her own room, with the lights out and the crisp linen sheets around her, that they still hadn't formed any precise plan for how to stop Preston Powell.

# CHAPTER FIVE

THE EARLY-MORNING sunshine pouring through the guest room windows had never bothered Deborah when she was a child. "But in those days," she told herself owlishly, as she pulled the blanket over her head, "Aunt Ida always sent me to bed straight after supper, so I suppose I was more than ready for a new day to come."

It was too close under the blanket to breathe, and in any case the pseudo-darkness didn't do any good. There were too many arguments going on in her brain to let her rest. So she put on pastel shorts and a matching striped shirt and searched out Henry in the kitchen to beg a cup of coffee.

"It's left from breakfast, Miss Deborah," he warned. "If you don't mind waiting a bit, I'll make some fresh."

"This will be fine, Henry." Deborah poured herself a cup and stared at it for a long time. It was very black. "What time was breakfast?" she asked doubtfully.

"About two hours ago. Miss Ida's gone to the garden, and Mr. Powell went to play golf."

It begins to sound as if the man doesn't do anything else, Deborah thought uncharitably. Then she reminded herself that it was Saturday, and a good many of Preston Powell's prospects would be spending the day at the country club. It would be an opportunity he couldn't afford to miss. She pulled a chair over to the heavy, knife-scarred table that served as a butcher block and island in the centre of the big old-fashioned room. "How long has Preston Powell been living here, Henry?"

"About three weeks, miss."

"He's put all this together in three weeks? The whole Paradise Valley project, I mean."

"Oh, no. He's been doing that for some months, I understand. I thought you meant how long he'd been at Lassiter House."

Deborah sipped her coffee and tried not to make a face. "Ida's put up with him for that long? You don't like him any better than I do, do you, Henry?"

"It's not my job to like him or not," the houseman said primly. He took his hands out of the dishwater and began to dry his fingers carefully, one at a time. "Now if you'll excuse me, I have to answer the telephone."

"Never mind. I'll get it." She left her coffee on the kitchen table without regret and dashed through the butler's pantry to the tiny telephone booth in the side hall. In Jacob Lassiter's day, one telephone was a luxury; more than that would have been scandalous, despite his standing in the community. And what was good enough for him had remained good enough for his family. Ida hadn't even installed an extension in her bedroom until she fell one winter, broke her leg and was confined to her room for weeks.

"Hello, Deborah darling!" William Ainsley sounded extraordinarily cheerful. "I have good news, I think."

She relaxed. "Hi, Daddy."

"I found my copy of the trust arrangement. Shall I send you— Oh, darling, I should have asked. Can you talk? If someone is listening in, just say 'bananas' and I'll understand."

Deborah laughed, but she looked over her shoulder before she said, "Daddy, this is not a CIA stakeout, for heaven's sake. Of course I can talk."

"Oh, good. I haven't forgotten what it's like in Ida's house. When I was visiting her I tried a time or two to call my broker, and she always walked through the hall at the wrong time. She seemed to think I was placing bets with a bookie or arranging an assignation with a hooker—"

"Oh, was her hearing going even then?" Deborah asked cheerfully.

"Just remember, dear, 'bananas', and I'll know what you mean. I'll send you a copy of the trust document."

She shifted her grip on the telephone. "How about giving me a rundown of the relevant parts now?"

"Let me see." She could imagine him arranging his half glasses on the bridge of his nose, and she could hear the rustling of paper. "As for money for the wedding—"

"Daddy, that is hardly my biggest concern at the moment."

"Of course not. Silly of me. The original trustees were Jacob's three children, Ralph and Ida and your grandmother. Now, of course, there's only Ida, and Riley is right—she's got total control. After her death, control passes to..." He flipped a page, and the telephone rattled as he almost dropped it. "To the trust department of Jacob's bank and to the senior partner of his law firm, jointly."

Deborah groaned. "And trying to get information out of either of them, or for that matter to get them involved in unseating Aunt Ida, will be impossible."

"Very likely."

"Wait a minute. What does he mean, the senior partner of his law firm? The one who handled his business? If he was Jacob's age, he'd be at least a hundred years old by now."

"It isn't terribly clear, but I suppose it means whoever is the senior partner at the moment. Law firms tend to go on and on, you know, they just change personnel over the years."

"Too bad Riley didn't make it through law school," Deborah said grumpily. "It might have been him, and he could have fought this battle all by himself."

William Ainsley made a noise that might have been agreement. "The firm's name at the time was Bowers and Milligan."

Deborah riffled through the telephone directory. "Well, there's no Bowers in Summerset now," she reported. "And no Milligan, either."

"Well, I'll send this to you. Maybe you and Riley can make something more of it than I have. Good luck, darling."

"Daddy, maybe you'd better send it to Riley. I'd hate to have it opened by mistake here at Lassiter House."

"So there is some spying going on, after all." There was satisfaction in William's tone. "As long as we're talking about intrigue, I stopped at the gallery yesterday to see how things were going in your absence, just to make sure there was no funny business."

"I'd only been gone a few hours," Deborah said dryly. "How bad could it have gotten?"

"You never know. That assistant of yours—Peggy, is that her name? She's very good, Deborah."

"Daddy," she said wistfully, "please don't tell me Peggy sold you something."

"Only a small watercolour."

"Oh, is that all? You traitor!"

"Well, if I'd waited for you to come back, someone

else might have got it," William Ainsley said reasonably. "I'll talk to you later, darling. Shall we set up a regular call schedule, so I can notify the authorities if I don't hear from you?"

IDA WAS TRIMMING the faded blooms off the old-fashioned roses in the walled garden behind the house. The huge old plants clambered up the walls, clinging tenaciously to the brick and mortar. Deborah wondered how badly scratched little Alec had been in his first few expeditions to the forbidden swimming pool. Had he come upon the hidden roses without warning, having climbed the wall and dropped into them? And how long, she wondered, had it taken him to pinpoint the safest spots for scaling the barricade? Not long, she suspected, remembering the beach ball ploy; Alec had a very well-developed sense of self-preservation.

"Good morning, Aunt Ida," she called from the French doors, and was annoyed when Ida glanced at the position of the sun before answering.

It's not all that late, Deborah told herself. In Chicago I'd only be starting for the gallery. But she swallowed her annoyance and circled the pool slowly to join her aunt. "May I help?"

Ida shook her head. "It's touchy, pruning these old plants."

"I thought I could learn."

Aunt Ida shot her a look. "Don't tell me you're bored with Summerset already."

"Of course not. I just haven't anything else to do at the moment."

"Riley hasn't offered to put you to work? I'm surprised at the boy, passing up a chance for free help."

Riley has better sense than to try, Deborah thought. She

sat down on the edge of a stone bench. "I suppose that comes later. He's picking me up in a few minutes, by the way. We're spending the day out at the farm."

"I gathered that. It's lucky he can take time off whenever he wants like that. I'd think it would concern him, leaving the hired help in charge."

"Aunt Ida, no one should work all the time. And if he's got good hired help..." Deborah pulled her heels up on the edge of the bench and hugged her knees. Then she added deliberately, "I thought you liked Riley."

Ida's pruning shears didn't pause. "And who said I didn't?"

"You certainly sounded yesterday as if you didn't approve."

"Of Riley?" Ida sounded more curious than surprised.

"Of our plans." Deborah bit her tongue and forced herself to actually say the words. "The whole idea of us getting married."

Ida turned around then, and it seemed to Deborah that there was nothing but honest amazement behind her old-fashioned wire eyeglasses. "That sounds a bit guilty, Deborah. I wonder why. Do you know of some reason why I shouldn't approve? Something you haven't told me?"

So much for the direct approach, Deborah thought. She shrugged. "Of course not. I just got that impression from you. Of course, Riley is a bit unorthodox." She congratulated herself; if that understatement didn't sound like a woman in love, nothing ever would!

"Yes," Ida said thoughtfully. "I must admit I was surprised."

"I thought perhaps you might be upset at the idea of me living in a warehouse, or something."

Ida had gone back to trimming the roses. "At least it's a *converted* warehouse," she pointed out. "And why should I care where you live? Just don't get any notions of living here."

Deborah stifled a shudder at the idea of Lassiter House as a honeymoon cottage. The mere suggestion of being part of a newlywed couple sharing that monstrosity on the hill with Aunt Ida made her feel ill. She said with perfect honesty, "The idea had never crossed my mind."

"Good. I'm putting it up for sale, you know."

"Lassiter House?" It was almost a croak. Lassiter House without Aunt Ida? No, this must be a colossal joke.

"It's too big," Ida went on, "and Henry's getting too old to keep up with it."

"You could hire more help," Deborah offered tentatively.

Ida shook her head decisively. "That would be a waste of money. As soon as it sells, I'm going to build a small place out at Preston's resort. I've already got my site picked out."

Deborah's uneasiness faded a bit. At least Ida was being sensible enough to wait for her house to sell before plunging into something new, and a sale could take months or years, or forever. Who would be fool enough to buy Lassiter House, anyway?

It's a dinosaur of a house, she told herself. It hasn't had an ounce of updating in the forty years since Jacob died. There's still no air-conditioning, the plumbing is beginning to be balky, and the kitchen could have come straight out of Wuthering Heights. Who would want the place?

It was with considerably more calmness that she said, "You're right. A smaller place would be much easier for you to manage, Aunt Ida."

Ida sniffed. "I can manage anything I choose. It's Henry I'm worried about. Besides, it's only sensible to keep an eye on my investment."

Deborah swallowed hard and told herself that there would be no advantage in arguing with Aunt Ida about Paradise Valley. Not just yet, at any rate.

Ida was watching her curiously. "You don't approve of the resort, do you?"

"That's not up to me," Deborah said steadily. Now I'm beginning to sound like Henry, she thought. "I'm certain that you'll look into it very carefully before you actually make any big investment. Especially with the trust's money, knowing as you do how determined your father was to keep his estate intact."

"And also because of the expense of your wedding coming up?" Aunt Ida asked mildly.

"I didn't say that. But as long as we're on the subject, perhaps you'll tell me if there is anything I should know before I start making plans."

"You mean if there are limits, or things you're not allowed to buy, and that sort of thing? No, there aren't— not really. I think sometimes that my father had no sense at all."

At least we agree on something, Deborah thought wryly. Personally, I'm beginning to think the man was a certifiable nut! Perhaps old Jacob wasn't so big on the idea of marriage after all. He must have managed to take all the joy out of weddings by making them into family fights.

Then she thought once more about what Ida had said, and asked suspiciously, "Exactly what do you mean, *not really?*"

Aunt Ida smiled. Her procelain-perfect teeth gleamed between the thin lips. "I have to approve all of the bills," she said gently.

"I expect that you'll look them over very carefully," Deborah said calmly. Thank heaven it isn't going to come to that, she thought. I wonder how Mother managed. But then she didn't have Paradise Valley and Preston Powell to contend with! "I'd hate to think I wasn't getting my money's worth."

"Or—to be painfully accurate, my father's money's worth," Ida agreed.

Before Deborah could get her breath back again after that jab, Ida went on, "Your mother had a small but very pretty wedding. Of course, your Uncle Ralph had a few things to say about that."

I suppose, Deborah thought, that means Ralph stood up to Ida, and took Vivien's part.

"And so we had to fight for everything," Ida mused. "This time it will be much easier. Do you know he didn't think that orchids were reasonable at all? Your poor mother had to settle for roses. And you should have heard the fuss he kicked up about the champagne. He actually thought it didn't need to be vintage or French—or even champagne at all!"

Deborah put out her hand experimentally, resting it against the warm brick wall. No, she was still upright on the bench. She hadn't fallen and hit her head against the tiles and concrete; for a moment she had thought that was the only explanation of the sounds she was hearing. It certainly sounded like Ida's voice, going on about taffeta and alençon lace and ice sculptures and a wedding breakfast that sounded like food for the gods....

She's flipped, Deborah told herself in astonishment. Yesterday she looked sour at the mere mention of Riley's name. Today...!

"Aunt Ida," she said. It was little more than a croak.

Ida stopped pruning and looked quizzically at Deborah. "Didn't anyone ever tell you?" she asked. "It's foolishly sentimental of me, I suppose, but I've always been crazy about weddings."

It was like biting into a bit of rare beefsteak and finding herself with a mouthful of marshmallow cream. Deborah almost choked on the taste of it.

"I'm glad you're going to be married here in Summerset so I can really be involved," Ida went on gently. "It will be fun to give you a wedding no one will ever forget. That reminds me—we'll have to talk to Father Adams right away and reserve the church. I'll call him and make an appointment for tomorrow after early services."

It took a moment for Deborah to find words. In the meantime, Ida continued to murmur happily to herself about the relative merits of limousines versus horse-drawn carriages; of white cake, chocolate cake, fruit cake or a many-tiered combination of all three; and of satin caps as opposed to flowers for holding a veil in place.

"You are going to wear a veil, aren't you, Deborah?" she asked anxiously. "It's hardly a wedding without one, but…well, you are eligible for one still, aren't you?"

Deborah, who had just cleared her throat, lost her power of speech again over that one. The idea of Aunt Ida matter-of-factly enquiring if she was still a virgin and therefore entitled to the symbolic veil…

Behind her, a husky voice said, "Of course she's going to wear a veil. I have dreams about Debbie in a veil." Riley's arms went around her and Deborah screamed weakly as he lifted her clear off the bench in an enthusiastic bear hug.

Ida's look of half-abstracted concern faded into something like genuine amusement. "What a lucky girl you are, dear," she murmured.

Riley let Deborah slide back to the ground, still holding her tightly against him, and pressed his lips to the side of her throat. "Yes, you are," he whispered. "A very lucky girl, that I came along just in time to stop that kind of question."

"Have a good time at the farm, children," Ida said with a dismissing wave of a gloved hand. "I suppose your mother is still being stubborn about poor Preston, Riley?"

"I wouldn't put it quite that way," Riley replied evasively.

"No, I'm sure you wouldn't. You're missing a wonderful opportunity yourself, you know. You really should make an investment for your future. I'm sure Preston would be happy to talk to you about the possibilities."

"I'm sure he would," Riley agreed. "But unfortunately, until I've married my heiress I don't have anything to invest." The smile he directed at Deborah was a kindly one.

Ida laughed. It was almost a girlish giggle.

They were halfway down the hill to his car when Riley asked casually, "By the way, can you wear a veil?"

Deborah's voice was pure ice. "What possible business is it of yours?"

"Oh, mere curiosity," he said cheerfully. "And a little ammunition for the next time we schedule a fight about the wedding plans. You can hardly have ten bridesmaids if you can't wear the established costume yourself. The symbol of innocence and purity and all that."

She wanted to kick him. "You busybody! You wouldn't dare bring that up in a public fight."

He looked thoughtful. "Probably only the final, climactic one."

"Well, if you aren't more careful about what you say, you aren't going to need the final, climactic fight, because you'll have messed things up long before that. You might as well have told Aunt Ida straight out just now that you're only marrying me for my money. Talk about asking for trouble, Riley."

"All the best dynastic alliances involve money," he said earnestly. "But in any case, she didn't believe me."

"Oh, really?"

"Really. And she shouldn't believe it, either, because no amount of money would be enough to make me marry you," he added blithely.

Deborah's anger deflated abruptly, like a punctured balloon. She thought about refusing to go with him at all, and stalking back to the house, but there was that hill, and Aunt Ida, who was probably writing the wedding vows by now. All in all, she'd rather put up with Riley. So she trailed along after him, still a bit bemused.

Riley said, as if he'd just noticed, "Why are you wearing pink shorts? Have you forgotten we're going to the farm?"

"I've outgrown my mud puddle days, thank you," Deborah told him grandly. "Unless you plan to put me to work stacking hay bales, I don't expect to have any trouble staying clean."

"No more hay. Just courgettes and cucumbers and tomatoes and cabbage and brussels sprouts and—" He interrupted himself as they sped through downtown. "Would you mind awfully if I bring someone else along?"

Deborah shrugged. "It's your party."

"He doesn't get a chance to get out in the country much, and his mother's working today."

A child, and obviously not one of Mary Beth's. It was silly of you, Deborah, she told herself, to assume that it would be female, and not a child. She had suspected he meant that gorgeous blonde hostess of his, and now she poked fun at herself for the very idea.

But it did startle her when they stopped in front of a small bungalow at the edge of the business district and a boy came racing across the lawn towards the car.

"It's Ruth's kid," Riley said. He sounded a little defensive. "And don't give me that I-told-you-so look, either. He's a friend of mine and his mother's a good worker and they're having a tough time—"

"And you're only trying to help out," Deborah finished. "Good intentions get more people in trouble than any other thing in the world. Hi, Alec."

The child's eyes rounded. "You're Riley's girl?"

Riley muttered, "I should have known you two would have met already. May I ask where?"

"You may not," Deborah said briefly.

It didn't take much of an invitation to persuade Alec to join them, but it did require a direct order from Riley to make him return to the house long enough to leave a note for his mother. Then he piled into the back of the car. He poked his head over the seat between them and began a nonstop monologue that lasted till they were well out of town.

Finally Deborah interrupted firmly. "Let's drive through Paradise Valley on the way."

"Why?"

"Because how am I supposed to be a detective without seeing the scene of the crime? Honestly, Riley, don't you ever read mysteries?"

"Crime?" Alec asked. "You mean like murder?"

"Now you've torn it," Riley muttered. "Deborah was speaking figuratively, Alec, which is just another way of saying she was making it up."

Alec looked disappointed.

"It will only take a minute to drive through," Deborah argued.

Riley shook his head. "We'd have to hike in. The snake put in a new security fence and gate so no one can drive in any more."

"I wonder why."

"Use your head, Deb," he said irritably. "He doesn't want visitors running around loose, poking into things. He wants to be on hand to do a sales pitch for every one of them. That's not the reason he gives, of course. He says it's a matter of liability insurance. Now that he's responsible for the place, he doesn't want anyone drowning without his permission. Are you up for a walk?"

Deborah held up one foot, in a sturdy walking shoe. "You're talking to someone who does miles every day on concrete."

"Not the same thing at all." Riley glanced at his watch. "We could come later this afternoon," he said. "It will take some time."

Alec's head popped up again from the back seat. "I want to go, too," he chimed in. "Mom and I are going to get rich from Paradise Valley, you know."

Deborah's gaze locked with Riley's for what seemed eternity. It could only have been a split second, however; the car had not even wavered when Riley looked back at the road and said, "Really, Alec? That's interesting."

Deborah could hear the strain in his voice; she didn't think Alec was likely to pick it up.

"Heck, yes," Alec said. "She told me it's a lot better than just leaving the money in the bank. Dad's insurance money, I mean," he added unnecessarily.

Deborah closed her eyes in pain, remembering Ruth's thin, eager face, the efficient way she had gone about her job—and the way Preston Powell had flirted with her last night. "Widows and children," she said under her breath. "Is there anything the man won't do?"

Nothing more was said, but neither was there any doubt about whether they were going to stop at Paradise Valley.

The resort lay several miles west of the city, in a natural

hollow. Local legend had it that Paradise Lake, fed by the Summer River, had been originally formed by beavers, generations before the first human settlers had seen it. Now the water was trapped by a huge engineering marvel of a man-made dam, and a much larger lake was the proud centerpiece of an Eden of opportunity for vacationers.

Except that here, as in that other Eden, humanity was no longer to be found on any regular basis.

Riley parked the car on the shoulder of the road just out of sight from the shiny new steel security gates, and they climbed through a ditch full of brush and weeds and random stale puddles—and probably poison ivy, Deborah thought—wriggled through the barbed-wire fence, and were inside.

A shell of a building near the entrance, a guard shack with a fallen-in roof, a great many twisting ribbons of concrete leading nowhere in particular and a filling station with gasoline pumps frozen at a ten-year-old price were all that remained of the original attempt to build a resort.

"It's like a concentration camp in here," Deborah muttered.

But once the fence was left behind, that impression dissipated. The whole resort looked faded and unkempt, as if it needed a good scrubbing. But it was easy to see what the plan had been.

"The streets look as if they're in pretty good shape," Deborah said, trying her best to be fair.

"Yes, they do—but I wouldn't care to vouch for the sewers and water mains and natural gas lines that run underneath."

"Oh. I hadn't thought of that." She scuffed the toe of her shoe against a kerb lined with weeds. She itched to pull them out. "He could at least hire someone to neaten up the place."

"He did, when he first came to town," Riley said sombrely. "If he was serious, he would keep it up."

"Well, I see why Preston wants to give the tours himself. So he can put the best possible explanations on everything. Keep people from asking too many questions."

"He does a good job of it, too. Over there the plans call for a five-hundred-room hotel." Riley made a sweeping gesture.

Deborah whistled faintly.

"And in this section there's room for about three hundred summer cottages. I'm using the term *cottages* lightly, because one of the conditions on the purchase of a lot is to set a minimum price for the house that's built on it."

"It's sizeable, I suppose?" Deborah hazarded.

"You probably wouldn't think so, compared to Chicago—considering what you must have paid for your apartment. But let's just say there were only a half dozen houses in that price range sold last year in all of Summerset."

"And he thinks people will build three hundred of them here?" Deborah added thoughtfully, "I wonder where Aunt Ida's lot is."

"She has one?"

"I thought you knew everything," she said sweetly. "Hasn't the grapevine told you that she's selling Lassiter House?"

"You're joking."

"No, I'm not. But I agree. Aunt Ida without Lassiter House is unthinkable. It's like bagels without cream cheese."

"Or Laurel without Hardy," Riley agreed.

"Peanut butter without jelly."

"I've got it. Politics without corruption!"

"I think you've missed the point, Riley. I wasn't playing a new game." She frowned.

Alec had run down the long slope to the lake. "Do you suppose we'd better go after him?" Riley asked.

Deborah nodded, and said absently, "When that boy gets around water he shows no sense at all. I'm afraid to ask...is it still a real lake? Or has it all silted in and it's only a mirage now?"

"Last time I checked, it was still deep enough to swim in. However, the beaches..."

From the top of the gentle hill, Paradise Lake itself was still the shining blue basin that Deborah remembered. But as they drew nearer she saw what Riley's unfinished sentence meant. The sandy beaches were only ghosts of their former inviting selves; one had grown up knee-high in weeds, another had been washed almost entirely away by seasons of heavy rain.

Alec was standing in the middle of the weeds, his face woebegone. Deborah could see the disappointment in the set of his shoulders; she could almost feel it radiating from him. She wanted to put her arms around him and tell him everything would be all right.

But she couldn't, because she was so terribly afraid it wouldn't be all right at all. Not for Alec, and not for Ruth, and not for any of the people of Summerset who had trusted their futures to a man like Preston Powell.

## CHAPTER SIX

DEBORAH WANTED to cry, or else go straight back to Summerset and commit assault and battery on Preston Powell. Instead she took out her frustration by pulling up a weed at her feet, and then eyed its deep, well-established root system with astonishment. It had left a gaping hole in the sand.

"The beach would have to be torn out, of course," Riley said meditatively. He was standing with feet planted firmly in the sand, his hands on his hips, looking at the expanse of weeds.

"The whole place needs to be redone," Deborah muttered. "It would be cheaper to start over somewhere else if you were really serious about a resort."

"Oh, it's probably not quite that bad. There's no sense in throwing out all the basic, expensive work that's been done—the streets, the utilities, the surveying."

"I thought you said you wouldn't vouch for the utilities."

"I wouldn't. Still, almost any amount of repairs would be less expensive than starting from scratch. Take the golf course, for instance. It was constructed last time around." He waved a hand at a rolling hill on the other side of the lake. "Of course it would take a whole lot of work to get it back into shape, but it's all still out there under the brush."

"And there's plenty of brush," Deborah said a bit

sourly as she waded through the overgrowth on the walk back to the car. Her unprotected shins felt as if they'd been sandpapered. "It's astounding," she added. "The size of the project. It doesn't make any logical sense at all."

Riley shrugged. "Since he's not going to actually build anything, why shouldn't he plan on a grand scale? Drawing lines on paper is cheap."

"But why is everyone falling for it? How can anyone look at this mess and actually believe that the project will come to anything, when he can't even get the weeds pulled?"

"Would you invest your life savings in a ten-unit hotel? Doesn't a five-hundred-room one sound a lot more stable and secure?"

"Neither one of them sounds exactly inviting to me," she said frankly. "I'm not big on taking financial risks, anyway."

Riley snorted. "You? As if starting a gallery in a city that already has five hundred isn't taking a risk!"

"That's different," she said. "I'm not exactly investing in old masters. I buy what I know and believe in, and I know when to ask for advice."

"Great," Riley groaned. "By that rule of thumb, Ida and Ruth are doing exactly the right thing!"

"And I'm not risking my daily bread and butter," she added morosely. "Though if Aunt Ida has her way, I'll have to."

Riley looked at her sharply, but he didn't comment.

Alec said, in a voice that just escaped being a whine, "I thought there would be a float to swim out to. And a playground. The pictures had a playground!"

It didn't take much imagination to know what he meant, even though Deborah hadn't seen the promotional brochures herself. She wondered if Alec's mother knew any more about Paradise Valley than the child did, or if her investment had been made solely on the basis of those slick promotional brochures.

DEBORAH HAD NOT FORGOTTEN the approach to Anna Maria Lassiter's farm, a long curving lane that led down a gently sloping hill to the buildings set well back from the road. Even though she knew it was no longer a grain farm, her memory had painted a cornfield framing the big white house, and it was almost a shock to see a neatly tended patchwork of vegetable gardens stretching as far as she could see, instead of the waving sea of shoulder-high green stalks.

The lawn seemed full of people. A couple of towheaded children ran towards the car. One of them, a girl just old enough to have lost both her front teeth, was calling, ''Uncle Riley!''

Mary Beth's kids, Deborah thought. The boy must be her big brother. I didn't realise they'd have grown up so much. And I don't even remember their names.

Deborah's gaze happened to be on the girl's face at the moment she saw Alec. Distaste dawned in the child's wide blue eyes, and she cast a scathing look at Riley as if to ask how he could do this to her. Deborah had to bite her lip to keep from smiling at the memories it evoked.

I must have looked just like that, she thought, when I was seven years old and my eyes fell unexpectedly on Riley! Not that things have changed so much, actually.

Alec seemed to have forgotten his disappointment at the lake. ''Zach!'' he called with delight, and the boys went tearing off towards the barns. Deborah thought she heard something about a bird's nest Zach had discovered.

Obviously Riley had heard it, too. ''There isn't a bird within a mile who's safe with those two around,'' he muttered, and swung the girl up into his arms. "Especially this one. How's my Robin?"

"Why did you have to bring Alec?" she asked.

"You're just like your mother, aren't you?" Riley asked. "Straight to the point and no nonsense. Give me the benefit of the doubt, won't you? At least Alec took Zach off and now neither of them is teasing you."

Robin tossed her head.

"Did I heard you talking about me again, Riley? Hello, Deborah—welcome home." Mary Beth disentangled herself from the blond child on her lap and held out her hand.

Riley had been right, Deborah thought. Mary Beth was no longer the lithe beauty she remembered. Matronly, that was the word for her now. She looked prosperous and sleek and well groomed and contented in her white skirt and red blouse.

"Where have you been?" she went on. "This is a bad habit, Riley, never being on time. I'm sure you've discovered already, Deborah, that something always conspires to make him late. In fact, you might want to tell Riley the wedding is half an hour before it really is."

Riley gave his sister a slow, lazy grin. "Debbie would wait for me forever, wouldn't you, darling?"

"With pleasure," Deborah returned gently. In fact, she wanted to add, the longer the wait, the better! It reminded her that she hadn't yet told him about Aunt Ida's enthusiastic plans. And she hadn't asked him about that law firm, either.

But there was no chance, then. Anna Maria had set up a picnic on the lawn, and she seemed to have invited half the county. Deborah scarcely got a chance to eat because of the continual procession of well-wishers.

But she couldn't help overhearing when the owner of a nearby farm asked Anna Maria when she was going to be sensible about her land, and whether it was fair to hold out for more than her neighbours had gotten. And a moment later, Mary Beth chimed in, "Mother, why don't you sell? Rod and I both think you're being foolish to pass up this wonderful opportunity, you know. You and Alan could retire and take it easy for a change, instead of slaving out here."

"And what would we live on?" Anna Maria asked absently, as if she had been through this discussion so many times she no longer had to think about it at all. "It's hard to spend stock certificates at the supermarket, that's sure. Boys, stop tormenting Robin and finish cranking the ice cream freezer."

Deborah had lost her appetite. She felt like a small boat adrift in a foggy harbour, unsure what direction to steer next but dead sure that if she didn't do something she was going to be run down by a freighter named Preston Powell.

She spotted Riley across the lawn, perched on top of the split-rail fence. He smiled at her, and the warm reassurance of that gesture made her put her plate aside and go over to him.

It's silly, she thought, but at least I know where I stand with him. I'm not sure about anyone else.

He reached for her hand and drew her close to him till she was leaning against the fence, her shoulder brushing his chest. She was slightly off balance, and so she put her arm around him to steady herself. He continued his conversation without a break while his fingertips drew patterns on the soft skin of her upper arm so idly that he seemed to have no idea that he was doing anything of the kind. The touch tickled, and every breath he released stirred her hair, and the soft resonance of his voice seemed to vibrate through her bones.

I'll bet, she thought idly, that if I tipped my head back, I'd be at just the right angle to steal a kiss...

It was an unsettling sort of sensation, as if the earth below her feet had suddenly turned to quivering gelatin. She shivered a little. And why would you want to steal a kiss? she asked herself sternly. Don't get caught up in your own one act play, Deborah, my girl.

Riley asked softly, "Shall we go for a walk?"

The matron he'd been talking to smiled knowingly. It annoyed Deborah a bit, but she did want to talk to him, so she nodded.

He jumped down from the fence and interlaced his fingers with Deborah's. "I'll take you down by the creek," he told her. "It's quiet there."

The route took them past a huge field of tomato vines, heavy with ripening fruit, and down a winding path to a rippling brook, its banks almost lined with trees and bushes and berry brambles. In one spot, however, the grassy meadow dipped almost to the water, and it was here that Riley stopped and dropped to the ground to sit cross-legged in the sun. "What's on your mind?" he asked bluntly.

Deborah shrugged. "I've said I'll try to help, but I don't even know where to begin," she said hopelessly. "I'm an outsider. No one's going to listen to me. And everybody seems to be sold on the idea, anyway." She pulled up her heels and hugged her knees tightly and didn't look at him as she said, "Riley, is it possible that *we're* the ones who are wrong? Maybe we're the ones who are prejudiced, or paranoid. It could be a good investment after all."

Riley sighed and threw himself back against the grass, full-length. "Not you, too."

"Not really," she admitted. "Personally, I wouldn't

trust Preston Powell enough to invest a subway token. But it's hard to be so outnumbered and still hold firm."

Riley pushed himself up on his elbows. "There's a man who used to live here, a businessman, who moved to Florida years ago," he said slowly. "He was back a couple of months ago for a visit, and when he heard the story of Paradise Valley, he went through the roof. I heard it. He was having lunch at the restaurant, and I happened to be seating a party at the next table. It seems he'd heard of Preston Powell before, in connection with an elaborate resort in the Everglades."

"One that went bankrupt and drained all the investors' money?" Deborah speculated.

"You've got it."

She glared at him. "And you didn't tell me that? Dammit, Riley, you didn't have to drag me into this at all! You could have just told Aunt Ida—"

"The man's a friend of Ida's, Deborah."

No *"Debbie darling,"* she noted idly.

"In fact," he said heavily, "it was Ida he was having lunch with."

Deborah's lips formed a soundless oh.

"I don't know what Ida had to say about it—I could scarcely stand behind her chair and eavesdrop—but I can tell you what Mary Beth's reaction was when I told her about it. She said that I shouldn't be foolish, that every venture capitalist has a failure now and then, and that he'd certainly learned from the problems in the Everglades so they wouldn't be repeated at Paradise Valley. Shall I go on?"

"No need," Deborah said glumly. "I get the picture."

"People believe what they want to believe, Deb."

She sighed. "So, it's back to the beginning, isn't it? Well, the only clue I have is that Daddy told me there was a law firm in Summerset called Bowers and Milligan that used to handle Jacob's business. Are they still around somewhere?"

Riley shrugged. "It doesn't ring a bell with me. Ask Mom, she'll know."

If I really thought it would make any difference, Deborah thought, I'd rush back there and ask her this minute. Instead, she stretched out beside him on the long grass. "Who is Ida's attorney now?"

"Mary Beth's husband."

"The one who thinks Paradise Valley is a great opportunity?" she said wryly.

He almost smiled. "That's the only husband she has, as far as I know. And he's a stickler for ethics, too. Nobody tries anything shady with Rod Walters."

"The irony of that simply defeats me." Deborah closed her eyes. If it weren't for the damned problem with the resort, she thought, she could have really enjoyed this. It was so peaceful out here, just the sigh of the breeze in the branches, a bird calling in the distance, the rustle of some small animal behind the big oak tree that arched above their heads. She listened to the tiny, hypnotic sounds of nature for a long time. "There used to be whippoorwills out here," she said sleepily.

"There still are, at twilight."

"Wake me up in time to hear them."

Riley warned, "You'll fry if you go to sleep out here in the open. And we were talking about Paradise Valley, anyway."

"I'm tired of Paradise Valley," Deborah said, without opening her eyes. "And I don't want to let it spoil my nap."

"All right," he said genially, and she relaxed. But when

he rolled away from her and jumped up a moment later, a warning bell sounded deep inside Deborah's head.

She looked up at him warily. "You wouldn't leave me out here, would you?"

"Of course not. I'm just going for a walk down by the water." It sounded too cheerful to be real, and a moment later she knew why. "I haven't gone frog-catching for years...."

She grabbed for him as he walked away and managed to lock both her hands around his ankle. He dragged her for a couple of steps and then stopped and put his hands on his hips, looking down at her with a sparkle in his eyes.

"You don't like that idea?" he hazarded.

"Not exactly. See what you've done to my clothes? Grass stains all over them!"

"I'm not the one who turned you into a human sleigh." He dropped down beside her. "But at least it got you into the shade, so you won't burn. Would you like me to kiss you and make it better?"

"Kiss the grass stains, you mean? I hardly think—"

He obviously didn't mean the grass stains, and her protest died to a soft little sigh under the first sultry touch of his mouth against hers. He smiled and eased her back against the grass, his forearm forming a pillow for her head. The whole length of him was warm against her side, and his thumb wandered down her throat, coming to rest in the hollow at the base of it, where it stayed to magnify the jerky beat of her pulse. Almost against her will, her hand slipped to the back of his neck, and he kissed her again.

There were fragments of grass caught in his hair, and he carried the scent of sunshine and soft breezes. It was the most sensual sort of cologne she'd ever smelled.

His hand wandered over her shoulder and down her arm,

and then tentatively brushed her breast. He nibbled at her lower lip, tugging at it softly with his teeth, and raised his head to smile at her.

There was something in his gaze that puzzled her a bit. Not triumph; it wasn't so cold as that. Satisfaction, perhaps—was that it? So few men seemed to enjoy this sort of caress for itself. She didn't mind admitting that she was enjoying it herself.

And that's the problem, she warned herself. You're enjoying it too much. This is a delightful way to pass a little time, but don't forget why you're really here.

Still, it had been an awfully long time since she had been kissed quite so enthusiastically, and she could feel the glow of lazy contentment spreading slowly through her veins.

There was a rustle in the tree above them, as if a large bird had been suddenly startled off a nest. In the same instant a girlish voice called from the top of the slope, "I see you, Zach! I'm going to tell!"

Riley turned his head just as a bright red blur dropped from the tree. Deborah screamed a wordless, futile warning just as the object struck Riley's nose and exploded with a wet gush, splashing over his face and hair and clothes. The overflow soaked her, as well.

Riley sat up and wiped his eyes with the back of his hand. Two chortling figures dropped from the tree and hit the ground running; they topped the hill with Robin staying a bare stride ahead of them, and Riley sank back against the grass. "There's no sense in chasing the little monsters," he muttered. "I'll catch up with them later, and they'll pay. Where did they get the damned water balloon, anyway?"

"And how long were they up there with it?" Deborah added.

"You might well ask. I suppose we were too absorbed to notice." He rubbed his sleeve across his face and shook drops of water from his hair as a dog would. "Shall we go on from where we were so rudely interrupted? The kids will probably have told everyone up at the house what we were doing anyway."

"We weren't doing anything so very terrible," Deborah said defensively.

"That's what I mean. We might as well enjoy ourselves. That's a very interesting new fashion twist, Debbie darling." He leaned back on one elbow and his index fingertip slid slowly from her still-dripping chin down the soaked front of her knit shirt.

She jumped up so suddenly that her head swam. "On the other hand, a hike up the ridge to see where Preston is going to put the toboggan run sounds awfully exciting."

Riley frowned and sat up. "Toboggan run? Here? Did Ida tell you that?"

"No. It just seemed like a logical next step. Maybe he's going to try to bring the Winter Olympics here."

"Please don't start talking like that in public, Deb," he said somberly. "Half the town would believe you, and the next thing you know you'd be reading it on the front page of the local paper as gospel truth."

Deborah ran her hands through her hair. "Talking of gospel truth reminds me. I hope you've got a good excuse not to go to church tomorrow."

"What? And risk my immortal soul?"

Deborah looked down at him disparagingly. "I doubt missing church once would be enough to make a difference."

He looked offended. "Are you implying I'm already in danger?"

"Well, if we lie to Father Adams—is that his name?"

Riley nodded.

"About our intentions of getting married, we'll both end up in big trouble."

"Why would we—"

"Because Aunt Ida is making an appointment for us to talk to him after the service tomorrow, that's why. Just when I thought I'd outgrown her rules about early church, she comes up with this!"

Riley thoughtfully pulled up a stalk of grass and began to chew it. "I don't like the sound of this."

"It gets worse, Riley. She's taking over the wedding plans. If we don't get out of this mess soon, Aunt Ida will have arranged for the entire Seventh Cavalry to show up and form an arch of swords outside the church on our wedding day."

"I really don't like the sound of this, Deb."

"Well, don't start blaming it on me! You're the one who announced that this supposed spectacle is coming off in Summerset, you idiot. If you'd let me have my way, Ida wouldn't have had any reason to dive into the plans. No one would have even wondered whether we were making headway!"

"All right," Riley conceded handsomely. "Perhaps I did mess up a bit on that one."

"Mess up? It looks to me as if you didn't just put your foot in your mouth, you stuck it all the way down your throat," she said grimly. "At the rate she's going she'll have spent the whole trust fund on this wedding."

"And wasted it," Riley agreed. "Because when the wedding doesn't happen, she'll have thrown away all that money for nothing."

They looked at each other in horror.

"No, she won't," he said.

Deborah sat down hard on the grass and said weakly,

"Because if we don't have a wedding after all, then the trust won't pay for anything. And the question becomes, who ends up stuck with the bills?"

"It was your idea," Riley said uncompromisingly.

Deborah sighed. "The engagement, maybe. But you wouldn't have caught me dead in this town if you hadn't begged me to come down here. And that makes you half-responsible."

"You're the one with the money."

"Not for long, at this rate!"

"We could just go through with it," Riley suggested.

"The trust pays for weddings, idiot. Divorces are not included. We wouldn't gain a thing."

"Well, at least that way we wouldn't be in debt for Ida's idea of a party."

"Good. You're finally admitting you share the responsibility for this fiasco!"

There was a long silence. "I think we'd better start by following up your one clue," Riley said. "Fast."

"Good idea." She stretched up her hands to him and he obligingly lifted her to her feet, without apparent effort.

Most of the crowd had dispersed. They found Anna Maria in the kitchen drinking tea; nearby Mary Beth sat in a rocking chair, with her four-year-old napping on her lap. She raised a well-plucked eyebrow when she saw the state of Deborah's clothes, but she made no comment.

Deborah had hoped to catch Anna Maria alone, but it looked as if Mary Beth wasn't going to move for a while, so she said, "Do you know where I could find an attorney by the name of Bowers? He used to practise here."

"The Summer River Cemetery," Mary Beth said dryly. "Why? Are you two writing a prenuptial agreement or something?"

"Yes," Riley said promptly. "I'm trying to protect all

my worldly goods from the possibility of Deb being a gold digger.''

Deborah stared him into silence. "How about his partner, Milligan, or something like that? Is he still alive?"

"The last I knew, yes. What's wrong with having Rod draw it up?" Mary Beth countered.

"Conflict of interest," Riley said. "He might be prejudiced. For me, of course."

"Don't bet on it," his sister told him dryly. "He knows you too well. In any case, I'm not going to beg for your business. But I wouldn't count on Fred Milligan. He went to Springfield to join the attorney general's office, and is out of private practice."

Attorney general's office? Deborah thought blankly. There was a special division of the state attorney general's office that handled fraud; he would know immediately what she was talking about. That, plus the fact that Milligan also knew and understood the Lassiter trust. All she would have to do was catch up with Mr. Milligan!

She flung a triumphant look at Riley, who glared at her and suggested, a little too promptly, that it was time for them to be going if he was to be at the restaurant by the time the evening crowd began to appear. "I don't suppose you know where we'd find Alec?" he asked his sister.

"Don't worry about him," Mary Beth said. "I'll round him up when I take my brood home. One more scarcely makes a difference."

"Except to Robin, of course," Riley said under his breath as they left the house. "But if you think I'm going to argue with Mary Beth over custody of that little scoundrel..."

"Honestly, Riley, I expected you'd be applauding. The water balloon was a trick worthy of you at your worst."

"Do you really think so?" He grinned at her. "I must admit, I never thought of doing anything like that."

"I'm humbly grateful." But she promptly forgot the matter in her delight over her discovery, and she almost danced out to his car. "I told you Bowers and Milligan would be important," she said gleefully as soon as they were safely away from the farm.

Riley gave a sort of half-believing grunt. "We'll see how important it is. You can't do anything about it till Monday."

"Big deal. Oh." It was a very small voice.

Riley eyed her with almost malicious concern. "Yes, that still leaves us with the problem of Father Adams tomorrow."

"I don't want to lie to a man of the cloth, Riley."

"All you have to do is smile and stick to generalities."

"And you'll do the actual lying? You comfort me more than you can possibly know."

He gave her a sideways, speculative look. "For someone who doesn't want to go to church at all you have an awfully sensitive conscience," he mused. "I think we should tell him we want a spring wedding."

"All right," Deborah said agreeably. "We just won't tell him which spring."

"Something like that. Surely Ida won't start committing money right away when the wedding is months away."

"Obviously you haven't been involved in many weddings."

"And you have? Do tell, Debbie darling!"

"Remember all those girls who'll want to be bridesmaids at my wedding?" Deborah said dryly. "Half of them are already married, and I walked every one of them down the aisle. And held their hands through all the months of organising and planning and budgeting...."

"Please, let's not talk about budgets," Riley said politely. "It makes my stomach ache."

"Mine, too," Deborah said glumly. "One of them took a full year, and it was on nothing like the scale Aunt Ida's got in mind. As a matter of fact, I can think of only one thing worse than having Aunt Ida planning my wedding, and that's watching her plan one for herself."

She was joking, and it startled her when Riley seemed to take her words seriously. He turned them over in his mind for almost a minute before he shook his head. "I don't think it will come to that," he said finally. "After all, the snake is getting everything he wants without any commitments, this way, and I don't see him changing that unless he has to."

It left her speechless.

They were almost back to Lassiter House before Riley said, "Correct me if I'm wrong, but I get the impression that you're not as sold on huge weddings as I thought you were."

Deborah was still thinking about the spectacle of an octogenarian bride in white satin and a veil—she would bet her life that Aunt Ida was eligible to wear one. On the other hand, she reminded herself, Aunt Ida was turning out to be full of surprises.

"Not exactly," she said absently. "My idea of a perfect wedding is a brief ceremony at nine in the morning, followed by a bash of a champagne brunch, followed by the departure of the bride and groom on a long, leisurely honeymoon in some romantic locale, not so far away that travel becomes a problem, and where there is nothing much to do but lie around and get to know each other."

Riley was grinning. "You could always pitch a tent at Paradise Lake," he said. "It sounds like just the place you're looking for!"

She made a face at him. "I said romantic, remember? But maybe I'll ask Preston to save me the bridal suite in his new hotel."

"That's an excellent idea if you're not planning to get married any time in the next twenty years." He started to whistle, slightly off-key. She would have liked to hit him with something.

He drove all the way to the top of the hill, since he was only dropping her off; Deborah was grateful to avoid the climb, and when the car stopped under the *porte-cochère* at the side of Lassiter House she said the most sincere thanks she had ever in her life expressed to Riley and got out.

"Hold it," he ordered, and came around the car.

"What? I said thank you."

"Not nicely enough," he murmured. "At least, not if Ida's watching. And this house has a zillion windows, so she probably is."

The prospect of an audience never seemed to bother him, Deborah thought a little hazily, during one of the most thorough kisses she had ever participated in. It was almost funny, she decided, that without ever moving his hands out of safe and approved zones, Riley could make her feel as if she'd been sensually assaulted. Of course, there had been that brief, warm touch against her breast this afternoon, but that scarcely counted; it had only been a brush of his hand against her shirt, really, brought to a sudden end by the water balloon.

Still, it was just as well they'd been interrupted, she thought. She'd been enjoying the game perhaps a little too much for safety's sake. And as for the comment he had made last night that whoever had taught her to kiss should start a school, she thought, privately, that Riley could give a few lessons himself.

I wonder, she mused, just where he learned all this....

# CHAPTER SEVEN

AUNT IDA HADN'T been watching. She was in the sun room at the back of the house, sitting on the wicker couch with a glossy magazine, so quiet and still that Deborah had almost stepped on the woman's toes before she realised she was there. Then, when she saw the photograph on the front cover of the magazine, she did her best to become invisible and sneak out before Ida noticed her. It was a vain effort, of course.

Aunt Ida waved the magazine in the air. "Look at this glorious white velvet gown," she said.

Deborah sighed inwardly. It was awfully warm in the sun room, with the afternoon light pouring through the beveled glass and not a breath of air moving, despite the open windows. How did Aunt Ida stand it? she wondered. Even more, how could the woman look admiringly at white velvet when the temperature inside Lassiter House must be above ninety degrees?

But talking about the temperature wouldn't make it cooler, so she obediently looked at the magazine. It was a beautiful dress, she had to admit, with a tailored bodice and a long full skirt sweeping to a short train. The collar was high and the beaded trim that twisted and curled across the soft velvet reminded her of military braid. The ensemble was something like a modified Cossack uniform, or was it only the fur headpiece that made her think of that? Yet somehow it was a very feminine dress, for an older and more sophisticated bride.

That's enough, Deborah, she told herself sternly. Show the tiniest bit of interest and Aunt Ida will order it shipped by overnight mail!

"I see leg-of-mutton sleeves are back in style again," she said with an air of casual unconcern.

"Yes. I swear, Deborah, I should have kept all those dresses I wore as a girl. They've been in and out of fashion a dozen times since then. I could have just had them remade."

Now that, Deborah thought, sounds a great deal more like the Aunt Ida I remember!

Ida held the magazine up at arm's length. "That headpiece is ermine," she remarked. "Lovely stuff. And velvet is always so elegant. Or would you rather have something in silk taffeta and marabou, or satin with an overlay of antique lace?" She glanced at Deborah's crumpled shorts and shirt, blinked and added dryly, "Though perhaps, to be on the safe side, you should consider something in polyester with a stain-resistant coating."

Deborah told herself that she should have seen that one coming. Razor-sharp sarcasm delivered without hesitation had always been Aunt Ida's strength, and there was no appropriate answer. "I'll think about it," she murmured.

Ida's gaze flickered as if she was disappointed by the meek response, but she said very smoothly, "When is the wedding going to be, anyway?"

"I don't know."

Aunt Ida cupped a hand behind her ear. "Do speak up, dear. It sounded as if you said you and Riley hadn't even discussed it."

Deborah gritted her teeth. "Riley said something about

next spring." There, she thought. That should be noncommittal enough to slow her down.

Aunt Ida almost clucked in concern. "Then we'll have to get busy. It will take every moment to be ready in time. What sort of theme are you going to have?"

Deborah was too startled to exercise caution. "A theme?" she asked weakly. "This isn't a high school prom, Aunt Ida."

"Of course not, but it should look as if it all goes together! Good heavens, Deborah, where is your head? I've always thought, for instance, that a summer wedding would be lovely with an ancient Grecian motif. Those high-waisted dresses in different pastel colours are so flattering, and there could be simple flowers in everyone's hair."

Deborah yielded to a sudden vision of Riley wearing a wreath of orange blossom, and had to turn a hysterical giggle into a choking cough. "I hadn't really considered a theme, Aunt Ida."

"Well, you should. Personally, I do love the Grecian idea. The wedding cake could be shaped like a miniature Parthenon...." She seemed to fade away for a minute, then went on briskly, as if she was resigned to the loss of her dream. "But I suppose spring would be a little cool for that style. And I doubt you'll want to wait a whole year from now if Riley wants to be married sooner."

Gladly, Deborah thought. I'd wait any number of years!

"Do think carefully about styles," Aunt Ida went on briskly. "I always think it's unfortunate when the bridesmaids end up looking like dumplings in ruffles, don't you?"

"I'll keep it in mind," Deborah murmured. She didn't realise she was twisting the diamond ring on her finger. In fact, it was so light she'd forgotten she was wearing it, until Ida's pale blue eyes came to rest on it thoughtfully.

"That's not much of a ring," she remarked. "I'm surprised at Riley, giving you Darlene's diamond chip instead of a decent stone."

Deborah glanced down at her hand. Darlene? She had forgotten, if she had ever known, Riley's grandmother's name. Then, automatically, she sprang to the defence. "It's got great sentimental value," she said. "And I wouldn't want a big stone if Riley had to put himself in debt for it."

Ida gave a nasal grunt. "You could have a different ring, you know. The trust would pay for it."

And afterward I could pawn it to pay for the divorce, Deborah thought. For a split second it actually made sense. Then she wanted to bang her head against the nearest wall for letting herself get carried away.

Don't even think of things like that, she ordered herself. Riley's remark about going through with the ceremony was the craziest thing she had ever heard. In fact, all she had to do now was to talk to Milligan, and he would soon straighten Ida out. *Voilà*! There wouldn't be any bills, there certainly wouldn't be any wedding. And there wouldn't be any Paradise Valley, either.

She finally made her break to freedom, but only by taking along the stack of bride's magazines that Ida had already finished. The woman must have bought out the local newsstand rack, Deborah thought in disbelief as she tossed the pile on the end of the guest room bed. She flung herself down on the fainting couch by the window, fanning her hot face with one of the lighter magazines.

This, she thought, is getting out of hand. I'm beginning to feel as if I'm never going to escape.

Chicago, and the gallery, had never seemed so far away.

IDA WAS LATE coming down for dinner that night. Preston Powell wasn't, and his company quickly began to wear on Deborah's nerves. She didn't like being told that champagne was the only drink that could possibly match her own effervescence, or that her voice was like carillon bells in beauty and clarity. And when he announced, after an unnervingly close inspection, that her eyes were the very color of Paradise Lake on a stormy day, Deborah had had it.

She sipped her sherry and said, "I've been wondering about something, Preston. If someone makes an investment in your project, and then later changes his mind and wants a refund, what happens?"

She had to give him credit for poise; he didn't even hesitate. "I'd give it, of course," he said. "I don't want any unwilling investors. We're all a team, and one pessimistic person will affect us all." He sat down on the arm of her chair. "Has anyone ever told you—"

She moved away to stand by the baby grand piano, her fingers trailing over the keys. "You'd just give the money back?" Deborah mused.

"Well, not instantly, of course."

She was intrigued. How did the man enunciate without ever moving his lips? He didn't even stop smiling to talk!

"I'd want to know what had changed his mind," Preston went on, "and I'd do my best to convince him that he was turning his back on a perfect opportunity."

"But if he was sincere in wanting out?" she persisted.

"Then I'd write him a cheque for the full amount of his investment."

And our nameless, mythical investor had better be careful to get it to the bank right away, too, Deborah speculated.

Preston had followed her over to the piano. "Why all

the questions, Deborah? Are you thinking of investing with me, and you want to be sure your money will be safe? I'd be happy to show you some projections.''

The telephone bell shrilled stridently in the hall, and Deborah jumped. ''I'd better get that,'' she said with a sigh of relief. ''You know how Henry hates to be interrupted when he's putting the finishing touches on dinner.''

It was Bristol, and for an instant when she heard that crisp, cultured Ivy League accent she was aghast, too upset even to speak. It wasn't only the idea of his calling her here at Lassiter House that was bothering her, she realised abruptly. It was the fact that she'd forgotten about him—in fact, she hadn't given him an instant's thought in the past two days. She hadn't missed him. She hadn't even wondered how he was, or how his business conference was progressing. Her mind had been so full of Riley.

My mind has been full of Paradise Valley, she corrected herself firmly. Not of Riley. It's no surprise that I haven't been thinking of Bristol. I've had too many other things on my mind. And it's just as well, too, with the part I'm having to play.

''Is there something wrong, my dear?'' Bristol asked in the polite, careful tone she knew so well.

Deborah seized the last shreds of her poise. She could hardly tell him, after all, that he could not call her, unless she was willing to explain the whole plot. ''Of course not. I was just surprised at hearing from you, that's all.''

''But surely you know I would have called earlier if I hadn't been so very busy.''

Heaven forbid, Deborah thought. ''Are you enjoying San Francisco?''

There was a brief silence. ''Darling, if I haven't had a spare moment to call you, surely you don't believe I've been out riding cable cars instead!''

"Of course not," Deborah said hastily. "How is the conference?"

"It's moving along wonderfully, thank you. There are so many implications for the foundation that it will take weeks to think them all through, of course. Ways to safely maximise the investment potential of the endowment funds, and—"

Deborah seized on one word. "Investment? Do you mean you're learning about all kinds of investments?"

There was another aching silence, and then Bristol said politely, "Yes, Deborah. I told you, I believe, that this was a seminar featuring the premier investment counsellors of the nation. But perhaps you were preoccupied at the time."

They'd been at Coq au Vin, and she'd been thinking of Riley; she remembered it, now. "I don't suppose they'd know anything about a resort development here in Summerset."

He laughed condescendingly. "My dear, these people keep track of everything. I'm sure they'd know. Are you looking for some free advice, or merely offering me a test case to use to evaluate their knowledge?"

"Neither. I'd just like to find out everything I can. Aunt Ida's got herself into this scheme, you see, and—"

"Oh, yes, your Aunt Ida. How is the dear old lady?"

For one mad moment, Deborah considered telling him about Aunt Ida, the wedding Czar of Summerset. Then she regained control of herself. She shot a look over her shoulder towards the parlour where Preston Powell was still drinking his Manhattan, and said in a low voice, "Look, Bristol, I can't take the time to give you all the details, but this is important. If you can find out anything for me about Paradise Valley, and Preston Powell, the guy who's promoting it…"

To Bristol's credit, he didn't demand an explanation. He

had her spell Preston's name and that of the resort, and he said, "She's financially over her head, do you think? It's such a shame, but these things do happen now and then. I'll see what I can do to help rescue the dear lady and put your mind at rest, Deborah."

After he'd said goodbye she sat there for a long moment with the telephone still in her hand. Good old Bristol, she thought. Always solid and predictable, and there. He was everything that Morgan had never been. What was it Riley had called Morgan? Her furry-faced friend? She smiled a little at the implication. He *had* been something of an animal, interested mainly in his own comfort.

Ida came down the staircase, her old-fashioned square-heeled shoes striking solidly against the wooden steps. "I do hope you're not going to expect us to delay dinner while you chat," she said.

"Of course not," Deborah said cordially. In fact, she thought, I can't wait for dinner to be over, so I can get out of this madhouse and go bring Riley up-to-date. I had no idea that conspiracy was a full-time job!

IT HAD APPARENTLY BEEN a slow night at the restaurant. Cars were sparse around the warehouse, and while she was parking she saw a figure in dark clothing silhouetted against the gathering twilight, leaning against the railing that separated the parking area from the drop to the river itself.

Riley turned from the rail and watched her come towards him. "That's a switch," he said, with a wave of his hand at her cocktail dress, a drifty thing in emerald green shot through with gold threads.

"I was trying to impress Aunt Ida," she said. "What are you doing out here?"

Riley grinned. "Don't you know?" He pointed down at the water. "I'm reflecting."

Deborah groaned. "I'm amazed that your mother didn't drown you by the time you were six."

"I resent that. I was a darling six-year-old. You, on the other hand, were a pudgy crybaby. Of course, that was nothing compared to what you were like at nine, when you started to giggle and didn't stop for two years. And then when you were twelve, you had braces as well as baby fat."

"Don't you ever forget anything? It's very troublesome of you, Riley." It should have annoyed her, she thought, having every embarrassing incident of her childhood dangled over her head that way. But somehow, it didn't bother her any more. In a way, she thought, it was rather pleasant to spend time with someone who knew every fracture, every fault, every wrinkle in her past. It was comfortable not to have to hide anything.

Not that she hid things from Bristol, exactly, she thought uncomfortably. It was just that there were subjects that never came up; childhood memories, and silly, unimportant, almost forgotten things like that. With Riley it was different. He might know every embarrassing detail there was to know about her, but she knew every wart on his character, too. They were even.

He leaned against the rail and looked at her for a long time. "You know what, kid?" he said finally. "You turned out pretty decent despite it all."

She pretended irritation. "Oh, is that all you can say for me? I'm pretty decent?"

He grinned. "What do you want? A poem? All right. 'Roses are red, and Debbie is blue, because I won't tell her she's beautiful, too.'"

She reached up to tousle his hair. He caught her wrists

and twisted her around—how, she was not quite sure—until she was firmly held between his body and the railing, with her back to him, his arms around her, her hands under his on the cool steel bar. She wriggled a little and then gave up with dignity. He hadn't been on the high school wrestling team for nothing.

The last rays of sunshine had turned the smooth surface of the river to liquid gold, tinged with violet and pink and blue.

Beautiful, Deborah was thinking idly. Did he mean that he does think I'm beautiful, and just won't feed my vanity by telling me, or did he mean that he has too much integrity to say something that isn't true? I wonder which it is.

She tipped back her head to look thoughtfully up at him. Sunset's glow had caught in his hair, turning the auburn threads to strands of fire. Deborah's breath caught in her throat.

He really has turned out to be one very good-looking man, she thought. But it wasn't only looks that made him attractive. There were lots of handsome men, but Riley was one of the rare ones who weren't stuck on themselves. The combination was deadly.

Good heavens, Deborah thought, he might have been telling the simple truth when he said there were hundreds of women in his life! If someone had asked me two weeks ago about my cousin Riley, the great lover, I'd have laughed till I choked. But at the moment it doesn't sound very funny. Even I…

Even I…what?

She swallowed hard and told herself deliberately, Even I have enjoyed his kisses. So what's wrong with that? Why shouldn't I have a little fun? I'm no prude, and I'm not a hypocrite, either.

They watched in silence until the fiery glow in the west

had died to shades of velvety grey, and streetlights began to form a glittering chain along the avenue that bordered the river.

Riley cleared his throat. "Seeing that always makes me want to go get my trumpet and play 'Taps'."

"I thought 'Taps' called for a bugle," Deborah mused. Her voice was husky, and she had to clear her throat.

"Sorry. I can't play a bugle."

She smiled up at him warmly. "Of course, you could never play the trumpet worth a darn, either." His arms tightened threateningly, and she said very quickly, "I didn't mean that, of course. Have you had a chance to talk to Ruth?"

Riley let her go. "Not yet," he said slowly. "And what in heaven's name am I supposed to tell her, anyway?"

It was chilly with the sun gone. Deborah turned her back to the rail and told him of Preston's offer to refund money to any unhappy investor.

Riley grunted. "I wouldn't care to make any bets on that. I doubt he's put it in writing anywhere. But I'll tell her."

"You don't think she'll change her mind?"

"No. And she may tell me to go to hell, that it's none of my business what she does with her money. And it's not, you know, but I suppose I have to try."

"For Alec's sake," Deborah reminded gently. When he didn't answer, she nudged him. "Riley?"

"I'm thinking about it," he said. "After that water balloon this afternoon, I'm not so sure."

"That's always the way with practical jokers," Deborah said. "They're poor sports themselves. Oh, I have good news, by the way. Father Adams is busy with a christening brunch after services tomorrow and can't talk to us until Wednesday."

"That's a relief."

"It certainly is. With any luck at all we'll be history by Wednesday, and there won't be any need to draw him into it at all."

"You think it will be that fast?" Riley said doubtfully.

"Of course. I'll call Milligan on Monday and explain what's going on, he'll call Aunt Ida and read her the riot act, and we'll be in the clear."

"By Wednesday." He sounded dissatisfied.

"Why not?" Deborah asked grandly. "I've left him Tuesday to ask around about Preston Powell. That should be plenty of time."

"You never cease to amaze me, Debbie darling." There was faint irony in his voice.

Deborah, who had been about to tell him that Bristol was now also on the trail, changed her mind. So Riley didn't think she could accomplish anything, hmm? Well, just let him wait; sooner or later he'd see what she could do!

"I'm not trying to break up the party," Riley said, "but I did just step out for a breath of fresh air, and by now the staff must be ready to report me as missing. Would you like to come in and have dessert while I close up the place?"

"Are you trying to corrupt me?"

His eyes brightened. "That depends. Are you corruptible?"

"I was referring to that cartload of calories I saw Ruth wheeling around last night," Deborah said with dignity.

"Well, you're certainly no fun at all. As a matter of fact, however, I happen to know that the dessert menu at Lassiter House consists of fruit with gelatin, or for a change now and then, gelatin with fruit."

Deborah sighed. "You're right, and it's not fresh fruit at that."

The dessert cart was just as tempting as she remembered it, and she fought a brief skirmish with her conscience before surrendering to the lure of a raspberry puff pastry, oozing whipped cream and nestled in a pool of caramel sauce on a crystal plate. She perched on a high stool at the bar to eat it, and was only halfway through when Riley appeared. He raised an eyebrow, but he didn't comment. He didn't have to; she knew what he was thinking.

Deborah speared a raspberry on the tines of her fork and waved it at him. "Fresh fruit," she said. "From your mother's garden, I presume?"

He caught her wrist and held it while he ate the berry. "Of course. The doors are locked, and everybody's gone."

"I know. I said goodnight to Ruth. Did you talk to her?"

"With everyone around? Of course not. And I didn't exactly want to ask her to stay late."

Deborah nodded wisely. "The hostess wouldn't have liked that at all," she murmured, and licked her fork. "I take back what I said about Ruth being infatuated with you," she went on. "It's the hostess I think you should watch out for. What is her name, anyway?"

"Suzannah. She prefers being called Zanne."

Deborah nodded. "It would be something like that. She doesn't like me, you know."

"She can't possibly have formed an opinion."

"Of course she can. I've got the prize. You." She frowned and dipped her fork into the caramel again, then let the sauce trail in strands over the top of the pastry.

"If you've finished playing with that—"

"I'm not playing with it. And I'm not finished."

"Then bring it along, but let's go somewhere that's

more comfortable than this, all right?" He turned out the lights. Deborah obediently picked up her plate and followed him through the dim glow of the security lights through the lobby and up the stairs.

"What's up here?" she asked, peering into the darkness at the first landing. "You've got the restaurant on the ground floor and your apartment at the top, but what's in between?"

"Lots of empty space," Riley said. "Would you like the tour?"

Deborah shook her head. "Not really. It was merely curiosity."

But he had already pulled out a ring of keys and unlocked a door. Bare fluorescent fixtures hummed quietly into life, casting a bluish glow over the single empty room that took up the entire floor. It was scrupulously clean, but the walls were bare brick, and the scratches and stains on the wooden floor were mute evidence of hard use. No amount of scrubbing could wipe them out. The ceiling had once been lined with acoustic tiles, but a good many of them were gone, and in the gaps Deborah could see the original ceiling level. The room was almost tall enough for a balcony to be added, she thought. It would make wonderful studio apartments.

She must have said something aloud, but she didn't realise it, and it startled her when Riley spoke. "I'd rather turn it into extra party rooms for the restaurant," he said. "As it is, when I've got a big dinner party or reception, I have to turn my regular customers away. But that's a long while off."

"Why? You've got the space, and you certainly need it."

"Remember what you said about the appearance of success not being cheap? Besides, have you priced elevators lately, Debbie darling?" He turned off the lights and snapped the lock tight. "There are regulations about things like that. And that's only the beginning. I also own the building next door."

She looked at him in astonishment.

"You may well ask why," Riley murmured. "I was having a weak moment, and the price was really ridiculously low, that's why. I'd like to turn it into a collection of antique shops or something of the sort."

"It would draw customers into the neighbourhood," she said.

"Bright girl. And after doing all that shopping, they'd be hungry, too. But by the time I got the leaks fixed in the roof, and all the broken glass repaired..." He sighed. "Maybe next year, if the snake doesn't succeed in throwing the whole town into an economic slump in the meantime."

They were at the door of his apartment. "He could do that?"

"Certainly. If he siphons off enough of the disposable cash that would otherwise have supported Summerset businesses."

"I see." Deborah had lost her appetite, and her voice sounded hollow.

"But of course there's no reason for concern, is there?" Riley's tone was light. "You're going to have it all fixed up by Wednesday."

The weight of what she was trying to do, of the responsibility she had taken on, was suddenly overwhelming. Deborah set down the crystal plate with a little crash and put one hand to her temple, where a blood vessel was throbbing with an alarming rhythm.

He turned from closing the door and said, "Deb? Are you all right?" He was beside her in two steps, his arms closing gently around her, taking her weight against him as her knees gave way. He carried her to the overstuffed couch and dropped to one knee beside her, his hand warm against her cheek. "Debbie darling, what is it?"

She tried to tell him, incoherent as she was, and he frowned through her sobs and tears and half sentences. Halfway through her attempt to explain, he moved to the couch and put both arms around her. Finally he seemed to have it all put together. "Is that all?" he said.

"All!" She was irate. "You're the one who said—"

"Dammit, Debbie, I was only teasing you. Don't take it so seriously."

"That was teasing?" She sat up straight and pushed him away.

"All right, it wasn't very tactful, but you were beginning to sound all-powerful, you know. It's not up to you to save the world."

"Only your corner of it, is that all?"

"Just try, Debbie. If it doesn't work—"

"Then your dreams go down the drain." Despite herself, she knew she sounded a little sad about that, and when his arm tightened, pulling her back against him, she didn't object.

Riley rubbed his chin against her hair. "Not me," he said gently. "Don't worry about me. And as for everyone else, well, it's a sad fact, but true, that everybody's got a right to be a damn fool, Deb."

He stopped. She sniffed, and nodded, and looked up at him, waiting for him to continue, and something in his face seemed to hold her paralysed.

Riley sighed. "Including me," he said under his breath. The palm of his hand flattened against the middle of her back and pulled her close against him.

She didn't resist. In fact, if she had been able to express

what she was thinking in that moment, she would probably have said that she didn't in the least mind the idea of a soft, comforting caress.

But that was far from the reality. There was no softness, no caressing comfort, in the way he kissed her. It was instead more like a summer thunderstorm that sprang fully developed from a clear sky, raging with thunder and lightning and wind, threatening anything that lay in its way, anything foolish enough not to seek shelter.

But she did not want to run for shelter. She did not want to hide herself from the storm. And so she kissed him in return and gloried in the taste of him, in the firmness of his body against hers as he eased her back against the overstuffed couch, and in the gentle touch of his hands against the thin emerald green of her dress. It was a sensation not much different than if he had actually been touching the heat-flushed skin underneath. And in a moment, she knew, he would be, for his fingers had gone unerringly to the tiny buttons that fastened the front of the dress.

You should stop this, she told herself. This is like playing Russian roulette. The longer it goes on the more dangerous it gets. You must stop this, Deborah....

But what actually came out of her mouth, in a feeble sort of croak, was, "Not here, Riley."

He did not unfasten the dress. Instead his hands slid down over the soft fabric until his palms were resting firmly over her breasts. The soft tips contracted under his touch, and an uncontrollable shiver racked her body.

It was not fear, she diagnosed with the one bit of her brain that still seemed to be functioning correctly. Certainly she was not afraid of Riley.

But was he afraid of her? He looked a little pale,

Deborah thought, as he pushed himself up and away from her, and rubbed his hand along his jaw.

She tried to laugh. "We just proved we're capable," she said unsteadily, and then realised that there were a dozen ways to interpret that. "Of being damn fools, I mean."

"Yes," Riley muttered. "Well. If there isn't any further business tonight, I mean, anything more to talk about…"

Deborah gathered herself together and surreptitiously tried out her feet to make sure they still worked before she attempted to stand up. "Nothing," she said. "I'll see you some time tomorrow then."

"I'll take you home."

"I've got my car, Riley."

"So I'll ride up with you and walk back."

"Honestly, I'll be fine! I drive around Chicago at night, you know."

"You'll be perfectly safe from me, too," he said levelly. "But you don't want Ida asking questions about why you came home alone, do you?"

That silenced her, and they walked down the long flights of stairs and out to the Jaguar without another word. Unlike the previous night, he made no effort to take her keys, and when she had parked the car at Lassiter House he gave her the merest brush of his lips against her cheek, and then, rather than walking her all the way up to the house, leaned against the car and watched until she was safely at the front door.

She glanced back at him from the terrace. He was a mere dark shadow in the little parking area halfway down the hill. As she watched, he seemed to merge with the night, and vanish.

That puts you in your place, Deborah told herself. You scared the poor man to death, that's obvious. Not here,

Riley. Good heavens, girl, you sounded like an overheated nymphomaniac. Fortunate for you that he didn't have the opposite reaction! Just what would you have done if he'd taken you at your word and led you off to his bedroom?

You'd have gone, said the tiny voice of conscience. And you'd have loved it.

# CHAPTER EIGHT

AND THAT, she told herself sternly, would have been the most deranged thing you could possibly have done. Going to bed with Riley was utterly out of the question. Certainly he was attractive. She could understand why women found him appealing, even why some of them fell in love with him. But Deborah Ainsley was not among them.

*Or am I?* she asked herself, half-astonished by the force of the question.

*Love?* It was insane, and yet...

She sat down on the bench of the carved walnut coat tree in the hall, and didn't even notice that the plush padding, the best available in Jacob's day, was no longer adequate.

I can't have fallen in love with Riley, she told herself desperately. Yes, it's true that he grew up to be a decent human being, despite all indications to the contrary when he was younger, but that's certainly no reason for me to fall in love with him. It's just that I'm stuck here in Summerset, with only Riley to confide in. When I get back to Chicago, back to Bristol, I'll laugh at the notion that I could have fallen for Riley.

Bristol. She seized on his name with a lighter heart, and was in her room before she remembered the odd feeling she'd had when he called earlier that evening, as if he was phoning from another planet altogether. How had she managed to tuck Bristol so far away into a corner of her heart that she hadn't even thought of him in two days? The resort, she told herself. Aunt Ida, Preston Powell, Ruth, the trust. It was no wonder she hadn't had time to daydream about Bristol.

She perched on the marble ledge of the open window and looked down across the town, where the stillness of night lay almost undisturbed under the moon's glow. In the quietness, the truth could not be denied.

It was not the resort and Aunt Ida and the trust that had kept her from thinking about Bristol, she admitted with slow and painful honesty. It was Riley who had interfered. The evidence was clear. Tonight, when she was with Riley, she had yet again forgotten Bristol altogether.

It's not important, she told herself firmly. It's not as if you were being unfaithful to Bristol, after all. You've made no promises to him. It would be a different matter altogether if you were engaged to him, if you were wearing his ring.

She looked for a long time at Darlene Lassiter's diamond, sparkling faintly on her finger. Then, with confusion in her heart, she undressed in the dark and crept into her bed. Surely, in the morning, everything would once more make sense.

ON SUNDAY MORNING, Deborah discovered that Preston Powell did not, after all, spend every minute of his time on the golf course. Despite the lure of a perfect, sunny day, he came downstairs dressed in sombre black and joined her and Aunt Ida in the back of the vintage Rolls for the short trip down the hill to the old stone church.

Deborah's heart skittered from toes to throat for most of the trip; she wasn't certain if it was because of Preston's presence or Henry's driving skills, which were rusty at best. Or, perhaps, it was her fear that Aunt Ida might prevail upon Father Adams to fit them into his morning's schedule after all. Or...

She manoeuvred into the pew first, to keep Aunt Ida between her and Preston, and spent the few minutes before the service began in refreshing her memories of the church. It really was not as huge and imposing as she had thought when she was a child and the stained glass wasn't garish at all. It was brilliantly jewelled and gloriously rich, a superb Victorian legacy.

The organ prelude had already begun when Riley came quickly down the side aisle and slid into the pew beside her. Late, she thought crisply, and remembered what Mary Beth had said about his habits. Then she realised what had really been bothering her earlier. It had not been Preston Powell or Henry, or even the prospect of a chat with Father Adams, but the fear that Riley wouldn't show up at all, that what had happened between them last night had shaken him so badly that nothing else mattered any more.

He smiled at her, a smile that didn't quite reach his eyes, and picked up the hymn book from the rack just as Father Adams began the service. The rich baritone rolled down over the congregation, and Deborah closed her eyes and imagined the way it would sound if the words were just a little different, if he was starting out instead with "Dearly beloved, we are gathered here today to witness the union of this man and this woman in holy matrimony...."

Her heart twisted a little, and it was then that she finally faced the truth. Last night it had not been imagination that had led to her suspicions that she had fallen in love with Riley. It had not been hormones running wild, or boredom with the lack of company in Summerset, that had sent her into his arms. The simple truth was that it wouldn't have mattered where she was; as long as Riley was there, too, she would have been content. The peacefulness she felt when she was with him—the comfortable feeling of having nothing to hide—those had been the symptoms of growing love, and she had been too innocent, or too egotistical, to recognise them. She had gone merrily on her way, falling harder with every moment she spent in his company.

Everybody's got a right to be a damn fool, Riley had said last night. It's true, she thought. And I've certainly exercised my right to be a fool by falling in love with him.

She kept her head bent respectfully, but she didn't hear much of the service. Her imagination kept filling in bits from the dozens of weddings she had attended. But it wasn't the elaborate decorations or the glorious voice of a professional musician or the glamorous costumes that she recalled. It was the beauty of the ritual, and the love that spilled across the church, and the softness in a young man's eyes as his bride came to him....

The dresses, the flowers, the music, the party, they were nice, to help set the stage, but all those things meant nothing at all, really. What mattered was the person who shared the hopes and the dreams, and the love that was more important than any material things.

She looked down at her left hand, at Darlene Lassiter's diamond ring. It was such a tiny thing, but it had meant so much to Riley's grandmother. It had been the symbol of her love, and the gift of the man who loved her. That had been enough. The number of carats mattered nothing, compared to that.

It would have been enough for me, too, Deborah thought humbly. If only Riley had loved me. If only that easy companionship we felt had grown into something more for him, as it did for me.

But it had not. And now even the easy companionship they had shared was a thing of the past. For now Deborah would have to keep up her guard, even if Riley offered her a return to the way things had been.

She could not bear it if he knew, and felt sorry for her, or even worse, if he was amused. She could not allow him to guess what had happened to her. And so she must guard herself with care, for now she had something that she must, at all costs, hide from the man she loved.

DEBORAH INTENDED to start her search for Fred Milligan at the earliest moment that the attorney general's office could possibly be open on Monday morning. The guest room's solar alarm clock did not fail her, though she moaned in resignation as usual when the sunlight crept across her pillow and into her eyes.

What she did not expect was to run into Aunt Ida at the breakfast table. It's not fair, she thought, as Ida looked at her with a mixture of approval and scepticism, or was that just Deborah's own guilty conscience speaking? She slid warily into her chair with a surreptitious glance at her wristwatch. No, it wasn't her imagination; it might be early for her, but it was certainly late for Aunt Ida to be still lingering over her coffee.

"It's nice to see you taking advantage of the best part of the day," Aunt Ida said calmly. "I'm glad you're up, Deborah. I need you to do a small favour for me this morning."

Deborah sighed inwardly as she poured herself a glass of orange juice. Great, she thought. Just what I need. She's probably decided to teach me to prune the roses, on the very day when I absolutely must get out of here and to a telephone where I can't be overheard. Now what do I do? she wondered. What kind of excuse can I safely give?

"I was planning to go down to the restaurant," she said tentatively.

Ida dismissed that with a wave of her hand. "It won't even be open for hours, and I'm sure you won't mind delaying your plans briefly. Henry will be out doing the marketing, you see, and Preston—"

"I know," Deborah said glumly. "He's on the golf course making up for yesterday."

Ida looked at her sharply. "As it happens, he's out at Paradise Valley, but that's beside the point. Someone has to be here this morning to let in the real estate agent."

Deborah choked on her orange juice. "The— Do you mean someone's coming to look at Lassiter House? Today?"

"Is there a reason why they shouldn't?" Ida asked crisply. "I'd take care of the matter myself, but I've been advised it's wiser for the owner to be absent when the house is shown."

I can't quarrel with that, Deborah thought. Especially in this case.

"All you have to do, really, is let them in. It isn't as if you'd be giving a tour or anything of the sort, and it won't take long. I just want to have someone here." Aunt Ida wiped her lips primly with her linen napkin and pushed back her chair. "I do so appreciate your help, Deborah."

And that, Deborah told herself wryly, is that!

Though, when she thought about it, it wouldn't be so terrible after all. With Ida gone, there was no reason she couldn't go right ahead with her call from Lassiter House. And there was poetic justice, as well as a bit of black humour, in the idea of telephoning Fred Milligan from Aunt Ida's own house, and charging the call to her bill.

Ida stopped at the door. "I've been meaning to ask you, Deborah," she went on. "This gallery of yours, in Chicago?"

Deborah braced herself.

"You're going to give it up, of course."

It was not a question, and it set Deborah's hair on end, despite Riley's warnings that the matter was certain to arise. "Why should I?" she asked coolly. "I might just take on a partner to run the Chicago operation, and start a branch office here."

Ida's eyebrows raised. "What a lovely idea," she said. "In Riley's extra building, no doubt? I'm glad you've given it so much thought. It's a much more prudent plan than for you to actually work for him as a hostess, or anything of that sort, until the children come along." She smiled approvingly and vanished toward the kitchen, calling Henry's name.

Deborah finished her orange juice slowly and deliberately, and waited for Ida to leave the house. She was getting an awful lot of experience in practising patience, she thought. It would no doubt come in handy some time.

But there was a pang of sadness in knowing that whatever happened, it would soon be finished. She would be back in Chicago, and these few days in Summerset would be history. In time, they would fade into distant memory.

And pigs will fly, too, she told herself tartly. It wasn't going to be so easy to forget the day at the farm, and the long warm evenings at Riley's apartment. Even yesterday at church and through a long afternoon at Lassiter House, despite that new undercurrent of uneasiness between them, there had been moments of warm harmony, of shared laughter, of joy.

Because, Deborah told herself honestly, in those moments I forgot that it was only a scene we were playing, and I allowed myself to believe that the way he held my hand and looked at me was the reality.

It was something of a miracle that she actually reached Fred Milligan on her second try, though it was only by talking very fast and using Ida's name to his secretary. Fred Milligan himself listened to her in such utter silence that Deborah began to wonder if he was still there at all, or if he had put down the telephone and gone off.

She broke off in midsentence. "Mr. Milligan?" she asked anxiously.

He grunted. "I'm still here, Miss Ainsley. So far you've told me that you think Ida's lost any business sense she ever had, but frankly I don't see why you're trying to get me involved in it."

"But surely you have some influence with her still!"

"Perhaps I do, and perhaps not. It's her own business, you know."

"Not entirely," Deborah said pointedly.

"Oh, yes. Now we're getting to the bottom of it. It's your trust fund you're really concerned about, isn't it?"

"It isn't exactly criminal to want to see it preserved, is it?" she snapped, and then thought better of it. "I'm not a gold digger, Mr. Milligan. I'm worried about Aunt Ida, and how she'll take it if—when—Preston Powell disappears with her cash and leaves her holding the bag. She's not a young woman, and the shock—"

The doorbell rang. Deborah looked distractedly towards the front of the house and then told herself that it would just have to wait. She propped her elbow on the small telephone table and put her head down into her palm.

"The preservation of the capital is certainly a concern," she went on steadily. "But it's not the only thing that is important to me. I do not want to see Aunt Ida defrauded and hurt."

Fred Milligan grunted again. "Very well, I'll talk to her as soon as I can," he said finally, with obvious resignation.

"Mr. Milligan, you have my deepest gratitude—"

"Don't thank me," he said bluntly. "I haven't done

anything yet, and I'm not sure I will. Anything more than to talk to her, that is."

"That's all I've asked for," Deborah said pointedly. She would have hung up on him if he had given her a chance.

The doorbell pealed again, longer and seemingly louder this time. She swore under her breath and hurried down the long hall to answer it.

The estate agent still had his finger on the bell when Deborah opened the door. The prospective buyers, a couple in their late thirties, were standing on the terrace, inspecting the roof through binoculars. They were no sooner inside the house than the woman wrinkled her nose and made a comment about the musty smell. Deborah had thought the same thing herself a hundred times, but she found herself resenting the remark from a stranger and wanting to usher the woman straight back out into the sunshine. Instead, she smiled cheerfully and retreated to her perch in the telephone booth in the back hallway while the estate agent and the prospective buyers began their tour.

The telephone at the gallery rang several times, and Peggy sounded a bit out of breath when she answered it. "I'll call back if you're busy," Deborah offered.

"Oh, no—no clients, that is. I was unpacking crates of sculpture that just came in from Michigan."

"How does it all look?"

"Wonderful, I think. It's just that there's so much of it, and I've got no room to put it! Deborah, have you considered renting the building next door and expanding?"

"Frequently." It was crisp. "But you know what rents are like on the Magnificent Mile."

"I know," Peggy said with resignation. "Well, I'll fit it all in somehow. When are you going to be back?"

Deborah forced herself to laugh. "Don't worry. You've

got a couple of days to work it out." She broke the connection and sat with the telephone in her hand, thinking glumly that if Ida persisted with her scheme, the Ainsley Gallery not only wouldn't be expanding, but she would probably be looking for a new and less expensive location altogether. It was not a pleasant thought, and to help banish it, she called her father at the foundation offices.

He was, as usual, cheerful. "Hello, darling. Is there something you want me to bring down for you?"

"You're coming to Summerset? Daddy, are you sure that's wise?"

"Didn't Ida tell you? She called me up yesterday and said she thought I should be there for your chat with the Reverend whatever-his-name-is, and of course I agreed." He chuckled. "It sounds as if you and Riley are doing a capital job with her!"

Deborah groaned. "Oh, we are. You should have been here yesterday, when she told us she didn't think the church would be big enough to hold everyone on her guest list and perhaps we should have the wedding in the high school auditorium where they held Uncle Ralph's funeral. Daddy, I can't take much more of this. You've got some influence at the state level, don't you?"

"Well, a bit perhaps. But—"

She told him about Fred Milligan. "And if you could just hint that your friend the governor might fire him if he doesn't co-operate..." she suggested.

"You're certainly sounding bloodthirsty. I'll see what I can do, and I'll be there tomorrow, darling, so go cry on Riley's shoulder if you need to, but don't say a word to Ida in the meantime. Everything will be all right. It's only a temporary measure, after all, and you'll be out of this mess before you know it."

Cry on Riley's shoulder? Deborah thought despairingly.

About what, for heaven's sake? The only thing that made her feel like crying was the fact that she didn't really want to be out of this mess. If only she could rearrange it a bit, this engagement would be not a nightmare, but a dream come true.

And if she told Riley that, he would be the one doing the crying, she told herself grimly. Unless that irrepressible sense of humour took over and he started to laugh instead.

She had almost forgotten the prospective buyers, until the clatter of feet descending the stairs reminded her. They stopped at the bottom, and in the quiet house Deborah could hear every word as the woman said, "It's not perfect, of course, but it's certainly got atmosphere, and we can make it work. In a way it's an advantage that it hasn't been remodelled or updated at all."

Deborah wanted to scream. She hoped Fred Milligan managed to make time to call Aunt Ida today. Tomorrow might be too late.

WITH HER TELEPHONE CALLS completed, there was no reason for her to go to the restaurant, but she found herself there anyway. Riley would want to know what had happened, she told herself, and squashed the tiny voice in the back of her brain that said she really had nothing to report and so it was only her desire to see him again that had brought her hotfooting it down to the old warehouse.

The back door was unlocked, but there was no answer at all when she called his name, so she went on in. She peeked into a pantry lined with boxes and crates and tubs, walked through the gleaming stainless steel kitchen where huge coolers hummed as if to keep themselves company, and almost tiptoed through the ghostly-silent dining room.

Riley was in his office, and the surface of his desk was

buried in bills and invoices and order forms and payroll records. His hair was rumpled; it was obvious he'd been running his fingers through it.

He didn't even bother to say hello. "You can use the phone in the bar. There won't be anyone around, and I've got to get through my bookkeeping this morning."

Deborah gingerly pushed papers back from the corner of his desk and perched on it. "I can see this is one of your favourite pastimes," she said, and waved a hand at the papers. "You look so very cheerful about it."

He gave a little snort. "Taking a few days off almost isn't worth it," he muttered, "with all the catching up there is to do."

"How well I know," she said, thinking of her own desk at the gallery. It was not an inviting prospect. "I don't need the phone, by the way. I've already reached Mr. Milligan."

He looked up at her warily. "And?"

"And he's going to talk to Aunt Ida."

He looked astounded, and then slowly warmth dawned in his eyes. "Good girl!"

Being on the receiving end of Riley's smile, she thought, was almost better than getting a trophy, and it was a long moment before she remembered that she wasn't as certain of her overall success as he seemed to be. But before she could warn him that Fred Milligan hadn't exactly promised to help them out, Riley had picked up his pen again.

"Mary Beth and Rod are having a party here tonight," he said, reaching for another envelope. "She wants us to join them."

"Great," Deborah muttered. "That's all I need, more people asking stupid questions."

"I don't suppose we have to go, but she was rather insistent."

"I'll bet she was." When Mary Beth wanted something, she could give new meaning to the word *insistent*.

Deborah saw what looked like her father's handwriting on the face of a fat envelope half-hidden under Riley's elbow, and she tried to twist her head to an impossible angle so she could inspect it more closely.

"She said she tried to call you at Lassiter House, but she couldn't get through."

"I don't doubt it." It sounded absentminded; she was still studying the penmanship. It was definitely William's, she decided.

Riley shifted his elbow and the envelope fell off the desk. "What's eating you this morning? Oh, people asking stupid questions. Has Ida started in on you again?"

"Whatever makes you think she might?" Deborah's voice was only faintly ironic; she was proud of herself. "She's been relatively calm since that outburst yesterday, and frankly, the lull terrifies me. Oh, this morning she approved my plans to open a branch gallery in your extra building, but other than that—"

Riley pushed back his chair and propped his feet on the corner of his desk. "That's not a bad idea at all," he said thoughtfully. "A high-class gallery, perhaps not quite as upscale as your Chicago operation, but with the same sort of style."

It did sound wonderful. In fact, Deborah could see it, without even having to close her eyes and imagine; a reincarnated Ainsley Gallery seemed to have sprung to life in her head in the space of an instant. She could have an entire floor—who cared if it had once been a warehouse? All the evidence of that could be erased easily enough. There would be high ceilings and natural light and airy space. The kind of space that she could never afford in Chicago.

Not possible, she reminded herself. Because whether you stay on Michigan Avenue or not, you'll be in Chicago. Not here in Summerset.

She shook her head. "Remodelling would take a ton of money," she said. The repressive tone of voice should have ended the conversation, but she'd forgotten for a moment that she wasn't talking to the average man, but to Riley.

"That's no problem. Not if Ida approves."

"What on earth do you mean?"

He sat up and began scrambling through the papers on his desk. "It's here somewhere...I was reading it just a little while ago."

"If you're talking about the copy of the trust document that Daddy sent," she said coolly, "I believe you'll find it under the wheels of your chair. And what do you mean, you were reading it?"

He grinned at her. "Well, it was addressed to me," he pointed out reasonably. "In fact, it's marked *Personal*." He stooped to retrieve the envelope and waved it at her with a flourish. "The trust allows you to get cash to develop a business opportunity, with the trustees' approval."

Deborah seized the envelope out of his hand. "No one ever told me that before!"

He shrugged. "Perhaps Ida didn't approve of your location in Chicago."

She buried her nose in the document, several closely spaced pages of legalese that soon had her floundering. "I can't believe this," she said. "No wonder Daddy always let the attorneys handle it. Listen to this bit."

Riley stopped writing a cheque and looked up at her. "I've read that bit," he pointed out. "And all the other bits, too. Would you mind doing that somewhere else? You make a very attractive paperweight, but I do need to get down to work.''

''I'm so sorry,'' she said sweetly, and slid off the desk. ''I thought perhaps you'd agree that this was important.''

He didn't even answer, and she stalked back through the restaurant and out to her car in a huff.

''Don't be ridiculous,'' she told herself. ''The man does have a job, after all, and he's running behind because he must have spent an hour or two this morning deciphering this mess.'' She tossed the envelope onto the dashboard. ''What are you fussing about, anyway? The fact that you didn't even get a kiss?''

It stopped her cold, because it was true.

Remember that, she told herself firmly. Remember it well. Today, he had not had an audience that needed to be impressed, and apparently he'd done all the research he felt necessary. So he had stopped exerting his right to be a damned fool....

She waved at Alec, who was walking his bicycle along Main Street, and was a block past him before she realised that the front tyre on the bike had been flat. She circled the block, pulled up beside him and called, ''Need a lift somewhere?''

They managed to wedge the bicycle into the back of the car, and she took him home. His mother was on her knees beside the front steps, weeding a flower bed. She looked up with dismay in her eyes. ''Not another flat tyre, Alec.''

''It's okay, Mom. I've got a patch kit.''

Ruth sighed. ''That tyre is going to be almost solid patches before long,'' she said, but Alec had already vanished around the corner of the house. ''Thank you for bringing him home.'' She stripped off her gloves. ''Would you like some coffee?''

Deborah must have looked startled.

Ruth said diffidently, "Coffee sounds sort of silly when it's so warm, doesn't it? But sometimes when the weather is like this, if I drink something hot it makes me feel cooler."

"I'll try it. Thanks."

It was pleasant inside the house, at least in comparison to the rising heat outdoors. There was a whisper of a breeze through the open kitchen windows, where crisp white curtains had been tied back out of the way. Deborah sat down at the small table and wondered if she dared to bring up the subject of Paradise Valley.

She had forgotten to ask Riley whether he had talked to Ruth yet. She suspected he had not, and she also thought that he'd rather forget the whole thing. Well, that was understandable, she supposed; he didn't want to take the chance of infuriating what was obviously a good and sincere employee. But Deborah didn't have that consideration holding her back. And now that she had been offered the chance...

Ruth pushed aside a sketch pad and a box of cheap watercolours and set two ceramic mugs on the table. Deborah picked up hers—Love Is Like a Mushroom, it said on the side, with a sketch of half a dozen toadstools—and sipped her coffee. Then, looking for a way to break the ice, she pointed at the box of watercolours. "I had the impression that Alec never sits still long enough to paint," she said.

"He doesn't," Ruth said a little stiffly. "I do. Just for something to pass the time. The days get long sometimes."

"May I look?" The question sprang automatically to Deborah's lips, and the cover of the sketchbook was open before she realised there had not been an answer.

Ruth's mouth had tightened into a firm line, but all she said was a quiet, "If you like."

When will you learn? Deborah asked herself. Ruth said it was only a way to pass the time. Of course she doesn't want to show you her work. A lot of people don't. Others—well, the mere fact that Deborah Ainsley had asked to look had convinced more than one hopeful amateur that she was the next Mary Cassatt, and that was even worse.

Just glance at the drawings, say something noncommittal and get out of here before you have another attack of tactlessness, Deborah ordered herself. Let Riley deal with the rest. She's his friend, after all, not yours.

She glanced. Then she set her coffee cup firmly out of the way, pulled the sketchbook closer and looked long and thoroughly at every sheet. At a small blonde girl with a jump rope, at a towheaded boy with a cat curled on his shoulders, at a child in a hooded yellow slicker squatting over a rain puddle.

She looked up finally and said sternly, "*This* is just a way to pass your time?"

Ruth coloured. "Not exactly," she said.

"Well, I should hope you know better than that. You should be ashamed of yourself for saying it. No wonder you asked about my gallery."

"I thought maybe if I could work up my nerve to ask you to look at my things... But then you said you were going to close it, so..." Ruth reached for the sketchbook almost protectively.

Deborah held it out of her reach and pulled out one of the larger drawings, of a tiny girl sitting at a miniature tea table with her three guests—a teddy bear, a china doll and a small dog wearing a baby's bonnet. "I'd like to buy this," she said.

"I—I've never sold anything," Ruth admitted. "I wouldn't even know how much to ask for it."

"Believe me, I know what it's worth," Deborah said firmly, and told her. "And as for the rest..."

Ruth swallowed hard, but all she said was, "Would you like more coffee?"

"I think you'd better make another pot," Deborah told her. "We've got a lot to talk about."

# CHAPTER NINE

It was the strangest thing Deborah had ever seen, actually watching as years peeled away from a woman's face as she glimpsed a new world opening up before her. But at the same time, she saw a sort of exalted strain come into Ruth's eyes, and finally the woman asked, in little more than a whisper, "What if I can't do it?"

"You're already doing it," Deborah said, and added dryly, "If you have trouble, just pretend you're only painting to pass the time!"

By the time she left a couple of hours later, the agreements were made; it was only a matter of the paperwork. Ruth had announced her intention of signing the contracts the moment they came into her hands.

"I'm gratified, but I'd feel better if you'd have an attorney look everything over first," Deborah told her. She drained her mug and thoughtfully read the rest of the motto, printed coyly on the bottom, where it was nearly always hidden by the contents of the cup. Ruth was right about the coffee, she thought. She did feel cooler after the hot drink.

And the wisdom printed in the mug? Was Ruth right about that, too?

Don't think about it, Deborah told herself. Just be glad that this trip hasn't been a total washout. Finding Ruth made it all worthwhile.

Just keep thinking that way, she told herself, and someday you might make yourself believe it. Finding Ruth. Finding Riley. There was no comparison.

She considered stopping at the restaurant again, but in the end she drove on past and went back to Lassiter House instead. Riley obviously hadn't been feeling desperate for her company this morning, and she didn't feel up to being rejected again. Besides, it was only fair to let Ruth have the joy of telling Riley, or the alternate fun of holding her good news close to her heart for a while, keeping it secret from the world.

The thought of secrets finally reminded her of Paradise Valley, and the talk she had originally meant to have with Ruth. She sighed. Perhaps it was just as well that she hadn't brought it up, and risked this fledgling partnership that promised so much for Ruth. No matter what happened to the resort, she and Alec wouldn't be destitute as long as Ruth kept painting.

You're beginning to sound cynical, Deborah told herself. Don't give up yet. Fred Milligan may come through with flying colours. And Aunt Ida may suddenly acquire wisdom, too, she mocked herself, and Preston Powell may have a massive attack of conscience and return everyone's money in the town square at high noon, but I wouldn't count on it!

She knew what was really bothering her, of course, and once back at the house she threw herself down on a chaise longue beside the pool and gave herself a good lecture.

It will pass, she told herself firmly. This entire infatuation of yours with Riley will go away. It's not surprising that you got caught up in it, but once you're away from him things will get back to normal. You always knew this was only temporary, anyway.

She sighed and put her hands over her eyes and tried again.

This is the strangest infatuation you've ever heard of, she reminded herself. How can you possibly be in love with a man you cordially detest half the time?

But I don't detest him, she corrected herself. And even though this is certainly not the normal, madly passionate sort of love affair...

"Don't kid yourself about that, either," she muttered. If what had happened in his apartment on Saturday night wasn't madly passionate, then Deborah Ainsley hadn't any idea what would be. If she was looking for fireworks, well, she had found out on Saturday night that the potential was certainly there.

For a full minute she lost herself in pleasant, dreamy memories of the way he had kissed her and the shivers of pleasure that had racked her body and made her want so much more. And then, finally, she sat up and reminded herself that while Riley had without a doubt shared the pleasure of those sensations, his reaction had been much different. He hadn't been able to get rid of her fast enough. And since then, he'd scarcely touched her at all.

He certainly doesn't find anything about me to be overwhelmingly attractive, she told herself bluntly, or he wouldn't have turned down that invitation I issued.

No amount of money would be enough to make me marry you, he had said once. It was painfully obvious, she thought, that he'd considered the question carefully, and found the price unbearable.

It's only infatuation, she told herself firmly. You can't actually be in love with someone who turns pale at the sight of you!

She knew, down deep, that infatuation was a bonfire that flared high and then burned out, but she also knew that the feeling she held in her heart for Riley was more like a furnace; not flashy, perhaps, but solid and reliable and always, always there.

And, even if there had ever been a chance of changing that, of backing out of loving him, it was too late to do anything about it now.

Ruth had been right about that, too.

Love Is Like a Mushroom, that silly ceramic mug of hers had proclaimed. You Never Know If It's the Real Thing Until It's Too Late.

When Mary Beth threw a party, she didn't waste effort on a small one, Deborah found herself thinking that evening. The two private dining rooms that overlooked the river had been opened into one for the event, and Mary Beth's friends filled it to the point of claustrophobia. Deborah suspected that if a third room had been available, Mary Beth could have filled that one, as well. She certainly had no shortage of friends, and she seemed to want Deborah to know them all, too.

It's a microcosm of what my wedding reception would have been like, Deborah thought. With Aunt Ida doing the planning for one half of the family and Mary Beth in charge on the other side, it would have been the biggest party southern Illinois ever saw. Aunt Ida was right; the church probably wouldn't be big enough!

"You're looking pensive," Riley murmured, beside her.

She tried to smile. "I was just thinking that if this wedding actually was taking place, you wouldn't have any choice about finishing your party rooms upstairs. I'm surprised Aunt Ida hasn't questioned you about when you'll be starting and how long it's going to take."

He glanced over his shoulder warily. "Thanks for the warning. I'll keep my distance from her."

"You mean she's here tonight?" Deborah was

astounded. "I thought this was a strange collection of people, but I never expected Aunt Ida would be on Mary Beth's list of friends!"

"Calling them all friends is a bit euphemistic, perhaps. The guest list also includes all of Rod's clients," Riley reminded her. "Preston Powell is here, too, for instance. Mary Beth has the politics of a small town laid out like a mathematical equation, and she makes it a practice not to leave out anyone."

"Oh, is that why she's been exhibiting me? I was beginning to feel like a scientific curiosity."

"Don't let it bother you. She's probably just rehearsing the receiving line for the wedding."

"That's such a comfort, Riley." She allowed a hint of sarcasm to creep in; at least it was better than sounding as if she was on the brink of tears.

She turned towards the buffet table, mostly so she didn't have to look up at him and smile convincingly. Ruth, in uniform, was replacing a half-empty pan of Swedish meatballs with one that was heaped full. From the corner of her eye, Deborah thought she saw a look of surprise flash across the woman's face, but an instant later all trace of it was gone, if it had ever been there at all, and Ruth offered her a plate with a conspiratorial smile.

You're seeing things, Deborah told herself.

Her nerves were shot; she admitted it. It was agony enough to stand beside him and play the public part of the adoring fiancée, when she wanted with every fibre of her being for it to be true instead of only a masquerade. But it was even more difficult to play the private role of slightly cynical Deborah, always willing to fence with good old Cousin Riley, when she wanted to fling herself into his arms instead and plead with him to love her.

It was a relief when Riley murmured that he had to

check on something in the main dining room, and went away. She didn't see him again for the better part of an hour, and by then she was starting to fret about his absence.

Dammit, Deborah, she finally told herself, I wish you'd make up your mind!

That was about the time that she realised the crowd was changing; it was quieter, for one thing, and everybody seemed to have stopped milling about. People were settling into groups, looking expectantly at Mary Beth, who stood near the windows with a small silver dinner bell in her hand.

Please, not party games, Deborah thought. If she starts something juvenile like musical chairs...

She did not. Instead Mary Beth called Riley to her side and thanked him, and summoned Deborah to introduce her, as if, Deborah thought, she hadn't already made introductions to everyone already! Then Mary Beth's laugh rang out, just as pleasant as the sound of the bell. ''And now that we have the guests of honour up here where they belong,'' she said, ''let's get down to the real intention of this party—the entertainment!'' She rang the bell furiously; the double doors across the room were flung open, and Ruth wheeled in a huge serving cart, heaped with boxes and parcels brightly wrapped and ribboned, a loving shower of gifts from good friends to a future bride and groom.

Deborah wanted to groan. She glanced at Riley; he looked just as startled as she felt, but she still wanted to kick him. Mary Beth was *his* sister, after all. He should have suspected what she was capable of doing!

Mary Beth's perfect smile reached almost from ear to ear. ''You didn't have a clue, did you?'' she said with a chuckle. "I'm so proud of us all. Nobody breathed a single hint!"

That must have been why Ruth looked surprised, Deborah thought. She thought it must have been obvious what was going on, and therefore no surprise at all. But of course Ruth would have known about the cartload of gifts building up outside the door....

She turned on Riley suspiciously. "Wait a minute," she said under her breath. "You told me you were going out to the main dining room. How could you not know about this? You must have seen that pile of packages!"

"I never got outside this room. Rod had some business." He sighed. "Damn. I should have seen this coming."

"That's right. You should have. Now what do we do? Have our final and climactic fight?"

"We open the gifts and say thank you and smile prettily."

Deborah glared at him. "Just be sure you keep track of which name goes with which gift," she muttered. "Because you are going to get the joy of returning all of them!"

No nightmare could have made her feel as crazily topsy-turvy as that simple bridal shower did. When she opened a box containing a cut-crystal vase, or a handmade pillow, or a set of napkins, she had to swallow hard to keep from imagining its place in the apartment upstairs. She managed to laugh her way through a thank you for the set of red satin sheets, while her heart shuddered with the pain of thinking of a wedding night that could never be. And she did her best to look modestly coy when Riley—and of course it had to be Riley who opened that particular gift—lifted a black lace negligee from a box, and someone at the back of the room called, "I thought the presents were supposed to be for both of them!"

"Don't worry about it," Riley assured the heckler, with a soulful look at Deborah. "I'm sure I'll enjoy this one just as much as Debbie does." Then, for good measure, he kissed her, a long and soft and lingering caress.

She thought fleetingly about using his own bow tie to strangle him, but before she could make up her mind whether the undoubted satisfaction would be worth it, a movement from the doorway caught her eye, and her father walked in, his silver hair ablaze under the glow of the chandeliers.

"Daddy?" she muttered. "But he's not supposed to be here till tomorrow!"

Riley had obviously seen him, too. "You seem to have failed to tell me that he was coming at all, Deb."

"Well, I'd have remembered to tell you if you hadn't been so short with me this morning." She pushed a big, silver-wrapped package aside and stood up. "Daddy!" she called, and hurried across the room to greet him, stretching up on her toes to kiss his cheek. It was at that instant she realised that the man who had come into the room behind William Ainsley didn't belong there, either. Not tonight, not tomorrow, not at all.

"And you've brought Bristol, too," she said weakly. "How—nice to see you."

Riley had a little more command of himself. He seized Bristol's hand and shook it heartily and at length. Under the cover of his loud and enthusiastic greeting, Deborah whispered, "Daddy, how could you do this to me?"

William shrugged. "He turned up at my office at the foundation this afternoon. He was on his way down here and wanted Ida's address," he said unhappily. "I certainly couldn't stop him from coming, so I decided the best thing to do was come along."

She glared at him. "I hope you explained it."

"Of course I did. But I must say—" he waved a hand at the table, strewn with wrapping paper and boxes and gifts "—I didn't expect to have to explain something like this. What the hell is going on, Deborah?"

Despite Riley's best efforts at holding him captive, Bristol had managed to disentangle himself. He looked sternly down at Deborah, but he didn't make a move to kiss her cheek, or even to touch her at all. "Deborah, where may I find your Aunt Ida? I must speak to her immediately concerning my discoveries."

"What discoveries?" Riley said.

Deborah was almost afraid to hope. "You found something out about Paradise Valley?"

Bristol drew himself up even straighter. "Deborah, time is critical," he reminded. "Where is your Aunt Ida?"

"Over there—" She waved a hand toward the windows.

A gravelly voice right behind her said, "What the devil is going on here? William, must you always poke your nose into things where you aren't wanted? You were invited for tomorrow. And who is this you've brought with you?"

"Oh," Deborah said faintly. "This is Aunt Ida, Bristol."

Bristol made a stiff little bow. "Madam," he began, "I am a friend of Deborah's—"

Riley whispered, "Friend? It looks to me as if he's rubbed you right off his list, Deb."

She stepped on his toe as hard as she could.

"I've come all the way from San Francisco to talk to you, Miss Lassiter. At first, when Deborah requested me to look into this matter of the Paradise Valley resort—"

"You asked for this, Deborah?" Riley's voice was no longer a whisper. Still, no one more than a couple of feet away could have heard him over the sudden surprised murmur of the crowd.

"I am not interested in discussing—" Ida began.

"Not here, certainly," Riley said hastily. One hand closed firmly on Ida's arm, the other on Bristol's, and he started for the door. "Deb, get the sna—I mean, ask Powell if he'd step out here."

Preston Powell shrugged and followed, with William and Deborah at his heels.

Bristol was still talking. "This kind of scam absolutely shocks and horrifies me. I had no idea such things went on—"

Riley kicked the door shut on the excited murmurs from the party room. The hallway just outside wasn't very big, and it was awfully crowded with all of them pressed in together. But there seemed to be nowhere else to go.

Bristol didn't even have to raise his voice here. Nevertheless, even Ida seemed to realise that there was no stopping him, so she merely glared at him instead as he summarised what he had discovered.

It was apparent, Deborah thought as she listened, that his interest had been piqued by the whole affair. She hadn't seen this much animation in Bristol's face in all the time she'd known him.

Preston Powell leaned against the door of the party room, smiling a little and shaking his head sadly every couple of minutes as he listened.

Finally, Bristol stopped, out of breath, indignation still seeping from every pore.

Ida was frowning. She looks confused, Deborah thought. That's good. Obviously Bristol has shaken her confidence.

Preston Powell didn't move. "Very interesting," he

said. "Very dramatic. Of course, that's all it is—drama. You've got no right to accuse me. I'm a decent, hardworking citizen who has never been convicted of anything. Now I'd like to return to the party, if you please. Ida?"

Deborah's jaw dropped. Could he really be so certain of Ida that he wasn't even going to defend himself? "Aunt Ida, please!" she pleaded, and seized the woman's elbow. "You have to listen to Bristol."

Ida shook her arm free. "No, Deborah, I don't have to. I've already asked my attorney to look into it."

"Rod? Some good that will do! He's so sold on the idea himself that he can't possibly be objective." It was out before she considered what she was saying, and Deborah glanced guiltily over her shoulder, half-afraid that Mary Beth might have followed them into the hall and overheard that tactless comment. Then she reminded herself that it wouldn't have mattered; she wasn't going to be Mary Beth's sister-in-law, anyway.

"No, I don't mean Rod," Ida said very clearly. "Rod's a very pleasant young man, but he isn't experienced in these things. I meant my former attorney. Mr. Milligan still advises me now and then. In fact, he called me just this afternoon."

Deborah almost sagged in relief. Good old Fred, she thought. He came through for me after all!

"And he's coming down tomorrow to look over the financial records and the...what is it, Preston? Oh, yes, the prospectus, that's what it's called."

Deborah had turned to look at Preston Powell in triumph, and she was watching him as Ida went on.

"I certainly hope that you will all take Mr. Milligan's word for it when he's looked everything over," Ida said. "He's in the fraud division of the state's attorney general's office now, and this is the kind of thing he looks into all the time.''

Preston Powell had turned deathly white, and his Adam's apple bobbed so furiously that Deborah thought it was going to burst.

"Ida—" His voice was little more than a croak. "You should have warned—" He gulped. "You should have let me know so I could have a presentation ready."

Ida's forehead wrinkled in concern. "Did I forget to tell you that Mr. Milligan was coming, Preston? So foolish of me. But then it's been such a busy day, with selling Lassiter House and—"

Even William was part of the outcry on that one. Paradise Valley was momentarily forgotten.

Deborah rolled her eyes and sat down on the nearest radiator. If there were any more shocks in the offing, she didn't think she could trust herself to remain standing up.

Ida held up a hand to her hearing aid. "Will you all stop?" she said petulantly. "It's just a jumble when you all talk at once, and it hurts my ears. Mr. Powell tells me that we need to have a chat, and I'm very tired, so I think we'll be going home now."

Deborah slid off the radiator. "Aunt Ida," she said desperately, "don't talk to him!"

Ida's eyebrows soared. "Why on earth shouldn't I?"

"At least wait till Fred Milligan gets here tomorrow."

"Oh, do you know Fred, Deborah? He's such a brilliant man, don't you think? I must be going now, dear. Enjoy the rest of your party."

Deborah was grasping at straws. "If you insist on doing this, then take Bristol with you," she said. "He can look after your interests, at least."

"My interests?" Ida said sternly. "What on earth do I know about the man, Deborah, except that he very rudely pushed his way into a private party and made some extremely serious charges without evidence to back them up? I don't care to take up the gentleman's time with my interests."

There seemed to be no answer to that, and before Deborah could even croak, Ida and Preston Powell were gone.

Deborah sagged into Riley's arms. For a long moment, the silence in the hallway was complete. Then Riley cleared his throat and said glumly, "Every human being has a right to be a damn fool."

"I am sick of hearing you say that," she snapped.

Riley looked as startled as if she'd slapped him.

"Never mind," she said helplessly. It was scarcely his fault that the phrase had been running through her mind for two days. "What on earth do we do now?"

"Go open the rest of the gifts?"

That didn't even deserve an answer; she simply stared up at him as if he'd grown a second head.

"Sorry," he said. "Keep Preston away from the books so he can't make last-minute alterations, I suppose."

"How? By setting fire to Lassiter House?"

William asked, "Has she really sold it?"

"Probably. What difference does it make?" Deborah shook her head, trying to clear it, and then remembered that Bristol was watching. She gathered her strength and pushed herself gently away from Riley. He let her go quite easily.

"We could all go up there," William offered.

"I doubt it would do any good," Deborah said. "I doubt anything would do any good, now. We'll just have to talk to Fred Milligan tomorrow, that's all. Surely with all of us chiming in, he'll have to listen. Thanks for trying, Bristol."

He nodded stiffly. "There were too many things interfering with my concentration. Next time..."

"Unfortunately, we aren't likely to get a second chance at him," Riley pointed out crisply.

"That's enough, both of you. Daddy, please."

William stepped forward. "Perhaps if we just got out of the way, Bristol."

"Of course." But Bristol stopped a couple of steps away and turned, a frown cutting into his forehead. "I don't understand you at all, Deborah," he said. "To have engaged yourself to this person... Don't you realise that your own children will also be your third cousins once removed? The chance you're taking—"

"Is minimal, so don't let it keep you up nights, Bristol," Riley recommended.

William tugged Bristol off down the hallway. "You and Deborah can talk about it tomorrow," he was saying as they went out of sight.

Deborah put one hand to her head, which felt as if it were about to explode. "He's taking the engagement seriously," she said helplessly.

"Of course he is. I told you even before I met him that the man has no sense of humour. What's it going to be, Debbie darling? Shall we have the rest of the gifts, or are you anxious to have our final and climactic fight, and get it over with?"

"The gifts," she said absently. "I don't have enough energy left for a messy public fight."

He smiled down at her, and his eyes lit to a brilliant hazel glow. "That's my girl," he said.

And Deborah thought, I only wish I were....

TUESDAY MORNING dawned with the sky overcast and threatening rain; still, Deborah was awake early, after a restless night in which she had not been able to uncoil her tense body enough even to rest. For all she knew, Ida and Preston Powell were still locked in the study, where they'd been closeted when Riley brought her home well after midnight. It had taken that long to get all those blasted gifts hauled up to his living room.

Finally she put on shorts and a shirt and padded downstairs, barefoot, to seek out a cup of coffee. At least with a dose of caffeine inside her, she'd have an easy excuse for being so jumpy, she reasoned.

She was not surprised to find her father and Bristol already in the dining room, each gloomily scanning a section of the morning newspaper. Her father, still stubbly-faced, was wrapped in his favourite disreputable bathrobe; Bristol, on the other hand, was wearing a charcoal-grey suit with a crisp white shirt and a red tie, as if he were on his way to a major negotiating session. Deborah sat down beside him with her coffee and almost choked on the cloud of after-shave that surrounded him.

"Has Aunt Ida been down?" she said finally.

William shook his head, without raising it from the sports section.

"I suppose that means Preston succeeded in explaining away any niggling doubts we might have given her, and he's gone out to the golf course to celebrate."

"Haven't seen him, either," William said.

"I have to give the man credit," Deborah murmured. "He certainly works hard at his chosen method of making a living."

Bristol merely looked at her.

Riley's right, Deborah thought. Bristol doesn't have so much as a shred of humour in his whole body. How could I ever have imagined that I might want to live with this rigid framework of a man? He'd have squeezed the joy right out of me.

Daddy was right, long ago, too, she thought. It was security I wanted, and so I chose Bristol. But even I knew, down deep inside my heart, that he wasn't right for me. That's why I haven't been in any hurry to marry him. And now that the wounds Morgan left on me have finally healed, I can see that Bristol would be every bit as bad for me. And so, she thought ironically, I've decided I want Riley instead. You're an idiot, Deborah Ainsley.

Riley came down the hall from the kitchen with a cup already in his hand and a bounce in his step. He was wearing cut-off jeans, running shoes and a polo shirt, and he was the only one who looked as if he'd had enough sleep.

That makes sense, Deborah thought. He's also the only one of us who's a little better off than he was yesterday. He may still be fighting the battle of Paradise Valley, but one of his problems is solved. He's all but rid of me!

"When are we expecting Fred Milligan?" he asked.

It was Ida who answered him, from the door that led into the main hallway. "He'll be here for lunch. I hope you'll all stay." There was a faint note of irony as she surveyed her four uninvited guests. "Preston sends his regrets, by the way."

"Regrets?" Deborah said blankly. "You mean, he's gone?"

"Yes. He left Lassiter House last night, quite late, after we finished our little talk."

"You kicked him out?" William asked. "Ida, I congratulate you."

Ida looked at him coldly. "I did not evict him, William. He chose to go."

"I'll bet," Deborah said. "And he's probably scooping up the money right now so he can run before Fred Milligan arrives." She propped her elbows on the table and stared morosely into her coffee cup.

"I'm quite sure he will avoid meeting Fred," Ida said. "But he's not taking any money, except for the certified cheque I gave him. I bought his entire interest in Paradise Valley, you see. I own it now—all of it." She looked around at them with a proud smile.

William put his head down on the newspaper. Riley and Deborah uttered a mutual groan. Bristol looked intrigued.

Ida seemed hurt. "It was a very small certified cheque actually, just enough to get him out of town, and make the transfer legal. And don't worry that he slipped any of the assets out from under my nose, either. I've been keeping a very close eye on them, along with my banker and Fred Milligan and a few other people who had their reasons to want to see Preston Powell taken down a few notches. As a matter of fact, I thought you'd all be pleased. Now we've got Paradise Valley out of the hands of the swindlers who have held it for ten years, and we can do something legitimate. I bought it for five cents on the dollar, and Preston was delighted to sign it over and get out of town before the fraud division showed up."

The silence that fell in the dining room was absolute. It was Riley who finally said, "You knew he was a crook?"

Ida sniffed. "I suppose I should be pleased at how well I obviously played my part. Still, I don't find it flattering that you all believed I was dizzy enough not to see through a scam like that. Especially you, Deborah." She shook her head primly. "To think that you had so little trust in me that you would go to such great lengths in an attempt to protect the Lassiter money!"

"Such lengths?" Deborah repeated. Her voice sounded a little hollow.

"Yes, dear," Ida said gently. "This nonsense of yours about being engaged to Riley."

Deborah, instantly suspicious, turned to stare at her father, but William looked just as awestruck as she was. Then she realised there was a dancing light in Riley's eyes—not a guilty gleam, however, but a dawning glimmer of appreciation. "We've been taken for a ride, Deb," he said.

"Aunt Ida," Deborah said helplessly. "You knew, and you didn't say anything?" It was impossible, she thought, and yet in a crazy way everything fit.

"It was very naughty of me, wasn't it? I didn't catch on at first, you know. I don't mind telling you that I played terrible bridge that first afternoon when you'd just made your announcement. I lost every rubber. But that night at the restaurant it all fell into place. You did a very convincing job, both of you, but it was the only explanation that made sense, you see. You and Riley..." She shook her head. "It was nonsense to think you could be serious about each other."

Right, Deborah thought morosely. It's nonsense. And if you've got any brains at all, Deborah, you'll remember that.

"I could hardly take you into my confidence," Ida went on. "You were far too useful in diverting Preston's attention from what I was doing. But I'm afraid I just couldn't resist egging you on a little."

Deborah sighed. "So that's when you started making wedding plans that kept getting wilder by the minute."

Ida looked just a tiny bit guilty. "I simply couldn't resist seeing how far I could go before you would protest. I found myself looking at it in very much the same way I thought about Preston Powell, you see."

"This ought to be good," Riley said under his breath.

Ida smiled at him gently, and said almost apologetically, "One good scam deserves another. And you had both asked for it, you know."

## CHAPTER TEN

RILEY GAVE a sudden shout of laughter. "Ida, you're priceless," he said. "But tell me, please, just what you plan to do with that decrepit resort, now that you own it. It's still going to cost a fortune to build hotels and ski ramps, you know."

"Old people like me don't want hotels and ski ramps," Ida said calmly. "They want good, pleasant housing without having to worry about upkeep and maintenance. They want community activities like a clubhouse and a swimming pool and a bingo hall, and they want—"

"You're turning it into a senior citizen complex?"

"Don't worry, Riley," Ida said dryly. "It will work. I've done my research."

He shook his head admiringly. "I don't doubt it for a minute."

"And as a matter of fact, there's a small and quiet waiting list for the apartments and town houses we're going to build in the place of all those summer palaces Preston had planned.

"*We* being you and Fred Milligan?" Deborah speculated.

"And a fair number of other investors, yes. Anyone who wants out will have no trouble selling those pretty stock certificates Preston gave them. Personally, I think they'll make more by staying in, but then sometimes—"

"Venture capital is a risky business," Deborah recited

in unison with her. "Tell me one thing, Aunt Ida. If Fred Milligan is in this up to his neck, why was he so suspicious when I called him?"

Ida looked at her as if she were a mildly stupid child. "Of course he was suspicious," she said. "He was sitting in Springfield chewing his nails while I laid the foundations. It's no wonder the poor man was getting nervous waiting for his cue. And then you called up and told him 'Aunt Ida's up to no good' or something of the sort, and he didn't even know which side you were on, for heaven's sake!"

"I'm glad *someone* in your crowd had an anxious moment over this," Deborah said disgustedly.

Bristol cleared his throat. "Since obviously none of this has anything to do with me, I am going back to Chicago. Shall I wait for you, William?" he asked, with a scathing look at the disreputable bathrobe.

"I suppose there's no need for me to stay to talk to the minister now, is there?" William said with a weak smile.

"That's right," Deborah told him coolly.

"Then unless you'd like me to keep you company..."

She took pity on him; he was so obviously grasping for an excuse. "Don't worry about Daddy, Bristol. I'll be driving back myself later today." She bit her lip and added, "I'm sorry you had to miss the rest of your seminar for nothing."

He nodded, matter-of-factly accepting the apology. "There will be other seminars. I found the matter quite interesting, actually." He nodded to Ida, and was gone.

Well! Deborah thought. He doesn't seem to care whether I'm engaged or not!

The loss of his company did not seem to disturb Ida. He was no more than out the door when she asked, "And the rest of you? Will you be staying to have lunch with Fred?''

"I don't think so, Aunt Ida," Deborah said dryly. "You seem to have everything well under control."

William excused himself to get dressed, and Ida murmured something about needing to get busy because she had wasted far too much time in the past couple of days. She hurried off towards the kitchen.

She's wasted time, Deborah thought. Studying bridal magazines, I suppose she means, and thinking up all those idiotic twists. How could I have been such a chump?

She didn't look at Riley. She toyed with her coffee cup instead. "I suppose I should go and pack, too," she said finally.

She knew he was watching her; he was sitting at an angle, one arm stretched over the high back of his chair, his long legs occupying a great deal of the space between her and the door. She thought for a moment that he wasn't going to answer, but finally he said, very quietly, "Deborah…"

She waited, but he didn't go on. Her nerves were stretched as taut as violin strings. She gave Darlene Lassiter's diamond ring a tug and succeeded only in jamming her knuckle. She gritted her teeth and twisted the narrow band on her finger, and finally it slid free, leaving a patch of reddened, abused skin. She held the ring for a single tick of the clock and then dropped it into his hand. "Thanks for the loan," she said. "I don't think I've hurt it." It sounded a little sad, and she tried to recover with a laugh. "We never got to have our final climactic fight, after all."

He smiled, a little. She saw the corner of his mouth quirk, even though she wasn't looking straight at him. "That's just as well, don't you think?"

She nodded. "I suppose so. This way you can just tell everyone we fought it out over the telephone, or something. Whatever you like. It doesn't matter." She bit her lip and looked down at her now bare hand, holding the edge of the table, waiting for him to go.

But he did not leave. Instead, his hand slipped from the back of his chair to the nape of her neck, and pulled her ever so gently towards him. By the time she realised his intention, it was too late; she could not stand up or lean away or even turn her head at all. All she could do was raise a hand and spread it across his chest, directly over the strong beat of his heart. "Please," she whispered, and he let her go.

Instantly, she regretted stopping him. Surely there would have been nothing so very wrong with allowing him to kiss her goodbye. She could have had one last warm, strong caress to tuck into her heart. But it was safer this way, she knew, for probably it would not have been the lover's kiss she craved, but a cousin's, and that would have been a memory to haunt her.

She walked with him to the front door, silently. On the terrace, in the brilliant sunshine that had burned away the morning's dull greyness, he said, "See you around, kid."

"Of course," she said, trying to sound casual. "We're family. Call me next time you come to Chicago."

"I'll do that." He flicked a careless finger across her cheek and down the line of her jaw. Then he was gone.

At the bottom of the hill, he stopped and turned, and automatically she raised an arm to wave to him. Her chest seemed to constrict, and her breath came in gasps. If I call to him, she thought, will he hear me? Will he come back? Is he having second thoughts about leaving me?

But it was not at her that he was looking, and he did not see her wave. Someone else had hailed him, then came down the street and dropped into step with him—a small figure with white-gold hair. Alec, she thought, and her arm dropped to her side as if the muscles had been cut. The man and the boy went out of sight beneath the trees, absorbed in conversation. Whatever they were talking about, Deborah knew, she had no part in it. She had already been forgotten.

She went back into Lassiter House and up the stairs to the guest room to pack her bags.

CHICAGO'S MAGNIFICENT MILE—the mad bustle of pedestrians surging in waves down the pavements, the constant roar of traffic on North Michigan Avenue, the distant wail of a dozen sirens scurrying in all directions. Once not so very long ago the city's busy roar had been Deborah's lifeblood. Now the packs of pedestrians gave her claustrophobia, and the noxious fumes of the cars and buses choked her, and the sirens made her head ache.

The Ainsley Gallery was quiet and peaceful, still a haven for the art lover, though it no longer was for the owner. She was honest enough to admit, however, that it was not the gallery, or the city that had changed; it was Deborah herself. And she knew that with one small change, she could again be very happy here. One very small addition, really, she thought. All it would take was six feet of masculinity, with rumpled reddish-brown hair and a dancing smile.

When the discreet doorbell sounded, Deborah stopped contemplating the calendar spread open on her desk—it had been a mere three weeks since she came back from Summerset, not the six months it seemed—and went out to greet the client who had just come in. Her first glimpse of him brought a tiny smile to her face. "Hi, Daddy," she said. "Happy birthday."

William Ainsley straightened from his inspection of a pastel sketch of a sailboat on Lake Michigan. "Don't remind me," he said with mock grumpiness. Then he pointed at the pastel. "Tell me about the artist."

Deborah glanced at it, and frowned. "I can't," she said, a bit puzzled. "I've never seen that piece before."

Peggy had just come out of the stockroom at the back of the gallery, wrestling with a large flat box. "Actually Deborah," she began hesitantly, "I took that on consignment while you were gone, and..."

Deborah gave her a long, thoughtful stare.

"The papers are on your desk," Peggy offered.

"It's beautiful," Deborah said. It's a good thing someone's minding the gallery, she thought. I haven't been doing a very attentive job of it.

Peggy's face lit. "I was afraid..." She stopped, as if thinking better of it. "This box just came for you. It's from Summerset."

From Summerset. For an instant Deborah's heart soared, and then she crashed back into reality. What was I hoping for, anyway? she asked herself cynically. A raspberry puff pastry, fresh from Riley's own hands?

The box was from Ruth Chastain instead, and it was heavy. Deborah carried it back to her office and opened it with a feeling of foreboding; three weeks wasn't much time for the woman to have produced this volume of work, and if it turned out to be less than good...

"I suppose you'll still accept my check," William said, following her into the office.

"With the proper identification," Deborah teased. She looked over her shoulder at Peggy, still in the gallery taking down the pastel. "Did you buy the sailboat? Daddy, you're addicted."

He shrugged. "A birthday gift to myself. What have you

got there?" He looked at the top watercolour—a little boy running down the street with his dog—with a reverent whistle. "That's superb. You've got enough there for a show, haven't you?"

"Yes," Deborah said thoughtfully. "I need to talk to Ruth about that, soon. I'm glad you like it. I've got one of her paintings set aside for you, for your birthday. Shall I take you out to dinner tonight and present it?"

"Oh." He sounded ill-at-ease. "I'm sorry, darling. I've already made plans. We're going to the Art Institute to see the new architecture show, but if you'd like to come along, I'm sure Peggy wouldn't mind."

Peggy? It should have been a surprise, but somehow it wasn't. William had been dropping into the gallery more often lately, and now that Deborah stopped to think about it, he and Peggy had seemed to get along rather well.

"I get lonely," he confessed softly. "Deborah, it's not as if I want her to take your mother's place, but—"

Deborah smiled. "Mother would," she said softly. "She'd be cheering you on."

William coloured a little. "I am sorry about not thinking of you, though," he said. "I just assumed...but you're not seeing as much of Bristol lately, are you?"

"I'm not seeing him at all," Deborah said crisply. "When he finally realised that I really had gotten myself into a completely fake engagement, he seemed to think I was incredibly loose, or perhaps just a fool, or an adventurer of the worst description.... I'm not sure what he believed—he couldn't seem to make up his mind. I must admit I didn't try very hard to convince him otherwise."

"I'm glad," William said simply. "He was never right for you."

"I only wonder why I couldn't see that," Deborah murmured.

But she knew, and long after her father had gone back to the foundation and the morning edged on towards noon, she was still thinking about it. Bristol's solid reliability had been just what she was looking for after those tumultuous months with Morgan. He had filled a gap in her life, and he had helped her to heal. Then that very same solid reliability threatened to choke her.

There has to be a happy middle ground, she thought. I want to know where I'm going, yes, but not if the price is having to give up all flexibility about how to get there. I want a certain amount of material comfort, but not at the cost of giving up my peace of mind. I want stability, but not if I have to give up the freedom to laugh at the world.

I want Riley, that's the bottom line, she admitted. And it hurts worse than any ache I have ever experienced to know that I cannot have him.

It was not getting better; three weeks without him had not made the desires fade. And three years won't, either, she told herself firmly, so you might just as well get down to work. You've got a great deal to do here.

She picked up the watercolour of the little boy and the dog. William was right; when all the paintings were framed and ready to hang, there would be enough for a show, and it would be time to introduce Ruth Chastain to the public. The trick, it was becoming apparent, was not going to be in getting Ruth to work to her capacity, but in properly marketing her, and in convincing her to promote herself. Deborah could already predict the answer if she was to call Ruth and ask her to come to Chicago for a show. The woman would have all kinds of excuses. It would be much easier to deal with Ruth's fear and her lack of self-confidence if they were face-to-face.

But the only way to do that just now was for Deborah

to go back to Summerset. And that would probably mean that she would have to face Riley.

But wasn't that inevitable, whether she ever set foot in Summerset again? she asked herself. Sooner or later, Riley was bound to come back to Chicago. He would call her; she had, after all, invited him to do that. Or, worse, he might simply drop in at the gallery unannounced. It would be the cousinly thing to do, after all.

And when that day comes, she told herself, you'll have to be polite and friendly and casual, without warning and without a chance to practise your family-reunion smile in your mirror. Wouldn't it be better to get it over with on your own terms? It will get easier after the first time.

She sat at her desk for a long time and thought about it. Then she pushed all the unfinished business into the top drawer, went back to her apartment and packed an overnight bag, and started out for Summerset.

SHE ALMOST TURNED back a half dozen times on the long drive, and even at the front entrance of the restaurant she nearly seized the Jaguar's keys back from the parking valet's hand.

Don't be ridiculous, she lectured herself. You're here to see Ruth, remember? Anyone— she paused and rephrased it sternly—anything else is incidental.

She squared her shoulders and went in. The blonde hostess was nowhere to be seen; Riley himself was in the foyer, studying the delicate drawing of a trumpet vine with what looked like scholarly contemplation. He turned to greet her with a professional smile that froze when he saw her.

Her heart seemed to settle down against her diaphragm with a thud. That, she thought, is not how I would have looked at him if he had walked unexpectedly through the door of the gallery. My reaction would have been much warmer, and ever so much more embarrassing.

Riley had recovered himself. "This is a surprise."

And not a particularly pleasant one, he seemed to imply. "I'm here on business." Her voice was huskier than she would have liked, but he didn't seem to notice. Why should he, after all? "Not business with you," she added too hastily.

"Of course not." There was an edge of ice in his voice.

"I'm sorry. I didn't mean it to sound that way. I came in to have dinner, actually."

For a moment she thought he was going to throw her out bodily, if only he could bear to bring himself to touch her. Then he reached for a leather-covered menu from the stack and asked quietly, "Will you be alone?"

Unless you'll join me... Despite it all, the invitation hovered on her lips. Finally sanity returned and she said, "Yes, I'll be alone. I'd like to have Ruth as my waitress if I could."

He had turned to lead her into the dining room, but he stopped abruptly in the doorway. Deborah, who had closed her eyes momentarily in an effort to keep the tears from forming, bumped into him and had to grab for his arm to steady herself. The scent of him, clean and fresh and masculine, tugged at her senses, and she gritted her teeth against the pain that slashed through her.

"She's not here tonight," Riley said. "She's taking a week off to paint her house."

"Her house?" Deborah said blankly.

There was a brief pause. "She said she was painting. So I assumed... But if you're here to see her on business, I gather she's not redecorating her living room, after all."

Deborah tried to laugh. "She'd better not be."

He looked down at her for a full minute. Finally,

Deborah realised that her hand was still braced against his arm.

She withdrew it hastily. "I don't think I'll come in after all."

He put the menu back. "As you wish." It was formal, polite.

There was nothing more to say. She started down the slightly angled ramp to the main entrance. She glanced back when she reached the door, cursing her own foolishness even as she did it—if he was watching her, it would only be to make certain she was gone. But he had already retreated to the dining room.

She glanced at the outer door, and then at the dark flight of stairs, and before she realised that she had made a decision, she found herself on the dimly lit landing just outside his apartment, almost out of breath, hoping that the sound of her feet on the stair treads had not echoed down throughout the building.

Downstairs, the massive main door closed with a thud. If anyone looks up, they'll see me, she thought, and she twisted the knob and slid into Riley's apartment with a sense of relief that lasted just over three seconds.

Then she leaned against the door and said under her breath, "You fool. Just how do you think you're going to creep back downstairs, with people coming and going all the time?"

Why had she come up here, anyway? Certainly it wasn't because she was embarrassed at having to ask the valet to return a car he had parked just moments ago!

She leaned her head against the door and sighed. She knew, of course, what had brought her here. With Riley fully occupied in the restaurant, she could sneak into his house for just a moment. It would be the last time she would ever step inside these four walls. She could stand here and feel his presence; she could soak up the quiet atmosphere. And perhaps she could begin to let go of the memories.

She pushed herself away from the door and walked cautiously across the room. The only light was the dim glow of street lamps reflected from far below. The only sound was the hum of the mechanical system. The building was too big and too well built for the laughter and conversation from the restaurant to find its way up here.

The apartment was quiet; it was full of his presence. But it was not peaceful—not for her. The feelings that she had hoped would lessen were not only still here, as if trapped in the very air of the room, but they seemed to have grown stronger with a few weeks' absence—the memories of his firm strength as he had held her, of the tender experiment of their first kiss, of how much she had wanted him to make love to her on that last night...

The sound of the doorknob turning froze her to the floor in the shadows, and she braced herself for the sudden flooding of light, and the questions, perhaps the accusations, that would follow.

But the light didn't come. The door closed, and Riley crossed the room in darkness, his step sure and firm as if he knew every square inch of the floor. An overstuffed chair yielded a tiny squawk of protest as he dropped into it, his hand over his eyes.

Deborah had to stifle a sudden, hysterical giggle. It's become a Laurel and Hardy skit, she thought frantically. Or a scene out of a situation comedy. What am I supposed to do now? Drop to my knees and crawl frantically for the door?

"I wish I knew what you were thinking." It was quiet, as if he was talking more to himself than to her. For an instant she was absolutely still; Riley's hand moved to the lamp beside his chair, and a pool of golden light sprang into life.

"How did you know I was here?" she parried.

"You make a lovely silhouette against the windows."

She gathered her dignity. "I shouldn't have trespassed. I'm sorry, Riley."

"Why did you come back here, anyway? Is there something you think you left undone? Or were you just playing Miss Manners and checking to be certain I'd returned all those gifts? Oh, I've got it—the engagement party wasn't enough of a practical joke, so you sneaked in and filled my bathtub with strawberry gelatin, right?"

She cringed at the harshness, for she could not understand his anger. "Riley, please..." she whispered.

"When you came in tonight, I thought..." He broke off and leaped up from his chair to pace across to the windows. "Why the hell did you come here, Deborah?" he asked sharply. "Ruth has a telephone. You know where she lives. If you hate the sight of me so much, why did you bother to come here at all?"

"Hate?" The denial came automatically. "I don't hate the sight of you."

"You seemed to think I was going to drag you back to the kitchen and use you to sharpen knives! You couldn't get out of the restaurant fast enough, and yet I find you up here. Why did you run up here?" he asked. "Aren't you afraid of what I might do?"

She shook her head. "Of course not. You don't have it in you to be violent, Riley. How did you know I was here, anyway? You did know, or you wouldn't have come upstairs at all."

"The valet said you hadn't come outside."

He had followed her, she thought blankly. But he had gone back into the dining room.

"That left this as the only place you could have gone. Does that frighten you even more, to know that I would have chased you down the street?"

"No," she whispered. "But why did you change your mind?"

He sighed heavily. "Because I couldn't let you go like that. Afraid of me."

Something was quivering deep inside her, a newborn hope so fragile that she was afraid to move, afraid to breathe, for fear of crushing it. "What did you mean..." She hardly recognised her own voice because the force of the blood pounding in her ears distorted it so. "Riley, what *did* you think tonight, when I came in?"

For a moment she believed he wasn't going to answer. He stared out the window, one hand braced against the glass. "I thought you might have come because you wanted to see me," he said in a voice so low that she almost couldn't hear. "Because...maybe...you missed me."

Her heart was skittering at such a rate that she couldn't get her breath. "I came because there is something here I want." She steadied her voice as best she could. "You."

He scowled. "That's not funny, Deborah."

"I didn't say it was." She moved very cautiously across the room until she stood behind the overstuffed couch; her fingers dug gratefully into the softly upholstered back, helping to take the strain off her shaking knees. "The practical joke turned itself inside out, Riley. I got caught in it. I fell in love."

She saw something flare in his eyes, something that looked liked fear, and it sent chills through her. My God, she thought, have I gone too far? Telling him I love him? I should not have said that, not yet.

No, she told herself. There is no room now for anything

but the truth. No matter how badly it hurts, and no matter how it ends, there is no other way. I have to know, that's all. And if the answer is the worst, then I'll have to deal with that. But at least I'll know...."

"I love you," she said quietly. "I'm sorry if you don't want to hear that, but it's true. And I just need to know if there's a place for me in your life. I don't know what you wanted to say to me downstairs...."

"Don't you?" There was something in his voice that was almost a tremor.

She looked down at her hands, and she didn't see him moving quietly toward her. "But if you missed me, too, and if you want me, I'll stay."

He was at her side. "I did. And I do."

The words almost echoed in the still room, and she wondered if he realised how very much like a vow they sounded. It hurt to know how desperately she wanted him to mean just that, and so she said, quickly and uncomfortably, "It doesn't have to be permanent, Riley."

"Yes, it does." It was uncompromising, as firm as his arms around her. "Very permanent," he said. "Just you and me, Deb."

She released a long, shivery breath, and his mouth came down against hers with an almost hungry urgency, as if he was seeking solace for a soul-deep pain. And since she could not answer him with words, she pressed herself against him and tried to tell him with her body how very glad she would be.

"You'll marry me," he said against the corner of her mouth.

She blinked slowly, and tried to pull herself out of the pleasant fog he had so skillfully induced. "You said there wasn't enough money in the world to make you marry me," she reminded.

He smiled down into her eyes. "I changed my mind," he said gently, and began to kiss her again, concentrating this time on the tender skin of her temple.

The blunt statement jolted her. When he'd said that, she remembered, it had looked as if her trust fund was going to vanish without a trace. But now that the money was safe—did it make a difference? Was that why he wanted permanence, with a marriage licence to ensure it?

She twisted uncomfortably in his arms, and he stopped kissing her. "A dowry is such a civilised custom," he murmured.

She pulled away from him. Misery was starting to rise in a wave, threatening to choke her.

Riley sat down on the couch and tugged her onto his lap. "Debbie, you little fool!" he said fiercely into her ear. "What I said was, no amount of money was enough to make me marry you."

"Isn't that the same thing?" she said uncertainly.

"Not at all." He captured a glossy brown curl and began to wrap it slowly around his finger, drawing her face nearer to his with each revolution. "How much cash have you got in your pockets?"

"What's it to you? About ten dollars, I suppose."

He raised one eyebrow. "It's mere curiosity, but how were you planning to pay for your dinner?"

She said stiffly, "I have a credit card. I left home in a hurry." She stopped abruptly.

He smiled a little. "I see."

She thought, vengefully, that all of a sudden he was seeing a great deal too much. He saw, for instance, that no matter what his reasons, she was too deeply in love to care.

"In any case," he said cheerfully, "ten dollars is plenty.

I'll marry you for it. And if you only had two cents, that would be enough, too."

Her nose was almost against his. "Oh," she said softly. "You mean that no amount of money—"

"Would make me marry you. Because money has nothing to do with it. Now will you marry me? Or do you have some general distaste for the state of matrimony that we need to deal with first?"

She would have answered him. But it was impossible to talk when she was being kissed with such skill, and such zeal. And in any case, she thought he probably already knew what she would have said.

It was a long time later that she recovered the power of speech. She was sitting beside him by then, with her head nestled against his shoulder and his arm around her. He was toying with her hair as if he still couldn't quite make himself believe that she was real.

"What if I hadn't come back?" she said finally.

"Well, I wasn't dim enough to sit back and wait for Ida's funeral—that's assuming she has one someday—in the hope that you'd show up to pay your respects. In fact, if you'd like to look at the reservations calendar downstairs you'll see that I've reserved myself all of next week to spend in Chicago."

"Really?"

"Yes. I was hoping that you'd had a chance to miss me, and I was going to do some serious stalking."

She sighed. "I missed you, all right. I'd probably have thrown myself into your arms the minute you showed up."

"Hmm. Perhaps in that case you should have waited for me. It would have been much tidier than this method." But the way he smiled at her made her heart turn over.

"When did you know?" she asked softly.

"That you were going to be the bane of my life again, in a different sort of way?"

She wrinkled her nose at him.

"Sorry," Riley said quickly. "I meant to say, when did I fall in love with you? At breakfast that first morning, I think. I'm absolutely certain I was past saving by dinner that night. The very idea of Bristol Wellington the fifth set my teeth on edge." He drew them along her index finger, as if to prove the point. "And then when you came up with the engagement scheme—"

She sighed. "Not the most brilliant thing I've ever done."

"Oh, I don't know about that. My life just sort of flashed in front of my eyes at that moment."

"You said you didn't want a fiancée," she reminded.

He smiled at her lovingly, and kissed the tip of her nose. "Not a fake one, that's for certain."

"So when you said you had dreams about me in a wedding gown and veil, and things like that—"

"Not a gown," he pointed out. "It was just a veil—and nothing else."

That sent shivers of pleasure up her spine. "Talking of wedding gowns reminds me," she said reluctantly. "We should call Aunt Ida. She's probably already heard from the grapevine that I'm in town."

"Does that mean you're not staying with her?"

Deborah said carefully, "I haven't arranged to do that, no."

He smiled very slowly. "I see. Well, let's not bother her tonight. She'd only start on wedding plans again." He began to nibble at her ear.

"We could elope," she said on a tiny breathless gasp.

"No...we'd better give the party ourselves, or Mary Beth will surprise us with one, and I don't think I could take another one of those." He picked up her hand. "I'm sorry, darling, but I don't have your ring yet. I was going to buy it in Chicago. Only a masochist buys a diamond ring in a town the size of Summerset unless he's quite sure of the answer he's going to get."

She had to smile at that, but she said, "A new ring? I'd much rather have your grandmother's diamond back."

"Are you certain?" It was softly surprised. "But it looked awfully tiny. I'd like to put a whopping big diamond here." He stroked the base of her finger.

She nodded firmly. "I'm certain."

"All right. I'll have the band resized tomorrow, but in the meantime, at least you can look at it." He dug the old velvet box out of his pocket.

"You've been carrying it?"

He admitted unsteadily, "It seemed to bring you closer, somehow."

She snuggled against him, took the ring out of the box and turned it under the light, watching the stone. In the lamplight the diamond seemed brighter, even perhaps more lively, than it had been before. As if it, too, was happy.

The light caught on the engraving inside the band. She tipped it so she could see better, and almost dropped the ring. "Riley, it's our initials!"

He shook his head. "You never looked at it before?"

"I couldn't get it off, remember? It's right there: *D.A. and R.L.*"

"Her name was Darlene Anderson—his was Roger Lassiter."

"It's perfect," she whispered. "And it also says *Forever Yours*."

"Remember that," he said, and gathered her close again. "Because this is forever ours, Debbie darling. We're all finished with temporary measures."

**Helen Brooks** lives in Northamptonshire and is married with three children. As she is a committed Christian, busy housewife and mother, her spare time is at a premium but her hobbies include reading, swimming, gardening and walking her two energetic, inquisitive and very endearing young dogs. Her long-cherished aspiration to write became a reality when she put pen to paper on reaching the age of forty, and sent the result off to Mills & Boon®.

# *AND THE BRIDE WORE BLACK*

by

HELEN BROOKS

# CHAPTER ONE

'Now I'm sure if we'd met before I wouldn't have forgotten.'

As the narrowed tawny eyes swept over her in warm appraisal Fabia had the strangest desire to bare her small white teeth in a snarl like a tigress objecting to a proposed mating.

'No...' As the hard, penetrating gaze came to rest on the dark gold silk of her hair the tall, beautifully dressed man in front of her shook his head slowly. 'I definitely wouldn't have forgotten.' He smiled a slow, predatory smile.

She had felt in her bones that this would happen! History had a macabre way of repeating itself at times! Why, oh, why had she been foolish enough to let Joanie persuade her to come here? He waited a moment for her to speak and then gently lifted her small chin with cool, experienced fingers, bringing her violet-blue eyes up to meet his amused gaze. 'Does the vision talk?' he asked mockingly.

It was in that moment of frustrated anger and embarrassment that the idea was born and, once given life, there was no stopping it. 'Well, landsakes, sure I do, honey...' She forced her normally clear warm voice into a harsh nasal twang, taking the accent of a Southern belle, the tone a good few decibels louder than normal. 'Mary-Lou Dixon at your service, honeychild, and I do mean service...'

She saw the shock register for a brief moment in the handsome face and then he recovered magnificently, taking the hand she held out to him with practised ease. 'Are you with anyone?' he asked politely. 'I didn't see—'

She interrupted him archly with a high, shrill little giggle, fluttering her thick eyelashes with an obviously flirtatious flick of her head. 'Well, sweetiepie, ya surely don' think little ole me would be runnin' around alone, now? Snakes alive!' She giggled again, squeezing his hand meaningfully and ignoring his attempts to retrieve it. 'My pa'd be madder than a pig in a poke!'

'Quite...' The unusual gold-flecked eyes had a slightly dazed glaze to them now and she saw him turn his head warily, glancing round the crowded room in hopes of rescue.

Not yet, mister, she thought determinedly, biting back the laughter with difficulty. You're going to squirm for a bit longer yet. 'Now ah just know ya wanna hear all about little ole me...'

She was still holding his hand and he seemed to have resigned himself to the fact that he was well and truly button-holed, for the moment.

'Now do ya know much about the deep South, honey?' she asked loudly as she pulled herself into his side, taking his arm in a way that suggested they had known each other for a good deal longer than two minutes.

'I'm afraid not,' he said quietly, the polite smile stitched on his face with noble fortitude.

Thank goodness for that, she thought delightedly, drawing on all the old films she had seen for the next few minutes as she drew a graphic picture of spoilt, empty-headed women and dashing young men. It was hard work to keep the accent flowing but oh, so enjoyable, she thought silently, to fool such a self-satisfied male chauvinist pig!

She had slowly drawn even closer as she had talked, engineering herself into the circle of his arm so that she was standing side-on, and, just as she was deciding, reluctantly, that she really would have to let him go, she caught sight of a tall, slim brunette watching them with narrowed cat-like eyes, her beautiful face tight with irritation.

The girlfriend? Her mind raced. He had tried to make a move on her when his girlfriend was here? Pay-off time, Mr Cade, she thought coldly.

As the woman moved towards them, her motive clear, Fabia drawled to a halt, looking up into the closed stony face with a sweet little smile of satisfaction. He hadn't liked the last few minutes, he hadn't liked them at all. 'Well, ah mustn' keep ya from all ya other guests now...' She laughed prettily. 'But before ya go, honeychild...' She had reached up and drawn the amazed face down to hers before he realised what was happening, taking his lips in a firm kiss that to anyone watching looked most enjoyable. 'To thank you for such a truly lovely party,' she murmured as she let him go just as the woman reached their sides.

'Alex?' She left them to it as the amusement that was bubbling to the surface threatened to overflow. She couldn't believe he had swallowed the outrageous parody so completely, but then, she reflected thoughtfully, in the world of mindless lackeys and shameless sycophants that he inhabited she doubted if anyone had ever tried to actually *repel* the great man!

Alexander Cade. Her lip curled as she thought of his name. Millionaire a hundred times over, playboy extraordinaire with film-star good looks and a lifestyle to match. She pictured the tall, muscled body clothed immaculately in the best that money could buy, the long—unusually long—rich, shining brown hair cut expertly to lie into his neck in a style that might look effeminate on the average man but on him merely served to emphasise the slanted tawny eyes, straight nose and hard square jaw.

'Handsome you might be but you don't do a thing for me,' she muttered to the tall figure across the far side of the room standing with his back towards her, probably, she suspected gleefully, because he was terrified of catching her eye again. 'And I haven't finished with you yet, Mr Cade, not by a long chalk!'

'Talking to yourself, Fabia?' Joanie's soft brown eyes were crinkled with laughter as she tapped her friend on the shoulder. 'I know you didn't want to come tonight but there must be someone in all this lot to catch your fancy?' She waved expansively at the huge ballroom.

'You must be joking!' Fabia's deep midnight-blue eyes were scathing and Joanie gave a little sigh of resignation. 'And where have you been anyway? You've missed all the fun.'

'Fun?' Joanie's plump face expressed her bewilderment. 'What fun? And I've been in the loo for half an hour. I should never have had that seafood in the nurses' dining-room at lunchtime.'

'Oh, Joanie.' Fabia smiled with a mixture of affection and annoyance at the woebegone expression on Joanie's face. She loved this friend dearly but at times she was sure she had been sent to this earth with the express purpose of providing her life with a little extra turmoil and irritation—like dragging her to this function tonight, for instance.

They had met in their teens when doing A levels at college, Joanie going on to fulfil her ambition to take up nursing and Fabia carving out a promising career in the world of advertising. The first tenuous thread of friendship had developed into a strong supportive bond that neither wished to break, and whenever either one needed assistance it was immediately given, no questions asked. Like tonight, Fabia thought again grimly, but this time Joanie had had no idea what she was asking.

'What fun, anyway?' Joanie repeated interestedly, catching the gleam of devilment in her friend's eyes with a slight feeling of apprehension. Many years of friendship had taught her that Fabia could be a force to be reckoned with. 'What have you done now?'

'Well, you did say if I came and stayed for a couple of hours you'd be satisfied, didn't you?' Fabia said lightly. 'Well—I have and I will, but how I spend that couple of hours is down to me, right?' She smiled sweetly.

'Fabia, I know that look. What have you done?' There was definite anxiety in Joanie's plain face now and Fabia couldn't resist a wicked chuckle at the undisguised panic in her friend's eyes.

'Nothing much,' she answered quietly. 'Just had a little chat with the great Alexander Cade himself. I mean, the whole point in coming to this fiasco was to gaze adoringly at him, wasn't it?'

'Oh, shut up.' Joanie poked her sharply as her plump face turned pink. 'I only wanted to see what he looked like in the flesh, and all these other famous people too. It's one thing to read about them in the papers but quite another to see them face to face.'

'It sure is,' Fabia said disparagingly, glancing round the room with a blatant look of disgust marring her beautiful face. 'I've never seen such a collection of painted dolls in one place, and that's just the men!'

'Oh, you...' Joanie's voice died away as she remembered the original start of the conversation. 'What happened, anyway? Did he really talk to you? Oh, Fabia, I wish it were me. Still, I knew no one would take any notice of me, not in this crowd. They're all so—'

'Pathetic!' Fabia cut in savagely. 'Don't run yourself down, Joanie; you'd make ten of any of these clowns.

Can't you see what these people are like, for goodness' sake? Open your eyes for a minute and wipe the stardust out. Most of them are weak and shallow and totally selfish. They aren't fit to wipe your boots.'

'But they're all so beautiful,' Joanie said wistfully, glancing down at her small heavily boned figure with a gesture of longing. 'And slim.'

'Scrawny, half of them,' Fabia returned scornfully.

'Well, it's all right for you,' Joanie said quietly without a trace of jealousy in her voice as she glanced at Fabia's tall, slender shape topped by the mass of long thick blonde hair and vivid blue eyes set like jewels in a flawless skin. 'You'd knock any one of the women here into a cocked hat. Alexander Cade knew that. I bet—'

'Joanie—'

Fabia's concerned voice was cut off as Joanie tapped her on the cheek affectionately. 'Don't worry, I'm not depressing myself, just stating facts. And I do appreciate your coming tonight. I know you didn't want to and I know you'll probably hate every minute but I so wanted to be at something like this just once. When Dr Campbell gave me the tickets after his wife got ill it was like the chance of a lifetime.'

'Well, we couldn't have afforded them,' Fabia agreed wryly. 'What charity is the great Cade donating to anyway?'

'Cancer research,' Joanie said soberly, 'and they sure need it. Anyway—' she gave a little shake of her plump body '—come on, spill the beans, what's happened?'

Her good-natured face got straighter and straighter as Fabia recounted the little episode, until her brown eyes were wide with horror. 'Don't say, it Joanie,' Fabia said warningly as she finished the account. 'I know I shouldn't have, but it was too good to resist. I shall have to keep it up now, of course,' she added with an innocent smile. 'Must be consistent.'

'Fabia, there are times—'

'Stand back and watch me in action.' Before Joanie could stop her Fabia was on her way across the room to where Alexander Cade was deep in conversation with a somewhat austere-looking elderly man, who had an even more severe-looking woman who was clearly his wife by his side. They glanced up as she reached their side and she had to admire Alexander Cade's self-control. She knew he had been avoiding her since their first encounter and she knew she was unwelcome, but he didn't betray his thoughts for a moment.

'Well, hello again,' he said warily, his smile cool as he looked directly into her eyes, and Fabia registered a slight jolt as the full power of that cold tawny gaze swept over her. 'I hope you are enjoying yourself, Miss Dixon?'

'Sure am, honey, but what's with the "Miss Dixon"?' she drawled playfully with a little roguish wink at the dour-faced couple by his side. 'He's a fast mover, this guy,' she continued knowingly as she placed a light hand on the woman's thin arm. 'Just been introduced and he's takin' honey from the flower, but I sure ain't complainin'.' She let her eyes wander over the strong-muscled body saucily, taking care not to meet his eyes which she knew were cold points of steel in the furious face. 'This sure is one hell of a bee.'

'Well, really!' The woman's outraged murmur of disgust was plainly audible to those about them and she caught one or two interested glances in their direction as she became aware of Joanie sidling round to stand in the background. See what a fool he is, Joanie, she thought bitterly to herself, see what fools they all are! His type were all the same, as she had good cause to know. A pretty face and they were into action like stud stallions!

But not this time, Mr Cade! Her eyelashes fluttered pertly as she turned to leave. 'Ah must leave ya for a minute, honey-pie,' she murmured slowly into the pregnant silence, 'but don' ya go flirtin' with no more of the girls, ya hear?' She reached up and kissed the edge of the hard mouth before he had time to resist.

'Who is that woman?' The man's clipped voice didn't make any effort to speak quietly and as Joanie took her arm and hurried her away Fabia saw that her friend's eyes were wet with laughter.

'Fabia, you're priceless, but I shouldn't laugh really. What if he ever finds out?'

'Well, he won't, will he?' Fabia said coolly with a little grin. 'We're hardly likely to ever get an invitation to anything like this again!'

'No, I guess not.' Joanie looked longingly at the laden tables of food at one end of the vast ballroom. 'Ready for something to eat?'

'Come on, then,' Fabia said indulgently.

She found to her surprise that she quite enjoyed the rest of the evening. Joanie had to make several trips to the loo but apart from that slight inconvenience the two girls appreciated every moment of the excellent floor-show that had been organised, one singer in particular having a pure, sweet quality to her voice that Fabia could have listened to for hours. She had to admit the deception with Alexander Cade have given her a terrific boost, although she wouldn't probe her feelings beyond that. The whys and wherefores were in the past and best left there.

When the party finally began to break up Fabia contemplated one last attack on the hapless Mr Cade and then decided, albeit reluctantly, that enough was enough. There had been something in that dark gold gaze that she had found disconcerting, and anyway, one thing was sure: he certainly wouldn't forget her in a hurry! She gave a small secretive smile as the thickly carpeted lift whisked her and Joanie and a few other guests down into the discreetly elegant foyer of the sumptuous hotel.

'Could I just make one last visit before the taxi comes? That seafood doesn't want to say die...' Joanie shot off before Fabia could reply and with a little sigh she seated herself in one of the huge soft silk-upholstered chairs that were dotted about the reception area, kicking off her shoes and stretching her toes with a small sigh. This was the sort of place Robin had taken her to. She brought herself upright with a small jerk. Don't think of him, Fabia, she told herself angrily. You haven't wasted a thought on him in months; don't start now! It was because she was tired, she thought grimly, tired and in the sort of place that brought back a host of unwelcome memories.

She heard the man fall before she saw him, the sound of a body hitting the carpet with a dull thud at the same time as a piercing shriek cut through the hushed atmosphere. 'Billy! Oh, Billy! Someone do something, somebody help him.' As the last word died away she had reached the side of the elderly couple who had just come out of the lift, pushing aside the small plump woman who was kneeling by the side of her equally small plump husband. His face was a ghastly caricature of pain, bulbous eyes distended and skin stretched tight over his red face as he gasped for breath.

It looked as though his wife was going into full-blown hysterics and Fabia glanced round quickly at the crowd of interested onlookers that was gathering as she fumbled with his tie. 'Is there a doctor here? Does anyone know how to deal with a heart attack?' Blank silence met her clear sharp voice and, as the man beside her made another strangled gulp for air that ended in a deadly choking sound, she shouted across to the stunned receptionist who was frozen by her desk, 'Get an ambulance, and quickly!'

He had stopped breathing. As she looked down at the twisted face she was aware that all signs of life had stopped and without pausing to think she went into the emergency procedure she had practised so often with Joanie when her friend was taking her nursing examinations. Loosening his tie and ripping open his clothing, she hit down on to the smooth rounded mass of flesh as hard as she possibly could, hearing the gasp of shock from the crowd gathered round them through the ringing in her ears. The wife increased her screaming at the second blow to her husband's chest and Fabia spared a second to push her aside. 'Will you be quiet? You aren't helping.'

'You're killing him!' At the third blow the woman tried to drag Fabia from her husband's side and then through her concentration she was aware of someone holding the unfortunate woman out of range and talking to her in a deadly quiet voice. Whatever was said worked, as the screams were shut off as though by magic.

On the fifth blow there was a great intake of air from the supine figure and a mingled gasp of relief from the onlookers, who had entered into this battle of life or death wholeheartedly now. Fabia continued to crouch by his side without taking her eyes off his dazed face, talking to him in a low, reassuring tone as he struggled to survive. He stopped breathing once more before the ambulance crew arrived but this time only one hard punch was needed to jolt the reluctant heart into action again, and as they whisked him out to the ambulance one of the crew patted Fabia swiftly on the shoulder. 'Well, done, lass. It was lucky for him you were around.'

It was all over in a second, and as Fabia sank back on her heels into the ankle-deep carpet she was suddenly aware that her hand was throbbing as though she had thumped a brick wall and her head was pounding. 'Oh...' For a moment everything faded in a misty haze.

'OK, folks, the show's over.' As a pair of hard male hands grasped her under her arms, drawing her carefully to her feet, the attentive audience melted away and the vast room once again took on the refined subdued murmur that was customary in such elegant surroundings.

It wasn't until she had been lowered on to the edge of the chair she had vacated a few frantic minutes ago that Fabia rallied sufficiently to raise her eyes, realising that the same voice that had taken charge of the screaming wife so capably earlier was now taking charge of her.

She froze in horror as Alexander Cade stared back at her silently, his strange tawny eyes glittering with unholy fire and his dark face set in lines of deadly cold anger. 'Yours, I think?' As he dangled her shoes in front of her white face a screaming blackness caused her ears to ring and his shape to blur into a tall shadow, and although he moved quickly with a muttered oath he was too late to save her from sliding into a graceful heap at his feet in a dead faint.

'What did you do to her?' She came to in disorientated panic to hear Joanie's soft voice whispering seemingly in her ear. 'What on earth did you do to her?'

'I didn't do anything, you stupid girl.' She recognised the bitingly frosty voice immediately and gave a little groan as she remembered where she was. This was all she needed!

She opened dazed eyes to see Joanie's anxious face two inches from her own. 'Are you all right?'

'Of course she isn't all right.' Joanie was plucked from her vision and a large balloon glass of brandy held in front of her nose. 'Drink that.' The tone was uncompromisingly severe with not a trace of warmth in its arctic depths. 'Now.'

The neat alcohol burnt as it hit her stomach but its reviving power was immediate, and as the colour came back into her face she became aware that she was lying on a remarkably uncomfortable leather sofa in what she presumed was the manager's office.

'Can you sit up?' the hard voice asked coldly above her head.

'Perhaps she shouldn't, we don't know—'

'Look, Miss...?' The two words held intense irritation.

'Fletcher. Joanie Fletcher.' Fabia detected a tremor in Joanie's soft voice and her hackles rose immediately.

'Look, Miss Fletcher, your friend just rendered somewhat extreme first aid on a poor unfortunate man who had the temerity to have a heart attack in front of her, owing to which, among other things, I should think he now has several broken ribs to contend with. If you'd seen what I'd seen you wouldn't be at all surprised at her collapse. I think the man's wife will need psychiatric care for some considerable time—'

'You lying hound!' The fierce adrenalin pumping vigorously through her system banished the last remains of faintness as she swung her feet off the sofa and rose in one swift leap. 'How dare you? I—'

'How dare *I*?' The incredulous note in the icy voice checked her flow of words and as she gazed into the livid countenance towering above her Fabia knew a moment of pure stomach-twisting fear. 'You ask *me* how I dare?' Joanie moved silently to her side in unspoken support, her plump round face as white as a sheet and her hands stretched out imploringly.

'Mr Cade, this isn't what you think—'

He cut off Joanie's anxious voice with a sharply raised hand without taking his eyes off Fabia's face. 'Don't insult my intelligence with excuses, Miss Fletcher, and keep quiet. Do you understand?' The last three words were a bark and now Fabia pushed Joanie to one side as she moved directly in front of him, glaring defiantly right up into his face, while a small part of her mind wondered at this change in him. There was no trace of the elegant, laconic man who had been present all evening. The cool charmer, the enigmatic philanderer, all the things that made up Alexander Cade had disappeared and in their place was a dangerously angry man with blazing eyes and a hard cruel mouth. Why hadn't she noticed his mouth before? she thought faintly. Maybe that was more an indication of the real man than all the glossy camouflage? But no, she shook her head mentally. He was just mad at being made to look such a complete and utter fool. Which he was.

'Why the little charade all evening?' The grim voice was stiff now and she had the impression he was exercising great self-control in speaking quietly. 'What was the point of all that?'

For a brief second she thought about trying to placate him, offer him an excuse that would be more acceptable than the bald truth, and then her spirit rebelled against the deception. He might be the king-pin in his world but not in hers! Oh, no, not in hers, she thought furiously.

'Because I'm sick to death of your type of man, Mr Cade,' she said clearly, her voice firm and strong. 'You think your money can buy anything and anyone and you control your little empire like a big fat spider drawing people into your web. You are vain and you're selfish and probably over-sexed too! What did it feel like to be the hunted for a change? To be backed into a corner by someone who repulsed you? Fun, was it?'

He listened to her angry tirade with narrowed eyes and folded arms and strangely, in view of the insults she had just hurled at him, seemed calmer when she had finished than when she had begun. 'What was his name?' he asked softly when she paused for breath.

'What?' Unconsciously she took a step backwards, her

wide eyes darkening to midnight-blue and her breath catching in her throat. 'I don't know what you're talking about.'

'No?' He was smiling now, a cruel hard calculating smile, a smile that robbed her of speech and seemed to strip her bare until she had the crazy notion he could read her mind. 'I think you do. And I was his substitute, eh? A nice convenient deputy ready to hand whom you could vent your venom on and make a laughing-stock of.'

'Look, no one knows, Mr Cade.' Joanie came back into the conversation after one glance at Fabia's white, shocked face.

'*I* know!' The words were an explosion of the fury he was keeping in check and Fabia flinched instinctively as she took another step backwards. What had she done? What *had* she done? 'You're going to pay for this, my golden-haired little beauty.'

The words were low and soft but with such acrimony in their depths that she shuddered as a shiver snaked down her spine. He looked like one of the old Greek gods as he stood there in front of them, the harsh artificial light directly over his head catching the tawny gleam in his dark brown hair and turning his eyes to pure gold, his tanned skin and great height adding to the impression of a blazingly beautiful golden statue come to life with a mission of revenge and destruction. He was...terrifying.

'Oh, I feel sick...' As Joanie slumped against her Fabia's arm instinctively reached out to support her. 'I've got to get to a loo again, Fabia.' She bowed her head helplessly.

'I don't believe this.' Alexander Cade's contemptuous voice bit through the air. 'What game are we playing now?'

'It's no game.' There was no mistaking the ring of truth in Fabia's indignant voice as she cradled Joanie in her arms. 'She's been ill on and off all night. She's a nurse, for goodness' sake. Don't you think when that man collapsed she would have helped if she hadn't been... indisposed? She—'

'All right, all right.' He waved his hand irritably. 'Help her to the ladies' powder-room but first...' He pressed a bell on the wall and immediately a small middle-aged man opened the door leading out into the reception hall, making Fabia think he had been listening outside. 'There you are, Swinton. Escort these...ladies to the powder-room and then wait outside so they won't get lost on the way back. OK?' His voice was icily controlled.

'OK, sir.' The man gave a quick nod, the ghost of a smile touching his lips as he turned to Fabia.

'And Swinton?'

'Yes, sir?'

'Tell the manager he can have his office back now. I won't be needing it any longer. These ladies are going to return upstairs.' The grim voice was chilling.

'Very good, sir.' Swinton gestured for them to follow him.

'You can't—' Fabia's furious voice was cut off as Joania moaned quietly by her side, her voice a soft whimper.

'Please...'

'OK, you're all right, don't worry.' All her attention was concentrated on Joanie as they left the room and she didn't even glance at the tall silent figure standing to one side of the doorway, his arms folded in silent scrutiny.

'Quick, Fabia!' As the door of the large and very luxurious powder-room closed behind them Joanie jerked herself off Fabia's arm and pulled her over to the row of pink shell-shaped washbasins lining one velvet-embossed wall. 'Come on.'

As Joanie lifted the hem of her shiny, sweetie-paper-style evening dress, exposing two rounded plump knees, Fabia stared at her in amazement.

'What on earth—?'

'Come on, you idiot! We haven't got much time.' With an agility that belied her stout build, her friend had climbed on to the veneered wood that supported the vanity unit before Fabia could blink, reaching up and loosening the catch to the narrow frosted window and peering outside carefully. 'I thought so. This leads into the yard where they keep the dustbins and there's a side door at one end into the street. *Come on*, Fabia!'

'You aren't seriously thinking of climbing through that little thing, are you?' Fabia looked up into Joanie's flushed face in horror. 'And I thought you felt ill?'

'And I thought I was supposed to be the dim one,' Joanie muttered irritably. 'Face facts, Fabia. There's a man out there who's loaded like a lethal weapon and he's definitely gunning for you. Now you can try sweet reason on him but I wouldn't give much for your chances.' Fabia pictured the narrowed cat-like eyes and cruel mouth and nodded slowly. 'The only other alternative as I see it is to remove the target from the firing-range.'

'You mean run away,' Fabia said flatly.

'I *mean*,' Joanie took a deep breath that vibrated with impatience, 'that just for once you should admit you're in a situation you can't handle and do the sensible thing. He's got more clout than a field full of turnips!' Fabia reflected wryly that in moments of extreme stress Joanie's country upbringing became more obvious. 'You can't beat him so let's make a dignified retreat!'

'Dignified?' Fabia stared aghast at the small window. 'And what if someone comes in?'

'Someone will in a minute,' Joanie said grimly, 'and he's about six feet four and hopping mad. Don't think about it, just take notice of me for once in your life, and *come on!*'

As Fabia joined Joanie in her precarious perch she had the insane urge to break into hysterical laughter. This wasn't at all how she had visualised finishing the evening, she reflected wryly, as she hoisted the soft blue silk of her evening dress about her waist, exposing the full length of her slim beautifully shaped legs to the blank gaze of the expensively ornate mirror opposite. 'Hang on a minute.' She jumped down again just as Joanie prepared to launch herself out of the window, and heard her friend's exasperated sigh as she rummaged frantically in her tiny evening-bag.

'What on earth are you doing, woman?' Joanie whispered nervously. 'You haven't got time to titivate.'

'I'm just leaving a little goodbye note,' she said softly as she wrote boldly on the clear glass with her lipstick. 'I don't want him to think I'm a complete chicken.'

'Who cares what he thinks?' Joanie muttered crossly. 'If you don't hurry up he'll be able to tell you himself.' She peered at what Fabia had written and groaned softly. 'There are times—'

'I know, I know.' Fabia climbed up beside her again and gave her a little nudge. 'Go on, then, be careful.' She heard a tiny muffled grunt as Joanie slid out of the window and then it was her turn. As the cold night air met her hot face a sense of adventure stirred her blood in a way it hadn't been stirred since she was a child. 'This is fun, isn't it?' she murmured as she landed beside Joanie against the brick wall. 'Cowboys and Indians!'

'Oh, wonderful,' Joanie said sarcastically as she glanced nervously around the small dark courtyard. 'And guess who'll end up with an arrow in her back if we're not careful!'

As they tiptoed across the shadowed and none too clean

yard Fabia found Joanie was gripping her arm tightly and glanced at her friend's set face as she patted her hand comfortingly. 'Don't worry, we're nearly home and dry.'

'You're enjoying this, aren't you?' Joanie accused softly. 'You're actually enjoying it.'

'I am rather,' Fabia agreed lightly, opening the bolted door into the narrow side-street and looking warily about her. The lights and traffic of the main thoroughfare a few yards away spelt safety and it was with a sense of anti-climax that she found herself hurrying, a few minutes later, along the brightly lit street and away from the hotel.

'Taxi!' As they collapsed into the back seat of the big London taxi Joanie leant back against the upholstered plastic with a small sigh, stretching her small plump legs wearily.

'What a night!'

'I thought you enjoyed it?' Fabia said cheerfully as she glanced at Joanie out of the corner of her eye. 'It made a change.'

'It did that all right.' Joanie's voice was loaded with feeling. 'And I'm dying for the loo again, and it's for real this time!'

It was an hour or two later as Fabia lay quietly in bed, hands behind her head and sleep a million miles away, that she felt the laughter that had been bubbling below the surface all evening begin to emerge as she pictured Alexander Cade's face when he saw the message she had scribbled on the mirror. 'Bye for now, sweet thing—catch ya later.' He wouldn't like it! She hugged herself as she giggled helplessly at the understatement. He wouldn't like it at all. To be made a fool of twice in the same evening; it would drive him crazy!

When the paroxysm of laughter had died away a slight feeling of disquiet took its place. How crazy would it drive him? Crazy enough to try and find her? She shook her head slowly, silky strands of corn-gold hair drifting across her face in a soft veil. It wouldn't matter if he did. He didn't even know her name. She relaxed again, snuggling further down under the duvet as she tried to empty her mind preparatory for sleep. She knew plenty about him; he was hardly ever out of the newspapers and glossy magazines with a different model-type girl gracing his arm, and no doubt his bed, each time. But he knew nothing about her. A smile touched her full pink lips as her eyelids grew heavy. And that was just the way she wanted it.

## CHAPTER TWO

THE radio was blaring forth a carol as Fabia whisked two eggs into fluffy lightness for the omelette she was preparing to accompany the solitary pork chop sizzling in its own juices under the grill.

The November day had a starkness that spoke of snow and it was the first of December tomorrow, two whole weeks since that eventful night. So why did her mind keep harping back to Alexander Cade? And why did everything seem so dull at the moment?

She glanced round the bright cheerful kitchen of her tiny flat. She had been so thrilled when she had first acquired this, a home of her own, five years ago. And she still was, really. It was just that... She paused in her thoughts. What was it exactly?

The doorbell interrupted her musing, chiming shrilly across the last chords of 'Once in Royal David's City', and she switched off the music as she went to answer the door. Not Brian again, she thought irritably as she glanced at her wristwatch. This was about the time her neighbour got home from work and lately he had intensified his relentless pursuit of her, her snubs sliding off his thick skin unheeded. For some reason he considered himself a special gift to womankind although she couldn't understand why; the thick lips and greedy pig-like eyes did absolutely nothing for her except to create a slight feeling of nausea.

'Joanie!' As she opened the door and saw Joanie standing outside, her face as white as a sheet, she moved forward with an exclamation of concern. 'What's wrong?'

'Fabia, I'm sorry, I had to—'

'It would seem your friend is feeling somewhat unwell again.' For a second all time was suspended in a weird kind of time-lock as her stunned eyes watched Alexander Cade's lean, tall body move to stand just behind Joanie in the doorway. 'Do you know how many nurses with the surname of Fletcher there are in London hospitals and the surrounding districts?' he asked conversationally, his eyes registering satisfaction at her shock. 'Of course I had to include private nursing homes and suchlike on the list. One has to be thorough.' His smile was chilling as his eyes swept insultingly down her body.

'Now look here, Mr Cade—'

He cut off her shaking voice as quickly as he shed the mantle of mildness. 'But I am looking...Fabia, I think Miss Fletcher just called you? An improvement on Mary-Lou, I would agree. I've done nothing *but* look over the last two weeks, incidentally. You've cost me a considerable amount of time and effort, not to mention money, Miss...?'

'Grant.' Her voice was flat. 'Fabia Grant.'

'A delightful name.' The icy eyes narrowed. 'And now, Miss Fabia Grant, you will explain exactly what the hell you have been playing at.' He turned to Joanie abruptly. 'My car will take you home, Miss Fletcher. Kindly tell my chauffeur to return here for me.'

'Please, Mr Cade.' Joanie spoke faintly into the heavy atmosphere. 'It was just a joke, a silly joke. Fabia didn't mean—'

'A joke?' The dark voice expressed exaggerated disappointment. 'And here was I thinking my fatal charm had won out after all in view of your farewell.'

'What?' Fabia stared at him for a moment in bewilderment.

'"Bye for now, sweet thing—catch you later".' As he repeated the words she had found so amusing at the time a slow shiver ran down Fabia's spine and she heard Joanie groan softly. 'Well, you wanted to catch me, Miss Grant, and now you have.' The tawny eyes held her fast. 'And what are you going to do with me?' As she stared at him, temporarily dumbstruck, he inclined his head towards Joanie. 'And please tell your friend to avail herself of my offer. The car is waiting for her.'

'It's all right, Joanie, you go,' Fabia muttered slowly as Joanie shook her head at Alexander Cade's words.

'No, I can't leave you, I—'

'You will leave now.' He turned the full force of his piercingly cold eyes on Joanie—she shrank back slightly and the numbness that had taken hold of Fabia melted as a tide of furious rage washed over her, bringing her snapping upright on her heels.

'Don't you dare talk to her like that. You have no right—'

'Don't talk to me of "rights", Miss Grant,' he snarled softly. 'You lost me a very important business deal with that little act you put on at my reception, so don't talk of "rights".' He turned to Joanie, his manner milder. 'You can go, Miss Fletcher. I have no intention of harming your friend in any way but I am determined to speak to her, and in private.'

'Fabia?'

'Go on, Joanie.' She pushed her gently towards the waiting lift. 'I'll be all right.'

As the doors closed on Joanie's white, troubled face Fabia looked up at Alexander Cade, her eyes huge in her pale face, and in the same instant he moved forward, taking her in his arms before she had time to protest.

'Well, sweet thing,' he drawled mockingly, his eyes fiery, 'as I said, you've caught me. Let's see if the promise in that delectable body holds true.'

When his mouth fastened on hers she was too surprised

at first to feel anything but furious outrage, and as she struggled helplessly in his iron grip she was aware of the wicked chuckle deep in his throat as he moulded her softness into his body. She wasn't quite sure when a subtle awareness of him as a man—and what a man!—crept into her consciousness, but when it did she renewed her efforts, struggling violently as a warm sweet languor threatened to take over her limbs.

'Stop it.' He raised his mouth a fraction to admonish her. 'You asked for this—enjoy it.'

Her words of protest were lost as the firm hard lips took her mouth again and she suddenly realised he wouldn't let her go till she submitted. As she forced herself to become still in his arms the dark head raised again, and this time there was a glow of satisfaction in the tawny eyes.

'Good girl.' His voice was bitingly mocking. 'I can see you're catching on already.'

'You're a brute.' Her voice was annoyingly breathless but she couldn't help it. She couldn't remember when a kiss had affected her like that.

'Now, now, no insults please.' He took a step backwards and smiled tauntingly. 'You had a head start on me, after all. I seem to remember you've kissed me twice already?'

'That was different.' She glared at him angrily as her shoulders squared for battle. 'And you know it.'

'The hell I do!' There was only anger in his voice now.

She glared at him helplessly. 'I suppose you'd better come in.'

'How kind.' He followed her into the small lounge, his eyes shooting to the window and then back to her angry face. 'And just remember we're three floors up now. The windows are hardly conducive to flight, unless you're a bird, that is, of the feathered kind.' There was a hard thread of steel in the contemptuous drawl but nothing could have stopped Fabia's rage from spilling over as she looked into the handsome cruel face.

'I suppose you think you've been very clever!' She took a step forward as she spoke, her voice a low hiss and her eyes glittering blue fire, but he merely smiled slowly, totally unperturbed.

'No more than usual.' He let his eyes wander down her body in taunting contempt. 'But it's you who should be getting the Oscar, isn't it? Such a riveting performance and so well executed. You had us all on the edge of our seats.'

She glared at him furiously. 'Did I, indeed?'

'You sure did.' The slanted eyes fixed firmly on to hers. 'And none more so than Mr Hymes.'

'Mr Hymes?' She stared at him blankly. 'I don't remember anyone called Mr Hymes.'

'No?' He smiled thinly. 'Well, Mr and Mrs Hymes certainly will remember you for a long, long time. Your little charade cost me a vital business contract and irreplaceable good will. I'd been setting that deal up for six months and you blew it in as many minutes. They are as strait-laced as they come and didn't appreciate your particular brand of...entertainment.'

'Oh.' She tried to remember exactly what she had said and then winced as she did so. 'I see.'

'"I see"?' He glared at her. 'Is that the best you can do?'

'Look, I can explain—' Fabia stopped suddenly. No, she couldn't explain, not even to herself. What madness had possessed her to take on someone as powerful as Alexander Cade?

'I'm almost tempted to let you try,' he said smoothly. He was aware of her discomfiture and loving every minute of it, Fabia thought furiously, her eyes shooting daggers.

'Instead we'll cut through the nonsense and I'll tell you what I've come for. But not here.' He glanced round him as though her home was distasteful to him. Which it probably was, she thought bitterly, in view of the indulgent splendour in which he normally lived.

'If you've got anything to say to me you say it here and now, Mr Cade,' Fabia said angrily. 'And for the record I'm not going anywhere with you. Not now, not ever.'

'Think again.' The two words were loaded with menance.

'On your bike, mister!' She would not be intimidated or threatened in her own home. She would not!

'"On your bike"?' He repeated her words with a trace of amusement lightening the dark face. 'It's been years since I had a bike, Miss Grant,' he said mockingly.

'Now that I can believe,' she said stonily. 'Born with a silver spoon, the original spoiled brat, am I right?'

'Would you believe me if I said no?' he asked in a tone to match hers, his eyes narrowing as she shook her head firmly. 'No, I thought not, so I'll save my breath.' He walked through to the kitchen, turning off the grill as he did so and peering at the charred remains of the chop. 'Was that your dinner?'

'This *is* my dinner, yes,' she said coldly. 'Not quite up to your pretentious standards of smoked caviare and oysters maybe, but it suits me.'

'What a nasty prickly little inverted snob you are, Miss Grant,' he said slowly. 'Are you always this obnoxious?' His eyes wandered in insulting appraisal over her slender figure, resting for a moment on the full high breasts before continuing up to her hot angry face. 'Such a shame, when the exterior promises so much,' he added meaningfully.

'I don't promise anything,' she said furiously, longing

to reach up and smack the coolness from his handsome face but not quite having the courage. How dared he? *How dared he*? He had done nothing but criticise her home since he came in and now he was doing the same to her.

'Look, it's obvious you think this place is a dump, so why don't you just leave?' she said flatly, forcing all emotion out of her voice by sheer will-power. 'You've made your point, you're omnipotent, the all-powerful one, you found me against all the odds and I'm suitably chastised.' Her hand moved unconsciously to her bruised lips. 'Can't we leave it at that?'

'I haven't made my point at all,' he said after a long moment of silence. 'And I do not think your flat is a...dump, I think you so quaintly termed it.' He glanced round the light painted walls and the windowsill full of flowering plants before turning to inflict the full gaze of his piercing eyes on her again. 'And I repeat, I wish to speak to you in private. That is no slur on your home, merely the wishes of a hungry man who wants to discuss a particular matter in private at the same time as filling his stomach. I take it you wouldn't like to cook me dinner?' She glared at him silently. 'No, I thought not.' He smiled coldly. 'Then you take the alternative. Yes?'

She still didn't speak.

'We can either do this the hard way or the easy way, Miss Grant,' he said after a full minute of taut silence had elapsed. 'I am not going to abduct you if you allow me to buy you dinner, I am not going to threaten you or mistreat you in any way, in fact I am not going to deal with you at all as you deserve.'

The last was said so matter-of-factly that for a moment she missed its import, and then she flushed angrily as his words registered. 'How do I know I can trust you?' she asked slowly. 'That you won't try to kiss me again?'

'You don't.' He leant lazily against the door as he spoke, his tawny eyes gleaming oddly. 'But this is what is called taking the consequences, Miss Grant. Unpleasant, maybe, but if you play games then you have to accept the forfeit. Understand?'

'I don't understand any of this,' she snapped angrily as she snatched the grill off the stove and placed it in water, opening the kitchen window to let the pungent smell of burnt meat fade. 'Not any of it!'

'No, maybe not,' he said complacently. 'It's for me to explain and you to listen. Now, get your coat and we'll go. Swinton should be back with the car by now.'

She marched past him, through the lounge and into the bedroom without a word. 'Look on it as a bonus, Miss Grant.' The hated voice followed her. 'You'll be fed and watered.'

'I'm not a dog,' she said stiffly as she marched out of the bedroom with her coat slung over her arm, and then blushed hotly at the look on his face as his eyes ran over her again.

'That you aren't, Fabia Grant,' he agreed softly, 'that you aren't.' His gaze fastened lingeringly on her swollen lips.

As they left the flat Brian was just entering his, next door, a bottle of cheap wine under his arm. The small eyes took in the situation as Alexander Cade took her arm. The feel of his hand through the soft material of her dress was disconcerting and she had to stop herself sighing audibly with relief when he loosened his hold as they waited for the lift, helping her on with her coat without speaking, his face expressionless.

Within moments they were downstairs in the somewhat dour entrance hall and as she walked by his side towards the big glass doors she found her legs were shaking along with a distinct trembling in the pit of her stomach, and it wasn't all due to fright, she acknowledged silently. Away from the affected, subservient hangers-on who were part of his entourage and the opulent sophisticated surroundings in which she had seen him, the sheer maleness of the man came across in a virile potency that was almost tangible. He was tall, very tall, and the big black overcoat that he wore made him seem even larger, his shoulders broad and powerful under the expensive cloth. His hair was brushing the collar of the coat, gleaming with rich life against the dark material, and he exuded a sensual, intoxicating, dominant mastery that made her feel helplessly feminine even as she chided herself for her weakness. He wasn't anything like Robin. As the thought came unbidden into her mind her footsteps faltered and his hand came out instantly to steady her. 'All right?'

'I'm fine.' She flinched from his touch and his hand fell immediately to his side, but apart from a slight tightening of the hard mouth he displayed no emotion at all, his face closed against her. He was suddenly a different man, icy and very distant.

'The car's over here.' She looked across the dark road to where a magnificent Bentley was waiting regally in the shadows, the man he had called Swinton sitting in the driving seat. 'Shall we...?' He took her arm again as they crossed the street and she forced herself to display no reaction to his touch even as her mouth dried with a mixture of fear and excitement. What on earth had she got herself into? He was right out of her league in every way. And that kiss!

'Now, Miss Grant.' As she seated herself in the spacious interior he slid in beside her, tapping on the glass that separated them from Swinton and indicating to him to drive on when he turned round. 'A couple of things we need to get straight before I take you for a meal.'

'You needn't take me for a meal,' she protested quickly, 'I really don't—'

'The first thing.' It was just as though she hadn't spoken, and she subsided against the soft leather, her senses reeling as she caught a whiff of deliciously expensive aftershave. 'I shall call you Fabia and you will call me Alex. OK?'

'OK.' Her voice was weak and she heard it with a trace of anger sharpening her mind. Don't go all soft and pathetic now, Fabia, she told herself tightly. You're going to need all your wits about you tonight. 'And the other thing?' she said more loudly, her voice firm. Sexual magnetism was wasted on her!

'The other thing is that, in spite of having every reason for the contrary, I am not your enemy, Fabia. Got it?' The sound of her name on his lips caused her heart to pound crazily but she kept her face bland as she nodded quietly, not trusting herself to speak. 'I don't know what prompted you to act as you did and I won't pretend I like it—' the deep voice harshened a little '—but I'm not here tonight for revenge so you can relax a little.' He glanced down at her hands bunched in two tight fists in her lap, and as she caught his glance hot colour raced across her cheekbones in humiliating awareness of how easily he read her mind. She hated him, she really did!

'What are you here for, then?' she asked stiffly. 'There must be hundreds of women all too ready to fall into your lap, Mr—Alex.'

'Undoubtedly,' he agreed laconically. 'Unfortunately wealth is a powerful aphrodisiac to certain women, Fabia, which can prove...irritating at times.'

'Can it?' she asked cynically, her gaze resting on the classic profile as he stared straight ahead. She doubted if he had ever needed any help in that area in his life.

'It can.' He glanced at her, catching her wide blue eyes

with his sharp gaze. 'Now correct me if I'm wrong but I rather suspect that, although you may have many failings, that is not one of them?' His voice was full of mocking amusement.

She nodded slowly. 'I've nothing against money and what it can buy, it's only the love of money that I find repellent.'

'Quite.' The light brown gaze intensified. 'You are quite right in your assumption that I was born into wealth, as it happens—extreme wealth. However, I was not spoiled.' She lowered her eyes but not before he had seen the disbelieving gleam in their dark blue depths. 'You don't believe me?'

'No, I don't,' she answered frankly. 'You probably wouldn't know what a normal childhood was, so how can you say for sure that you weren't spoiled? And your lifestyle now is so outrageous, I don't think—'

'Outrageous?' He looked at her keenly. 'Do you really believe everything you read in the sordid little tabloids? I would have thought a woman of your intelligence would have kept an open mind on such sensationalism, but maybe that was before?'

'Before?' Her voice expressed her puzzlement. 'Before what?'

'Before whoever hurt you so badly left.' As the hot colour flared under her high cheekbones he turned away to look out of the window. 'I'm not ashamed of my wealth, Fabia,' he continued quickly before she had a chance to speak. 'I make it work for me and I use it wisely, but because of the amount I have any anonymity is merely a pipe-dream.'

'Oh, come on,' she said sceptically. 'Do you really expect me to believe that all those fabulous parties and different women for each day of the week are a figment of the Press's imagination? And you love every minute.' Her voice was bitter now. 'You know you do.'

'I don't expect you to believe anything,' he said quietly. 'It's not important anyway. I was merely trying to give you a little background information in view of what I intend to ask you later. One thing.' He paused and looked at her hard. 'I was not spoilt as a child, not at all. I don't know if you are aware of it but my parents were killed when I was three months old and I inherited everything. I was brought up by my paternal grandmother, who is a quite exceptional old lady. If you met her you would understand.' He moved to the edge of his seat as the car drew to a smooth halt. 'We've arrived—shall we...?'

'Please.' She caught hold of his coat-sleeve as he opened the door and he turned in surprise. 'Stop the cat-and-mouse game. What do you want from me?'

'All in good time.' He climbed out of the car and moved round to open her door, helping her out into the busy London street carefully. 'Give us a couple of hours, Swinton.' Swinton nodded blandly and the big car nosed gently into the traffic again to the usual blaring of horns from impatient city traffic.

The restaurant was quietly elegant and discreetly lit, full of secluded alcoves and attentive waiters who greeted Alex with an almost reverential respect that he seemed quite oblivious to. But he would be, wouldn't he? Fabia thought bitterly; he was used to this every day of his life. 'Your usual table, Mr Cade?' The manager appeared from nowhere, almost touching his forelock as he escorted them to a small table, out of sight of the general diners, already set for two with a large bowl of hothouse orchids gracing the snow-white linen cloth. Fabia sat down gingerly, hardly daring to breathe.

'An aperitif?' Alex looked across at her, the manager standing to attention by his side, and she suddenly rebelled against the ostentation, the ostentation that had trapped and degraded her all those years ago.

'No, thank you.' She smiled sweetly up at the waiter hovering at the manager's elbow. 'Could I have a glass of water, please?'

'A glass of water?' The young waiter was openmouthed but the manager stepped in smoothly, his voice expressionless and his face bland.

'Certainly, miss. And your usual champagne cocktail, Mr Cade?'

Alex hadn't taken his eyes off her during the little exchange and now he smiled slowly, his face enigmatically intent. 'I think I'll join Miss Grant, Xavier. Could I have ice and lemon in mine, please?'

'Er—yes, Mr Cade, certainly.' From the delighted expression on the waiter's face Fabia assumed it wasn't often the young lad had seen his prestigious superior at a loss for words but it was happening now. Xavier opened his mouth to speak, closed it again and then backed away silently, clicking his fingers at the waiter who set a gold menu-card in front of them before quickly following his boss.

Fabia opened her menu silently, a pink flush on her cheeks, and glanced down the contents with a feeling of apprehension. French. She might have known. She glanced up to find Alex's eyes still fixed on her. 'Would you like me to order for you? There are some dishes that are always exceptional here.' He was giving her an easy get-out but she didn't take it, her eyes steady on his as she stared into their tawny depths. He knew. He knew she couldn't speak French.

'Yes, please, this is all double Dutch to me.' There was a slightly defiant tilt to her chin as she spoke and he smiled that slow deep smile again, his eyes warm as they flickered over her beautiful face. She was feeling distinctly under-dressed for her surroundings, which didn't help, the pencil-slim black skirt and heavy gold blouse that had been just right for the office lamentably out of place next to the exclusive creations most of the women were wearing. Still, no one could see her here. She relaxed slightly. And it was his fault! If he was embarrassed by her it was his fault.

Alex didn't seem at all embarrassed, leaning back in his chair with his hands on the table, his dark face implacable and his eyes alive with laughter. 'Did you enjoy that?'

'What?' She knew exactly what he meant and glared at him as he gave a soft chuckle.

'Poor Xavier, and he so prides himself on his creative cocktails; you've quite ruined his night.'

'You didn't have to join me, you could have had what you wanted,' she said tartly, her eyes flashing.

'I wanted to join you, Fabia,' he said softly as all amusement left his face. 'I've got exactly what I wanted.' There was a strange expression on his face and she stared at him uncertainly for a moment or two before he leant forward to touch her cheek with the tip of one finger, his eyes unreadable. 'I thought so—soft as silk.'

'Don't!' She jerked back so violently from his touch that she almost knocked the glass of water that the waiter was presenting over her shoulder out of his hand.

'Sorry.' She smiled up at the young lad quickly. 'My fault.'

'Thank you, miss.' He placed the beautifully cut crystal wine glass in front of her carefully. 'I was told to put it in this glass, is that all right, miss?' She grinned wryly and he gave an answering smile, communicating without words, totally on her wave-length.

'Well, if that's the best there is I suppose it will have to do,' she said.

'I wondered how you'd look with a real smile and I know now, don't I?' There was a note in Alex's voice that made her raise her head sharply in surprise but his face was quite expressionless apart from a strange glow in the piercing eyes as he held her glance with his. 'Do I have to take up waiting at tables to get under that beautiful skin?'

'Don't be ridiculous,' she said coldly, forcing her gaze not to drop before his.

'Ridiculous...?' He leant forward again and lifted a strand of hair with one finger. 'I don't think it's ridiculous. I'm sure that even now you are constraining yourself to show no emotion, although everything in you wants to jerk away from my touch. Do I repel you in some way, Fabia? Is that it?'

'Don't be—' She stopped abruptly at the fiery gleam that flashed for a second in the gold eyes. 'You're nothing to me. I don't know you, do I, so how could you repel me?' Repel? That would have been almost funny in other circumstances. She breathed a quick prayer of thanks that they were not alone, that there were other people near by. There was a sensual charm, a fascination, that pulled her in spite of herself, and she willed herself not to show it.

'You're very beautiful, Fabia.' His voice was like velvet now. 'But I suppose you're tired of hearing men say that.' His fingers left her hair and moved to her cheek, slowly wandering down her face to trace the outline of her mouth and then continuing to the hollow of her throat where a tiny pulse was beating madly.

'Don't...' She sat as though turned to stone, her eyes brilliant in the stillness of her face.

'That's twice you've said that in as many minutes.' He smiled slowly. 'It's very...challenging.' He bent forward and lightly kissed her lips before settling back into his seat again, his face wry. 'Something tells me I shall have to dig deep before I get to the bottom of this particular Southern belle.'

She didn't know how to reply and so she said nothing, taking a sip of the ice-cold water before raising her face to his again. 'What is it you want to say to me, anyway? I want to know,' she said determinedly, her eyes wary.

'I need your help,' he said softly, his eyes narrowing as they watched her start of surprise.

'My help?' She realised her voice was too shrill and lowered it quickly as her face turned scarlet. 'Mr—Alex, I'm sure there's nothing I can do to help you; if anyone is in control, you are!' There was a bite in the last words.

'You don't know what it is yet,' he said quietly. 'Didn't your mother ever tell you to look before you leap?'

'I've no intention of leaping anywhere,' she answered quickly, 'and I never had a mother, well, only in the biological sense, of course.' Why reveal that to him? she asked herself crossly.

She sensed a stiffening in the big body but his face was cool and remote when she glanced up, his expression unfathomable. 'Meaning?'

'I was an abandoned baby,' she said lightly, forcing an airy note into her voice. 'You know, "the police need to contact the mother at once as they fear she is in need of urgent medical attention" and all that.' She waited for him to speak, to express the usual surface sympathy, but when he said nothing she continued slowly. 'I was in a children's home until I was two and then a succession of foster homes until I was sixteen. Took my A levels when I was eighteen—that's how I met Joanie—and then out into the big world to earn my living. End of story.'

'I see.' He hadn't moved. 'So we've both been orphans all our lives in a way.'

'I hardly think our two situations were similar.' She

smiled as she spoke but his face was straight as he looked hard at her.

'No?' He sighed softly as he leant back in his chair again. 'A lonely child is still a lonely child whether it has ten pence or ten pounds.'

'Or ten million?' Her voice was without humour. He didn't reply, just continuing to stare straight at her, and she flushed again as she realised the presumption of her words. 'I'm sorry, I shouldn't have said that,' she said quickly. 'I have no right to judge—'

'Well, it hasn't stopped you this far, so please don't change the habit of a lifetime just for me.' He was angry, very angry, she could feel it in the throb of his voice although his face was quite bland. She was beginning to realise that he gave little away, either in facial expression or body language, and that didn't fit into the mental picture she had of him at all. Playboy, socialite... She hadn't made a mistake, had she? An overwhelmingly catastrophic mistake?

'Do you work?' It came out quite baldly because she didn't stop to think, and she saw his surprise in the widening of those tawny-gold eyes seconds before the thick brown lashes came down to shield his face. There was silence for a moment.

'Yes, I do work, Fabia.' He glanced up again and now the careful mask was back in place. 'I have a large and very demanding business empire to manipulate with countless jobs and livelihoods hanging on the right decisions at the right time. But that isn't good news.' He smiled cynically. 'The latest social gathering I attend or the linking of my name with such and such an actress— now that—' he paused as his eyes sharpened '—that is good journalism.'

'Yes...' She looked up with immense relief as Xavier appeared at their side again to take their order. She would never have dreamt a few minutes before that she would actually be pleased to see the dapper little man, but now she gave him such a beaming smile that he was clearly quite taken aback. She felt at a complete and utter loss. All the preconceived ideas she had held about Alexander Cade seemed to be falling by the wayside and yet she didn't trust him. She looked at him from under her long silky lashes as he gave Xavier their order in fluent French. No, she didn't trust him an inch. He was too handsome, too rich, too powerful, a sight too much of everything, she reflected wryly. And what could a man like him possibly want with her? Fabia had no false modesty; she had been forced to evaluate herself from an early age and draw on any assets she had to the best of her ability.

True, she thought carefully, she was physically attractive and reasonably bright, but so were half the girls in London. In the world in which he moved beautiful people were ten a penny, so why had he taken the trouble to find her if not to punish her for the trick she had played on him and the financial loss it had caused? Panic became uppermost again and as her heart began to pound she took a hasty sip of water, holding the glass carefully in hands that trembled slightly. His power was frightening.

'There is no need to be frightened of me.' The golden-brown eyes were trained on her face again. 'I won't hurt you.'

'I'm not frightened of you,' she lied firmly with an upward tilt to her small chin. 'I don't frighten easily.'

'Better and better,' he drawled sardonically, and although he appeared to have taken her words at face value she had the uneasy feeling that the sharp cat gaze was alarmingly perceptive. She had been foolish, very foolish, to tangle with him, she thought tensely, and in spite of all his reassurances she felt instinctively that she was going to have to pay for her mistake. The debonair, rakish philanderer had been a mirage and instead she had been left facing a prowling lion, and indeed the simile seemed more than apt as she glanced at his mane of dark tawny-brown hair and the curiously gold eyes with their thick lashes that could be as clear and transparent as those of the king of the great cats, and just as unreadable. There was something about him, a hard brooding ruthlessness; he would fit into the inhospitable, cruel plains of Africa beautifully, stalking his prey carefully under a fierce burning sun and then just at the right moment—

'Your salmon soufflé, miss.' As the young waiter placed the glass bowl in front of her she almost jumped out of her skin, hiding her embarrassment with a cool smile as he disappeared again after placing Alex's dish in front of him.

'I was dreaming,' she said lightly to the attentive gaze.

'Really?' he said quietly, his voice smooth. 'I don't normally have my lady companions going off into a world of their own, but there have been several firsts with you, Fabia, in our somewhat short acquaintance. I have the distinct impression that life round you is never dull.'

There was no answer to that one and she didn't attempt to find one, suddenly finding that in spite of the enormous butterflies that were racing around her stomach she was really quite hungry. Lunch had been hours ago and had consisted of a snatched sandwich and paper cup of tepid coffee due to one of the ceaseless panics that cropped up every few days in the advertising world. She dipped a fork into the light, fluffy soufflé.

She didn't know what he was paying for the meal but whatever it was it was worth every penny, she reflected wryly as she tucked into the main course of trout, cooked in a wonderful concoction of orange liqueur and lemon, with baby new potatoes and fresh green beans and carrots. 'This is gorgeous...' She looked up as she spoke to find his amused gaze stroking her face, a sensuality in his eyes that caused her heart to pound.

'I'm glad you're enjoying it.' He let his glance wander for a moment down her slim shape. 'I didn't know if you were on a strict diet to keep that figure so perfect.'

'No fear.' Keep it friendly and general, Fabia, she thought silently, and you might just get away with this fiasco with nothing more alarming than an over-full stomach! Don't let him see how he affects you. 'I don't have weight problems; I suppose my job helps.'

'Really?' He leant forward slightly, amusement pulling at the firm mouth. 'Don't tell me you're a PE teacher or weight-lifter or some such thing?' His eyes were wicked.

'No.' For some reason she didn't want to tell him anything more about herself—she had regretted the earlier revelation as soon as it had slipped out—but there was no way she could not do so without appearing churlish. 'I work in advertising actually—nothing physical, except that we seem to race about from morning to dusk in a state of panic most days. If I remember to eat, which isn't often, I should think I've burned it all off again within minutes!' She smiled dismissively.

'I see.' His voice was casual but she had the feeling that every little thing she told him was being computed into an extensive memory bank and filed for future reference. She could believe now he managed a billion-turnover business. There was something very intimidating about this man, a sharp directness, an astuteness that lit the cold, handsome face from within. He was like a chameleon, she thought suddenly, able to change from one facet of his complicated personality to another at the blink of an eyelid. Tonight there had just been glimpses of the socialite flirt, but it was a mask that could instantly be brought out and donned in a second. Why hadn't she realised she had grabbed a tiger by the tail? Because he had fooled her as he fooled most people, she suspected, and he wanted it that way.

She glanced at him from under her lashes as she ate. He would be a dangerous adversary to contend with and hopefully she wouldn't have to, but if necessary... Her thoughts raced as her stomach filled. If necessary she would fight him. He might not be quite like Robin but he *had* been used to money and power all his life, and no doubt he thought he could acquire anything and anyone. But not this girl! Oh, no, not this girl.

'Dessert?' They had been sitting in silence sipping the excellent white wine he had ordered for some moments and as the waiter came to clear their plates Alex smiled at the shake of her head. 'Oh, come on, there must still be a little hole waiting to be filled.' He turned to the attentive waiter easily. 'Two helpings of that delicious berry trifle gâteau your chef does so marvellously.'

'Yes, Mr Cade.'

When they were alone again she glared at him across the small space, her eyes flashing blue sparks. 'Are you always so dictatorial?' she said sharply. 'Don't you listen to other people at all?' She suddenly felt trapped and overwhelmingly intimidated by the sheer presence of the man and it wasn't pleasant.

'I apologise,' he said calmly as the beautiful eyes turned icy, and she felt a little shiver snake down her back. Why didn't she just keep quiet, why antagonise him further? But she just couldn't help herself. It wasn't the dessert that had fired her but his dominant masculinity, which reached out to subdue her in a hundred and one ways.

She stared at him silently. She was behaving very badly and she didn't like herself this way but she disliked still more the strange melting feeling he could produce in her if they weren't fighting. 'I'm sorry,' she said tightly as she lowered her eyes to the wine glass in her hand. 'I'm on edge and as I said before, I don't think I can help you with anything, Mr Cade. I didn't want to come here and now I'm feeling—'

'Manoeuvred?' The cool sardonic voice brought her eyes shooting up to his. 'But you *are* being manoeuvred, my dear Fabia, and the name is Alex, remember?' He smiled slowly. 'I think you are honest enough to recognise that you owe me, yes?' She stared at him blankly as her heart began to pound. 'Yes?' His voice was cruelly insistent.

'But—' Her protest was cut off by the arrival of the berry trifle gâteau, and as the waiter placed the mouth-watering slice of soft cake running with brandy, whipped cream and ripe sugared berries in front of her Alex caught her eye, his expression enigmatic.

'Eat and enjoy.' His tone was uncompromising and she suddenly realised that what she did or did not eat would have very little bearing on the outcome of this disastrous evening. He had brought her out to be alone with her and for a purpose that had yet to be made clear. It could be he was just like all the other men she seemed to come into contact with these days, one thing on their minds and one thing only. But she doubted it. She looked again at the hard, handsome face. No, it wasn't as simple as that with him. He could have any girl he wanted. He didn't need to coerce a reluctant woman into his bed. Then what on earth *was* it? She gave up for the moment, picked up her spoon and dug into the rich sweet mixture with a guilty feeling of pleasure, secretly pleased that in this instance he had won the battle, and then instantly disgusted with herself.

'Now.' As she poured a liberal helping of cream into the dark aromatic depths of her coffee he finally spoke, and in spite of the portent of what was to come she felt a sense of relief. His silence over the last few minutes had been a little unnerving and she had known instinctively that he was collecting his thoughts in order to make plain to her what the evening had been about. 'I have a proposal to put to you which I want you to consider carefully over the next day or two, after which time I shall be in contact with you for your decision.' He cleared his throat.

'Yes?' He was speaking as though he were in the boardroom but the controlled, distant voice had a calming effect on the fluttering in her stomach until the tawny eyes fixed her again.

'I am in need of some assistance in a somewhat...delicate area and I would be grateful if you would listen quietly to what I have to say until I have finished. Do you understand?'

She nodded slowly, quelling the spurt of anger the formal, authoritative voice had caused. He was an enigma, this Alexander Cade, she thought silently as she looked into the stiff restrained face. Definitely an enigma.

'As I mentioned to you earlier, I was brought up by my paternal grandmother on her estate in Cumbria until school age, after which time I divided my life between boarding-school and her home in the holidays. She took the place of mother and father in my life and did it very well considering that when I was first foisted on her she was already in her early fifties.'

'I don't see—'

He cut her voice off abruptly, his face darkening. 'Please be quiet, Fabia, and let me get on with it.' Just for a fleeting moment she had the impression he was finding this difficult, but then she dismissed the thought as fanciful.

'My grandmother is eighty-seven and has been in poor health the last six months. I have had a word with her consultant and she isn't expected to live beyond a few months. Her heart is very tired.' He looked at her intently. 'I care very much for my grandmother, Fabia.'

'Yes, well, that's only natural...' She had no idea where this strange conversation was leading but a little trickle of apprehension was running down her spine at the determined expression in the beautiful gold eyes watching her so closely.

'She is a rather...forceful old lady who speaks her mind with less tact than is comfortable at times.' A slight smile touched the hard mouth. 'You would have a lot in common with her, I think. However—' he raised his hand quickly as she opened her mouth to speak '—that is by the by. As you have already pointed out, repeatedly, my name has often been linked with various young ladies who have come and gone through the years, some of which I have introduced to my grandmother and some not. It would give her a great deal of pleasure if she thought that I had a...particular friend at the moment. She is a born matchmaker, probably due to having an Italian mother herself—who knows?'

She was staring at him very hard now with a faintly incredulous expression turning her large eyes navy blue. He couldn't be suggesting...? No, it was ridiculous. She had misunderstood him.

'As I said, time is short. I would like her last Christmas to be a happy one with the feeling that everything is right in her small world. Do you understand what I mean, Fabia?'

She shook her head dazedly. 'There are several women I could take home to meet her but none of them would appeal to her and *all* of them would present me with interminable problems once the festive season is over. I have neither the time nor the inclination for such complications at the moment. I am in the middle of several important business transactions and can't waste time on trivia.' He was still speaking in the distant, unemotional tone he had used throughout, which made the whole thing even more preposterous. He couldn't mean—

'I need a nice steady two-feet-on-the-ground girl who knows exactly where she stands with me long-term but is confident enough to charm my grandmother into thinking that maybe, just maybe, this is the one for her grandson. No lies, no promises; I shall take you there as merely a friend but I know my grandmother—she will immediately plan for all sorts of possibilities, and for once I shall let her.'

'Take me...?' Her voice was a breathless squeak and now the full barrage of that tawny feline gaze was trained on her and his voice was anything but impassive as he leant forward until he was just a breath away, his eyes liquid gold.

'Yes, you, my golden-haired little beauty,' he said softly. 'In spite of looking like the fairy on top of the Christmas tree you have more guts than most men I know. Anyone who can make the sort of escape you did from that washroom in full evening dress after plucking a man back from the jaws of death and putting on a great show for me all night will find a piece of harmless deception child's play. I want you to accompany me to my grandmother's home for Christmas, Fabia Grant, as my girlfriend. Now, finish your coffee and don't say a word for at least five minutes.'

## CHAPTER THREE

'You can't be serious!' Fabia didn't wait five seconds to explode, let alone five minutes. 'I've never heard of such a crazy idea in my life!'

'Crazy? Why crazy?' There was a softness to the deep voice that spoke of molten steel but she was too incensed to notice.

'Me, accompany you, to goodness knows where and as your girlfriend? You must think I was born yesterday! I suppose this charade would involve us sharing the same room and so on? All friends together?' She glared at him furiously. 'At the risk of repeating an old cliché, Mr Alexander Cade, I'm not that sort of girl.' Sheer anger had quelled the trembling in her stomach.

'I'm fully aware what sort of girl you are,' he said icily, 'which is why I have made the suggestion in the first place. I don't mince words when I'm setting up a business deal, Fabia. All the facts are out in the open and there are no hidden "punches" involved. I don't know what sort of men you are used to dealing with but don't make the mistake of putting me in that catagory! This would be an arrangement between the two of us, in writing if you like, for a specified amount of time and with a set fee of your choosing. You would sleep alone. I would sleep alone. Got it?'

'Now look—'

He brought her indignant voice to an abrupt halt. 'And I have made it perfectly clear exactly where we are going. Cumbria. You have heard of that part of the country, I take it?' he asked derisively.

'Of course I have,' she hissed angrily. 'But this whole idea is preposterous. I *can't* believe you're serious.'

'Of course I am serious,' he returned coldly, 'and there is nothing preposterous whatsoever in what I am suggesting. I need a service which you may or may not be able to supply... Have you already made arrangements for the Christmas period?' he asked suddenly, his eyes narrowing on the heavy blonde hair and fragile face. 'I am quite prepared to pay for any cancellations. Or to soothe any irate boyfriend...?' His voice hardened slightly.

There was a question in the last words which she chose to ignore. 'My plans are my own affair,' she said sharply, her eyes glittering angrily as he leant forward to take her left hand in his.

'Of course they are,' he agreed smoothly. 'However, I think we have ascertained that there is no immediate family to complicate matters, and you aren't wearing a ring on the third finger of your left hand, so I assume the boyfriend, if is one, is not serious?' The feel of his warm flesh on hers was curling her toes. The question was there again and she was furious at his autocratic assumption that he had the right to interrogate her about the state of her love-life, and even more furious at the effect his touch was having.

'You really have got a cheek,' she spat angrily, jerking her hand away so violently that it hit the table with a dull thud. 'I don't even know how to play your girl-friend! We are worlds apart, as you very well know. Take this restaurant, for instance—'

'Yes?' He leant forward, his face intent.

'It's just so...plush, so removed from anything I would normally go to. You eat at this sort of place all the time, don't you?' she finished accusingly.

'And that is the main cause of your concern about my proposal? That we eat at different restaurants?' His voice was mocking and cool and in that moment she felt a stab of sheer hate pierce her as she looked into the narrowed amber eyes. He thought he only had to say the word and things would fall magically into place. Well, perhaps that happened if you were rich enough to buy and sell half of London, but everyone had to be disappointed some time! Her thoughts were mirrored in the clear blue of her eyes and as he kept his gaze fixed on her face he smiled slowly, his face unreadable.

'I told you I wouldn't accept any decision tonight,' he said blandly after a full minute of tense silence had ensued. 'I will contact you in forty-eight hours when you have had time to consider my suggestion properly.' He settled back in his chair.

'Oh, it is a suggestion, then?' she said bitingly. 'For a minute there I thought it was an order.'

'Not at all,' he said calmly. 'However, a few things I would just reiterate. First, you do owe me, Fabia, whether you care to admit it or not, and this would be a perfect way to cancel your debt—and, believe me, it's quite a large one.'

'I don't have a debt,' she began furiously, but he held up his hand for silence and something in the hard, handsome face made her bite her lip as her voice faltered away.

'Secondly, I am in something of a fix for the reasons I have explained. I need to approach this situation as a business deal, something separate from my private life, you understand?' She glared at him silently. 'And the point that you are not used to my kind of lifestyle is quite unimportant. If you accept this offer you are at liberty to just be yourself; I would expect nothing more. The only thing I would ask you to do is to force some degree of warmth into our relationship.' He smiled at her angry face. 'Only when we are in company, of course. In private you could be your normal waspish little self shrinking from my touch like the original shy violet.'

What she would give to slap that mocking smirk off his handsome face! She schooled her features into a cool mask with considerable effort.

'And if I did agree to this mad idea—not that I would do, of course,' she added coldly, 'how do you explain to your grandmother that we met? What am I supposed to be, one of your employees who caught the boss's eye or a modern-day Cinderella taken out of the gutter by a passing noble?'

'You really must try to curb this enormous inferiority complex, Fabia,' he said smoothly. 'Maybe a course of psychoanalysis would help. You are just as good as me, my dear.'

'*I* know that!' she snarled ferociously, eyeing him with angry antagonism as he began to shake with silent laughter, his eyes aglow. 'And you haven't answered my question.'

'Why, I would just tell it as it is,' he replied after a few moments when he could restrain his amusement. 'I don't suppose for a moment you and your friend were the original recipients of those tickets. What was it, a last-minute gift?' She nodded slowly. 'There you are, then, that's all anyone needs to know. I met you there for the first time, our eyes met across a crowded room and from that point the rest of the world faded into oblivion.' There was a strange note in his voice that she couldn't place and she stared at him hard. 'Simple, eh?'

'I'm not doing this, Mr Cade,' she said flatly.

'It's Alex!' This time the voice was stone-cold and his face was grim. 'And I've told you, I won't accept any decision now. I will contact you as arranged. Now, have you finished?' He raised a hand and immediately the waiter was at their side with their coats.

'Don't you pay?' she asked in amazement as he escorted her from the restaurant with a firm hand under her elbow, to the smiles and nods of most people present.

'I have an account here which is settled monthly,' he answered quietly, his face hardening at her satisfied little nod. 'And don't start that "we're so different" rubbish again,' he warned coldly as they stepped on to the icy pavement.

'Well, it's true,' she protested as the Bentley glided to a halt in front of them as though by magic. 'You must see it.'

'Are you seriously telling me that you don't believe two people from different backgrounds can meet and fall in love and live together happily all their lives?' His eyes were piercing her as she sat uncomfortably in the warm lush interior of the car. 'Is that what you're saying?' He was uncomfortably close.

'Of course not.' She flushed hotly. 'But it's rare. It can happen, but it's rare. And that isn't what we're talking about. We are discussing persuading your grandmother that you find me attractive.' Did he *have* to be so darned good-looking?

'And what's so strange about that?' he asked carefully.

'With all the women you've—' she nearly said 'had' and altered it quickly '—known? They're beautiful and famous and—'

'Boring,' he finished quietly. 'Not all, I admit, but a surfeit of rich goodies becomes unpalatable after a time.'

'You didn't find that meal tonight unpalatable,' she said quickly, deliberately misunderstanding him. There was a stillness in his profile that unnerved her a little although she didn't know why, but she disliked the way this conversation was heading.

'No, the meal tonight was wonderful,' he agreed quietly, turning to look at her for just a fleeting second.

As his eyes met hers in the shadowed darkness of the car she felt something akin to an electric shock shoot down her spine and drew back sharply into her seat, her eyes widening in unspoken protest. It was as though he was making love to her, without touching her, without even speaking. He was dangerous! Dangerous and seductive and compelling. He held her glance for a long moment before turning to look out of the window at the brightly lit busy London street, full of small wine bars, tiny restaurants and the odd fish and chip shop incongruous against its upper-class neighbours. 'Of course the salad at that particular restaurant is delicious,' he said blandly as the car sped smoothly along. 'I often have that along with a chop or seafood.' The mind-stunning moment passed but the vibrations were still with Fabia when the car drew up outside the dismal block of flats, and she stiffened as he left the car and opened the door for her, helping her out with old-fashioned courtesy, his face inscrutable.

'Thank you for the meal; it was lovely,' she said hurriedly as she stepped on to the uneven paving slabs that led over to the big glass doors of the silent building, holding out her hand dismissively. 'Goodnight, Alex.'

'I'll see you to the door,' he said quietly, his eyes travelling over her flushed cheeks and coming to rest on the wide full mouth. 'Just to the door.' He looked down at her silently.

'There's no need...' Her voice died away as he took her arm again, his hand firm. She was wearing three-inch heels but in spite of that he still towered over her by a good four inches, and she found it peculiarly gratifying to be in the company of a man who was a good deal taller than herself for once. At five feet nine inches plus heels she normally found that she was on a level with most men, a fact which in the past had not bothered her at all. Nevertheless, his height was...satisfying. She caught the thought and brought it severely to heel. There was nothing about him she liked! Nothing!

As the old grimy lift took them jerkily upwards she glanced at him from the corner of her eye. I wonder what he's thinking? she thought curiously. This grubby, somewhat seedy part of London had been the best that she could afford in the early days, and as she had progressed in her career she had found herself loath to move from the cosy little flat, having renovated it with loving care and a good deal of elbow grease. It was bright and clean and unusual, a reflection of the complicated personality who lived within its walls, each room alive with colour and comfort.

As the lift shuddered to a halt on her floor and the faded yellow doors slowly opened she stuck out her hand again. 'We've arrived,' she said brightly. 'Thank you again.'

'I said to the door,' he returned coolly, stepping out of the metal box with her and walking along the corridor that always seemed to smell slightly of cooked cabbage. 'Safely home?' He leaned against the wall as she hunted in her handbag for her key, annoyed to find herself all fingers and thumbs as he stared at her, his expression sardonic and his powerful body relaxed. 'Against all the odds?'

'Not at all.' She smiled cautiously. A few more seconds and she was home and dry. As she retrieved her key from the muddle at the bottom of her handbag he stepped forward suddenly, taking her completely by surprise.

'I'm probably going to regret this in view of the fact that I shall be completely blotting my copybook as far as you are concerned,' he said huskily, pulling her in his arms and taking her mouth in a long, hard kiss as he moved her round so that her back was against the wall and his body pressing against hers. For a moment she was too stunned to react and then, as the kiss deepened into a seductively sensual caress and she felt the length of his hard body moulded intimately against hers, she realised, with a shock of horror, that part of her had been waiting for this, hoping for it.

The expensively delicious smell of him was intoxicating, surrounding her with an undeniable aura of masculinity that both thrilled and repelled her, repelled because she must remember, *she had to remember*, that she was just one of many, a trinket to play with for a time and then thrown away without a moment's thought. A rich man's toy!

Hadn't that agonising time with Robin taught her anything? Was she completely crazy? As the condemning thoughts hit her mind like a deluge of cold water she froze in his arms and he immediately sensed it, moving away as he ran a hand through the dark brown hair, his eyes rueful. 'Stupid, Alex, my boy, real stupid...' He was muttering as though to himself and the next instant, without a word of goodbye, he was walking away towards the waiting lift, entering its doors without a backward glance, his walk easy and free like a big relaxed cat.

She stood for a moment as though transfixed to the spot, listening to the sounds of the ancient machinery grinding downwards, her thoughts in turmoil and her body on fire. There was an ache in her body that was almost painful, each nerve-ending vitally alive and seeking relief. What was the matter with her? What *was* the matter? She almost stamped her foot in impotent rage and disgust at her weakness and heard the phone ringing in her flat with a mixture of irritation and relief. It would be Joanie, no doubt. 'Hi, it's me,' Joanie said breathlessly. 'Well, what's happened? Are you all right? Did it go well? What did he say?'

'It's OK, it's OK, no problem,' Fabia said reassuringly,

but the words sounded hollow even to herself. 'I'm shattered though, Joanie. Can we talk in the morning?'

'But what did he want?' Joanie persisted doggedly.

'Suffice to say the ball's well and truly in my court and I'm not starting to play, but as I said I'll explain in the morning. Night, Joanie.' She couldn't make small talk, she just couldn't!

She put down the receiver on further protestations and after collapsing in a heap on the bed flailed herself yet again.

Why had she ever agreed to go with Joanie to that ill-fated function in the first place and, once there, what on earth had possessed her to act in such a way? She lay back on the bed as her thoughts raced. She knew why. Everything had so resembled the first time she had met Robin and she had rebelled, hotly and violently, against ever being put in the same position again.

The thoughts that she had kept back for months surfaced in excruciating clearness and she was too exhausted to fight them, giving in to their agony as she went back in time to that night, seven years ago, when she had been eighteen and thought the world was out there just for her.

She had been wearing red, she remembered tiredly, a red velvet evening dress that had moulded itself to her figure like a second skin, sleeveless, backless and incredibly daring. It had been hired specially for the great night; it wasn't often a working girl like her won tickets for a ball that people would kill for, and the women in the shop had urged her to take that particular dress in preference to the one she had chosen, a more subdued little number in pale green.

She had only been in London four weeks and living in digs at the time, at a loss to understand the great city or its people, nervous, excited and wonderfully aware that every man's eyes were being drawn to her that night, picking her out from the three other girls she had gone with in a manner that brought a flush to her cheeks and glitter to her eyes.

Robin had noticed her in the first five minutes, appearing at her side with two glasses of champagne, his light blue eyes frankly appreciative and his smooth, almost white blond hair and unusual good looks bowling her over. He had turned on the charm and she had been lost, a little girl alone in the big city and the perfect pushover, she thought bitterly, her mouth hardening.

Robin had been clever, she had to give him that. So caring, so gentle, so considerate at first. And then... 'If you love me you'll want us to be as one, darling,' he had murmured night after night as they had kissed and fondled in his magnificently luxurious apartment or in the back of his white Rolls-Royce. 'I love you so much, I want to know everything about you.' He had wined and dined her, taking her to the best restaurants, the most exciting shows, dazzling and bewitching her, picking her up from work now and again, insisting that nothing was too much trouble for his 'darling'.

She had realised later, when it was far, far too late, that he had used his limitless wealth and influence like a drug, increasing the dosage little by little until she was completely hooked. It hadn't mattered that he was twenty years older than her at the time. 'Age means nothing to us, sweetheart,' he had assured her over and over again and, loving him as she did, trusting him implicitly, unable to believe her luck that this caring, handsome, tender man actually loved her, she had agreed wholeheartedly. Indeed there were times when, exhausted from a grinding day at the office, the very bottom rung in a massively tall ladder, she had felt years older than him.

He had assured her that the playboy image, the fact that he lived on the vast wealth he had inherited from his father without ever dirtying a finger in work, was all a figment of people's imagination, and although, secretly, she had wondered at times, she had accepted that along with all the other lies.

Three months after they had met, when he'd considered she was ripe, he had issued an ultimatum, his eyes full of pain and his face woebegone. 'If you love me, darling, really love me, you can't let anything separate us,' he had said mournfully, shaking his head gently. 'This is killing me, to love you, to hold you in my arms and then have you draw back at the last moment. I can't take any more, Fabia. It has to be all or nothing.' He had ridiculed her idea of keeping herself chaste until she was married. 'We don't need to wait for that, darling. You know I love you, that I'll always love you.' And she had believed him. Utterly, completely. It had been so wonderful to have someone tell her that she mattered after the long years of being moved from one home to another, never really belonging, never knowing if she dared presume to put down tentative roots.

And so she had promised him. That weekend she would come to him. In his flat. She would stay the weekend, cook and care for him, and love him as he asked. Be everything he wanted.

'Stupid, stupid, stupid...' She groaned at the memory, rolling over into a tight little ball and putting her hands over her ears as though she could shut out the sounds of that woman's screaming when she had discovered her and Robin in the huge bed with black silk sheets. And Robin's rage. Rage that his mistress had come back from her trip to Paris too soon. Rage that he hadn't consummated his affair with Fabia. Rage that he had been found out. Rage that his careful manipulating had gone wrong.

'No more.' She rose, pale and shaking, from the bed and, after stripping off her clothes, padded into the bathroom, standing under the hot shower with her head raised to the water and letting the cleansing flow wash over her until it turned cool. A twenty-five-year-old virgin in London. She smiled to herself soberly. There were probably more about than met the eye. She wasn't unique.

Something had died in her that night. The humiliation and the aftermath had hurt too deeply, destroyed too many childish dreams of a knight on a white charger, for her ever to be the same again. She had lost all her self-respect for a long, long time but she had regained it now and nobody, *nobody*, would ever take it away again. She had had the odd boyfriend after a time but none of them had remotely stirred her dead heart. She viewed the whole male sex without rose-coloured glasses, seeing them as vain, selfish and shallow most of the time with the odd exception here and there proving the rule. And she *would not* be fooled again! Not by a tawny-eyed giant with a glib line in persuasion whose kisses were out of this world. She caught herself with a sense of shock. She didn't need kisses and she didn't need any complications in her life! She was a career girl who had got everything very nicely under control, thank you, and if, occasionally, in the dark of the night when sleep was a million miles away, she yearned for a different life, the cold harsh light of day soon put her to rights. White knights and white weddings were in story-books.

A pale watery dawn was creeping into the small bedroom when at last her eyelids closed in sleep, and she slept soundly and deeply until the shrill ring of the doorbell brought her jerking awake.

It had to be Brian, she thought furiously as she stumbled to the door, pulling a robe over the blue silk pyjamas she was wearing. Only Brian would be inconsiderate enough to ring the bell at eight o'clock on a Saturday morning.

'Just returning the coffee.' Brian's face was a picture of innocence. 'Didn't get you up, did I?'

'Yes!' She was too tired to be polite, reaching out for the coffee jar as she spoke.

'Sorry.' He didn't look it. 'Who was that guy I saw you with last night? New boyfriend?'

His tone was distinctly hostile and brought her fully awake with a little thud. What now? She really didn't need this on top of everything else. 'I think that's my business, Brian, don't you?' She made no effort to soften her words. 'Now I'd really like to get back to bed if you don't mind.'

'Don't mind at all.' He had pushed past her into the flat before she was aware of it and walked into the small lounge with swaggering steps. 'Busy night, was it? Strenuous?' His meaning was unmistakable, as was the leer on his face, and for a second she felt a stab of fear before hot anger rose to take its place.

'Get out of my flat, Brian,' she said coldly. 'I don't remember inviting you in.'

'You never do, do you?' he said softly, his thick lips wet as the small eyes ran over her body. 'Got to have a Bentley or something first, eh? Like lover-boy?'

'You followed us out into the street?' The windows were on the other side of the flats so he couldn't have seen Alex's car from there. 'Just who do you think you are?'

'Someone who can give you a good time if you'd let me.' He took a step towards her. 'How about it?'

'I suggest you leave now, Brian.' She stood her ground and he shambled to a halt, picking nervously at his nails as he faced her.

'Why?' Again she felt that stab of fear but kept her voice cool and firm as she spoke.

'Because my new boyfriend would be most upset to

find you bothering me and, as you can imagine, he is rich enough to buy and sell you ten times over. He could make things very unpleasant for you, believe me; he knows people.'

'Oh, yeah?' The threat had worked, it was there in the reddening of his plump face.

'Yes.' She looked at him hard.

'You mean you're seeing him again?' he said slowly.

'Yes, I am,' she said quickly, too quickly; he caught the inflexion in her voice as she spoke the lie.

'I don't believe you.' He looked at her hard. 'Men like him don't bother with the likes of you once they've had their fun.' She agreed perfectly with the sentiment but wasn't about to let him know that.

'As it happens I'm spending Christmas with him, OK?' she said firmly. 'And please get out, Brian, I'm getting cold standing here talking to you.' The ease with which the lie had fallen from her lips plus her matter-of-fact tone seemed to defuse the situation and he glanced at her again before walking slowly to the open door.

'Huh!' What exactly the exclamation was meant to express she didn't know and didn't care as she shut the door quickly, sliding the bolt in place for extra comfort.

What a creep! She found she was shaking slightly as she ran a shower, sleep being a million miles away now. The warm water did a lot to calm her and as she dressed slowly she began to berate herself for being panicked into telling such a ridiculous story. She wasn't going anywhere with anyone—especially not Alexander Cade. Still, no one would be any the wiser, she thought comfortably after a time as she made herself tea and toast, and it had served a purpose. She had been looking for a way to get through to Brian for weeks and it looked as though it had been dropped in her lap. She ought to be grateful to Alex really.

She spent a lazy day at home doing a hundred and one

jobs she had been putting off for weeks, ringing Joanie in the evening and putting her mind at rest before falling into bed at the ridiculously early time of nine o'clock, tired out.

She had been invited to spend the Sunday with a married colleague from work whose husband was in Saudi Arabia and meet her children, and she was glad now that she had accepted. They had a wonderful day, lighting a bonfire in the garden in the afternoon after a huge dinner of roast beef and Yorkshire pudding and then taking the family dog, a comical little mongrel called Rambo— 'You'd know why if you lived with him,' her friend said wryly—to Hyde Park for a long walk before muffins and tea in front of the fire.

She arrived home late, tired but glowing from a day in the fresh air, to find Alex leaning lazily against the door of her flat as she stepped out of the lift.

'Good evening, Fabia.' His voice stopped her in her tracks and as she met the cool gold eyes she was aware of Brian's door being slightly ajar. 'I've just been having a little chat with your neighbour. Seedy individual, isn't he?' The door closed with a definite click and she glanced at Alex's face to see he was smiling wryly. 'I've warned him off in no uncertain terms. I'm afraid he won't dare speak to you again. Right or wrong?'

'Dead right and long overdue.' She looked at him carefully. 'What has he been saying?'

'I've no intention of having a conversation in the middle of this corridor,' he said coolly. 'Shall we...?' He indicated her front door with a wave of his hand and she had no choice but to step past him and unlock it. 'Now...' He looked at her tightly as she shut the front door. 'I understand I shall have the pleasure of your company at Christmas? A delightful prospect.' His eyes were speculative as they met her shocked blue gaze, narrowing slightly in silent enquiry at the stunned expression on her face. 'That *is* what you told love's young dream next door?' She had forgotten how devastatingly handsome he was.

'Yes, no; I didn't mean...' Her voice trailed away helplessly. 'I just...' She stopped again.

'Yes?' She couldn't read anything from his bland face and as her mind searched for a way out of what had turned into a monstrous parody she finally decided she would have to tell him the truth. There was absolutely no way she was going to spend Christmas as his leading lady in some macabre play so the only alternative was to explain things properly and throw herself on his mercy. Mercy? She shut her eyes briefly and then took courage and glanced at him carefully under her eyelashes. He had been relatively reasonable up to now considering the circumstances of their first encounter, and he had left the choice of whether she accompany him to Cumbria or not up to her, so it should be all right. Shouldn't it?

Just for a moment, as she looked directly at him, there was something quite ruthless in the brilliant golden-brown eyes that made her shiver, but when she looked again his face appeared quite bland, even pleasant, and she gave herself a little admonitory shake. You're getting paranoid, she told herself firmly, and it's got to stop.

'Fabia? Shall we be seated?' He settled himself comfortably into an easy-chair as he spoke, crossing one leg over his knee as his hands stretched along the back of the chair. For some reason the action seemed intimidating, perhaps because it highlighted the strong muscular shoulders, broad chest and long powerful legs. She gulped silently.

She had never met a man whose masculinity was worn so powerfully before; it was almost tangible, virile and dangerous, and she didn't like the tremors that snaked down her spine, she didn't like them at all. She didn't want to respond to the message his body was sending to her femininity. He was the enemy—all his type were. 'Well?' he said softly when she still didn't speak. 'Let's have it.'

'What?' She stared at him in consternation. 'What do you mean?' Was he psychic as well?

'That's for you to tell me,' he said quietly. 'You've been like a cat on a hot tin roof since you came in. What's wrong?' He smiled slowly. 'Or is it my animal magnetism?'

'Alex...' She leant forward imploringly, her hair glowing like liquid gold in the shadowed room and her blue eyes enormous. 'It's all a mistake, about me coming to Cumbria with you, I mean. I never meant you to know, I only told Brian—' She paused helplessly. She wasn't making a very good job of this, she thought miserably, searching her mind for a way to explain things that wouldn't make a bad situation ten times worse.

'I think you'd better start at the beginning.' In her anxiety she didn't notice the coldness in his soft voice or the way the teasing glow had died from his eyes, leaving them two hard chips of yellow glass. 'Let's have it all.'

So she told him, stumbling a little and keeping her eyes on her hands clenched into fists and when at last she ground to a halt she waited a moment before raising her face to meet his gaze. What she saw there made her blood run cold. If she had thought he was angry that first night it was mere irritation compared to the black rage that had his whole body in a tight grip now. He was furiously, violently angry.

'You really are priceless.' The words were ground out slowly through gritted teeth, a savagery in his voice that made her breath catch nervously in her throat. 'An absolute twenty-four-carat winner.' She shrank back in her chair as he came to crouch over her, his face twisted into a black satanic mask and his eyes flashing fire. 'What do you think I am? First you attempt to make me the laughing-stock of London with that cute little trick you pulled, losing me a great deal of money in the process, and then you duck out and vanish into thin air, leaving me with the proverbial egg on my face! Not content with that you now propose to use me in some duplicitous plan of your own without even informing me I'm bailing you out. I can't believe you, I really can't believe what I've just heard.'

'I told you, Brian—'

'Forget Brian,' he snarled savagely. 'I've made it clear to that scum that you are strictly out of bounds. Just concentrate on me for now.' He straightened slowly, staring at her from eyes that were slanted into narrow gold slits. 'Brian is the least of your problems, angel-face, believe me.'

She remained frozen in her chair, her face upturned to his, hardly daring to breathe.

'No one has ever been foolish enough to treat me like this before and I'm going to make damn sure you never make that mistake again. I don't know what's gone on in your life and at this moment in time I don't care, but you are going to be brought to heel, my girl, severely to heel.'

'Alex—'

'Don't "Alex" me.' His voice was soft now with a quiet deadliness that chilled her blood. 'From now on we play the game my way, understand? I've tried the softly-softly approach but you don't understand normal reasonable behaviour, do you?' His eyes glittered furiously. 'No matter, angel-face, we'll communicate on your terms. You will come with me to my grandmother's home for Christmas whether it fits into your plans or not, and you will do *exactly* as I tell you. Is that clear?' His eyes raked her ferociously as he spoke.

'I will not!' She had been too stunned by his unexpected rage to react before but now an anger to match his had her in its grip. 'You can't make me! With all your money you can't make me!' She made to rise but he pushed her down violently.

'Don't make me show you what I can or can't do,' he said slowly, the authority in his voice intimidating her even as she tried to fight it. 'You'll regret it, bitterly, if you do. I won't be taken for a ride by you or anyone else.'

'I wasn't—'

Her voice strangled in her throat as he reached out a hand and grasped a handful of hair, drawing her up to him slowly. 'How can anyone who looks so...fragile be so hard?'

'I'm not hard!' Her body was pressed into his now and her head tilted to look up into his dark face.

'No?' His mouth twisted in the semblance of a smile. 'You mean there's another side I haven't been privileged enough to glimpse yet?' His fingers loosened in her hair, slowly moving across her head to the back of her neck as his breathing thickened. 'I don't know why the hell I'm bothering with you at all except that maybe I believe that other side is there after all.' She stood absolutely still, hardly daring to breathe. The look on his face and the stirring in the hard male body pressed against hers told her more clearly than words of his arousal and she had never felt more vulnerable in her life, more threatened. Not so much because of his rage or passion, she was honest enough to admit to herself, but more because she couldn't trust herself not to respond.

'Fabia...' Her name was a groan on his lips as he bent to nuzzle his face in the soft silk of her hair, his mouth moving to her ears and throat in soft feather-like kisses that brought an immediate hot ache trembling forth in her lower stomach, and as his mouth fastened on hers with a touch of violence in its intensity she found herself straining to meet his need with her body even as her mind told her this was madness.

'Why do you fight me when it could always be like this?' His voice was so soft that she could barely hear it and as she felt his fingers on the tiny pearl buttons of her blouse she shut her eyes tightly. She had to stop this; what was she doing...?

'No, please, Alex...' Her voice was lost as he claimed her mouth again, and as she felt her bra slip and his fingers move to cup the silky fullness of her breasts a piercingly sweet pleasure took over her senses at the same time as a little cold voice hammered into her brain, Again? You are inviting all this again? And with him?

'I said no!' As she wrenched herself backwards out of his arms she pulled her blouse so violently across her chest that she felt the thin material tear. 'Don't touch me!'

'What the—?' As he saw the panic in her eyes his hands, which had gone out to grasp her, froze in mid-air, a stillness taking over his features as he turned away, walking over to the other side of the room and standing with his back bent and his hands resting palm down on the small coffee-table as he struggled for control.

She sank down into the chair she had vacated, her mind numbed and blank and her breath coming in little panting sobs. They remained suspended in a frozen tableau for a full minute and then he raised himself slowly, turning and looking over to where she sat huddled in the chair, his eyes as cold as ice.

'I don't know what all that was about, Fabia, but if you thought you could twist your way out of doing what I want you are dead wrong.' She stared at him silently, her eyes huge in her white face. 'You owe me and you are going to pay your debt. You'll come to Cumbria and behave beautifully, not a foot—not a toe—out of place. Do you understand?'

'I hate you.' As her whispered words reached him his face stiffened.

'Maybe.' His voice grew softer. 'But you're still coming. And afterwards I shall let you go, a few days older but a whole lot wiser.'

'You can't make me—'

'I can and I will, sweetheart.' He was calmer now but with a ruthless severity that was more chilling than his anger. 'I've given you every chance and you've blown it. Well, such is life.' He shook his head slowly as he walked to the door, his eyes resting on her face with a touch of biting contempt in their gold depths.

'I don't like to be played with, and, until you learn that, life is going to be very difficult.' He paused with his hand on the handle. 'And a word of warning: don't try and escape again, Fabia. The world isn't big enough to hide you. One of the advantages of having money is that it makes the world considerably smaller. I'll be in touch. Goodnight.'

It was a full minute before she could persuade her trembling legs to move after he had left, and then she stumbled over to the door, shooting the bolt into place with shaking hands and sinking down on to the carpet weakly.

He had trapped her! She groaned softly. Or maybe she had trapped herself? Why, oh, why had she told Brian she was spending Christmas with Alex? She could have handled Brian, but not this man. Not this man with his tawny cat-like eyes that could harden into stone and his limitless, terrifying wealth. He was too powerful to fight, with his sensual charm and compelling sexuality, and she seemed to have no defence against him. At the last thought she stiffened. No! He could *attempt* to subjugate her, impose his will over hers, but the final outcome would be up to her. She raised herself from the floor slowly. And, as sure as she drew breath, never, never again in the whole of her life would she allow herself to be crushed and defeated, broken at the feet of some man. She would rather die first.

She straightened her slender shoulders for battle, her mouth set in grim determination. She would go with Alexander Cade to his grandmother's home and act the part that fate, and a big golden-eyed barbarian, had allotted to her to the best of her ability. She had no other choice. But if he thought he had won he was wrong! Her eyes narrowed ominously.

He would never reach the real Fabia Grant, never touch the woman who had been born that night seven years ago amid heartbreak, disillusion and bitter humiliation, never touch the core on which she had built a new life.

She simply wouldn't let him.

## CHAPTER FOUR

'ARE you warm enough?' Fabia started violently as Alex's cool, quiet voice interrupted her thoughts.

'I'm fine, thank you,' she replied stiffly, and he nodded slowly with his eyes fixed on the road ahead, the windscreen wipers clearing the snow from the glass in steady monotonous rhythm. They had been driving for an hour and the snow was coming down thicker now, fat starry flakes patterning the cold glass for a split-second before the wipers cleared them relentlessly from view, the midday sky heavy and bleak.

She flexed her toes in the warmth from the car heater, reflecting silently that the smart high-heeled shoes that had seemed so appropriate in London were fast becoming most unsuitable in view of the worsening weather. The snow was already several inches thick and showed no signs of abating; in fact the thick grey sky promised much more. Still, it couldn't be helped. She glanced at Alex's severe profile from under her lashes, her stomach tightening as it dawned on her afresh that she was committed to this man's company for a whole week. Christmas had never arrived so quickly, she thought wryly.

'Having second thoughts?' As the flecked gold eyes pierced her own for a moment, she forced herself to show no reaction to the taunt, waiting a full minute before she replied.

'Second thoughts don't apply to this situation, do they? You forced me to come with you; I had no choice.'

'Not at all,' he said calmly. 'The choice was very clear—take the consequences of your actions or join me for a pleasurable break from routine. I would agree that it wasn't a very difficult choice in the circumstances, but a choice nevertheless.' The hard tawny eyes gleamed at her. 'Don't you agree?' He was close, much too close for comfort.

She shrugged her answer, turning her gaze from his to stare out into the sparkling silver world surrounding them, the trees and bushes proudly displaying their new coats of glittering virginal white, as she struggled to control her traitorous body. 'Don't sulk, Fabia, it's a most unattractive habit.' Her eyes shot up to meet his again and she saw he was smiling coolly as hot colour flooded into her face.

'I'm not sulking,' she said furiously. 'I've got nothing to say and so I'm keeping quiet.'

'A woman who knows when to be quiet?' The dark voice was tauntingly soft. 'There is no end to the surprises that you foist upon me, Miss Grant, is there? A veritable Pandora's box of wonders.' The velvet tones were mockingly warm.

'Oh, shut up.' It was weak, but the best she could do, and for the next few minutes they continued in silence.

Then he spoke again, his deep voice faintly disapproving. 'Haven't you got any boots? You're going to be soaked as soon as we leave the car.'

She flushed at his glance at her tiny feet. 'Of course I've got some boots,' she replied tersely. 'If you remember, it wasn't snowing when we left London and I just didn't choose to wear them.'

'A somewhat unwise decision in the present circumstances.' He slanted a quick glance at her stiff profile. 'And do stop looking as though you're being led to your execution.'

'Why?' she countered quickly. 'That's exactly how I feel.'

'Fabia, Fabia, Fabia...' He sighed mockingly. 'What am I going to do with you?'

'That's exactly what's worrying me,' she said with more than a grain of truth in the sarcasm. She was conscious of his eyes narrowing as all amusement left the hard face, and when he next spoke his voice was devoid of all banter.

'Look, Fabia, there are probably a couple of things we need to get clear,' he said slowly, his eyes intent on the road ahead. Her heart lurched sickeningly as she glanced at the grim face and then her chin rose in unspoken defiance. Here it came, the iron hand in a velvet glove. This was the moment he explained, ever so nicely, the sleeping arrangements...

'The last time we met I wasn't quite myself.' There was a trace of derision in the deep voice but not, she felt, directed at her. 'I may have given you the impression—' He stopped abruptly. 'Well, that last little trick was the straw that broke the camel's back and this particular camel is not known for his patience.' She could believe it. The firm hard mouth was a give-away. 'I have no intention of using you as one of Santa's playmates. You understand me?' She nodded slowly. 'And if this next week isn't going to be a nightmare for us both I would suggest we reach some sort of amicable agreement and keep to it. I will respect your space and you'll respect mine but in public we will be...believable.' The big body was quite motionless.

'How believable?' she asked carefully as her heart pounded.

He gave a harsh bark of a laugh, his expression unreadable. 'You're quite refreshing, you know, like a douse of cold water on a summer's day.' She glanced at him warily, unsure if he was laughing at her or not, but the closed enigmatic face gave nothing away. Her nerves jangled as she looked at him, really looked at him, for the first time that day. Why did he have to be so deliciously attractive? 'I mean it.' The gold eyes flicked over her for a spine-tingling moment. 'Most of the women I know are only too pleased to claim an alliance with the Cade name.' His tone was full of self-mockery and she stared at him for a moment. She didn't understand him, not at all.

'Well, extreme wealth carries its own set of problems, as you've said,' she said quietly. 'That's one of the penalties—'

'There is no need to offer sympathy,' he said scathingly, his voice cutting. 'I'm quite aware of all my assets, Fabia, and how to use them.' She flushed scarlet at the icy rebuff, at the same time as a flood of hot anger turned her eyes brilliant. He was a pig! An autocratic, handsome pig, maybe, but still a pig! 'So...a truce?' She glared at him, but the gesture was lost as he concentrated on the snow-covered road ahead. 'Fabia?' he persisted.

'OK,' she muttered grudgingly. 'If that's what you want.'

'Ah, what I want,' he said thoughtfully. 'Now that is a whole different ball-game, but let's not digress. "Sufficient unto the day" and all that...' He was playing with her, she could feel it. She stared straight ahead into the pale wintry world outside as her thoughts raced. She didn't trust him an inch and especially not when he was being cool and imperturbable, like now. He was so used to everything just falling into his lap! The thought of being on his lap suddenly made her quite hot and she forced her mind into safer areas.

'There's a little pub up ahead,' he said some time later, as the powerful car nosed carefully through the swirling snowstorm which had reached blizzard proportions. 'Fancy a bite to eat?'

She was about to refuse and then realised that his large

sturdy frame had been crouched over the wheel of the low-slung sports car for almost two hours while he negotiated them round drifts and past snow-obscured obstacles as they ventured ever deeper into the silent countryside. She had tentatively suggested half an hour ago that it might be wiser to turn back, but the low growl that had greeted her words had dissuaded her from repeating them. 'Lovely,' she said instead, her voice over-bright as he narrowly missed a large bird that flew out of nowhere, wings flapping madly.

'Damn pheasants,' he muttered irritably, and in spite of her concern for the hapless pheasant she felt a quick rush of pleasure that he could be caught off guard like any ordinary mortal. Because he *wasn't* like any other man she had come into contact with! The thought speared her mind and she was glad he was concentrating so hard on his driving and couldn't notice her face. It wasn't his wealth or his influence that attracted the women, she acknowledged silently, but the man himself. He had an aura of mystery, of fascination, aloof and cold and withdrawn at the same time as exuding a bewitching charm that beckoned even as it rebuffed. He was so...complete. She nodded mentally to herself. He was the most complete man she had ever met. Did he have any weaknesses? She doubted it.

'That's it, up ahead, where the lights are.' She looked into the distance and could just make out a faint glimmer now and again in the seconds when the windscreen was clear. 'I could murder those weathermen,' he added grimly. 'This little lot was supposed to hold off until tomorrow. If I'd known we were in for this we could have left yesterday.'

'I couldn't,' she said quickly. 'It was difficult enough to leave two days early for Christmas as it was. I—'

'Oh, you would have, Fabia,' he said quietly without

looking at her. 'You would have.' There wasn't a shred of doubt in his voice.

She bit back the hot angry words hovering on her tongue with enormous self-control, realising that at this moment in time he needed all his energy and concentration if they were to make the little inn safely, let alone his grandmother's home.

When they drew into the tiny space in the car park that wasn't covered by mountainous powdery drifts she sighed audibly with relief. 'Thank goodness. I didn't think we'd make it this far back there.'

He glanced at her in surprise, his light brown eyes with their thick lashes enquiring. 'You didn't? But there was no problem.' His face was calm and relaxed.

'No problem?' She stared at him. He seemed even closer now that the engine was stilled and she was conscious of the delicious male smell of aftershave on clean taut skin.

'No problem at all,' he repeated softly, turning in his seat and sliding one arm at the back of her shoulders. 'In the unlikely event that the car should break down I'd carry you to safety. I wouldn't let any harm come to you. Do you believe that?' She sensed he was asking her more than the surface question his words held, and for a moment in time she let her eyes be held by the hypnotic power of his tawny gaze before turning abruptly away, lowering her head so that the silky mass of her hair hid her face from his piercing eyes. He was too close, too…knowing.

'No, I don't think I do,' she said shakily, annoyed to hear the tremor in her voice. If she could hear it, so could he.

'I hope one day you will,' he said softly, so softly that she could barely hear him. She didn't look up and after a moment he opened his door and walked round the car to her side, stopping her as she made to climb out. 'Wait.' Before she realised what he was about to do he had bent down and scooped her out of the warm interior as though she were a small child, straightening with her in his arms and kicking the door shut with his foot.

'Alex! Put me down.' Her voice wasn't as indignant as she would have liked it to be. The feel of his arms about her and the hard strong face just an inch from her own was doing crazy things to her insides, and he was holding her so tightly.

'Why?' He smiled down at her lazily as the snowflakes fell into the tawny brown richness of his hair. 'You don't want wet feet, do you?' He brushed his lips against the silk of her hair.

Wet feet were the least of her worries at this moment in time, Fabia reflected faintly as he began to walk with her towards the small arched pub door. It felt deceptively good to be held close to his heart like this, deceptive because the rich promise of his big body and strong arms wouldn't be worth the price she would have to pay ultimately. When it ended. As it inevitably would.

He's not Robin, a little voice whispered tantalisingly in her head as they reached the snow-covered steps leading to the pub door, but the other voice was stronger, the voice that said coldly and quite dispassionately that she was here providing a service, for a time. He hadn't even tried to lie about that. She was an available commodity hired for a specific purpose and when her work was done he would dispatch her back into her own life without another thought. Just like Robin. They came from a different world, these wealthy, spoilt men, a world where they spoke and it was done. She had to remember that, *had to*!

'There we are.' He set her down just outside the door and leant over her to push it open, his snow-covered coat brushing against her face. 'In you go.'

The warmth and colour of a blazing log fire at one end of the small room reached out to greet them as they entered and almost immediately a large burly red-faced giant of a man appeared from a small passageway to one side of the bar. 'Didn't expect anyone to venture out tonight,' he began jovially, his face breaking into a grin as he saw who his customers were. 'Why, it's Mr Cade, isn't it? Come down for the Christmas break, sir? You picked the right day for it!'

'Didn't I just, George,' Alex returned easily with a warm smile. 'Meet Miss Grant. Come to keep me company in case I get lonely.' He turned to Fabia with a wicked gleam in his eyes. 'Isn't that right, sweetheart?'

She looked at him hard for a moment, disliking the innuendo, and then smiled carefully. 'Anything you say, o lord and master. I'm yours to command.' She curtsied prettily, her eyes cold.

George laughed cheerfully in the background, his rough face frankly envious. 'Been trying to get the missus to say that for years,' he said as he began polishing a tray of glasses standing to one side of the ancient till. 'You'll have to let me know your secret some time, Mr Cade.'

Alex smiled at the man as he took Fabia's arm, drawing her over towards the seat by the fire, but she could sense he hadn't liked her little act. It was there in the tightening of his hard jaw and the grip of his fingers on her flesh. 'What would you like to drink? A glass of water?' His smile had a twist in it that she didn't miss, and she glanced up at him defiantly as she sat down, her eyes fiery and her back stiff.

'Anything; I don't mind. They don't do hot drinks, do they?' She shivered as the heat from the fire warmed her cold face. 'I'd love a cup of coffee or hot chocolate.'

'Your wish is my command, o favoured one,' he said

softly. 'Who can refuse the favourite of the harem anything?'

She looked up at him warily, her eyes rebellious. 'You started that, Alex,' she said hotly, her face tight. 'Insinuating to that man that I was here as your...your...'

'My what?' His face was genuinely puzzled. 'You're *supposed* to be down here as my girlfriend, for crying out loud, aren't you?'

'You didn't make it sound like that,' she said quickly. 'Not your girlfriend, more...something else.'

'Like hell I did,' he said flatly, his eyes narrowing. 'If any of your other boyfriends had made a remark like that you would have taken it in the spirit it was meant. It was a joke, just a casual everyday joke. You really have got quite a chip on your shoulder where I'm concerned, haven't you? What is it about me, Fabia—my wealth, the lifestyle, my physical appearance? What is it that reminds you so much of him?'

'I've never said there was a "him",' she said coldly, 'and even if there were it's none of your business. You've asked me to do a job and that's what I'm here for. That doesn't give you the right to pry into my personal life.'

'No, you're dead right,' he said icily as he straightened up away from her, his face stony. 'But when you let your personal life interfere with the work in hand it becomes my business, and that's exactly what you're doing. I don't care whether you like me or not but we might as well get it clear now that I won't tolerate snide remarks and sarcasm for a week. I meant nothing by what I said and whether you believe me or not you're going to have to accept that. I've no intention of watching everything I say for the next few days in case you take offence. Got it?' He marched over to the bar before she could reply and she sat where she was, cheeks burning and hands clenched in impotent rage.

As her cheeks cooled along with her anger she was forced to admit to herself, albeit reluctantly, that he did have a point. She wouldn't have taken umbrage at the remark from anyone else, it was true. She eyed him with distinct irritation as he stood talking to George at the bar. She was in the wrong, again! Why do you have to be so altogether perfect? she thought balefully as she stared at him across the room. And why can you read me like a book? She suddenly wished with all her heart that she hadn't agreed to this crazy idea. She should have let him do his worst, let him unleash his anger—anything rather than be with him like this. She was standing on the edge of a precipice and it felt as if she were blindfolded.

'One cup of coffee.' As he placed the steaming cup in front of her she blinked and realised with a start that she hadn't seen him cross the room. 'Dreaming?' He smiled slowly, the cold anger of a few minutes before seemingly evaporated.

'I'm sorry, Alex.' She spoke quickly before she lost her nerve. 'I was being touchy. I can see you didn't mean anything in what you said.' She touched his arm in a gesture of apology.

He sat down beside her, a strange expression on his face as his eyes rested on the small hand resting on his arm. He smiled slowly. 'And you apologise when you're wrong? You really are quite an enigma, Miss Fabia Grant. I'm not at all sure if it was a good day or a bad day for me when you blazed over my horizon.'

'Blazed?' She risked a shaky smile. There had been something in the deep voice, something tender, that she preferred not to dwell on. It stirred too many discarded dreams.

'Definitely blazed,' he said lazily. 'You stood out from the other women like—'

'Shall we eat?' She broke in with a smile to soften the

abruptness but she couldn't listen to any more. Those had been the very words Robin had said to her all those years ago. 'You stood out from the other women like an exotic flower in a field of daisies'. She hadn't understood at the time that some men were fascinated by a challenge, the unattainable, but later, much later, how she had envied those daisies.

'Sure.' She sensed those sharp gold eyes missed nothing, but he accepted the change of conversation gracefully as he settled back in his seat. 'The steak in red wine sauce is excellent here. George's brother is a butcher and George gets preferential treatment for all the best cuts of meat. Care to try it?'

'Thank you.' She passed him the menu, her face enquiring. 'Do you often eat here, then?'

'I normally stop off and see old George if I'm down this way,' he said blandly, his eyes narrowing on her surprised face. 'I grew up in this neck of the woods, remember.'

'Yes.' She looked at him carefully. 'Of course.'

'You find that surprising?' There was a soft note in his voice that warned her she was on dangerous ground and she hesitated for a moment before answering him.

'Not exactly.' She chose her words cautiously. 'It's just so different from your normal sort of place...that restaurant in London, you know...' As her voice trailed away he didn't move for a long moment, looking at her silently from frosted eyes.

'No, I don't know, Fabia. Do I take it you assume I'm the sort of clown who only likes to be seen in the "right" places? Who carries a social *Who's Who* in his pocket? Is that it?'

It was so close to what she did think, how Robin had behaved, that a flood of betraying colour stained her cheeks pink.

'I see.' His voice was still cool and quiet but his eyes were deadly. 'Charming. And how did you arrive at this delightful piece of supposition? No, let me guess.' He held up his hand mockingly. 'It's none of my business, right?'

She stared at him miserably. The last couple of hours had been a wonderful start to the holiday!

'Well, let's just suppose, for a short while, that there are a few things about me you don't know? Ridiculous, you're thinking, but humour me.' The contempt in his voice was matched only by the scorn in his face. 'I am—surprise, surprise—quite normal in some respects. I eat, I sleep, I breathe and if you cut me I bleed.' He smiled coldly. 'I enjoy doing ordinary things,' he continued, his voice lifted in exaggerated surprise. 'I sometimes drive my own car, take the dogs for a walk, go to the pub. I *even*—' he paused dramatically '—cook a meal for myself now and again. "What?" you're asking. "This leader of the social whirl, this heartless seducer of women—can this be true?"' He paused and took a deep breath. 'I work hard and I play hard and I don't intend to apologise to you for either.' She stared at him silently, quite unable to speak. 'And for crying out loud stop looking at me like that!'

He moved so violently that his chair scraped harshly against the red tiles of the hearth, and as George raised his grizzled head in surprise Alex forced a smile to his face. 'Two steaks in red wine, George, and a nice bottle of wine, OK?'

'OK, Mr Cade. Ten minutes.'

Fabia sat in stunned silence for a few seconds more and then opened her mouth to speak at the same moment as she caught his eye. 'Not a word, Fabia, not a word.'

She flushed angrily. 'I was only—'

'I said not a word.' She suddenly understood how he

controlled his empire. There was a savage ruthlessness in his voice that stopped her in her tracks. She didn't dare speak! She was furious and she wanted to, but she didn't dare. She glared at him nevertheless, her dark blue eyes flashing sparks. 'And drink your coffee.' There was a thread of amusement in the dark voice that seared her stretched nerves like fire. 'You can rest assured that your objections, although not verbal, have been taken note of.'

They didn't speak again until George brought their meal. Alex seemed perfectly calm and untroubled, his big body relaxed and easy and his dark, handsome face quiet. She, on the other hand, Fabia reflected bitterly, was as tight as a coiled spring! It wasn't fair. None of this was fair!

The meal was delicious but she could only eat a small portion of the succulent meat and one potato. There was a huge lump in her throat that defied all food and the churning in her stomach was rendering eating impossible.

'What's the matter?' She became aware that his eyes were fixed on her face as she moved a piece of steak around on her plate for the umpteenth time. 'Are you worried about meeting my grandmother?'

Your grandmother? For an awful moment she thought she had voiced her amazement out loud. His grandmother was the last person she was concerned about, she thought wryly as she looked into the tawny gold eyes. If she were Lucretia Borgia personified the lady would be a pussycat to handle beside this man.

'I'm just not hungry,' she answered quietly. 'Too much breakfast.'

His eyes were frankly disbelieving. 'You'll be all right.' He reached out a hand suddenly and touched her arm gently. 'I told you, I won't let any harm come to you.' His eyes held hers in a tight grip. 'Trust me.' Her flesh tingled faintly where he'd touched.

'I can't.' It was a faint whisper and for a long moment they were locked in a silent world of their own.

'I could kill him.' His voice was flat. 'Whoever he was or is I could kill him. He's here with us now, isn't he?'

'Please don't,' she said weakly. It wasn't real, this concern, this caring. She lowered her eyes, stroking the top of her wine glass distractedly. She had been here before. She mustn't forget. Physical attraction meant little to a man like him.

When they left the cosy shelter of the small, warm pub it was to find that although the worst of the blizzard had abated an icy northerly wind was slicing the air with savage fingers and it was quite dark. Alex lifted her into his arms without a word and this time she didn't protest, steeling herself to show no emotion when he set her down by the car, his face tight.

'One thing, Fabia.' There was a strange tenseness in his voice and his arms were still about her as he spoke, his breath a white cloud on the frosty air. 'Which is it?'

'What?' She stared up at him in the circle of his arms, her eyes dark midnight-blue and her hair a pale glow in the darkness. 'I don't understand...'

'No, of course.' His voice was husky. 'I'm not expressing myself very well. This man, is he a "was" or an "is"?' His eyes were piercingly intent on her face. 'It's not idle curiosity, I need to know. The present circumstances and so on...' It was almost as though he wanted to say more and she waited a moment, her heart pounding and her hands clammy in spite of the freezing air. She wished he would kiss her... The thought jolted her out of the odd stillness that seemed to have her in its grasp and she shut her eyes for a brief moment before replying.

'Was.' She looked up and caught a flash of emotion in his eyes seconds before a shutter came down and blanked it out. 'He's a was.'

'Right.' Although he hadn't moved a muscle and his facial expression was just the same she felt he had changed, that some pressure, a tautness, had drained away. He opened the car door without letting go of her, easing her into the seat, and reaching into the back for a big fluffy car-rug which he draped about her lap before shutting the door carefully. He didn't speak when he joined her a moment later, starting the engine and clearing the windows of their burden of icy snow in silence.

As they continued on their way along white deserted roads the wind was vicious in its intensity, stirring the powdery flakes of snow that had settled on trees and bushes into mad flurries now and again and jostling the car with its force. They passed the odd solitary car crawling along at a pace to match theirs but otherwise the world seemed quite empty, the starlit clear sky overhead and the cold white earth beneath in perfect harmony.

'We've made it.' She came to with a start and realised she must have been dozing; the cosy warmth of the car had been deliciously seductive. She looked about her with wide eyes, seeing nothing but a huge snow-covered stone wall in which were set an enormous pair of wrought-iron gates.

'We have?' She realised there had been a note of great thankfulness in his voice although he had displayed no anxiety or concern during the journey at all. But then he wouldn't, would he? she thought intuitively. She was beginning to realise that Alexander Cade was not an easy man to understand. 'I don't see anything.'

'No, the house is down the drive a way, but first...' He cut the engine and leant over towards her, taking her lips in a firm, hard kiss before she could move. As his mouth covered hers she knew she wouldn't resist, that she didn't want to resist, that she had been waiting for this moment all day. 'So sweet, so fresh...' His passion was growing as he felt her response to him, his tongue plundering her mouth and his hands crushing her against him so that her hair hung in a golden veil over his arm.

The kiss was all-consuming and like before it amazed her with its power, a sweet drugging sensation taking hold of her senses as she melted into him, her hands caught against his hard chest and her head bent backwards. He was running his hands up and down her back now as he covered her eyes, cheeks and mouth in tiny burning kisses, his breathing harsh and uneven.

'Fabia?' There was a note of undisguised surprise in his voice as she opened her eyes to find his face an inch away from hers. She sensed that the blazing passion that had sprung up between them the moment he had touched her lips with his had taken him by surprise as much as it had amazed her. Surely people didn't normally feel like this? This wasn't usual, was it? She stared at him, her eyes huge in her pink-tinted face.

'I was going to kiss you and say I hope you'll have a wonderful Christmas,' he said ruefully as he let go of her, moving back into his seat slowly and brushing a lock of tawny-brown hair off his forehead. 'The...ardour wasn't premeditated.'

'Thank you,' she said shakily, quite unable to muster a casual reply to ease the situation. 'I hope you have a good Christmas too.'

'Yes.' He stared at her for another long moment before turning the ignition key so that the car sprang into life, easing his way between the gates and on to a long tree-lined drive that seemed to stretch into the distance forever, winding and turning as it went. Someone had obviously cleared the drive of snow in anticipation of their arrival; it was heaped in great shining banks either side of them and there was a thin scattering of dark sand beneath the car's tyres. It was a full minute before the house came into view and when it did it merely added to the sense of unreality that had taken hold of her in the last few hours.

The building was palatial, huge and regally beautiful in mellow white stone, set on a slight incline with massive weathered oaks either side like dutiful sentries. It was grand, imposing, like a magnificent stately home, and as she looked at it she felt slightly sick. I must be mad! she thought faintly. This cool, controlled man at her side had grown up in surroundings fit for a king, as far removed from her beginnings as it was possible to imagine, and here she was thinking that he might just be different from Robin, that perhaps he could be genuine.

You fool, she thought harshly. You stupid, pathetic fool. You have maybe caught his fancy for a brief moment in time, something different in his normal well ordered life that he can turn to his advantage, but don't forget you're here doing a job, no more, no less. You couldn't begin to function in his world; you don't even know the ground rules. She remembered the last words Robin had flung at her as she had left the flat that day, with the sound of his mistress's sobs in the background. 'You didn't seriously think you were expected to last, did you? You were a change, my dear, like good old-fashioned ice-cream after an excess of soufflé.' His face had been cruel, red with frustrated passion and rage, the short bathrobe he had pulled on to cover his nakedness revealing white hairless legs that were curiously repugnant. She had concentrated on his legs for a long time, she reflected bitterly; it had helped to get the rest of the miserable fiasco into balance.

'Penny for them?' As they glided to a halt in front of the massive oak door flanked by two imposing stone lions at the top of the circular steps Fabia raised her eyes to Alex's watching face, her expression guarded.

'They aren't worth a penny.' She smiled carefully. 'I would be robbing you.'

'I doubt that.' He was looking at her hard, his eyes noting the tight line of her lips and shadowed eyes, her hands bunched nervously in her lap. 'I doubt that very much. You intrigue me, Miss Fabia Grant; I've never met a woman who houses so many different facets in one lovely body. Playful, wicked, defensive, vulnerable...which is the real you?' She stared at him without answering, her eyes almost black against the whiteness of her face. 'But maybe they are all you?' he continued thoughtfully. 'A grand composite of a hundred men's dreams just waiting to be released.'

'There's nothing mystical about me, I assure you, so don't waste your time trying to make me into something I'm not,' she said sharply, the colour returning to her face as her anger sent a burst of welcome adrenalin to banish the past and provide help for the present. 'I'm a perfectly ordinary average working girl with two flat feet firmly on the ground. You needn't try to charm me into thinking I'm something wonderful, Mr Cade. I know what I am.'

'Maybe.' He smiled slowly. 'But do you know *who* you are? That's different, my prickly little siren. I have a feeling that the real Fabia Grant is in there somewhere, just waiting to be let out. She just got lost for a while.'

'Look—'

He cut her indignant response off with a lazy chuckle. 'And the name is Alex, angel-face, remember? I hardly think "Mr Cade" holds sufficient warmth to make our relationship believable, do you?'

She looked at him as he sat, perfectly relaxed and self-assured, long dark hair perfectly groomed and gleaming against the black coat and his tawny eyes glittering at her discomfiture, and felt a moment's blinding panic at what she had taken on. But it was too late now. As the big door at the top of the steps swung open the thought repeated itself like a ominous tolling bell. It was far, far too late.

## CHAPTER FIVE

THE next few minutes were a confused jumble of larger than life images and noise which gradually sorted themselves into order as they stood in the baronial splendour of the vast hall. The seeming crowd of people that had surrounded them as they had stepped out of Alex's car had shrunk into four elderly servants plus two huge German shepherd dogs which were clearly delighted to see Alex and ignored her with magnificent disregard.

'This is Mary.' Alex hugged the small plump grey-haired woman whose plain face was wreathed in a beaming smile of welcome. 'Best housekeeper in the world, eh, Mary?' The little woman giggled and pushed at him with the flat of her hand.

'Oh, you, Mr Alex, always the flatterer!'

'And this is Jenny, who cooks for us, and Christine, my grandmother's companion.' The two elderly women bobbed their heads smilingly. 'And to keep this house of females in order I rely on the very capable services of John.' He shook the ageing butler's hand as he spoke. 'How is she, John?'

'Looking forward to seeing you, sir.' John was obviously of the old school, Fabia reflected silently as the tall elderly man bowed his head to her solemnly, his face carefully polite. Somehow he seemed the odd one out in this atmosphere of easy informality where even the dogs seemed part of one huge family.

She had a moment's vivid recollection of Robin's coldness with what he termed 'inferiors', which had frequently bordered on rudeness. It had been one of the many things which she had pushed to the back of her mind at the time, dazzled and bewitched as she had been, but which had made perfect sense after the event.

'We'd better go straight in or else she'll be complaining we've kept her waiting,' Alex said smilingly to John, who nodded approvingly, a slight smile touching the severe line of his thin mouth.

'Very wise, sir.'

'Hey, behave, you two.' He stopped after two steps, his hand holding Fabia's arm, and turned to the two dogs, who had slunk behind them ingratiatingly. 'You know you aren't allowed in the drawing-room. Take them into my sitting-room, John—I'll be along in a few minutes.'

'Very good, sir.' When John, the dogs and the three women had disappeared, making the huge hall even larger, he turned to her, his eyes warm, his arms slipping casually round her waist.

'That wasn't too bad, was it?' he asked softly, his gaze drifting to her mouth and then back to her wide-eyed stare as she struggled to take in the opulence of her surroundings.

'No, they seem very nice,' she said weakly.

'Salt of the earth,' he agreed immediately. 'They've all been with my grandmother for years, John since she came to the house as a young and very nervous bride some sixty-five years ago, although he was just a kitchen boy then. He's absolutely devoted to her although she plagues him unmercifully.'

'Is that all the household?' she asked as he walked with her along the hall, pausing in front of a pair of beautifully carved oak doors with curving, ornate brass handles.

'No.' He looked down at her slowly. 'With a house this size it takes some upkeep, so there are a couple of women who come in from the village a few times a week to clean and then two gardeners who double as chauffeurs when necessary. They don't live in.'

'Oh.' Her voice was flat.

'You knew my financial situation, Fabia,' he said softly, lifting her chin so her gaze was forced to meet his. 'What did you expect?' His eyes raked her troubled face intently.

'I don't know.' She shook her head distractedly. 'It's just so... I don't know if I can be what you want me to be for your grandmother.' Blue eyes met gold defiantly.

'I want you to be yourself,' he said firmly, his eyes hooded. 'And don't forget this is an estate that has been in the Cade family for generations; we have no choice in the matter. I would prefer to just have my house in London and the couple of properties abroad, but there it is...' His eyes narrowed on her face. 'My ancestors would haunt me if I let it go.'

'You?' She paused uncertainly. 'But I thought it was your grandmother's home?'

'So it is.' He nodded confirmation. 'But with death duties and other annoying liabilities my grandmother made the estate over to me lock, stock and barrel when I was twenty-one. She didn't expect to live so long.' He smiled at her face. 'Should I have refused it then?'

'No, of course not.' She lowered her eyes quickly. 'And I didn't mean to pry, this is none of my business.' She raised her head as a sudden thought struck her. 'She must have trusted you very much, to give you everything like that.'

'We love each other,' he said simply, his eyes fixed piercingly on her confused face as he opened the doors quietly. 'There's perfect trust where the heart is involved.'

'And about time!' The voice that greeted them was strong and loud, a total antithesis to the tiny, shrivelled-up little figure seated in the massive armchair at the far end of the room almost on top of a huge blazing fire. 'Where have you been? Gossiping with John about me, no doubt? Don't you believe a thing that fool of a doctor has told him, Alexander! I've no intention of dying yet.'

'I've brought someone to meet you, Grandmama,' Alex said stolidly, patently ignoring the whole content of the tiny woman's words as he urged Fabia forward, his arm holding her close to his side.

'I can see that.' Isabella Cade glared at her grandson from the depths of the armchair. 'I might be old and disagreeable, Alexander, but I am *not* senile! Come here, my dear.'

The change in both voice and appearance as the old woman smiled beguilingly at her caught Fabia by surprise and she blinked nervously, glad of the support of Alex's arm as they walked down the beautifully furnished, opulent room, her feet sinking into the thick cream carpet which was ankle-deep.

'This is Miss Fabia Grant, Grandmama; she has agreed to spend Christmas with us.' Alex's voice was almost without expression as they stopped in front of the small figure, his face calm and smiling, but Fabia had eyes for no one but the diminutive little woman staring back at her so interestedly, bright black button eyes and thick white hair belying her great age. She looked like an old, and very mischievous, little gnome.

'Miss Fabia Grant.' The strong, slightly aristocratic voice repeated her name slowly. 'And do you work for your living, Miss Grant?' The lined, paper-thin face stared up at her.

Fabia blinked again in surprise, the formal introductory small talk she had rehearsed in her mind dying in the path of such directness. 'Yes, I do, Mrs Cade,' she said clearly and firmly. 'I am an advertising executive in a large firm.'

'Is that a real job or just one Daddy has purchased for

you?' The piercing black eyes were holding her soft violet ones tight now, and as Fabia felt Alex tense by her side and open his mouth to speak she intervened quickly, her voice staunch and unflinching. Grandmother or not, she would deal with this herself!

'It's a real job, Mrs Cade, worked for *by* myself *for* myself with no help from anyone else at all.' She held the tiny woman's glance unwaveringly. 'That's the way I like it.'

'Looking the way you do?' The tone was faintly disbelieving. 'I can't believe there haven't been many men who would have liked to smooth your path.' The beady eyes flickered over her face.

'I wouldn't deny it.' Fabia was pale-faced and unsmiling now. 'Unfortunately, even in today's liberated society, there are still some men who are egotistical enough to consider a woman as a body with cotton wool for a brain, and, *more* unfortunately, still some women who agree with that opinion.' She held the hard eyes fast. 'You know the sort of woman I mean, Mrs Cade?' It was a blunt criticism and the ancient face knew it.

Young and old stared into each other's minds for a long searching moment and then Isabella Cade sank back into her cushions tiredly, patting the arm of her chair with a tiny wrinkled frail hand. 'I like you, Fabia. I can call you Fabia, can't I?' Fabia nodded dumbly, dazed by the mercurial change of mood. 'I was worried when you walked in that door that you would be a flopsy with no mind of her own or a poor little rich girl becrying Daddy's millions. But you are neither of those things, are you, Miss Fabia Grant?' The old lady smiled wickedly at her grandson who was shaking his head slightly. 'And stop glaring at me, Alexander. I'm too long in the tooth to change and you should allow an old woman her indulgences.'

'Age has nothing to do with it, Grandmama, as you

well know,' Alex said severely with just the trace of a smile to soften his words. 'You've always been the same; your age has just grown into your tongue now and is a convenient excuse.'

'Very convenient.' She smiled roguishly, turning back to Fabia now and looking up at her enquiringly. 'Do you like my grandson, Fabia?' The meaning was painfully clear and now Alex stepped in firmly, his tone abrupt and his face losing the indulgent expression it had hitherto held.

'Enough, Isabella!'

'He only calls me that when I've overstepped the mark,' the bright voice explained to Fabia comfortably, 'although I don't see why in this case. Still, no matter.' The scrawny hands pulled the knitted shawl covering her legs more closely round her. 'Do you find it chilly, Fabia?'

The heat from the fire was enough to roast one alive, Fabia thought faintly. Already she could feel her cheeks glowing scarlet and small beads of moisture dampening her upper lip. 'It's icy outside,' she said quickly, parrying the question adroitly with a nod to the curtained windows.

'Tactful too.' The wafer-thin hand lifted slowly to pat her tentatively on her arm. 'I didn't feel the cold at your age either, but this miserable collection of bones lets me down now.' The deep-socketed eyes closed slowly. 'I'm feeling a little tired, children. Run away and play until dinner.'

As Alex signalled to Fabia to rise he bent and kissed the top of the white head gently, his eyes tender. 'Till dinner, then, you wicked old lady.'

'You wouldn't have me any different,' his grandmother returned immediately, still with her eyes shut.

'Is she always like that?' Fabia asked weakly as they

entered Alex's private sitting-room at the back of the house a few minutes later.

'Always.' He gestured for her to be seated in one of the big winged armchairs pulled close to the crackling log fire in front of which both dogs had been stretched comfortably until their arrival when they had leapt up to greet Alex, long furry tails wagging and tongues lolling ridiculously.

'These are Major and Minor, by the way, father and son.' He stroked the long fur for a few seconds before snapping his fingers, at which signal both dogs slunk back to their original position. 'They're supposed to be guard dogs, bought to swell the effectiveness of the security system, but are both as soft as butter. Everyone blames me.' He smiled at her, his white teeth flashing in his tanned face and the gold eyes creasing at the corners. She caught her breath suddenly as she stared into his face. Why couldn't he have been ordinary, an everyday man working hard for his daily bread and butter? Why did he have to be so far out of her reach? Her eyes widened at the path her thoughts were following and she slammed a door shut in her mind with ferocious determination.

'Just hearing them bark would be enough for the average burglar,' she said lightly, reaching down to pat one noble head. 'And seeing them would do the trick; they're quite magnificent.'

'Long-haired German shepherds are beautiful dogs,' he agreed softly without taking his eyes off her flushed face. She had the feeling that although they were talking quite normally something had sprung up between them that was curiously intimate in its intensity. 'She liked you, you know—you made quite a hit.' She stared at him as he took a step nearer. 'But I knew she would. The first time I saw you—'

She laughed nervously, trying to dispel the mood. 'The

first moment you saw me? I seem to remember you avoided me after that first moment all evening.'

'I should have trusted my initial instincts,' he said slowly as he reached her side and drew her up by her hand until she was standing within the circle of his arms. 'They've never let me down yet.' The moment to resist was there but she let it slip away.

This time his embrace was hard and fierce, and as his head lowered to take her lips she knew a moment's breathtaking panic before the feel of his mouth drove all lucid thought from her mind. He's done this so many times before, he's too good at it! The thought hammered in her mind but in spite of his expertise she couldn't help responding feverishly as he pulled her into his body, moulding her to the hard firm planes of his male frame, leaving her in no doubt as to the desire she had raised in him. His mouth was ravaging hers in an agony of need now and that tiny part of her she had kept locked away since Robin's cruelty had broken the key suddenly unlocked in a sweet response that had her straining against him, giving back kiss for kiss, moaning softly as his lips searched every contour of her hot face, wanting more as his hands travelled over her body in gentle exploration, his flesh warm against hers.

'You are so beautiful, my darling...' As he murmured quiet words of endearment against her lips she found herself wanting to believe him, wanting to trust him. She was so tired of being alone, of fighting her natural yearning for someone to share things with, someone to belong to... Her breath was coming in sobbing pants now and she wound her arms tightly round his neck, revelling in the smell, the feel, the completeness of him. It would be all right. She needed it to be all right. He wasn't Robin, he wasn't at all like Robin. And she wanted to trust him.

'Mr Alexander?' The polite knock at the door took

them both by surprise and as Alex moved her from him she knew a moment's deep, blindingly strong protest inside her. 'I have your tea-trolley, sir.'

'Just a moment, John.' As Alex raked back his hair with hard fingers and smoothed his tie into place she wondered at his composure. He was so cool, so unruffled, whereas she felt as if... Her cheeks burnt still hotter. She felt as if he had already made love to her. She sat down abruptly in the chair she had vacated, adjusting her clothing with shaking hands before bending quickly to stroke Major's coarse, springy fur as Alex opened the door. She didn't know herself any more. How could he sweep away seven years of hard-won cool remoteness in half as many weeks? This was madness, but oh, so sweet.

As John served them tea her cheeks cooled and the trembling deep inside that his passion had induced quietened. As the old man left, the little housekeeper came bustling in with a pot of water to replenish the teapot, loading their plates with still further sandwiches and cake, and standing to chat while they ate. She sensed that Alex wanted to tell the small woman to leave but his innate courtesy won through and he talked amiably with Mary, who was clearly delighted to have 'Mr Alex' home, her round cheeks bobbing animatedly and her brown eyes soft with pleasure.

'I'll show you your room. I'm sure you would like to have a rest before dinner.' As Mary wheeled the tea-trolley from the room he took her arm, leading her to another huge winding staircase at the back of the house.

'I'll get lost here.' The moment of closeness had passed and she needed time now to formulate this new thing that was happening, take in the enormity of what she was feeling. 'I've never been in such a huge place.' She shrugged his arm away carefully.

'It is vast,' he agreed lightly with a discerning glance

at her pale face, 'but your rooms are close to the main staircase so you can't go far wrong. I'll show you around properly later.' He didn't press her to acknowledge their earlier intimacy and for that she was grateful as he led her along several thickly carpeted corridors hung with beautifully framed pictures and dotted with small upholstered easy-chairs in tiny alcoves. 'We've come the long way,' he said as he drew to a halt outside a door identical to the others they had passed. 'The main stairs are just down there but if you get lost, shout.'

'I doubt if anyone would hear me,' she said quietly as he opened the door to reveal what looked like a suite of rooms, the small sitting-room they stepped into regal in white and gold.

'Oh, I'd hear you, Fabia,' he said softly, his voice husky and low. 'You could go to the ends of the earth and I'd still hear you if you called for me.' He moved to take her in his arms but she backed away suddenly, the tenderness and desire in his eyes causing an alarm she couldn't hide.

'I'm rushing you.' He stopped immediately and turned from her, his voice controlled now with its customary coolness. 'I didn't mean to; I planned...' He stopped and straightened his shoulders before turning to her, his face distant now and very cold. 'I'll see you later at dinner, eight o'clock.'

When the door shut behind him and she was really alone she suddenly felt as though her legs couldn't hold her any more. She sank on to a small, heavily embroidered chair in soft gold as she glanced round the room distractedly. It was beautiful, like everything else here. She shut her eyes for an instant and breathed deeply. 'This is crazy, you know it's crazy,' she said out loud, the sound of her voice bringing her eyes open with a quick snap. 'Look around you, girl, just open your eyes and look. What could he possibly want with you, apart from a quick fling for convenience's sake?' She shut her eyes again as the thoughts hammered relentlessly in her mind. But he was different, she felt he was different... She sat for a long time in the quietness of the graceful room, the soft warming glow from the wall-lights reflecting back the gold of the heavy brocade curtains, which had been pulled to banish the cold world outside. She had never felt so confused in her life.

After a time she wandered into the large and very ornate bathroom, deciding to have a bath and luxuriate in the sumptuous surroundings rather than a quick shower. Half an hour later, with her wet hair swathed in a small hand-towel and her body enfolded in a warm fluffy bathsheet, she padded through again to the sitting-room and through to the bedroom beyond, opening the large walk-in wardrobe and wondering what to wear as she gazed at her entire stock of clothes which seemed lost in the vastness.

The sound of high laughter beneath the window caught her attention and made her stiffen. Hugging the towel tightly round her, she walked across to the curtains and pulled them aside, peering down the ivy-covered stone wall outside to the snow-covered drive. She could just see a woman standing in the light from the house, the drifting snowflakes that were caught in the slight breeze now the storm had burnt itself out falling on to sleek black hair and the lovely young upturned face. She laughed again, her full red lips a soft pout in the whiteness of her face, and although Fabia couldn't see her expression clearly in the dim light she felt the beautiful face was alight with some emotion, alive with feeling. It was the girl from the reception, his girlfriend!

As Alex stepped into view, taking the woman's arm in the way he had so often taken hers, she felt no shred of surprise. With a feeling of doom she realised she had expected the inevitable from the first moment the carefree laughter had met her ears. It had been too good to be true, the hope, the expectation. She had known really, deep inside.

She wanted to turn away but remained glued to the window in an agony of self-torture. He walked the woman over to a Land Rover parked haphazardly to one side of the drive, bending down to hear something she was saying so the lighter brown of his hair merged with the darkness of hers. As she saw the woman's arms come round his neck and Alex's head being drawn down to meet the half-open bright red lips Fabia shot away from the window as though it had burnt her, the towel falling from her hair and the damp golden strands tumbling down on to the bare skin of her shoulders.

'Fool, fool, fool...' She ground the words out through tightly clenched teeth as she strode round the room in an agony of feeling before collapsing on the softness of the bed. 'It doesn't matter, he means nothing to you.' She was talking to herself in earnest now but she didn't care, she reflected wildly as she buried her face in the sweet-smelling duvet. There was nothing to get upset about; he hadn't done anything after all, had he? Hadn't promised a thing. She sat up suddenly, her eyes widening in shock. Just the opposite, in fact! He had been absolutely honest with her when he had explained his reasons for wanting her to accompany him here. He needed someone who was quite clear as to where she stood, no strings attached and certainly *not* heart-strings. She pulled his words out of the depths of her mind. 'I am in the middle of several important business transactions and can't waste time on trivia.' She bit her lip hard. What had he said? Oh, yes, he didn't want 'interminable problems once the festive season is over'. That woman down there, there were probably lots more like her and now he was counting her as of the same ilk. She tasted blood in her mouth. How could she have been so stupid? Of course he wouldn't say no to a little light diversion during her stay here; what man would? Of course he was going to try it on and see how she responded. And had she responded! She groaned as she kicked at the duvet viciously with her legs. But she hadn't meant it like that, she had felt—

She froze on the bed. What had she felt? She sat up, her hair a tangled mass of gold around her heart-shaped face in which her eyes shone out a vivid violet-blue in the whiteness. 'I felt a darn sight too much,' she murmured in the emptiness. But it was just physical attraction, of course it was. She nodded vigorously. The raw sexuality between them couldn't be denied but from this moment on she would keep it in its place. If she couldn't be remembered for anything else he would remember her as the one he *didn't* sleep with!

By the time she was ready for dinner she was the epitome of the cool blonde, long golden hair swept into a soft loose bun on the top of her head and a little discreet make-up to give some colour to her over-pale face. She had bought two new evening dresses, along with a long black skirt and several glittery tops, expecting they would dress for dinner each night, and now the soft gold silk of the ridiculously expensive dress gave her the courage she needed to face him again. She looked good, she knew she did, and for the moment that was all she must think of. She had brought this whole mess on herself, she would admit that, but she was blowed if she was going to become one of Alexander Cade's 'fancies'. 'No way, Mr Cade,' she said bitterly into the mirror as she checked herself for the last time. 'You're just like all the rest; the only difference with you is that you're honest about it. Well, thanks for the warning. I shan't forget again.' The tenderness, the sweet words, they were a familiar pattern, probably genuine at the time but swiftly forgotten. How easy it had been to persuade herself differently.

She eased her mouth into a smile as she caught its tightness in the mirror. He had told her he was a busy man with no time for commitment. Well, fine; that suited her just fine! He had nothing she wanted. She despised all his kind.

Her thoughts were mirrored on her face as she opened the door, starting visibly as she almost cannoned into the focus of her malevolence, who was standing just outside, hand raised to knock. 'What's happened?' The smile on his face died as his rapier-sharp glance swept over her face seconds before she schooled her features into blankness.

'Happened?' She forced a short laugh and then wished she hadn't as the sound died in a croak. 'Nothing's happened.'

'You're upset.' He looked at her keenly. 'You weren't like this when I left you a couple of hours ago.'

Before I saw you in a passionate clinch with Miss Happy-Go-Lucky? she thought balefully. How dared he? How dared he look at her as though he really cared how she felt when just half an hour before he had held another woman in his arms? She still wasn't quite sure what his little game was but she didn't like it, she didn't like it at all!

'Nonsense.' She smiled casually. 'You just startled me, that's all.'

'Well, if you look like that when you're startled, angel-face, I sure dread to think how you appear when you're angry.' He leant back against the far wall as he spoke, his eyes lazy as they wandered over her slender form. 'You look gorgeous, absolutely gorgeous, by the way.'

Cut the charm, she thought to herself angrily, this girl's

immune. 'I'm here to do a job and I intend to do it to the best of my ability,' she said coolly, driving back all treacherous thoughts of how delicious he looked in his evening suit with rigid determination. 'You kept your part of the arrangement; now I do my bit, OK?'

He straightened abruptly, the warmth in his face dying as he took in her stony face and hard voice. 'I see, a business deal, nothing else. That's what this little episode is trying to tell me, right?' She nodded coldly. 'And the little scene in the sitting-room? That meant nothing, I suppose?'

'Absolutely nothing.'

'What is it with you, Fabia?' He took a step towards her and then seemed to force himself to stand still, his big body taut and restrained. 'Why are we back to the ice-maiden act? It won't wash any more. I know you want me as much as I want you. I felt your need downstairs when we were making love.'

'We weren't doing anything of the sort,' she said icily as inside her whole being jolted with the force of his words. So he thought he only had to click his fingers and she would succumb, did he? The arrogance! The sheer male arrogance! 'We exchanged a few kisses, that's all; "love" had nothing to do with it! That phrase is dreadfully misused.'

'Well, excuse me...' he drawled slowly, resuming his former position against the wall, his eyes hooded against her. Somehow she felt the casual stance was a pose, a sham, but then she couldn't trust her feelings where he was concerned. The last few hours had made that plain. 'Do I take it you are still prepared to play the part allotted to you in public?' She nodded again, her eyes wary. 'Well, that's good of you, that's really benevolent,' he said smoothly. 'But let me make one thing plain, Fabia— I thought I already had but it would appear you had missed my point.' The gold eyes had turned to marble. 'In private there is no need to continue the charade. I'm not starved of female companionship, as you well know.' His face was expressionless but she suddenly knew, without a shadow of a doubt, that he was furiously angry. 'Neither would I intentionally force myself where I'm not wanted. I obviously misunderstood your...enthusiasm for the role as something else. Nevertheless you are here and you'll behave yourself in front of my grandmother. Do you understand me?'

'Perfectly.' She glared at him furiously and for a long moment they were like two contestants in a boxing-ring seconds before the bell went for the next round.

'Hell, Fabia,' he shook his head as he levered himself off the wall, 'why do I always bite back with you? Look, I don't know what's going on in that head of yours but how about giving me a break, girl? Letting down the drawbridge for just a short time? You don't know me, fine, I accept that, but how about throwing out all the preconceived rubbish that you've taken in and giving us a chance to get to know each other better? If nothing else it's going to make the next few days a lot easier for everyone concerned.'

For a moment, just a moment, the sincerity in his deep rich voice reached her and she felt herself weakening, and then the icy hand of logic pulled her backwards with a sharp jerk. Fool, she told herself bitterly, how many times do you have to be burnt before you stop playing with fire? The man's lethal. You thought Robin had got a good line but he was a mere novice beside Alex.

'I'm here to do a job for you and nothing else,' she repeated as she shut the door behind her, turning back to see his face close against her, his features setting into the cold autocratic lines she knew so well.

'OK, Fabia, have it your way,' he said unemotionally,

his eyes looking through her as they walked along the corridor. 'If you want to live in that little box you've made for yourself, who am I to try and dissuade you?' The tone was casual and uncaring and hurt her more than anything that had gone before, but she said nothing. Her emotions were too raw for more verbal sparring.

Isabella was sitting in solitary splendour as they entered the huge dining-room, a tiny little figure at the end of the vast dining-table, and somehow, in spite of the little woman's caustic tongue, the sight touched Fabia deeply.

'You look quite charming, my dear,' Isabella said warmly as they reached her side, patting the chair to the left of her as she spoke.

'Thank you.' Fabia looked into the wrinkled old face warily. She had the distinct impression that those bright black button eyes saw far more than Isabella revealed.

'I like to have young people around me,' Isabella said comfortably as John began serving the soup from a large silver tureen. 'Makes me feel young. Too many old fogies in this house, eh, John?' She smiled wickedly at the elderly butler, whose face remained in its impassive lines.

'As you say, madam,' he replied blandly.

Isabella gave a cackle of laughter as she turned again to Fabia. 'He thinks I'm a dreadful old lady,' she said with a wave of her hand at John. 'Quite dreadful. Isn't that right, John?'

'As you say, madam,' he said again, his face dead-pan, but as the old man's eyes met those of his mistress over the soup tureen Fabia saw a smile in their watery blueness that matched a light in Isabella's. The two understood each other, she realised suddenly, perfectly.

'How long have you known my grandson, Fabia?' Isabella asked after a few minutes of silence.

'Just a few weeks.' Fabia had practised this little speech in her head for so long it came out quite naturally. 'We met at a social function Alex was holding. My friend and I had been given tickets at the last moment and we thought it was a shame to waste them.'

'Another of your charity dos, Alexander?' Isabella asked disapprovingly. Alex nodded without speaking and his grandmother turned to Fabia again, her lined face irritable. 'I keep telling him, he's too busy to bother with such things, he works all hours of the day and night as it is. Work, work, work...' She eyed her grandson morosely. 'But he says just giving a donation himself is not enough, that other people's consciences need to be awakened, those who can afford it, that is.' She looked at Fabia sharply. 'What do you think?'

The abrupt question, coming on top of the surprising revelations that Alex worked too hard and actually cared about the charities he supported, temporarily robbed Fabia of speech and she stared at Isabella for a second, her mouth opening and then closing.

'I think Fabia would like to eat her dinner in peace,' Alex said smoothly, meeting her eyes for a split-second over the dining-table. 'All right, Grandmama?' His tone was mild but there was a touch of steel in the softness that the old woman clearly recognised.

'So I'm talking too much, so what's new?' Fabia had a sudden urge to giggle but restrained it with difficulty. This irascible old woman was outrageous but she liked her brand of unpretentious honesty and uncompromising veracity. There was an integrity about Isabella that was unmistakable, very much like her grandson—she caught her thoughts sharply. No, she hadn't thought that, she *wouldn't* be fooled again.

As the meal progressed she found that playing the part allotted to her became more and more difficult, due mainly to the close proximity of Alex rather than anything else. He reached across the table a couple of times, taking her hand briefly in a little show of affection that had her wanting to snatch it back at once. She didn't like the feel of his hard warm flesh on hers; it was...unsettling. Added to which those sharp bird-like eyes of his grandmother seemed to be watching her every move. She forced her mouth to smile, talked lightly of this and that, but had the distinct impression that she wasn't fooling Isabella for a second. The old woman knew there was something wrong, she just didn't know what it was—for the moment.

Yet the old lady seemed to like her. As Fabia talked frankly about her humble beginnings, her job, the little flat that she called home, she sensed she had gained Isabella's friendship. Isabella became quite animated at one point, reminiscing about her equally modest childhood as the youngest daughter of a poor Italian family in a little obscure village deep in the countryside of rural Italy. 'Then Henry comes along one day,' she said dreamily, 'Alexander's grandfather. His parents had sent him to do a tour of Europe; they still did it in those days.' She nodded to herself. 'And he couldn't speak a word of Italian and I knew no English. But we communicated.' She raised dark eyes to Fabia's interested gaze. 'In a manner as old as time.' Alexander shifted uneasily but the old lady was not going to be silenced this time. 'When Henry wanted to marry me his parents were horrified, and mine...' She laughed softly. 'They dragged me off to the priest and asked him to keep me locked in a room at the church. It was shameful, you see; I was a Catholic Italian girl and he was English and not of the same religion.'

'What did you do?' asked Fabia, fascinated.

'Alexander will tell you, won't you, my dear?' Isabella sank back in her chair. 'I'm tired.'

'Oh, it doesn't matter, please, leave it if—' The old lady interrupted her forcibly, waving her hands at Fabia irritably, her strong voice belying the excuse of exhaustion.

'Alexander knows the tale, he's heard it often enough. Tell Fabia what happened, my boy.' Fabia looked keenly into the dried-up old face. For some reason known only to herself Isabella wanted Alex to tell her the rest of the story.

'If you insist,' Alex said lazily, his flecked eyes with their strange golden light fastening on Fabia's pale, beautiful face tightly. 'My grandfather was determined to have her; he would listen to no one. Late one night he got a ladder and rescued her from the church. They eloped. For a time both sets of families would have nothing to do with them but then my father was born and...babies have a way of smoothing family feuds out.' He paused, his darkly tanned face and long thick burnished hair giving him the aura of a fierce brigand in the dim light from the shaded standard lamps, one at each end of the room. 'He had to have her, you see. Once he had found her there was no way on earth anyone would have persuaded him to let her go. He would have died first.' There was an emotion in his voice that had her transfixed now, her eyes locked with his, her head refusing to accept the message her heart was giving her as she looked into his waiting face. 'There's an old story about the Cade men; it goes on from generation to generation. We only love once, just once in our lives, but when we do it's for eternity.'

'Is it true?' she whispered breathlessly, mesmerised by the atmosphere that had thickened like a powerful drug.

'Oh, yes.' His eyes were burning into her. 'Quite true.'

Isabella expelled a satisfied sigh, nodding her head like a wise old owl. 'So now you know, my dear.' She looked hard at Fabia. 'Don't you?' There seemed to be more in the question than its face value and Fabia stared at her silently, trying to read the razor-sharp mind behind those bright black eyes.

'Yes, of course, thank you for telling me your story,' she said carefully, fighting the urge to lift her gaze to Alex's and see what was written in the hard face, afraid of what she might see. Laughter? Mockery? Scorn? He was sitting as still as a statue and she was vitally conscious of every line of his body as though she were looking at him.

She wondered what he *really* thought of the old story. He would have had to agree with it in front of his grandmother, knowing it meant so much to her, but what of him, and all those countless women he had known?

The rest of the evening passed pleasantly enough and when Isabella retired for bed, at just after ten, Fabia waited until the old lady had disappeared with the ever faithful John at her side, it being Christine's half-day off, and then made her escape from Alex's sombre presence. He nodded slowly at her hesitant 'goodnight', his dark face enigmatically distant, but she was conscious of his eyes on her as she climbed the long curving staircase, their heat burning into her back as though their light came from the sun itself. She glanced round just before disappearing from view to find his gaze tightly fixed on her as she had expected, the big body taut and still, the goblet of brandy in his left hand motionless. Everything in his stance suggested an attitude of waiting and it unnerved her without reason; she didn't understand him and she understood herself still less.

Later, in the soft downy warmth of the huge double bed, she cried for the first time in years, long racking sobs that did nothing to ease the ache inside her, the sense of loss and despair that had grown all day.

I'm just tired, tired and nervous, she told herself firmly when the worst of the weeping had passed. I'm in an unfamiliar environment, an alien in a different, fabulously seductive world where I don't know the rules and I'm surrounded by strangers who talk in riddles and expect me to understand. She bounced her head in agreement with herself.

She'd be different in the morning. In the cold clear light of day all the forgotten dreams and hopes that a certain six-foot-four, tawny-eyed stranger had resurrected would sink back to their rightful place, buried deep in the hidden recesses of her mind, locked away from prying eyes.

'I *am* happy,' she whispered defiantly into the beautiful empty room. 'No one has everything they want, after all.' She was a career girl now, a totally different creature from the childlike romantic whom Robin had picked up and discarded so brutally. And she wanted it that way. *She did*!

## CHAPTER SIX

'It's beautiful, Alex.' Fabia stood awe-struck in the doorway of the main drawing-room, her eyes wide with wonder as she looked up at the magnificent seven-foot tree towering above her, its sweet-smelling pine branches covered in red ribbon, glittering white stars and small delicately formed candles in red and white twists. 'I've never seen such a gorgeous tree.'

'I get one each year for Isabella,' Alex said quietly as his eyes stroked her glowing face, a warmth in their gold depths that caused her breath to shudder in her throat. 'In Italy, when she was a child, each house couldn't afford a tree with decorations and presents so all the villagers would get together and bring a tree down from the mountainside for the village square. I know the story by heart and you'll be hearing it soon, no doubt.' He smiled slowly. 'Each family would give what trimming they could, a ribbon there, an ornament here; she pines for those times now she's alone.'

'She has you,' she said softly, meeting his gaze, before her eyes were drawn to the mass of gaily wrapped parcels piled around the huge terracotta pot filled with earth in which the tree's roots were embedded.

'Isabella assures me the adults made sure even the poorest child had a gift on the Saviour's birthday. There aren't too many barefoot little ragamuffins round here but we donate the presents to the children's ward at the hospital on Christmas Eve.' He shrugged lightly. 'It's become something of a tradition.'

'I think that's lovely.' She smiled up into his watching

eyes and for a moment he looked as though he was going to say more, but then he turned away dismissively.

'I have my moments of weakness,' he drawled with mocking sarcasm, and she flushed at the taunting note in his voice. She had woken that morning deep in the luxurious warmth of the big bed and decided that the only way she was going to get through the next week was to take each day as it came. No more heart-searching, no more dissecting things that were better left alone. She was nothing to Alex, she had to remember that; he could have as many girlfriends as he liked, it was *absolutely* nothing to do with her. He was used to sophisticated worldly women to whom love-affairs were merely pleasant diversions for a limited time. She knew that...so why did the picture of a tall dark-haired woman with pouting red lips keep flashing into her mind in taunting ridicule?

They ate alone in the large breakfast-room—Isabella never rose before lunchtime—and just as they finished the doorbell rang. The morning was filled with visits from friends and relations and several of the women, Fabia noticed wryly, put great enthusiasm into greeting Alex. He remained his normal charming self, acting his part magnificently as he drew Fabia to his side time and time again, dropping a kiss on her fair head or hugging her close in a swift embrace. 'You don't need to keep doing that,' she whispered angrily after one long unexpected kiss on the lips, emerging flushed and breathless with a strange little tremor in her stomach.

'I like it,' he murmured unrepentantly in her ear, his warm breath causing her to shudder helplessly. 'Don't you?'

'No, I do not,' she snapped back quickly, all the finer feelings of the morning melting into hot rage. 'I'm here acting as your girlfriend, not your...your—'

'But I kiss my girlfriends, angel-face; I kiss them a lot,'

Alex said softly with his eyes tight on her pink face. She could hear a thread of amusement in the deep voice and longed to slap the cool, handsome face, hard! 'Don't the men in your life like to express their appreciation of your finer qualities?'

She glared at him ferociously and spoke without thinking, provoked by his cynical mockery. 'I don't have any—' She stopped abruptly as his eyes narrowed into gold slits. 'I mean...' She paused again, searching for the right words that wouldn't betray her.

'What *do* you mean, Fabia?' There was no trace of amusement or mockery in the hard face now, more a slightly incredulous intentness that totally unnerved her. 'Are you seriously telling me—?'

'I'm not telling you anything,' she said bitterly as she jerked away from his side, walking over to the other side of the crowded room without turning round. How could she have been so stupid as to let that little snippet of news slip? Maybe he would assume she had meant there was no one special at the moment? The hope died as it was born. No, he was too astute by half. She had unwittingly divulged her chaste state and to a man like him it would be like the ultimate challenge. Damn, damn, damn! She was making a real mess of all this.

It was as they all walked through to the dining-room for a buffet-style lunch and Fabia caught a glimpse of yet more presents piled high on one of the occasional tables in the hall that the dreadful realisation dawned on her. She hadn't brought any presents! She stopped so that Alex, a step behind her, cannoned into her back, his arms going out to hold her as she stumbled forwards. 'Very nice, but what's the matter?' he said softly as he caught sight of her stricken face.

'I didn't bring any presents, Alex.' She stared up at him in horror. 'How could I have forgotten? I should have got your grandmother something, I just wasn't thinking straight. What shall I do?' She glanced round helplessly.

'Don't look so tragic.' He smiled at her consternation, his voice wry. 'It's Christmas Eve, remember? The shops will stay open until they've extracted the last penny from the happy public who wander around in a daze of goodwill and whisky.' She didn't like the cynicism and turned away sharply, her face expressing her feelings more adequately than words.

'Sorry.' He turned her to him again and this time his face was clear of all sarcasm. 'I'll take you into town when we've had lunch,' he said quietly. 'You can do your shopping there.'

'No, I don't want to take you away from all your guests,' she said quickly with a little gesture of repudiation. 'You stay here—I'll call a taxi.'

'No need.' His voice was tight. 'It's open house here on Christmas Eve, everyone knows that. People just come and go as they please. I'll take you.'

'No, really.' She suddenly couldn't face the thought of being close to him again in the car, those long muscled legs stretched out so close to hers and the subtle, distinctly male smell of him filling the air round her with sensual promise. 'You stay here—your grandmother—'

'For crying out loud, woman!' He swung her round so quickly as she made to turn away that her head snapped on her shoulders, her hair flying over her face in silken disarray. 'Can't you bear my company for as short a time as that? Am I really so obnoxious to you?' She stared at him as he glared down at her, his face as black as thunder. 'I'm trying, I'm really trying to keep my temper with you, Fabia, but you know how to push a man to the limit, don't you? Now whether you like it or not I'm going to take you into the damn town. Another word and so help me I won't be responsible for my reactions.' After one more furious scowl he walked past her into the gaiety beyond, leaving her standing shaking and silent in the deserted hall.

This was ridiculous; he had no right to talk to her like that, she thought angrily as she smoothed the soft woollen dress she was wearing over her hips with shaking hands and flung back the thick gold hair from her face. She wasn't going to fall at his feet in gratitude for his company whatever the other women did. A vision of clinging arms round his neck and a bright red mouth close to his made her wince with sudden pain. He was arrogant and overbearing and everything she disliked in a man, and if he couldn't take the way she felt about him he should let her go home, where she belonged.

The air was bitingly cold and crystal-clear as they left the warm brightness of the house some time later. A weak yellow sun lit the white snow into blinding silver, the stark black branches of the bare trees standing out against the pale hoary sky in vivid contrast. She stood for a moment at the top of the steps as Alex walked past her to the car parked below and drew deeply on the fragrant icy air, shutting her eyes as she let its cold clear breath stir her lungs. After the close warmth of the house it felt wonderfully good.

It was a beautiful winter's day and it was Christmas Eve, she thought suddenly, and life was good. Whatever, life was good.

'You look like the spirit of winter with your head back like that and the sun on your hair,' Alex said gruffly, and as she opened her eyes and caught the full force of his golden gaze she stood transfixed for a long moment, caught by the magic of the moment. 'Come on, you'll get cold.' He broke the spell abruptly, turning away with a brusque nod of his head, his voice terse and his body stiff as though he was holding himself in control.

'This is a beautiful car.' She ran her hand down the smooth red paint of the Ferrari as she sank down into the soft leather seat. 'It isn't the one we came in, is it?'

'No, I have several cars,' he said shortly, his face cold as though she had said the words in criticism. She glanced at him as he shut her door and strode round the car to the driving side. He looked bad-tempered and angry, and undeniably gorgeous. She caught herself quickly. None of that, Fabia, she said silently to that other self she seemed to be talking to a lot recently. He's your employer and this is a temporary job, nothing else. Concentrate on that and that only.

It would have been a short journey into the town in normal conditions but due to the thick snow blanketing the countryside the powerful car was forced to crawl along, nosing its way through the space cleared in the middle of the main roads, which were narrow enough at the best of times. The wooded hills rolling southwards were frozen in pale silent beauty, sheltered farms and hamlets motionless except for thin spirals of smoke rising from weathered chimneys.

They made the journey in almost total silence and, although she tried to concentrate on the beauty of the countryside in its mantle of bridal white, her thoughts were drawn back time and time again to the dark-haired woman who had flung her arms round his neck with such familiarity. How many women had he known? How many did he still know? She bit her lip silently. He wasn't the sort of man to be without female companionship too long. No doubt he was in the middle of some sort of liaison right now. He had said that there were several women he could have asked to spend Christmas with him except that all of them would prove difficult to unload once the holiday was over. She glanced at him under her lashes, the strong firm hands that she knew by experience could be devastatingly gentle, the hard powerful body so vitally male—

'Would you like me to come in with you?'

As his voice jerked her out of her perusal she glanced out of the window and saw they were just entering the town, an enchanting little maze of narrow streets, snug squares and brightly lit low-tiled shops, timelessly picturesque under the snow-filled white sky. 'Sorry?'

'The shops. Would you like me to come with you?' he repeated patiently, easing the car along slowly in the nose-to-tail traffic, the packed pavements on either side of the narrow street threatening to thrust their burden of scurrying humans into their path at every turn.

'Not if you've something else to do,' she said quickly and then caught his sigh of exasperation as he drew into the 'reserved' space in a bulgingly full car park outside a large store.

'Does that mean yes or no?' he asked drily as he cut the ignition with a small sigh. 'Translate for me.'

'Well, I suppose I might get lost,' she said carefully, and after one searing glance he stretched lazily before opening his door.

'I've had sweeter offers but that will have to do,' he said with heavy sarcasm as he walked round the car and opened her door. 'I think I realised very early on in our acquaintance that as an ego-booster you were a non-starter.'

'I wouldn't have thought you of all people would need one,' she said quickly as she climbed out of the car, his hand on her arm.

'Oh, yes?' he said mildly but with a faint narrowing of the cat-like eyes. 'And why is that?' He turned her to face him, tucking her collar up round her neck as though she were a child and kissing the tip of her nose with warm lips.

The unexpected tenderness took her completely by surprise and she stared at him stupidly for a moment, her violet eyes with their heavy fringe of lashes wide with confusion.

'Why is that?' he repeated softly, tilting her chin up to him with one finger and drawing her against him so that she was tight within the circle of his arm. 'Tell me.'

'You're so...' Her voice trailed away as he kissed the tip of her nose again. 'Don't do that, I've told you.'

'You've told me a lot of things, angel-face,' he said comfortably as he tucked her arm in his and led her towards the shop. 'Whether I'm prepared to listen to them is another story, of course.' She tried to wrench her arm from his but his grip tightened until she was forced to give in.

'Mr Cade, how nice to see you, sir.' They had only been in the hot perfumed atmosphere of the shop for sixty seconds when a smartly dressed little man in a pin-striped suit came hurrying over to Alex's side, his jowls bobbing with delight. 'We've kept your space in the car park free for the last few days, sir, in case you decided to shop with us. I hope it was available for you?'

'Yes, it was clear, thank you.' Alex smiled dismissively, and after a long curious look at Fabia the small man backed away carefully, his head still nodding ingratiatingly, in much the same way that the common herd left the presence of a king in days gone by.

'What was all that about?' Fabia asked, stopping to look up into Alex's closed face. 'Who's that man?'

'The manager of this store,' Alex replied shortly. 'Now shall we—?'

She ignored the proffered hand and remained where she was. 'That space in the car park—is it kept specially for you, then, always?'

'Yes.' He looked down at her quietly. 'It is.'

'Why?' She stared up at him, noticing as she did so, in a strangely detached sort of way, that he was head and shoulders above any other of the men milling round them in the crowded store, his tanned skin and tawny colouring accentuated by the lights overhead.

'Because I own this building.' A dry smile twisted his lips. 'Another nail in my coffin?'

'You own it?' She glanced round the fabulously elegant store in amazement.

'I own the whole block,' he said slowly with a resigned expression on his face, 'and I'm blowed if I know why I'm trying to keep it from you except that it places a few more bricks in place, doesn't it?'

'Bricks?' This conversation was becoming more bizarre each moment.

'Yes, bricks,' he said shortly. 'As in "building", you know, like the ones you use so well in the construction of this wall to stop me getting inside that strange little head of yours.'

'I don't know what you're talking about,' she said shakily. The hard golden glare was unnerving.

'No?' He smiled coldly. 'I think you do. I think you know exactly what I mean, Fabia, and for the record—'

'Alex, darling...' As an overdressed, gushing matron of considerable years caught his arm Fabia made her escape.

'I'll be back here in ten minutes,' she muttered shortly and, ignoring his call, dived into the mêlée quickly, avoiding his restraining hand with a turn of her body as she went. She fought her way over to a relatively clear space beside a massive Christmas tree and stood for a moment, more shaken than she cared to admit. What did he mean when he said things like that? It was almost as though he cared, really cared about her opinion of him. She shook herself. Stop it, she thought grimly, you're trying to believe what you want to believe. Of course he'd like to get under your skin—for a time. Once you'd served your purpose it would be 'bye bye, Fabia' without a second thought. Wake up, girl!

Taking the lift up to the next floor, she wandered about for five minutes wondering what on earth she could buy a woman of eighty-seven who had everything she wanted and had for the last sixty-five years! The ten minutes were nearly up when she noticed a display of gaily worked tapestry blankets in a corner, and, remembering the heavy blanket wrapped round Isabella's legs on their first meeting, she decided that would do. It was ridiculously expensive but she bought it anyway and was just standing waiting for the lift to take her down to the ground floor again when she spied a tiny hoop of silver key-rings on the cosmetics counter. Each one had a minute mirror attached to it, and as she stood looking at them she made up her mind. He would see the joke, wouldn't he?

'Would you like me to gift-wrap it for you?' The tall, beautifully dressed willowy blonde was all long red-painted nails and flashing gold bracelets as she carefully placed the small key-ring in a tiny box and wrapped it with a small white bow, fixing a little card to the outside and handing Fabia a pen.

'Oh...thank you.' She thought for a moment and then wrote swiftly, 'Who caught who?' Would he tie it in with that first message?

Alex was standing just where she had left him when she stepped out of the lift and as she glanced over and saw his big dark figure quite detached from the rest of the noisy milling throng she felt a jolting sensation in her heart region. He looked severe and distant, and absolutely gorgeous.

The golden gaze fixed on her when she was a few yards away and he smiled lazily, his eyes travelling to the huge box in her hands which contained Isabella's gift. The key-ring was in her pocket. 'You don't mean to say you've chosen something already?' he said mockingly as she reached his side. '"Curiouser and curiouser", as Lewis Carroll wrote. You're a real little Alice, aren't you?'

'Am I?' She smiled nonchalantly, her stomach churning as he wrapped an arm protectively round her shoulders, pulling her into his side, fighting the pleasure the act of possession aroused.

'You sure are.' He looked down at her, his eyes travelling over the tousled blonde hair and huge violet eyes before they fastened on her lips. There was a heat in their depths that caused the fluttering in her stomach to intensify a hundredfold. 'Most of the women I know take a couple of hours to choose a lipstick!'

'Do they?' She smiled again, forcing her lips to turn upwards as his words rang painfully in her ears. 'Most of the women I know'. Oh, she hated all this, she did!

'Fancy a coffee before we leave?' He took the box from her, tucking it under his arm.

'Where?' They were moving towards the lift and he glanced down at her, a wry smile on his face.

'Well, we could go to my office on the top floor. It's nice and warm there and quite secluded, and once Tomkins has brought the coffee I could make sure we are quite alone. Or...' the tawny gaze was mocking '...we could go to the coffee lounge on the third floor.'

They stepped into the lift and he smiled down at her pink face as he pressed the button for the third floor. 'When I think of the girls who would have jumped at that offer,' he said lazily into her ear as they stood pressed together in the close confines of the crowded lift. 'You don't know what you're missing.'

'Why don't you ask one of them, then?' she said snappily as the metal doors swished open on the third floor.

His answering chuckle made her teeth grind in helpless

defiance and she eyed him balefully as he led her over to the fresh aroma of percolating coffee.

It was dusk when they stepped back into the icy air, the pavements treacherous underfoot and the heavy sky a pale pink against the white world beneath. The long, low car was forced to pick its way carefully through the crowded streets, growling softly at the indignity, and then they were in the open countryside again, the hedges and trees picked out in startling clarity against the darkening red sky.

'There's a picture-book view at the top of this hill,' Alex said quietly when they had been driving for ten minutes or so. As they reached the peak of the gently rising fell he drew to a halt, letting the slow purr of the car's engine fall silent as the grandeur of the sweeping wooded slopes dotted with the odd stone farmhouse and tiny isolated village tucked away in the snow-covered expanse worked their timeless magic.

Fabia forgot the flutter of panic she had felt when he had stopped the car, forgot that the man sitting next to her so quietly was a ruthless man of the world used to having his smallest whim granted with immediate deference, forgot everything as she gazed out into the miles upon miles of Christmas-card countryside frozen in exquisitely pale beauty beneath a darkening sky of red and gold. It was breathtaking, and the heavens had turned a light milky grey before she glanced at him, coming back to the world surrounding her with a small sigh that expressed what words couldn't.

His eyes were fixed tight on her face, a sensual slumberous warmth in their browny-gold depths that had her breath catching in her throat and her lips half opening in anticipation. His mouth was warm and mobile as it covered hers demandingly until he was crouched over her in her seat and she felt as if time itself had been suspended.

His hands moved beneath the warm tweed of her coat without her realising it, drawing her into him with sensuous ease as they caressed each curve and contour of her melting body. She was utterly lost in the moment, the beauty of the world outside and the scent of his light tangy aftershave creating a heady sensation of pliant, soft oneness that had her moaning his name against his hard mouth. His breathing was harsh and ragged as he felt her response and now his lips were exploring her face as though he were blind, moving over her flushed skin in tiny darting kisses that had her straining against him for more, her arms reaching up to the broad shoulders above her in wordless abandonment.

It was when she felt the coolness of air tighten her breasts that realisation dawned. She had been unaware that he had unbuttoned her dress, unaware of anything except the sweet pressure of his mouth and the feel of the hard, dominant body next to hers, but now she recoiled as though he had struck her, moving violently beneath him so that his hands were stilled and his mouth raised from hers.

'What is it?' He raised his head to stare into the wide, shocked blue eyes. 'I won't hurt you—don't be frightened.'

'No...' She struggled against him, pushing his hard chest with the flat of her hands, and he moved away immediately, his face settling into the expressionless mould she knew so well that hid his feelings like a cold blank mask.

'It's him, isn't it,' he said quietly and with no trace of emotion in his voice, making the words a statement rather than a question. 'It might be over but you're still thinking of him, aren't you?' The slanted eyes swept over her flushed face as he raked back his heavy fall of hair with his fingers. 'Do you love him that much? He must have left you, finished it, and yet you still want him that badly?' As he turned from her and rested his hands on the steering-wheel she noticed, with a detached numbness, that they were shaking slightly, but apart from that he betrayed no feeling at all. They could have been discussing the weather all those moments before, such was the quietness of his whole being now.

'I can't explain...' She knew she was going to cry in another moment and bit hard on her bottom lip to still the tears as she buttoned her dress with shaking hands, staring out of the side-window into the colourless world outside as she pulled her coat more closely round her.

After a full minute he relaxed back into his seat with a deep sigh, his hands still on the steering-wheel and his eyes straight ahead. 'I'm sorry, Fabia; believe it or not, that wasn't planned,' he said quietly. 'I'm not the sort of man to seize upon any advantage and it's been years since I've made love in a car.' He stopped suddenly. 'Hell, I'm making things worse, aren't I? What I'm trying to say is—'

'I know, I know.' She couldn't look at him—if she did she would be lost—so she stared out through the side-window, her face as white as the snow outside. 'Could we go back now, please...?'

He said nothing, adjusting his long legs in the close confines of the car as he turned the key in the ignition, his face grim and cold as he checked the mirrors before turning the car fully into the road and continuing down the hill, the car lights gleaming yellow in the darkness.

She felt sick with mounting horror as she remembered how easily he had overcome all the barriers erected so firmly during the last seven years. She had barely allowed a man to kiss her in all that time, earning a reputation for frigidity, she knew, but hugging it to her as though it were a prize. She hadn't wanted to be involved with anyone again—even the nicest of the men she had occasionally dated had left her cold—and here she had virtually thrown herself into his arms, inviting— She closed her eyes for a second and forced back the tears that were threatening to overflow. Inviting a lot more than she had got, she admitted honestly. She couldn't have blamed him if he had been unable to stop; all her signals had been bright green... She moaned silently. What was he thinking? She dared not risk a glance at his face.

The short drive home seemed like hours, so rigid and tense was her body, and as they drove through the gates and into the sweep of the long drive she uncurled her hands from her lap and tried to soften the tightness in her face. It was Christmas Eve, there was bound to be a houseful when they got in, and she had to appear relatively normal if only for Isabella's sake.

It seemed as though every light in the house was glaring as they drew to a scrunchy halt outside the door, and as Alex noticed a large white Mercedes to one side of the driveway he frowned, his eyes narrowing in protest. 'Great, just what we need—Susan and family *en masse*, if I'm not mistaken. I told everyone to keep their visits confined to the day for once; Isabella can't take too much excitement and she'll be exhausted by now.'

'Susan?' Her timid enquiry was lost as he opened his door abruptly and marched round to her side of the car, opening her door and helping her out with his eyes fixed on the house. Almost as though he had willed it, the door opened a second later to reveal a horribly familiar figure, the sleek dark hair swept up into an elegant chignon, each strand beautifully in place.

'Alex, darling, we've been waiting absolutely ages. We couldn't go without saying hello, now, could we?' The woman moved gracefully towards them down the steps, and as she placed herself unasked into Alex's arms Fabia realised she was a little older than she had first supposed, probably thirty or so, and as the lovely face glanced at her for a piercing moment with big beautiful green eyes Fabia knew something akin to an electric shock shoot down her spine. She had never before in her life experienced a look of such angry, undisguised hate; there had been something in those jade-green eyes that was positively malignant, something that reached out at her through the icy air with fierce animal viciousness and curled her insides in protest.

'Susan.' Alex gently disentangled the slim arms from around his neck and placed them firmly at the woman's sides, softening the gesture with a warm smile as he looked down at the beautiful face staring up at him. 'Are your parents with you, and the children?'

'Of course.' Seemingly unrebuffed, Susan placed her arm in his, ignoring Fabia as though she didn't exist. 'Daddy had to drive. You know I daren't take the car out on roads like these.' She smiled helplessly up into his face like a little girl asking for approval.

'I'd like you to meet Fabia.' He uncoiled Susan's arm with amazing dexterity and reached out for Fabia, curving her into the crook of his arm as he moved slightly to one side. 'Fabia, meet Susan, an old friend of the family.'

'Hello.' Fabia smiled into the beautifully made-up face, noticing as she did so that Susan's large green eyes had turned glacial the moment they had fixed on her.

'Hello, sweetie.' Susan held out a soft manicured white hand. 'I've seen you before, haven't I, at one of Alex's receptions?' She smiled a sugar-sweet smile that didn't reach the cold jade eyes. 'I didn't realise you were one of Alex's...girlfriends.'

The brief but very definite hesitation before the word 'girlfriend' was a subtle insult that only another woman would recognise, and Fabia looked hard at the other woman, her face straight. 'Probably because I'm not *one* of them,' she said coolly. 'I've never been one for sharing what belongs to me. I am *the* girlfriend.' She smiled a slow, long deliberate smile.

Both Susan and Alex were staring at her with equal astonishment on their faces if for different reasons. Alex clearly had no idea why Fabia had stated her case so firmly and Susan was obviously astounded that the gauntlet had been taken up with such speed. She opened her mouth to say more and then caught the glint in Fabia's eye and decided against it. 'How nice...'

Fabia smiled sweetly. 'We think so, don't we, darling?' She looked up into Alex's face, which had a distinctly mesmerised tinge to it now. He had said he wanted her to be herself, hadn't he? Well, there was no way she was going to let a spoilt little rich girl like Susan put her down without a fight.

'Uncle Alex! Uncle Alex!' As two small figures came hurtling through the open doorway and launched themselves into Alex's arms she caught an expression of what could almost be termed triumph on Susan's face. What now? It was clear the children adored him and he them, and as Fabia walked by Alex's side into the house, a child perched on each of his arms, she wondered with a feeling of dread gripping her heart what other little surprises Alex had in store for her this Christmas.

## CHAPTER SEVEN

BY THE time Susan's parents left an hour later with their daughter and grandchildren in tow, Fabia had passed through so many different emotions that she felt quite exhausted. The initial feeling of outrage at the other woman's deliberate snub and continued offhand disregard that bordered on rudeness had first changed to exasperation, then contemptuous disgust, to finish in such a mixture of feelings that even she couldn't have named them. Apart from one—anger. That alone had remained constant throughout.

The instinctive dislike that had first risen with Susan's discourtesy had been swiftly replaced by revulsion at the way the other woman quite blatantly used her children to further her friendship with Alex, encouraging them to sit on his knee and exulting openly in his easy relationship with them. 'Isn't Alex just a darling with the kiddies?' Susan said in a soft undertone to Fabia as she was preparing to leave. 'I just don't like to think how I would have coped without him when poor William died.'

'William?' Fabia asked coolly.

'My late husband, such a dear, dear man,' Susan said unemotionally. 'Heaps older than me, of course, but he was so in love with me and I was too young then to know what I really wanted.' The hard green eyes fastened on Alex hungrily.

'But of course you are quite a few years older now?' Fabia said drily, deciding enough was enough, and effectively finishing further conversation as Susan departed with head held high and cheeks burning, her eyes glacial.

Alex seemed to take an inordinate amount of time seeing them all off and his smile as he re-entered the room seemed like the last straw. 'Anything wrong, Fabia?' He looked at her oddly.

'Fabia has a headache,' Isabella intervened firmly and smoothly with an understanding glance at her stiff face. 'Why don't you go and have a rest before dinner, Fabia? I intend to.'

Those sharp black eyes missed very little, Fabia thought wryly as she smiled gratefully at Isabella. The tiny woman had been aware of every little subtle snub Susan had sent in her direction and Fabia had noticed Isabella's coldness with the lovely brunette. 'I will, thank you,' she said quietly, leaving the room quickly with just a cool nod at Alex as she passed him. The fact that he appeared quite oblivious both to Susan's behaviour and her own fury made her doubly irritated as she lay down on the soft bed, turning out the main light and leaving just the subdued glow from one small lamp to light the large room.

Men can be so blind, she thought bitterly as she lay in the warm semi-darkness, her mind buzzing with a thousand images. Alex chasing Gemma, Susan's little five-year-old, on all fours, growling madly while pretending to be a lion. Alex listening seriously with complete concentration while Jeremy, at eight years old, explained the rudiments of football. Alex— 'Stop it, stop it!' Her voice was loud in the empty room and she rolled over on the bed, hands on her ears as she endeavoured to shut out the pictures.

It had hurt to see him like that and she didn't understand why. She could cope with the ruthless millionaire businessman image or charming philanderer—just—but seeing him playing with the children, his male strength more marked against their fragility, had touched something deep inside her that was acutely painful.

He's nothing to you, so it doesn't matter, she told herself firmly as she glanced at her watch, deciding to have a leisurely bath before dinner. Susan isn't the first and she won't be the last, you know that. *You know it.*

So why, when she knew the inescapable truth, did it hurt so much? she thought later as she lay soaking in the warm, scented water. Why was there a permanent ache in her heart these days, and why the mad churning in her stomach every time she so much as thought of him?

I wish I could go back to the flat, she thought suddenly. Back to a safe little hidey-hole where I could lick my wounds in peace. But I haven't got any wounds, she argued hotly with that voice in her mind, sitting bolt upright in the bubbles, slopping water over the edge of the bath on to the thick fluffy carpet. I won't let there be any!

She heard the knock on the door and tensed before remembering that it was Mary's time to come and turn down the beds, a ritual she never missed and insisted on doing. The small woman had taken to spending five minutes with her when possible, filling her in on the history of the house and its occupants.

'Come in...' She slid back down under the bubbles as she spoke.

'Now I'd love to take you up on that, I really would, but as I suspect the invitation was given in error I'll restrain my natural tendencies with noble self-control.'

'Alex?' Her voice was a panic-stricken squeak. 'I thought you were Mary. *Don't* come in!'

The sound of a lazy rich chuckle did amazing things to her insides and she curled her toes in the water, her heart jumping. 'You really haven't got the spirit of Christmas at all, angel-face—goodwill to all men and so on.' There was a moment's silence and when she didn't speak he tapped the door again gently. 'I just called by to say that Isabella is feeling rather tired and is going to have dinner in her room.' There was a faint note of concern for his grandmother in the dark voice in spite of his efforts to hide it. 'It will just be the two of us downstairs so don't bother to dress for dinner—we'll be relaxed and casual. OK?'

She knew what he meant but a sudden vision of them both sitting at the magnificent dining-table stark naked brought a smile to her lips and hot colour to her cheeks. Where had that thought come from? 'OK, see you in a minute,' she said reluctantly, suddenly realising that without Isabella's presence the meal would become subtly more intimate.

She dressed simply in a plain blue dress that perfectly matched the colour of her eyes, adding tiny gold studs to her ears and a small dab of perfume to her wrists. She debated on whether to put her hair up but a tiny nagging memory of a long white neck and gleaming black hair coiled perfectly in place decided her against it. She would not lower herself to compete for a prize she had no intention of claiming anyway!

He was sitting in one of the easy-chairs at the bottom of the curving staircase as she made her way downstairs, rising instantly he heard her approach, his hard handsome face unreadable. 'You look lovely, Fabia,' he said softly. 'One can't improve on perfection but perhaps you'd like to wear this anyway.' He handed her a small transparent box through which the creamy furled petals of an exotic orchid were visible.

'Oh, it's beautiful, Alex.' She looked up into his face in delight, the flawless purity of the hothouse flower touching something deep inside her.

'They had more brilliant colours and shapes but that one seemed right for you.' He took the bloom out of its box and she saw that the petals were veined with faint blue and gold towards the centre of the flower, culminating in a deep vibrant violet at its heart. 'The correct name is unpronounceable but it's known as "unawakened",' he said blandly as he fixed the orchid carefully on her dress, his hands accidentally brushing the side of her breast as he did so and causing a deep heat to rise in her flesh. He seemed quite oblivious to her agitation, taking a strand of long corn-coloured hair in his fingers and letting the smooth silk slip through them as he finished.

'Thank you.' She stepped back a pace as she spoke, her hand nervously touching the flower as she stared, unsmiling now, into the sombre darkness of his face. He had discarded the formal dinner-jacket he usually wore for light trousers and a pale Aran sweater, the cream of the wool throwing his tanned skin and rich brown hair into stark contrast, and somehow emphasising his great height. He looked powerful and dangerous and irresistibly attractive and the blood drummed crazily in her ears as he took her hand and led her into the dimly lit dining-room.

The table was beautifully decorated in Christmas colours of red and green, the glittering silver cutlery and fine crystal glassware enriched with looped scrolled ribbons and sprays of holly, the centrepiece a magnificent arrangement of sweet-smelling deep red roses, red and green ribbon and soft feathery fern.

'Mary does tend to go overboard at Christmas,' Alex said drily as he pulled out the chair for her to sit down. 'Would you like a sherry or a glass of wine before we eat? Dinner will be promptly served in exactly,' he consulted the heavy gold watch on his wrist, 'eight minutes if I know anything about this household.'

'A sherry, please.' She was feeling distinctly uncomfortable and painfully shy and both sensations made her jumpy. He seemed different tonight somehow, although she didn't know why. She was just conscious of the fact that every inflexion of his voice, every little movement he made, registered on her taut nerves like an electric shock.

As he placed the glass of sherry in her hand he slipped a long gold package on the table at the side of her fork. 'Merry Christmas.' She raised startled eyes to find him looking down at her with that strange expression on his face she had seen once or twice before and once again it was swiftly veiled as he caught her glance.

'What is it?' She looked down at the box as though it were alive.

'Open it and see,' he said lightly, turning away from her and walking round to his place at the table opposite her, his big body easy and his face closed.

'Alex! I can't possibly accept this!' She stared down at the brilliant solitaire diamond surrounded by a little star of lacy gold fixed on a thin gold chain. It flashed its radiance from a bed of deep blue velvet and she almost stopped breathing as she thought of what the exquisitely wrought necklace must have cost. Why had he done this? The flower had been a piercingly sweet gesture, but this? This was a whole different ball-game.

'Don't you like it?' he asked mildly as he sipped a glass of wine slowly. 'You are at liberty to change it for something else if you like.'

'It's not that, you know it's not that,' she said quickly. 'No woman could fail to appreciate such a beautiful thing, but I can't possibly accept it. It must have cost a fortune.'

'The cost is incidental.' He leant forward suddenly, his eyes tight on her face. 'The flower reminded me of you and so did this, that's all there was to it. I saw them and liked them and it has given me pleasure to acquire them for you. Do you understand?'

'Alex…' She shook her head helplessly, her soft golden hair shining like silk. 'That's not the point. It's far, far too expensive. What would people think?'

'Does it matter?' The golden gaze narrowed. 'It's no one's business but our own. Do you really care what people think?'

She dropped her eyes before the directness, frightened her face would reveal her thoughts. She didn't care what misconstruction other people might put on the gift, it was true. That abrasive fire she had passed through all those years ago with Robin had cleansed her forever of needing people's approval. As long as she was right in her own heart nothing else had mattered since that purifying time. It wasn't the nameless crowd that worried her but him. She was worried what *he* would think if she accepted such a valuable present. Robin had tried to buy her in just the same way although she had been too naïve then to understand. She had no such excuse now. She couldn't accept the gift.

'I'm sorry, Alex.' She raised bruised blue eyes to meet his waiting face. 'It was very kind of you but I can't take this.' She snapped the lid shut and proffered the box to him. 'The flower is lovely—can we just leave it at that?'

He looked at her for a long moment, the rapier-sharp eyes boring into her mind as a coldness settled over the chiselled features, and then shook his head slowly. 'You think I'm trying to coax you into my bed with something like that?' His hand flicked scornfully at the box she still held. 'That I'm trying to tempt you into selling yourself? You do, don't you? Don't deny it.'

'I wouldn't deny it.' She held his glance bravely. 'It wouldn't be the first time someone in your position did something like that with a woman.'

'Well, it sure as hell would be the first time *I* did,' he snarled savagely, rising from the table violently and striding across to the huge full-length windows, pulling the heavy velvet curtains aside and standing with his back towards her, looking out into the snow-covered gardens beyond. She heard him swear softly to himself and then long minutes ticked by as he stood unmoving and she too remained like a statue, all thoughts numbed by the sudden storm. She heard him take a long deep breath as his shoulders straightened and then he turned to face her, his eyes hooded.

'That was the last thing on my mind, Fabia,' he said quietly. 'I know you well enough by now to understand that my wealth works against me, not for me, where you are concerned. I don't like the picture of me you have in your mind. I'm trying to understand, make allowances, but you sure don't make it easy. When I hold you in my arms your body tells me one thing but the rest of the time—' He stopped abruptly. 'What is it, Fabia? What makes you hate me?'

'I don't hate you, Alex,' she said painfully, the numbness melting in the face of his unexpected gentleness. 'I don't even know you—'

'Exactly.' He stared at her, his brow furrowed as his eyes bored into hers. 'And you don't intend to try to rectify that, do you.' It wasn't a question and she didn't try to answer it, her eyes falling down as her head lowered.

'Keep the pendant.' Her gaze raised to meet his. 'I would like to think of you wearing it some time, that's all. It's a Christmas gift, a thank-you for coming here with me if you like. You said you wouldn't accept any payment and I've taken a week of your time and placed you in difficult circumstances. Keep it.'

'Oh, Alex...' Her voice was soft but his face had set into harsh cold lines and he didn't look at her again as he resumed his place at the table, his movements abrupt. She had hurt him, she realised in amazement. Offended him.

As Mary served the first course, her round plump face beaming and a sprig of holly fixed in the tight knot on the top of her head, Fabia sat in miserable silence, her head spinning. There was Susan, and maybe others like her, and yet he seemed so...sincere. But then maybe he was, she thought grimly, sincere in wanting a brief affair with her, sincere in telling her exactly where she stood from the word go, sincere in letting her see Susan. He hadn't tried to keep Susan from her and maybe he honestly believed he wasn't trying to buy her, but it all boiled down to the same thing in the end. As she spooned the delicious rich beef soup into her mouth her resolve strengthened. She couldn't be what he wanted her to be and if she tried the only person who would get hurt was her. She sensed instinctively that, if she had found the episode with Robin hard, *this* man could destroy her. She wasn't sure why—she kept the door to that avenue of thought firmly closed—but she knew it.

'A glass of wine?' She looked up to see Alex smiling coolly at her, his face bland, and like an actor taking a cue from a director she adopted the same pose as the meal progressed. She had five more days to get through and then she would be free and she would make sure she never, ever came into contact with Alexander Cade again.

'Mrs Cade has finished her meal, Mr Alexander.' Christine, Isabella's companion, stood in the doorway as they sipped their coffee. 'Are you coming to say goodnight?'

'Of course, Christine,' Alex said easily. 'Mary did us proud, didn't she? But it was a shame you and my grandmother couldn't join us.'

'Oh, we had our own little party upstairs, Mr Alexander,' Christine said comfortably. She paused and then moved closer to him, lowering her voice as she spoke again. 'I've suggested to Mrs Cade that she doesn't get up at all tomorrow. The company over the last two days has tired her more than she will admit.'

'I was thinking the same myself,' Alex agreed thoughtfully. 'She really seems very frail. Don't worry, Christine, I'll take care of it when I come up shortly.'

As the tall elderly woman left the room he turned to Fabia, his face polite but withdrawn. 'I shall be going to midnight mass in the village later. It's something that Isabella expects and it's little enough to do to please her. You are welcome to come along if you'd like to.' She hesitated, the instinctive refusal dying on her lips. She didn't want to be alone with him tonight with the atmosphere so tense and brittle, and yet... Neither did she want him to think she was nervous of him and the uncaring casualness of the invitation had made her feel contrary. He obviously didn't care one way or the other and she intended to let him see she felt exactly the same!

'I may as well,' she said lightly in the same tone he had used. 'I always find a Christmas Eve mass rather lovely.'

'Yes.' He smiled at her and there was something in the tawny-brown gaze that made her think, just for a minute, that in some way she had just played right into his hands. But that was nonsense and she was getting far too imaginative. She gave herself a mental shake.

'Just dress for warmth, a couple of jumpers and thick trousers,' he said nonchalantly. 'The dogs are in need of a walk and they'll wait outside while we're in the church so I thought it would be nice to go by foot rather than car. It isn't far, just a mile or so across the fields.'

'Fine,' she agreed quickly. If she was going to be alone with him it would be less dangerous to be in the great outdoors with the temperature well below freezing and two frisky dogs bounding by their side than in the warm intimacy of his car.

'You'll need a warm coat and boots,' he cautioned as he stood up to leave the room. 'The church is always only slightly warmer than the temperature outside and once one is sitting down the cold can really bite. I'll see you down here in an hour or so?'

She took him at his word and joined him in the hall some time later, buried under her big thick duffel coat, long scarf and mittens with her feet as warm as toast in sheepskin boots. He smiled slowly. 'You look like all the Christmas presents in the world rolled into one waiting to be unwrapped,' he said softly, touching the smooth softness of her cheek before donning his own thick car gloves. 'Come on, Major, Minor!' The two dogs bounded round their heels excitedly, tails wagging and shiny black noses ready for action.

As they stepped outside the shock of the icy frost-laden air made her gasp, but it was wonderfully exhilarating. The frost on top of the smooth white blanket of snow made the silver world surrounding them sparkle magically, the clear black sky overhead alive with a million twinkling stars.

'There's a short-cut through the grounds,' Alex said in her ear as he tucked her arm in his, 'then a mile over the fields and we're there. Are you game?'

She nodded, laughing suddenly as the two big dogs, wild with delight at the unexpected outing, rolled each other in the snow, barking madly in a confused welter of heads, paws and tails. 'Crazy pair of mixed-up kids,' Alex said indulgently. She glanced at his handsome face, alight with laughter and affection as he watched the antics of the dogs, and her heart lurched uncomfortably and then raced at twice its normal rate.

The night was clear and the moon was full, and as they walked through the fields arm in arm, following the path that other feet had trod that day but that was still inches thick in snow, she had a blinding sense of the significance of the moment. The starlit sky overhead, the rolling countryside clearly visible in its mantle of white, the exuberant animals and...Alex. She drank it all in without trying to understand why she felt so sweetly sad; now was not the time.

She felt dwarfed at his side in the flat-heeled boots but it was a good feeling. They didn't speak and curiously that was more intimate than any spoken words, and as the Christmas bells began to call the faithful to worship she knew a poignant shaft of pain in her heart that was more piercing than any of the agony she had endured with Robin.

'There's the church.' He looked down at her as he spoke, pointing across the white expanse in front of them to where a small stone-clad church complete with pencil-thin spire stood picturesquely under the dark sky. She had known it would look like that. The magic that had her in its grip had decreed it.

She couldn't remember the details of the service afterwards, just the heavy sweet smell of incense, the timeless beauty of the carols and the small crib at the front of the altar containing the Christ child. As they walked out into the cold crisp air to the waiting dogs she felt more miserable than she had ever felt in her life, and totally, helplessly confused.

'I'm glad you came.' He pressed her into his side as he spoke. 'Isabella was pleased when I told her.'

She looked up into his face slowly. And you, she wanted to ask; what, if anything, did it mean to you? The dogs walked quietly at their side now as if they too had been touched by the mystery of the night, and as they left the village lights and retraced their steps over the snow-lit fields he put an arm round her shoulders, drawing her close.

'It's Christmas Day,' he said softly as he brought her to a standstill, lifting her chin up to meet his gaze. 'Happy

Christmas, angel-face.' His kiss was deep and fierce, his cold face touching hers as his lips plundered the sweetness of her mouth as though he was slaking a deep-rooted thirst.

She had known it would happen, planned that she would remain cool and unmoved, but the second she felt the pressure of his arms holding her close into the big body and his warm lips opening hers she was lost. The flame roared savagely, brightly, and when at last he lifted his mouth from hers they were both panting slightly, her eyes wide and dazed and his narrowed into bright gold slits.

'There's magic in the air, angel-face.' He slipped her arm through his and started walking, the dogs leaping up and padding by their side again, looking slightly puzzled at the strange behaviour of the humans who controlled their world.

'Magic?' Her voice was shaking slightly as she spoke and she hoped he wouldn't notice.

'Can't you feel it?' He looked down at her again, his face alive with emotion. 'The world decked out in bridal white as though it's waiting for us to—' He stopped abruptly and she licked suddenly dry lips, her heart thudding. For us to make love? she asked silently. It still comes down to that?

'Magic fades in the cold light of day,' she said quietly, 'and bridal white has a nasty habit of turning to black.'

'You don't believe that, not really.' He stopped again to look deeply into her face. 'You must believe in the power of love.'

'Why?' she asked coldly. 'It was love that put me on the steps of a hospital when I was a few hours old wrapped in an old newspaper. It was love that—' She stopped. She couldn't tell him about Robin; the humiliation had run too deep. 'I don't believe in love,' she finished expressionlessly.

'But you must want to get married one day, have children?' he persisted. 'Every girl wants a white wedding.'

'If I ever get married it will be in black as befits the occasion,' she said bitterly. 'Why pretend? Why play the game that everything is going to turn out all right in the end? It's fairy-tale nonsense.' She heard herself speaking the words with something akin to horror. Did she really believe that? she asked herself even as the words left her lips. She didn't want to feel like this, be this person she could hear talking so coldly, but it was the only way she could protect herself and stop the vulnerability from showing. Argue with me, Alex, she begged silently, convince me I'm wrong, give me some hope that I'm not going to spend the rest of my life alone.

He did none of those things as they continued their walk in silence, and as she glanced at his face from under her eyelashes she saw it was set in cold and austere lines now, the light that had been there a few minutes before just a memory.

As they reached the lights of the house he still didn't speak, not until they had divested themselves of their outer garments in the hall and she walked towards the stairs. 'You go up,' he said quietly as she turned to face him on the bottom step. 'I need a drink.'

He turned and walked into his empty sitting-room, the dogs following at his heels, as she walked slowly up the stairs and away from him, and suddenly that seemed forebodingly appropriate as the last drop of magic melted away.

## CHAPTER EIGHT

IT WAS snowing again when Fabia awoke late Christmas morning after a restless, troubled night. Mary was pulling back the blinds, her good-natured face smiling as always, and Fabia saw a tray on the small table by her bed that the housekeeper must have brought in with her. 'Just a light snack of grapefruit and toast,' Mary said as she followed Fabia's gaze. 'Don't want to spoil your Christmas dinner and it's ten o'clock already.'

'Oh, I'm sorry, Mary,' Fabia apologised as she struggled into a sitting position in the soft bed. 'You shouldn't have bothered with a tray for me, you must have heaps to do.'

'No bother, Miss Fabia,' Mary replied warmly. 'I came in earlier but you looked so peaceful I didn't like to wake you.'

Peaceful? Fabia thought miserably. She hadn't known a moment's peace since she had met the master of this household, if the truth be known.

'Mr Alex has taken the dogs for a walk,' Mary continued cheerfully, 'but he'll be back in about half an hour and wondered if you'd like to come and see the mistress with him?'

'Yes, that'd be fine,' Fabia said quietly. 'I'll have breakfast and get dressed and come down, Mary. Is there anything I can do to help you this morning?'

'Help me?' Mary looked horrified. 'Oh, no, Miss Fabia, Cook and I have got everything under control. It wouldn't do for you to help.'

'No, I suppose not,' Fabia agreed slowly, 'but I'm not

used to doing nothing. With looking after myself and the flat and doing a full-time job I usually haven't got a minute to spare.'

'Well, you just enjoy the luxury while it lasts, then,' Mary said brightly, 'but it was nice of you to ask, Miss Fabia, very nice.' She bustled off after placing the tray on Fabia's lap, her small body consumed with energy, and as Fabia ate she considered the small woman's words.

'Enjoy it while it lasts,' she repeated thoughtfully. The staff didn't expect her to be around again, then? The thought depressed her even though she had decided the same thing.

She was downstairs waiting for Alex when he returned from his walk, his face glowing and his bare head covered in snow. 'You should have worn a hat,' she admonished as he stood in the hall melting all over the thick carpet. 'You lose most of your body heat from the top of your head.'

'Really?' He cast a sardonic eye at her. 'And would you care if I was cold?' He was smiling as he spoke but she knew he meant the message the words were asking. 'Silly question, really,' he added as he gazed at her troubled face, 'and as I'm sure it's one you've got no intention of answering I won't wait for a reply.'

He glanced at the huge box she was holding in her arms. 'Isabella's present?' She nodded slowly. The tiny mirror was in her skirt pocket but she was wondering whether to give it to him or not now. 'Shall we go up, then?' He picked up several presents from under the tree in the main drawing-room first and then followed her up the stairs to his grandmother's room, where they spent a pleasant hour with the old lady, who was looking considerably better, but acceded grudgingly to Alex's repeated orders for her to stay in bed.

Fabia was touched to find that Isabella had bought her

a gift, a superb dark leather handbag with a matching purse inside.

'You shouldn't have,' she said gratefully, her face expressing her pleasure more adequately than words, to which Isabella replied with a loud snort, although the old face was soft as it glanced at the young woman sitting on the bed.

Dinner was a traditional affair, a huge turkey with all the trimmings followed by plum pudding doused in brandy. It felt strange to be sitting with Alex at the beautifully decorated festive table in the lovely room surrounded by all the evidence of his wealth. She glanced at him as he spooned thick cream on to the rich pudding and her heart twisted painfully. At that moment she would have given the world for him to be a normal working man struggling to make ends meet—maybe then she would have had a chance? She caught at her thoughts abruptly. It was madness to think like this.

'I'm glad you're wearing it.' As the deep slumberous voice broke into her thoughts she raised her eyes to meet his. 'The pendant.' He touched his own neck. 'It suits you.'

'It's beautiful.' She forced a smile to her lips as she spoke and he nodded slowly, his eyes warm and soft with their strange glowing gold light.

'It has its own kind of loveliness but I prefer the flesh and blood kind...like yours.' He wasn't smiling as he spoke, and there was a strange kind of intimacy that had crept unbidden into the room. She stared at him dumbly. 'Thank you for coming here with me, Fabia,' he said softly as their eyes held and locked. 'It's been...good.'

'Good?' She laughed sharply, purposely trying to break the mood before it took hold of her and her mind spiralled into the inevitable confusion he always managed to evoke. 'I got the impression I'm a trial and tribulation to you.'

'Did you?' He smiled slowly, his eyes dancing as he glanced at her defiant face. 'Well, maybe I'm due for a little trouble in my life right now.'

She didn't like him in this conciliatory mood, it was too...seductive. 'Yes...' For the life of her she couldn't think up a suitable crushing reply when faced with the questioning intensity that had now taken hold of his whole body. She sat, hardly daring to breathe, as he slowly rose from his chair, only to relax with an almost painful sense of anticlimax as the phone rang piercingly in the hall, shattering the mood into a hundred tiny pieces.

'Mr Alex?' Mary stood in the doorway as he resumed his seat, his face expressing his irritation. 'It's Miss Susan on the phone. She wonders what time the party begins tomorrow.'

'Susan?' He glared at poor Mary as though she were to blame for the spoilt moment. 'Same time as it does every year, I suppose,' he said abruptly. 'What's the matter with the woman?'

'I think she wants a word,' Mary said apologetically, and Alex snorted crossly.

'Tell her I'm eating,' he said coldly, ignoring his empty plate with regal indifference as Mary scuttled away.

'Party?' Fabia's heart had dropped like a stone.

'Oh, haven't I mentioned it?' he said with a little frown of annoyance. 'I meant to. It's one of Isabella's established laws that the whole of Cumbria congregates here on Boxing Day afternoon and unfortunately this year is no different.'

'Oh.' Fabia's voice was very small.

'We don't do much Christmas afternoon,' Alex said after the silence had stretched on and on interminably, 'but I hear one of the big lakes near by is frozen and being used for skating at the moment. We can either watch TV here or go there, whichever you'd prefer?' She caught his eyes fixed on her with a curious intensity as she glanced up but the next instant his expression had cleared into its usual remoteness.

'I'd love to go and watch at least,' she said eagerly, 'but I can't skate. I don't know how.'

'I'll teach you,' he said with a deep softness in his voice that brought a sudden hot flush to her face. 'We've several pairs of old skates somewhere; I'm sure we can find a pair to fit you.'

In ten minutes they were in the car with two pairs of skates on the back seat. It had stopped snowing but the sky was heavy and white and the air bitingly cold, all nature transfixed in its arctic grip. It was the start of a wonderful afternoon. When they arrived at the lakeside Fabia had the strangest impression that she had stepped back into Victorian times. The ice was alive with brightly coloured figures muffled to the eyebrows in long skirts and warm trousers and on the bank a man was selling hot roasted chestnuts, his glowing brazier vivid against the white snow.

The very air was intoxicating and Fabia made a sudden decision to take this afternoon, just this one, for herself, to enjoy this time with the tall handsome man at her side as though there had been no past and would be no future. Just the glorious present in all its poignant sweetness.

She discovered, to her delight, that she was a natural skater, and with Alex's arm about her waist and his hand holding hers in a firm supportive grip she found herself flying over the ice like a bird, gaining confidence every minute.

As the sky began to turn a soft rosy red they stopped for a cone of hot chestnuts, warming their hands in the heat of the brazier as they chatted to the other couples standing near by. She noticed that several of the women's eyes turned again and again to the tall and darkly vital man at her side but each time she glanced up into his face the golden-brown gaze was fixed on her, and when one of the women, more daring than the others, suggested they all swap partners for a time, he firmly declined, stating that as this was Fabia's first time on the ice he would trust her with no one but himself.

Even as the thrill of satisfaction shivered along her spine she found that other self cautioning her carefully, warning her silently that this was still Alexander Cade—just another facet that she hadn't seen before.

'I would have thought you would have liked to skate with that little redhead for a while,' she said lightly as they returned to the ice turned pink by the sky's fire overhead.

'Why?' he asked baldly, his eyes narrowed against the cold.

'Why?' The direct question floored her temporarily. 'Well...' She paused again. 'She's a very good skater,' she finished a little aggressively.

'Oh, I see,' he drawled softly, 'a very good skater? Maybe I prefer to stumble about with a very poor skater.' There was a coldness in the mocking taunt that warned her to leave the subject of the redhead alone, and after a few moments Alex began to show her how to spin and weave, laughing with her as in his efforts to save her from falling they both finished up in a heap on the ice.

'Nice state of affairs, this,' he grumbled laughingly as he helped her up from the ice, brushing the white flakes from her coat and adjusting her scarf more cosily round her face. She found little gestures like this almost unbearably painful, awakening as they did a whole host of abandoned dreams. There was something in his tenderness, his caring, that was more seductive than any lovemaking.

'You're a very complex man, aren't you, Alex?' she

said softly, resisting his attempt to draw her back into the whirling arc of skaters. 'I wish I knew which was the real you.'

'The real me?' There was an expression of genuine bewilderment on his face. 'You've seen the real me, Fabia. What you see is what you get.'

'I don't believe that.' There was no amusement in her face now as she looked up into the dark golden gaze. 'I've heard you can be ruthless in business and I've seen you in action in the social scene, remember. All that doesn't tie up with...' She paused, uncertain of whether to continue.

'With the family man?' He had known how the sentence would finish. 'I thought you had more sense than that, Fabia. Of course I can't wear my heart on my sleeve when I'm conducting business negotiations; that side of my life is completely separate. As for my public face...that's what it is, a face. I put it on when necessary, it's as simple as that.'

'And the women?' She had to ask. 'Do you fool them the way you fool everyone else?'

'You're deliberately misunderstanding me.' He drew her away from the crowd and off the ice to a more secluded spot. 'If you are asking me if there have been women in my life then yes, Fabia, there have. *Have*, in the past. Each one meant something at the time although there was no great love story, I admit, but I have no intention of apologising to you or anyone else.' His eyes held hers intently. 'I'm a man, angel-face, an ordinary man with normal needs. I haven't lived like a monk but the things that are reported in the papers are absolute rubbish. If only a small fraction of them were true I'd probably be dead by now with physical exhaustion! I don't show everyone the real me, I grant you, but can you honestly say you do? That anyone does? There are very few people that one meets in a lifetime who really reach the core.'

'Oh, come on, Alex.' She took a step backwards as she spoke, away from his hand holding hers. The reference to the women he had known had hurt more than she would have thought possible in spite of her prompting it. 'On the one hand you are part of the jet-set and you said yourself you work hard and play hard—'

'There's nothing wrong with that,' he interrupted harshly, 'and I resent the term "jet-set". It implies something I am not. First and foremost I control my business empire, and that takes a great deal of time and effort. I have neither the time nor the inclination to waste my talents, and I do have a certain flair for the cut and thrust of my occupation, whether you believe it or not.' His face was cold and proud now and his big body stiff with pride. 'That is a separate part of my life, as I have said. It doesn't mean that ultimately I don't want what every man wants: a loving wife, happy home, children and so on.'

'You really believe that's what most men want?' she asked bitterly as a whole host of burning memories swept over her. 'Then your experience of the male sex must be very different from mine.'

'Unfortunately some men are arrogant and foolish,' he said slowly. 'They will discard a pearl along with the common stones in their avid search for the deception of experience. And some of the most heartless men I've known didn't have a penny to their names, incidentally.'

'We were talking about men, not money,' she said slowly, and he shook his head thoughtfully, his eyes glittering in the last rays of the dying sun.

'I have the feeling it's the same thing with you and that the two together add up to something...harmful?' She didn't answer the query in his voice and he stared at her for a full minute before turning away with a little gesture of disappointment. 'Still determined not to let me in, Fabia?' he asked grimly as he glanced at the darkening sky. 'The light's gone. We'd better get home.'

It was a cold, distant stranger who drove home, and as she glanced at his face once or twice under her lashes all the old doubts and suspicions came bubbling to the surface. He was still manipulating her, she thought wretchedly. He had admitted to it at the beginning of their relationship and nothing had changed, not really. He was rich and powerful and used to getting his own way, and unfortunately their circumstances, the season, the beauty all around them, everything was working to his advantage.

But she couldn't let her guard down. She had done it once all those years ago and nearly been destroyed in the process. She couldn't risk that again.

Mary served high tea in front of a huge roaring fire in the drawing-room later that evening and in spite of the mouth-watering sandwiches and light fluffy cakes Fabia found her appetite had deserted her completely. She had to stop this pointless longing for something that was as distant as the moon, it was tearing her apart, but the sight of him stretched out in the chair on the other side of the fire, his long legs toasting comfortably and his plate piled high with food, invoked a positively painful ache in her throat that made her eyes burn and her hands clench.

Mary came to collect the tea-trolley, cluck-clucking at the amount of food still left. 'Don't blame me, Mary,' Alex said teasingly, glancing at Fabia meaningfully.

'Aren't you hungry, Miss Fabia?' Mary asked quickly. 'You do look a bit peaky.'

'I'm fine, Mary, really.' Fabia smiled brightly. 'I made rather a pig of myself at lunchtime, I'm afraid.'

'Oh, as long as you're all right, then.' Mary bustled off as Alex lifted wry eyebrows.

'Another of your admirers, I'll be bound.' He joined

her on the small two-seater sofa as he spoke, placing a casual arm round her shoulders as he sat down. 'Still, I suppose it's no surprise that she likes you; they all do.' She had stiffened at his approach and now turned to him, her face cold.

'There have been people who didn't,' she said coolly as she moved a fraction of an inch away from him, 'and please take your arm away, Alex. We're alone now, there's no need to act.'

'Is that what I'm doing?' A certain inflexion in his voice had changed now, its tone deeper and with a trace of iron in its depths. 'I can't put a friendly arm around you now?'

'No.' And you're not going to put me in the wrong again, she thought silently as she stared coldly into the handsome face inches away from her own.

'Why so hostile, Fabia?' His body hadn't moved an inch but in some subtle way it seemed more menacing now than affectionate. 'I'm getting a little tired of the constant assumption that I'm only capable of having one thing on my mind.'

'I'm not assuming anything,' she said quickly, 'but as far as I'm concerned *you* made the suggestion that you employ me for a specific task and nothing else. Not a foot or a toe out of place, I think you said? Well, that works both ways.'

'Does it, indeed?' He turned in the seat to stare straight into her face, his eyes slanted dangerously. 'What a bossy little female you are, my pet.' As he leaned towards her he moved his arms and body in such a way that she found herself pinned against the sofa so that she couldn't move, his hard rigid body trapping her as his face moved down towards hers.

She had expected a hard fierce kiss to follow through on the act of dominance, but instead she found his lips brushing down on hers, tracing the outline of her face with light feathery kisses in between parting her lips tantalisingly and circling her ears with his hot clean breath. It was impossible to stop the flood of desire that began to rise as he continued the sensual teasing game. She could feel every inch of his steel-hard frame against her melting softness and tried desperately to hide the quivering response the practised seduction was bringing forth, hating herself for her weakness at the same time as she wanted to moan her pleasure against his hard face.

The probing tongue reached deeper now with each return to her mouth, tasting the sweetness within greedily before leaving to burn a fiery trail over her upturned face and throat, his hands moving over her body with sure knowledge of how to please as he brought forth little whimpers of exquisite pain. She had never felt like this in her life, as though a blazing inferno was eating her up, but even as the storm of passion carried her along she knew it was a calculated exercise on his part, and despair at her vulnerability gnawed at her pride.

'There, now.' As he raised his head she lay for a moment stunned in his arms before opening dazed blue eyes as he rose slowly to his feet. 'Before you give out your orders to me again just think long and hard, would you, about who wants what?' The honey-brown eyes raked her flushed face mockingly as he walked towards the door. 'I'm not some sort of animal waiting to leap on you and have my wicked way, angel-face. If I had wanted you it wouldn't have been rape, would it?' He turned at the door and surveyed her once again as she sat up hastily, smoothing her hair with shaking, numb fingers. 'I happen to feel it would be necessary for you to want me as much as I want you before anything would happen, and I don't mean just in the physical sense.' The eyes were razor-sharp now. 'When you come to me it will be because you want to, heart, mind *and* body.'

'Never.' The whisper was faint, but he heard it, and the handsome face hardened.

'Never is a long time, little girl.'

As the door closed behind him Fabia sat in front of the hot, leaping flames, feeling icy cold right through, her thoughts spinning in a whirling circle of confusion. She had known he could be ruthless but the cold-blooded determination he had displayed in setting out to prove to her that she was defenceless against him had unnerved her more than she had thought possible.

'I don't understand you, Alexander Cade,' she murmured into the empty room after long, slow minutes had ticked by in the stillness broken only by the crackle of the burning coal. She wanted to think he had been trying to humiliate her, crush her; that would fall into line with what she thought of him, and yet...

Her mind ground to a halt. He could have had her tonight, they both knew that, and he hadn't. It hadn't been because he didn't want to either; the hard firm body pressed so close to hers had revealed his thrusting desire too clearly for that. Did she believe him when he said that he wanted her to want him in the way he had described, and, if so, why? Why not be content with her body and leave it at that? She brushed her hand across her eyes and saw it was wet with tears, and yet she hadn't been aware she was weeping. She didn't understand him!

Much later, as she lay in the warm softness of her bed, her eyes seeking the darkness for an answer to her despair, bitter memories of Robin's cruelty crept unbidden into the confusion. She had trusted him implicitly, and was he really any different from Alex in what he wanted? Alex had already said that the main reason for her being here was because he wanted no entanglements, no romantic involvement to complicate his busy life once the Christmas season was over. Why was she even considering trusting him? Once she had served her purpose he would return to Susan and her kind without a backward glance.

Susan... She pictured the brunette's long, glossy dark hair and deep green eyes with their thick black lashes and shivered despite the warmth of the covers. And there were the children too. Alex clearly adored them and Susan knew it.

She turned over in the bed, bringing the pillow down on her head as though it could shut out the thoughts that were tormenting her. It was hopeless, absolutely hopeless.

She rose early the next morning before the rest of the household was awake, taking a long leisurely shower before washing her hair and drying it slowly, brushing its sleek richness into shining golden waves. Somehow she needed to look her best the next time she saw him. She applied light, careful make-up before donning tight, figure-hugging trousers in a soft cream wool and a big baggy fluffy jumper of the same shade. It was a casual outfit but one she knew complemented her colouring perfectly, and she needed all the help she could get today. Later, at the party... She forced her mind away from Susan with dogged determination.

Alex appeared briefly at breakfast, his face tight and restrained, and then closed himself in his study with terse instructions that he wasn't to be disturbed. 'Is everything all right, Miss Fabia?' Mary asked anxiously as she bustled in with fresh coffee mid-morning as Fabia sat idly looking through a stack of magazines in the main drawing-room.

'I suppose so, Mary,' Fabia said as lightly as she could, 'but to be honest I'm bored out of my mind without something to do. Alex is busy and Isabella is still sleeping and

I'm just not used to doing nothing.' She smiled wryly at the little housekeeper. 'I'd never make one of the idle rich, would I?'

'I don't know about that, Miss Fabia, but you could do the flowers for the party tonight if you really do want something to do. Jenny is rushed off her feet with the amount of cooking there's still to do and I'm tied up with a million and one last-minute details. It'd really be a help if you wouldn't mind.'

'Would it?' Fabia smiled delightedly. 'I'd love to. Lead me to them.' Anything to keep her mind from the destructive circle it seemed intent on following, she thought gratefully.

By mid-afternoon all the preparations were complete and with Isabella installed in the drawing-room ready to greet the first guests Fabia hurried upstairs to change. She hadn't seen Alex since morning. He had ordered sandwiches and coffee in the study at lunchtime and she understood he had paid a brief visit to his grandmother's room before lunch, but apart from that he was incommunicado.

It was as she was finishing putting the last touches to her make-up that the light knock sounded at the door, and, thinking it was Mary or Christine with a message from Isabella, she called a cheerful 'come in' as she turned round on the tiny dressing-table stool.

'I wanted a word with you before we go downstairs.' Alex stood in the doorway, devastatingly handsome in an off-white lounge suit with pale blue shirt and tie, his long hair slicked back and his golden-brown eyes glinting strangely.

'Oh...' She stared at him mesmerised as he walked towards her, stopping a foot or so away and leaning against the wall as he took in her slender shape in the dark wine cocktail dress she had decided to wear for the evening's gaiety. She had twisted her hair into a casual knot on the top of her head, leaving several silky floating strands of hair wisping about her neck, the diamond pendant lying in the hollow of her throat like a piercingly beautiful teardrop.

'I think an apology is in order.' For a crazy moment she thought he was asking that she apologise to him, and then he cleared his throat slowly and spoke again. 'I'm sorry for acting in such a...cavalier way last night, Fabia. It was unforgivable and it won't happen again. I thought when I brought you here that you would understand—' He stopped abruptly. 'That you would see—' He stopped again and swore softly. 'Suffice it to say I won't be troubling you with my unwelcome intentions again. OK?'

It wasn't, but she couldn't explain to him what she didn't understand herself, and she merely nodded slowly as he inclined his head towards her and strode from the room, shutting the door firmly behind him. She took a long deep breath before turning slowly on the delicate little stool and looking at her reflection in the long, ornate mirror. That was that, then. She had sensed that he had reached some sort of decision. Maybe he would ask her to leave early tomorrow, but then how could he explain such action to Isabella? She shut her eyes for a moment and swayed back and forwards with her arms tight around her waist as a shaft of pure agony pierced her heart. She didn't want to leave him. The thought shocked her with its fierceness and she opened bruised blue eyes to stare reproachfully at the pale, slim girl in the mirror. 'Don't be so pathetic,' she said softly. 'You go down there now and you act like you've never acted before. None of this is real, it never was.'

As the guests began to arrive she was aware, as she stood by Isabella's side, that she was waiting for just one beautiful face in the throng that was slowly filling the huge house. She saw the children before she saw Susan, Gemma looking like a little angel in a frothy party dress of white velvet and Jeremy trying to act the man in a small cream suit with a little red dicky-bow. They looked delightful...and they were, she thought miserably. How someone like Susan came to have such warm, natural children she would never know. The answer to that was revealed later as she watched Susan's parents attend to their grandchildren's needs while Susan floated about in an elegant swirl of dark green silk, looking as though she had spent all day getting ready—which she probably had, Fabia thought tightly.

'Their father adored them,' Isabella said softly in her ear at one point early into the party as she watched the children standing dutifully by the side of their grandparents, their small hands clasped in those of the grown-ups. 'They were the only bright spots in the poor man's life once he'd taken Susan on,' she carried on quietly. 'She made poor William's life hell.'

'Did she?' Fabia looked sharply at the old lady, who smiled at her understandingly.

'Anything in trousers, my dear,' Isabella said blithely, unaware of how incongruous the term sounded on her lips. 'Poor William was sent to an early grave.'

'*She* called him "poor William",' Fabia said thoughtfully, making up her mind in that instant that she was going to stand no nonsense from Susan tonight. Or any other time, if it came to it!

'Crocodile tears, my dear,' the old lady said firmly. 'The girl's bad all through.' Fabia glanced at the tiny figure affectionately. Like a true Italian Isabella loved and hated with equal passion; there was nothing lukewarm about her emotions even at her great age.

Within minutes Alex appeared at her side and remained close by for the next hour or two although Fabia got the distinct impression that it was more to further Isabella's pipe-dreams than any wish to be near to her. She couldn't quite place what was missing in that cool gold gaze, but something had gone and she felt the loss.

It was when they were called into the huge dining-room for the buffet tea that she heard the middle-aged couple in front of her discussing Susan, and once Alex's name had been mentioned she was powerless to walk away although she knew instinctively that she wouldn't like what she was about to hear.

'Such sweet children, after all, and dear Alex appears to love them dearly,' the overdressed matron on the right was gushing enthusiastically, her mauve-tinted hair clashing horribly with the shocking-pink dress she had squeezed her ample figure into.

'Oh, I know...' The other woman was more conservatively dressed but equally vehement in her love of gossip. 'It would be *so* nice for Susan to be married again and the little ones to have a daddy, wouldn't it?' She smiled a slow smile. 'After all,' she whispered in a loud hiss, 'it's plain they've been more than friends for years. Susan is never off the doorstep when Alex is home.'

'Oh, my dear, you know the story of course,' the 'pink' lady said in tones that stated clearly she knew her friend didn't and that she was going to enjoy immensely the telling of it. 'About Alex and Susan, I mean?'

'No...?' The other woman leant forward eagerly, her eyes bright.

'Well, I have it on good authority that before Susan met William she was, well, you know, *with* Alex. They were going to be married, so the story goes, and then the next minute she ups and takes poor William instead. No one could understand it at the time but now it looks as though it could all turn out all right in the end, doesn't it?'

'But how long ago—?'

Fabia turned abruptly and left the two women to their prattling, noticing as she did so that the focus of their tittle-tattle had joined Susan's parents, lifting a child on to each knee as he smiled at something Susan's father was saying. As she expected Susan homed in like a nuclear missile, face aglow with triumph as she glanced up and saw Fabia watching the cosy little scene.

The evening deteriorated rapidly from that point. When Isabella retired to bed shortly after everyone had finished eating, Susan became a veritable octopus, arms wrapped round some part of Alex's anatomy at every opportunity. Fabia had noticed that the lovely brunette was a little wary of Isabella, probably having felt the lash of her tongue on more than one occasion, she surmised, but with the old lady gone she let her natural boldness have free rein, although Alex seemed quite oblivious to the pathetic display which began to make Fabia feel slightly sick.

She endured the travesty of a party for another hour or so and then as the clock struck eleven discreetly slipped away from the drawing-room where the main body of people had gathered, escaping to her room as quickly as she could and heaving a long sigh of relief as she shut the door behind her.

She wanted to scream and shout and lie down and drum her heels on the floor to banish the pain that was threatening to tear her in two, but in the end she did none of those things. Instead she ran a hot bath and soaked for a good hour in the warm comfort of the silky water before slipping into bed just after midnight, immensely relieved now she had had time to think that she hadn't given way to her natural feminine impulse to enter into a kind of contest and had emerged from the evening with self-respect intact.

She didn't know what time it was that Alex woke her,

but was suddenly aware of being harshly pulled out of sleep by a hard, furious hand shaking her shoulder at the same time as his clipped voice sounded in her ear. 'Wake up, young lady! You've got some explaining to do.'

'What...?' She jolted upright, her heart pounding, coming to as she took in her surroundings and saw Alex bent over her, his dark face breathing fire. 'What on earth do you want and what time is it?'

'What time is it?' He repeated her words in cold mockery as he stood upright, his eyes searing over her creamy full breasts, revealed clearly through the whisper-thin nightie she was wearing. 'If you had been where you should be, next to me in full view of all my guests, you would know what damn time it was! Why did you disappear like that?'

'Why did I...?' She spluttered out of words as sheer unadulterated rage took her over, her anger making her quite unaware of the seductive figure she made as she sat amid the tumbled covers with her hair streaming across her shoulders and her violet eyes huge in her flushed face. 'You dare to ask me that!' She knelt up in her rage, her hand going out to strike the handsome face above her, but he caught her wrist in an iron grip as his eyes narrowed.

'No, you don't, angel-face.' His grip tightened as she struggled until she gasped with pain. 'And I repeat my question. Why did you leave the party like that without even telling me you were going? If nothing else it was the height of rudeness.'

She stared at him angrily without speaking. If he thought she was going to object verbally to him making a fool of himself with Susan he had another think coming. He could do what he liked with whom he liked but she was blowed if she was going to sit and watch like some pathetic little bimbo grateful for crumbs from the great man's table.

'Well?' As his gaze lowered to her body she suddenly became aware of just how little she had on at the same time as she realised his breathing had thickened. 'Are you going to answer me?'

She pulled the duvet up round her breasts with her free hand, glaring at him ferociously. 'You're the one who controls an empire,' she spat furiously. 'You figure it out.'

He held her glance tightly, speaking quietly now through clenched teeth. 'You drive me to the limit, woman,' he said thickly. 'Right at this moment I want to take you until you're crying out for more, until the things I do to you drive you crazy with desire and there is no one in your world except me.'

'I'd hate you,' she said bitterly, trying to wrestle her wrist free, and then froze as he laughed softly, his eyes glittering in the dim light.

'You do anyway.' His gaze lowered again to her body, the duvet having slipped in her frantic struggles, and suddenly his arm swept round her waist as he pulled her close, his body falling against her on the softness of the bed.

She wanted to fight him and in those first few seconds she did, silently and with all her might, and then she became aware of the hard muscular thighs pressed close to hers and the trembling that caught hold of her limbs drove all the strength from her body.

He hadn't kissed her until that point but now his lips fastened on hers and she felt as though every nerve-ending in her body had been sensitised into one glorious whole. As his hands stroked down her body, ruthlessly determined at first and then, as he sensed her compliance, dizzyingly, erotically soothing, she knew she was lost. She was enthralled by the sensations he invoked so easily, entranced by the sheer heady excitement that he wanted her, wanted her so badly that he was groaning her name against her hot flesh. She hadn't expected it to feel so right.

She knew, as his body shuddered against her, that he was holding himself in an iron restraint as he coaxed her desire still further, and the more she responded, the more she gave of herself, the more unhurried and restrained he seemed to be, kissing her face, her throat, her breasts with soft, sensual, undemanding kisses that, even as they reassured, fired her to strain against him in an agony of need.

'Do you understand now, Fabia?' he whispered softly as he stroked her with long, sensitive movements that caused an exquisite pleasure to pulse in time with her heartbeat. 'It could be so good, I can make you want me as much as I want you. All you have to do is let me...' She could barely hear him, her senses disorientated and lost in an explosion of feeling, and as she sighed mindlessly his voice became more insistent.

'Fabia? Listen to me. You have to want this in your mind as much as your body; I'm not settling for second-best. Do you hear me?'

'Second-best...?' As she pulled herself back into the cold light of reason it was to see his face, inches from her own, his dark gold eyes blazing with passion and... something else, something she couldn't understand.

'I'm me, Alexander Cade, I won't be a substitute for anyone else, in bed or out of it.' They were still entwined in each other's arms and for a fleeting moment she wished he hadn't spoken, wished his hands and mouth had continued to do their devastating work which would have ended in only one conclusion. And then she realised where she was, who she was and the fact that she was stark naked in his arms, her nightie having obviously been discarded some time along the way without her even being aware of it.

'Do you care for me, even a little?' As she tried to jerk herself out of his embrace he held her still tighter. 'Do you?'

'Let go of me.' How could he ask her that? What sort of woman did he think she was? That she invited this from anyone? Of course she cared for him; she— The door in her mind slammed shut. He had got under her skin, that was all. That had to be all. 'Please, Alex, let me go.'

He held her for one long moment more and then slid his feet over the side of the bed flinging the duvet over her nakedness as he did so, his face set in a mask of tight control although she noticed, with a small dart of surprise, that his hands were shaking as he stood up and moved across to the dressing-table, resting both hands on the smooth marble surface as he bent down with head lowered and legs apart. 'That's that, then.' His voice was husky and deep. 'Now I know where I stand.' She couldn't reply, she was beyond speech, her mind spiralling in such a whirlwind of confusion that it was a physical pain.

As he kept his head lowered she saw his hand move out to touch something on the dressing-table top and realised with a little dart of horror that she had left his present there the day before, unable to make up her mind whether to give it to him or not, unsure of how he would react.

He picked it up, reading the little card as he did so, and then turned to look at her, his eyes remote and unfathomable. 'Do I take it this was meant for me, or is the Alex on the top of the card someone else?'

'Of course it was meant for you,' she said shakily. 'I just changed my mind, that's all.'

'A woman's prerogative.' His eyes returned to the tiny package in his hands. 'May I?' She nodded helplessly, her face white.

As he opened the small box and held the tiny key-ring aloft the little mirror flashed in a ray of moonlight from the window and he remained perfectly still for a moment. 'Thank you.' He slipped the box into his pocket. 'I shall treasure this, whatever the motive was in buying it.'

She stared at him, mesmerised by the compelling look on his face, a composite of pain, hunger, anger and... something else she couldn't place. He turned and walked to the door, twisting on the threshold to glance across at her again, the strangeness still visible in his tight jaw and shadowed eyes. 'And I do know, Fabia,' he said quietly, his voice now devoid of all emotion.

'You know?' she whispered in bewilderment.

'Who caught who.' A tiny muscle flickered for a moment in the hard jaw. 'But how was I to know how much it would hurt?'

As the door slammed behind him she shuddered for a second at the constrained savagery with which he had closed it, and then buried her head deep in the soft pillow as hot tears flooded her eyes.

'But how was I to know how much it would hurt?' What did that mean—after an evening spent with Susan? This whole thing was a maze, a minefield of half-spoken suggestions and confusing innuendoes, and if she took the wrong path... She shook her head as the wet pillow stuck to her cheeks. Alex, oh, Alex... There had been something in his face as he had left that had frightened her, a tight coldness, as though he had reached a decision that was painful but irrevocable. She fell asleep as dawn touched the night sky with tentative fingers, confused, frightened and desperately alone.

# CHAPTER NINE

THE next three days passed as if in a dream. The arctic weather still held the world outside in a breathtakingly beautiful icy grip but Alex didn't suggest they visit the lake again. They went on a couple of long walks with the dogs and visited some old friends of Isabella's, but Alex had departed from her in some unfathomable way, although he was as attentive and polite to her in private as when they were in company. He made no effort to touch her now when they were alone and even his endearments for Isabella's benefit were restrained. If his grandmother noticed that something was amiss she didn't mention it, although Fabia caught the bright robin eyes glancing at them more than once.

When she awoke on the morning of her departure she lay for some time in the big warm bed, gazing out of the window at the white lacy pattern Jack Frost had painted on the glass, unable to believe that she was going to say goodbye to Isabella and the rest of the household that day. Now the time was here she felt suddenly bereft and utterly alone, her stomach clenched in a giant knot and a feeling of something like panic sending fluttering shivers down her limbs. She wouldn't allow herself to think of Alex, not for a minute, a second.

She had packed the night before and now, after a quick shower, she dressed slowly in trousers and a warm jumper, looping her hair into a high ponytail and wearing no make-up except for a light touch of blue on her eyelids.

As she entered the big breakfast-room Alex looked up from behind his paper and just for a moment, before the heavy veil dropped down over his eyes, she thought she saw a flash of something almost like pain in the tawny gaze. 'Good morning, Fabia.' As the deep rich voice spoke her name it registered on her for the first time that there had been no 'angel-face' since the day of the party, and again she felt a loss she had no right to feel. 'Your day of release.' He smiled grimly. 'All good things come to those who wait.'

He wasn't joking and she didn't smile, merely inclining her head towards him before going to the long sideboard and helping herself from the covered dishes of scrambled egg, mushrooms, tomatoes and fried ham and sausages. 'What time do you want to leave?' she asked quietly as she seated herself at the table.

'After lunch.' His voice was abrupt. 'The roads aren't too bad now we haven't had any fresh falls of snow for a few days so we should be able to drive straight back without too much difficulty.'

She nodded slowly. He obviously wanted to get rid of her as quickly as possible now her mission was accomplished. The shaft of pain she felt almost took her breath away but as she continued eating, mechanically, the little voice of logic reassured her that it was probably the best thing. She had no place in his world so the sooner she left it the better.

'Miss Fabia?' Christine's grey head peered round the breakfast-room door. 'Mrs Cade would like a word with you later if that's all right. She's feeling tired so she isn't getting up today. Perhaps you'd take mid-morning coffee with her about eleven?'

'Of course.' Fabia looked at the elderly companion in concern. 'Is she well, Christine? I mean, she's not—?'

'I think all the excitement of the last few days has worn her out,' Alex said quietly. 'She would insist on having a grand sort of Christmas despite all advice to the contrary, almost as if she senses...' His voice trailed away and he rose from the table stony faced. 'She's just tired, Fabia, that's all. She is eighty-seven, after all.'

She wanted to offer some word of comfort to him as he strode from the room but there was nothing she could say. His grandmother *was* an old, old lady with a weak heart and she knew her imminent death would hit him hard. She had been mother and father to him all his life, after all. Maybe it was his anxiety for Isabella that had turned him into this cold, reserved stranger with his carefully polite voice and distant smiles? Or maybe he's just fed up with me, she thought miserably. Their relationship had hardly been a smooth one, after all.

The big grandfather clock in the hall was chiming eleven as she knocked on Isabella's door later that morning. As before, the tiny woman seemed lost in the huge bed, but Fabia was relieved to see that she was as bright-eyed as usual, with vocal cords intact.

'Come and sit by me, child, don't dither!' Fabia joined her by the bed with a wry smile twisting her lips. It would take more than exhaustion to quell Isabella's sharp tongue. 'Now, you're leaving after lunch, so Alexander tells me?' Fabia nodded slowly.

'I'd like to thank you for such a lovely holiday,' she began politely, but Isabella's lined face pulled itself into an irritated grimace and she waved a hand in front of Fabia's face, bidding her silence.

'Be quiet, girl. I want to have a little talk with you and we haven't got much time. I can never be alone in this house for long, always someone coming to bother me.' She glanced up at Fabia, her black eyes piercing under the shock of snow-white hair. 'Now, then, I like you, Fabia Grant, I like you very much.'

'Thank you.' Fabia stared at her in surprise.

'And because I like you I am going to say things which

you may think impertinent, but then I'm an old lady, so...' She shrugged graphically with the twist of her shoulders that was pure Latin.

'I don't usually care for the women my grandson attracts,' she said blandly as Fabia stared at her wide-eyed. 'There have been one or two who have been...acceptable, but not what I would choose for him, not at all.' Fabia flushed scarlet, her cheeks burning hot. 'You, as I say, are different and he knows it. I brought him up to recognise the wheat from the chaff and I wouldn't like to see him hurt.'

'I don't understand.' Fabia stared into the lined old face in confusion.

'I'm not saying he hasn't sown some wild oats, mind, but then you'd hardly expect him to have reached the age of thirty-five without having had a few...encounters, would you?' Fabia shook her head dazedly. 'But he knows a diamond when he sees one.' The black eyes held hers fast. 'You understand me, child?'

'Look, Isabella...' Fabia paused, uncertain of how to continue. The whole point of her being here had been to give Isabella's last days the comfort of thinking that her grandson just might have met the right girl at last, but it was all supposed to have been vague hopes and dreams. This direct confrontation was not at all what she had supposed but then, knowing Isabella as she now did, she *should* have known, she thought wryly!

'You know he cares for you, girl? That he cares very deeply indeed?' Now Fabia rose from the chair at the side of the bed with a little gesture of repudiation that was instinctive rather than tactful in the circumstances.

'I'm sorry, Isabella, I don't think things are quite what you think, not yet at any rate,' she added hastily. 'Alex—'

'Alex is in love with you, my dear,' the old lady said flatly.

'Has he told you that?' Fabia forgot to pretend as she met the old lady's tight gaze.

'No, not in so many words,' Isabella admitted slowly. 'But I've seen the way he looks at you, child. He's never looked at another woman like that and besides,' she paused reflectively, 'it's just the way my dear husband used to look at me.'

'It is?' Fabia realised her mouth was wide open and shut it with a little snap. 'But I don't think—'

'This is a cosy little huddle.' The deep voice from the doorway interrupted them seconds after a brief cursory knock. 'Is it private or can anyone join in?'

'See what I mean?' Isabella said to Fabia with a resigned little shrug. 'Never a minute to myself, visitors, visitors all day long. And then they wonder why I'm tired...?' She looked up at her grandson as he crossed the room to stand by her side, the wealth of love in her eyes belying the harshness of her words. 'You can both kiss me goodbye now,' she added grandly. 'I shall sleep directly afer lunch.'

They left the room a few minutes later with Isabella's words ringing in Fabia's ears, and as she ate the light lunch Mary had prepared for them in the comfort of Alex's sitting-room she glanced at his sombre, distant face once or twice, seeking something, anything, that would indicate Isabella was right. But there was nothing in the cold, slightly cruel slanted eyes that gave her any hope and his face could have been cut in stone, such was the lack of expression on the chiselled features.

They left the house just after one, with Mary's goodbyes ringing in her ears and the dogs' mournful eyes when they spotted the suitcases making her more depressed than ever.

'Isabella asked me to tell you that she would like you to visit again soon,' Alex said suddenly after they had driven a few miles in complete silence. 'Do you think that may be possible?' There was a certain inflexion in his voice, a tilt to his head, that made a surge of wild hope flare briefly, only to die as quickly as cold reason inserted itself grimly into her head.

He wanted what he considered was the best for his grandmother at the moment, she told herself flatly, and he had warned her at the outset of all this that Isabella was a born matchmaker. 'Maybe,' she said quietly. 'Let's just play it by ear, shall we?'

He turned quickly to give her a flash of a smile that had some of the old warmth in it, and as he did so her heart turned over. 'Suits me,' he said lightly. 'I'll be in touch.' That wasn't quite what she had meant but somehow the feeling that had swamped her so fiercely had taken her breath away and she let his remark go unanswered, more shaken than she cared to admit. It's just physical attraction, she told herself as the powerful car ate up the miles effortlessly, that's all. He's stirred your senses, but so what? It doesn't mean anything.

By the time they reached the grey streets of London, filled with black watery slush and tall austere buildings grimy and grim in the dim half-light, the light, crisp white world she had left behind seemed a million miles away. This is reality, she told herself silently as Alex drove towards her flat; come down to earth, girl, before he breaks you into a hundred little pieces.

'You're a wonderful advertisement for the beauties of Cumbria,' Alex said drily as they drew up outside her block of flats which looked even grubbier than normal. 'Could you just try and pretend that you've enjoyed yourself, if only to ease my guilt?' There was a dark mockery in the words that hurt her but she forced her voice to be as light as his as she replied.

'I've had a lovely time, thank you, Alex, and I'm sure

the guilt is only a momentary lapse. There's no need to come up,' she added hastily as he reached for her suitcase on the back seat, 'it's not heavy.'

'Don't be silly,' he said mildly as he helped her out of the car and followed her into the building after locking the car doors. 'Isabella would never forgive me if you were accosted on the last lap.' She smiled tightly. Damn Isabella, she thought suddenly, and you and the whole caboodle!

As she opened the door and switched on the light the little flat reached out to her welcomingly, and foolishly she had to bite back the tears before turning to Alex, her hand held out in farewell. 'Goodbye, Alex, and thank you again.'

He raised an eyebrow at the outstretched hand but took it anyway, raising it to his mouth before turning it over and gently kissing the palm in a long lingering caress. She had the urge to snatch it away but controlled it masterfully, keeping a bland smile on her face as he raised his head and looked straight into her face. 'I'll phone you,' he said huskily, his eyes bright in the artificial light.

She shrugged carefully. 'If you get time,' she said coolly as he let go of her hand that was burning where his lips had touched. 'I know you're a very busy man.'

He gave her one last long unsmiling look and then stepped backwards out of the door, closing it behind him as he went, and she was alone.

The next few days limped by in a confusion of disorientated thinking, sudden flashes of sharp knife-like pain and nights of crying. She made more mistakes at work in seven days than she had in the whole of the seven years she had worked there, couldn't eat, couldn't sleep and began to feel she was going slowly crazy...and still Alex didn't call.

As she left work on the Friday night, ten days after Alex had brought her home and disappeared out of her life, she found she was dreading the weekend ahead.

All this has just brought back all the old memories about Robin, she told herself for the hundredth time as she made her way through the busy London streets crowded with dour-faced commuters; it's no more than that. Give it a few more days and you'll be back to your old self. He's just unsettled you, that's all. Was he seeing Susan again? He could be with her now, this second—how would she ever know? He had obviously decided not to contact her again, anyway—that much at least was clear.

As a solitary snowflake landed on her nose she glanced up into the heavy white sky angrily. And now it was going to snow again! Even the elements seemed intent on reminding her of him at every turn. Well, she'd had enough of this! She *was* going to stop feeling sorry for herself, she *was* going to get back to being the old Fabia who was in control of her life and her destiny, and no six-foot-four Adonis with dark hair and tawny eyes was going to stop her.

As she turned the corner and saw the big sedate Bentley parked outside the flats her stomach jumped into her mouth and she came to an abrupt stop, causing several people behind her to cannon into each other like a human train. She didn't even hear the irate man behind her growling an insult about women pedestrians; all her energies were concentrated on the big tall figure uncurling himself from the car interior, his honey-flecked eyes tight on her face across the distance separating them. Calm, now, calm, she warned herself silently as she walked towards him on legs that were suddenly wobbly.

'Fabia.' Her name was a caress in itself as the low rich voice reached out to her and as he reached her side he bent and deposited a swift kiss on her wet hair. The sky was full of whirling flakes of snow now and already the ground was turning a virginal white. 'How are you?'

'I'm fine, thank you,' she said quietly as she inwardly mocked herself for the inanity of her reply. I'm terrible, Alex, she told him silently, and I don't know why. I'm falling apart, can't you see?

'I've been abroad,' he said slowly. 'America. Only got back today.' He stared at her silently.

'I see.' She nodded quietly. Say something, Alex, she said silently. Tell me you're pleased to see me, that you wanted to come, anything!

'I'm here to ask you a favour, again,' he said softly, and she noticed that there were tight lines of strain round his mouth and a weary hunch to his broad shoulders under the black coat. 'It's Isabella.'

For a brief piercingly painful moment she acknowledged that he hadn't come to see her because he had wanted to but because he needed something from her, and then that realisation was pushed aside as anxiety for the old lady who had been so kind to her asserted itself. 'What's wrong?' She stared at him wide-eyed. 'She's not—?'

'She's taken a turn for the worse.' He brushed his hair back from his forehead and she noticed there was a grey tint of exhaustion to the handsome face. 'John called me back from America because he was concerned about her and by the time I arrived she wasn't too good.' He flexed his shoulders tiredly. 'I had a few minutes with her but she's got it in her head that she wants to see you and nothing I said could dissuade her.' You wanted to dissuade her, she asked him silently, you didn't want to see me?

'Would you mind coming with me again, Fabia?' he

asked softly. 'I know it's a lot to ask, feeling about me the way you do.'

'Feeling about you...?' she asked bewilderedly.

'I know I'm probably the last person in the world you want to see right now, but it's important to her,' he continued slowly. 'Could you put your dislike of me aside for a day or two? Please?' His voice was infinitely weary.

'Of course I'll come with you, Alex,' she said quietly. 'Come inside and I'll pack a bag.' As she hurriedly filled her small overnight case she purposely kept her mind blank, numbing her emotions in case they let her down. He looks ill, she thought as she left her bedroom to find him waiting by the open front door, leaning against the wall, eyes shut.

'Why didn't you sit down?' She indicated an easy-chair in the lounge, her eyes wide with concern.

'If I sit down I'm worried I shan't get up again,' he said with a poor attempt at a smile. 'I haven't slept in the last thirty-six hours and I wasn't sleeping too well before then. Don't worry, Swinton's driving.'

'I wasn't thinking about who was driving,' she said sharply, and he winced slightly at her tone.

'Not tonight, Fabia,' he said softly. 'I really do believe I'm at the end of my tether, so just be a good girl and come quietly.' He smiled again but it didn't reach the glazed gold of his eyes. 'Are you ready?'

Once in the warm interior of the big car he stretched out his legs with a weary groan, taking her hand in his as she sat beside him. 'You don't mind, do you?' he asked with a nod at his hand holding hers. 'I just need to hang on to something at the moment.'

'Glad to oblige,' she said lightly past the lump in her throat. He looked suddenly vulnerable, younger, quite different from the hard, ruthless image of him she had carefully built up in her mind over the last ten days.

'That's all right, then.' Even as he murmured the words he was asleep, and as the weather worsened into the blizzard conditions they had endured on the first journey she was immensely grateful for the big powerful car and the solid Swinton sitting silently behind the wheel. More than once her heart was in her mouth during the long drive and although the backs of her eyes ached with tiredness she couldn't relax, vitally conscious of the dangerous conditions and even more of the exhausted man at her side, his dark head resting on her shoulder. She tried to quell the tenderness that was uppermost as she glanced down at him now and again but it was a tide that was unstoppable, and by the time the car drove into the long winding drive her emotions were raw.

'Alex.' She shook him gently and he opened dazed eyes that widened on seeing her face so close to his.

'Fabia.' He had taken her mouth in a long slow kiss before she realised what was happening and for a moment time was suspended as they clung together in the quietness of the car. Then Swinton coughed loudly as he climbed out of the driver's seat and opened the door on Alex's side.

'We've arrived, Mr Cade.' Alex came to with almost a start of surprise and stared vacantly for one more moment before realisation dawned.

'Of course.' Suddenly he was the efficient executive again, out of the car and round to her side before she could move and taking her arm as they walked through the thick snow to the front door. 'I must have slept the journey away,' he said in tones of comical amazement. 'I'm sorry, Fabia, very rude of me.'

'Don't be silly,' she said lightly. 'You were absolutely tired out.' The feel of his mouth on hers was still with her as they entered the house, and its warmth stayed with her until they entered Isabella's room and she saw just how ill the old lady was. The mauve lips tried to say her name as she leant over the bed but there was just the faintest whisper on the air and even that slight effort seemed to tire the tiny figure.

'Don't try and talk, Isabella,' Fabia said gently. 'I just wanted you to know I'm here with Alex and we're staying with you until you're better.' She saw a glimmer of understanding in the tired eyes fixed on hers and then the old lady shut her eyes peacefully.

It was a long night. Alex tried to persuade her to rest on the sofa he had moved close to the bed and she tried to coax him to do the same, but when both realised neither was going to budge they sat side by side in the shadowed room, talking occasionally but mostly dozing, an ease in their relationship that had never been there before.

'This is real life, isn't it?' he said abruptly at one point in the night when Isabella's breathing had become more shallow. 'All the tinsel and glitter of that crazy world I'm involved with, it doesn't mean a thing.'

'Do you really mean that?' she asked quietly, and he glanced at her from the corner of his eye, a touch of the old arrogance in his face.

'Of course I mean it,' he said flatly. 'I've got no illusions about some of the people I have to deal with both on a business and social level but that's life.' He shrugged slowly. 'My grandmother made sure from an early age that I knew the difference between right and wrong—on her terms, and frankly her terms are good enough for me. We don't always see eye to eye, of course,' he smiled slightly, 'but our values are the same.'

'But Susan?' She stopped abruptly and stared at him, horrified that she had blurted out the woman's name.

'Susan?' He stared at her, puzzled. 'What has Susan got to do with anything?' The tawny eyes fixed on her tightly.

'I thought you liked her,' she said quickly. 'People talk, you know...' Her voice drifted away helplessly.

'Oh, I know all right,' he said bitterly. 'If anyone knows, I do! Susan is an old friend, nothing more. I find the children delightful but I'm afraid their mother—' He stopped suddenly. 'Well, let's just say my grandmother's initial feeling about her many years ago proved itself valid.'

'Did it?' The surge of joy that swept through her was so strong that she lowered her eyes swiftly, afraid he would read her mind. Isabella had been scathing about Susan and he was saying he agreed with it!

'I'm afraid Isabella is not one of Susan's biggest fans,' he said drily. 'Let's just leave it at that, shall we?' He glanced down at her bent head and when he spoke again his voice was deep and soft. 'I've learnt that the best things in life are often the hardest to get, but when you succeed it makes all the effort and heartache worthwhile. The trick is to keep trying, not to give up even when it appears hopeless. Sometimes you have to step back a while, bide your time, but that's just tactics. Not defeat.'

'I see.' She stared at him, her violet eyes huge in the shadowed darkness.

'I doubt it,' he said huskily. 'But maybe you will one day.'

At some point in the night they must have both drifted off into a deeper sleep because the arrival of John with a pot of coffee at about six woke them suddenly. 'How is she?' Alex opened bleary eyes and peered up at John who was bending over the bed.

'*She* is much better, thank you, Alexander,' a feeble old voice croaked irritably from the depths of the covers. 'And please don't refer to me in the way you would to a female cat.'

'Grandmama?' As Alex rose and bent over the tiny

figure Fabia joined him, and both breathed a sigh of relief at the pink tinge to the face that stared back at them crossly.

'Such a fuss about nothing,' Isabella wheezed testily, giving John a long sharp glance in the process. 'I told him not to call you—a little rest and I knew I'd be fine. I was trying to juggle my tablets,' she admitted with a slightly sheepish glance at her grandson. 'I get tired of taking all that lot every day; I thought I'd cut down on one or two.'

'Isabella!' Fabia stared at the old lady in horror. 'Don't you ever do that again. That's really stupid; you could have killed yourself.'

'Nonsense.' The bright black eyes had their sharpness back again. 'And it's brought you two here to see me, hasn't it?' The dark eyes held Fabia's in a long considering gaze. 'And you weren't going to come back, were you?'

'Of course she was,' Alex said easily, unaware of the message passing between the two women. 'And now we're going to have some breakfast while you rest. And behave yourself,' he added warningly as he took Fabia's arm. 'I mean it, Isabella.'

'Just like your grandfather,' the old lady muttered crossly. 'Always thought he knew best, too.'

'Mary has some bacon and eggs on the go, sir, if you'd like to go down,' John said softly. 'I'll stay with Miss Isabella for now.'

'Thanks, John.' Alex patted the old man's arm as they left and the lined face smiled back at him understandingly.

'What on earth is going on?' They had just finished breakfast and were sitting in weary silence staring out of the huge full-length windows of the breakfast-room into the cold white world outside when Alex's gaze sharpened on a small figure in the distance. Fabia had been feeling acutely uncomfortable for the last few minutes, regretting the intimacy that seemed to have sprung up between them as some of the old doubts and fears were resurrected in the cold light of day. He had asked her to come here for Isabella's sake—fact. He hadn't contacted her once since the Christmas break—fact. He was a very attractive man in a world of beautiful women—fact.

'That's one of my gardeners.' As Alex's voice interrupted her thoughts again she heard the note of concern in his voice. 'And he's only got one dog with him. They don't usually separate.'

They met the red-faced man on the doorstep and he took a moment to catch his breath before he spoke, Major bounding up to Alex with a bark of delight but then running halfway across the lawn before barking again loudly.

'We've lost one of the dogs, sir.' The man looked up at Alex anxiously. 'My lad took them for a short walk this morning before breakfast, knowing how things were in the house, and one of them didn't come back when he called.'

'Where did he take them?' Alex asked quickly as he turned back into the hall and reached for his coat.

'Down by Sabre Wood, sir.' The man raised a hand as Alex went to speak. 'I know, sir, I know. I told him not to go there but the lad's young and he forgot.'

Alex swore softly. 'Young be damned, Mike. That wood is lethal at the best of times with the bog and sudden drops in height. It's been a no-go area for years. There are stretches there I wouldn't like to wander into on a summer's day.' He turned to Fabia suddenly as if he had just remembered she was standing by his side.

'It's all right,' he said calmly. 'I'll be back shortly. Keep an eye on Isabella for me and don't tell her anything; she doesn't need another set-back.'

'Where are you going?' Her voice was shrill with fear but she didn't care.

'You know where I'm going,' he said quietly. 'Minor is out there somewhere, either in the wood or the surrounding fields. He could be hurt or worse. You don't expect me to leave him there, do you?'

'I wouldn't go, sir,' the gardener said at the back of them. 'There are some wicked drifts out there and—'

'That's enough, Mike,' Alex said coldly. 'You're going to worry the lady unnecessarily.'

'He could be dead already,' Fabia said desperately. 'You know he could.'

'Or waiting to be rescued,' Alex said softly. 'Listening, waiting, probably scared out of his wits. I can't leave him out there, Fabia, I'm sorry.' He had pulled on a large pair of wellington boots as he was talking and clicked his fingers at Major as he straightened. The big dog bounded immediately to his side. 'I'm tempted to leave him here for safety but he can probably guide me right to where Minor is,' Alex said slowly. 'I'll be back before you know it.' He touched her cheek gently with leather-clad fingers and then he was gone, down the steps into the snow, shouting orders at Mike as he went, with Major barking enthusiastically by his side.

'Alex...' She watched the two figures until they disappeared from sight and then started violently as Mary touched her shoulder gently.

'Come on in, lass, you'll catch your death,' the housekeeper said gently. 'I've made the fire up in Mr Alexander's sitting-room and you can stretch out on the sofa there until he comes back—unless you'd like to go upstairs for a rest?'

'No, I'll wait in the sitting-room,' Fabia said gratefully. It had Alex's presence stamped all over it, and somehow she needed that security just at the moment. She felt sick with tiredness.

She was convinced she wouldn't sleep a wink but the next time she opened her eyes it was early afternoon and the weather had worsened if anything. 'All the phone lines are down, Miss Fabia,' Mary said worriedly after Fabia had wandered into the kitchen to find Mary and Jenny in a huddle by the window. 'And the wind's getting up.' Fabia's stomach knotted with fear.

After a quick cup of coffee she went upstairs to Isabella's room to check on the old lady and was relieved to find she was almost her old self, sitting up in bed in a quilted bed-jacket with her hair brushed into order and her reading glasses perched on the end of her nose.

'Is Alexander awake yet?' Isabella asked as she entered the room. 'John said he was asleep.' Fabia glanced swiftly at the old butler sitting by Isabella's side.

'Not yet,' she said brightly. 'He shot back from America to see you, don't forget, and has only had cat naps over the last forty-eight hours. The poor man's exhausted.' As she spoke she glanced out of the window into the swirling, whining blizzard outside and her heart almost stopped with fear. He was tired and cold and he was out there!

She turned back to see Isabella looking at her strangely. 'What's the matter, Fabia?' the old lady asked quietly. 'Is there something I should know about?'

'Of course not.' Fabia forced an easy smile to her stiff lips.

'Come and sit by me, then,' Isabella said regally. 'I've got an old photo album here that might interest you.' As the afternoon darkened slowly into an ominous dusk her fear became all-consuming. It didn't help that Alex's face was staring back at her from the photo album! Alex as a rosy-cheeked baby; Alex looking heartbreakingly vulnerable as he smiled bravely at the camera on his first day at school, painfully smart in his new uniform; Alex in his first long trousers; Alex going to his first dance.

'Isn't that Susan?' Fabia peered more closely at one of the photos that featured a crowd of laughing teenagers grouped round a sports car.

'Yes,' Isabella said calmly. 'The car was Alexander's twenty-first present from me. Susan was his girlfriend then, you know.' She glanced at Fabia sharply. 'It was just after that that he finished with her, if I remember.'

'*He* finished with *her*?' Fabia asked slowly, remembering the women's conversation that night.

'Hasn't he told you?' Isabella asked quietly. 'He was no fool, my Alexander, even at that age. Susan wanted to marry a rich man and that's what she did—after Alexander had told her they were friends, nothing more.'

'I see.' A sudden gust of wind shook the window and Fabia reared anxiously from the bed. 'I'll just see if tea is on the way,' she said quickly to Isabella as she left the room, 'and stretch my legs a bit.'

'Look in on Alexander, would you?' Isabella called after her. 'I'd like to see him if he's awake.'

You'd like to see him? As she walked downstairs she realised it was now pitch-black and he was out there, in the worst storm for years, and she loved him. Strangely the realisation didn't terrify her, considering she had been fighting it for weeks. He had been gone for over eight hours now and besides that cold fact everything else paled into insignificance. Mary had told her the wood was about an hour's walk away—on a summer's day. Even allowing for double the time owing to the weather, and then the return journey, that still left four hours—four hours too long.

He had been mad to go, she had been mad to let him go, the world was mad! Why hadn't she contacted the police, ambulance, someone? She took a deep breath as her heart began to pound painfully. She loved him and he'd never know. He *was* dead. She felt it in her bones. Why had she looked at him, even for a moment, in the same light as Robin? Would Robin go out into arctic conditions looking for a human, let alone a dog? She sobbed suddenly into the stillness. This was judgement on her. She hadn't had the courage to reach out and trust her innermost heart when it had been telling her all along he was different. Maybe he would never love her, maybe she would just be another passing affair to him, but if she didn't give them the chance she would never know, would she? She ground her teeth in an agony of regret. Physical attraction was a start, wasn't it? Maybe she could *make* him love her, building on that?

She paced back and forwards, ignoring the sound of Isabella's bell overhead, until John appeared in the doorway, his severe face soft in his distress. 'I'm sorry, but Miss Isabella wonders what's keeping you,' he said apologetically as he glanced at her tear-washed face. 'Shall I tell her you'll be up shortly?'

'I can't, John, not yet.' She couldn't endure more small talk when her heart was being slashed into tiny pieces. 'Tell her I'm having a bath or a rest or something.'

'What possessed him to go out in this?' John murmured anxiously, forgetting his stiffness in the face of another crisis in less than twenty-four hours. 'The dog might have come home by itself. Did MacKay go with him?'

'Is that the man called Mike?' Fabia asked quietly and when the old man nodded she nodded herself in answer.

'Well, he couldn't have a better man with him for conditions like these,' John said comfortably. 'Knows the area round here like the back of his hand. Mr Alexander will be all right, Miss Fabia, don't worry.'

Don't worry! As the old man disappeared upstairs she

had the mad impulse to run out into the snow and keep running until she found him. For the first time she felt she knew exactly how the big cats felt at the zoo when they prowled round a tiny confining cage, growling with frustrated rage and helplessness.

When she heard the faint sound of a dog barking in the distance she experienced such a feeling of relief that for a moment everything swam in a dark hazy mist, and then as she lifted her head towards the sound her blood froze. There was just one dog barking. What if Minor had found his way home by himself and the others were lost out there?

She raced into the hall, pulling on her coat as she went and not stopping to slip her feet into boots. Her light shoes were soaked within seconds as she stood at the top of the snow-covered steps and then, as a large bulky figure in thick coat and wellingtons appeared round a corner in the drive with a dog bounding at his side, the feeling of indescribable relief was replaced by hot blinding rage such as she had never known before. She flew down the steps and across the lawns towards him, stumbling in the two feet of snow that had covered everything in a thick white blanket, but righting herself as her fury drove her forwards.

'You stupid, stupid man!' she cried over the few yards separating them as she neared his side. 'How could you have been so incredibly stupid? You could have died out there! Everyone's been worried to death!'

'You didn't tell my grandmother, did you?' His face was a dull grey colour and he was walking as though each step would be his last, but she was too enraged with painful relief to notice.

'No, I didn't tell her.' She reached his side as she spoke and beat on his chest angrily. 'But what about me?' she asked with each blow. 'How could you do this to me?'

He stared at her silently as she continued in her tirade, hot tears stinging the numbed coldness of her face as she ranted and raved her grief.

'Come here.' As he lifted her up into his arms she clung on to him as though she would never let him go, collapsing against his wet body with a little inarticulate cry of relief.

'I thought you were dead, Alex, I thought you were dead.' As he carried her towards the house he looked down into her face with a strange smile hovering on his lips.

'Would you have minded?' There was no mockery in his voice, just a deep hard question that she answered immediately.

'I'd have died too.'

He stopped again in the middle of the snow-covered lawns as more lights flashed on in the house when Mary and the others realised he was home. 'What does that mean? Explain.' As she buried her head against the roughness of his coat his voice was threaded with wonder as he spoke again. 'I love you, Fabia. I've loved you from the very minute I saw you in the middle of that room amid a crowd of awful people who paled into insignificance beside you. I couldn't believe it when you turned out to be a Mary-Lou.' He hugged her to him as he started walking again. 'And when I found out what sort of a trick you'd played on me I knew you were the only woman I'd ever love. So beautiful, so defiant, so touchingly fierce.'

'You didn't mind?' She stared up into his face.

'I minded like hell,' he said grimly. 'But it was too late then. The die had been cast, the Cade curse had struck again. You were the one I'd been waiting for all my life and you loathed the very ground I walked on!'

'Not really,' she whispered against his chest. 'I was fighting myself as much as you.'

'Well, you went the full ten rounds, angel-face,' he said wryly as he reached the bottom of the steps. 'Is there anything there for me?' He stopped again and looked down into her face. 'Tell me, I want to hear it. I want to know this is not a dream, that it's real. Tell me, Fabia.'

'I love you, Alex.' As she spoke the last black thread of bitterness was loosened and her heart broke out into the glorious light.

'You love me?' He clasped her to him again. 'That was worth turning into a block of ice to hear. I thought I was going to have a hell of a fight on my hands before I'd hear you say that but I wasn't going to give up. Weeks, months, years—I'd have waited. Not patiently, maybe, but I'd have waited.'

'There are things you've got to know, Alex.' As he put her down inside the hall he looked at her for a long moment and then touched her face gently.

'Nothing would make any difference to the way I feel about you but let me get out of these wet things and then we'll talk.'

'Minor?' She looked down at Major with a little start of guilt. 'You didn't find him? Oh, Alex—'

'We found him.' As Mary and John appeared in the hall, faces wreathed in smiles, he took the dry clothes from John's hands with a little gesture of thanks. 'He'd managed to fall down one of the pot-holes that damn wood is littered with and break his leg besides getting his other paw stuck in some tree roots. There was no way he could have freed himself. We took him to the vet's in the next village before we came back; that's where he is now. I tried to phone but the lines are down.'

She stood, just feasting her eyes on him as he spoke, and as he returned the look John and Mary glanced at each other and then retraced their steps, leaving the two of them alone.

'Come in here.' As he pulled her into his sitting-room she felt his shaking through the hand holding hers and pushed him towards the roaring fire with a little cry.

'Get your things off, Alex.'

'Music to my ears.' He smiled wickedly at her blushes as he stripped down to nothing, donning his dry clothes with mocking reluctance and then drawing her into his arms as they sat in front of the fire. Mary had placed a flask of hot coffee liberally laced with brandy by his chair and Fabia made him drink two cupfuls before she would relax on his lap, snuggling against him as she did so.

He kissed her until she was breathless but as their caresses grew more feverish she pushed him away slightly, putting her finger on his lips as she did so. 'I want to tell you something, to make you understand why I'm like I am.'

He listened silently while she told him about Robin, leaving nothing out, and his face was dark with rage when she finished. 'I'd give the world for five minutes alone with him,' he said grimly.

'It's over now,' she said with an overwhelming sense of relief that she really was free at last, free to love again, free to live again. 'I just wish I'd never met him, that's all.'

'The past is past,' he said gently. 'I don't care about it as long as you love me now. Any other men—'

'There haven't been any others,' she said quietly. 'You will be the first, Alex, the first and the last.'

'Oh, my love...' As he gathered her close the look on his face made her want to cry again, but within a few minutes weeping was the last thing on her mind...

'Kiss the bride, sir! We want a nice friendly wedding, now, don't we!' As titters of laughter greeted the photographer's quip Alex leant towards her, moving the soft white silk of her veil aside as he bent to whisper in her ear.

'What happened to the little lady who informed me she was going to wear black on her wedding-day?'

She smiled wickedly, content and gloriously fulfilled on this her special day, and as she caught Isabella's eye in the background she lifted up her dress to reveal a saucy black garter on the top of one slim, beautifully shaped leg. 'I was going to keep this till later, but if you insist...'

He laughed delightedly, his eyes devouring her as she stood beside him, exquisite in her wedding finery, and as the photographer called again he gathered her up into his arms, holding her aloft in triumphant victory before claiming her lips as the camera flashed.

# Marriages that were meant to last!

# Husbands & Wives

*Available at branches of WH Smith, Tesco, Martins, Borders, Easons, Volume One/James Thin and most good paperback bookshops*

Together for the first time
3 compelling novels by
bestselling author

# PENNY JORDAN

## The Bride's BOUQUET

One wedding — one bouquet —
leads to three trips to the altar

*Published on 22nd September*

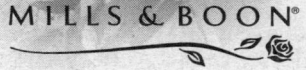

MILLS & BOON

# Modern Romance™

### THE PLEASURE KING'S BRIDE by Emma Darcy
Fleeing from a dangerous situation, Christabel Valdez can't afford to fall in love. But she can't resist one night of passion with Jared King. And will one night be enough…?

### DON JOAQUIN'S PRIDE by Lynne Graham
Joaquin Del Castillo believed Lucy owed his elderly employee money and so had taken her to Guatemala until she agreed to repay her debt. But he hadn't expected his contempt for his captive to be rivalled only by his blazing desire!

### THE HIRED FIANCÉE by Lindsay Armstrong
Vivian badly wanted to win an advertising account with Lleyton Dexter's company—but enough to act the role of his fiancée? Vivian told herself it was just a business arrangement. Yet the tension between her and Lleyton was anything but professional!

### THE DETERMINED HUSBAND by Lee Wilkinson
Having once been Keir Sutherland's fiancée, Sera had got engaged to his greatest rival. Now Keir had walked back into her life, seemingly determined to marry her after all. But did Keir love her or was he simply driven by revenge?

### On sale 3rd November 2000

*Available at most branches of WH Smith, Tesco, Martins, Borders, Easons, Volume One/James Thin and most good paperback bookshops*

# MILLS & BOON®

# Modern Romance™

### SANCHIA'S SECRET by Robyn Donald

It had been three years since Sanchia had set eyes on Caid Hunter, but the passion she felt for him still had the power to take her breath away. His reaction to her now was one of steely control—and she knew that this time there would be no escape...

### THE ENGAGEMENT DEAL by Kim Lawrence

Years ago, Niall had rejected Holly, making her vow that next time she saw him she'd be irresistible. Now he was back—except it was Holly's sister he wanted to be his fake fiancée! And Niall was enjoying Holly's efforts to convince him otherwise!

### THEIR CONVENIENT MARRIAGE by Mary Lyons

In the past Gina was humiliated after throwing herself at gorgeous Spaniard Antonio Ramirez. Now, however, Antonio seems more than interested...and soon Gina's only desire is to be his wife. Then, days after their honeymoon, Gina discovers the truth...

### THE PATERNITY CLAIM by Sharon Kendrick

Pregnant and alone, Isabella has fled to England and the only man she trusts—Paulo Dantas. Paulo feels honour-bound to help his family friend and claiming paternity of her child is the only way. But Isabella's father expects a wedding...

## On sale 3rd November 2000

*Available at most branches of WH Smith, Tesco, Martins, Borders, Easons, Volume One/James Thin and most good paperback bookshops*

MILLS & BOON

# Historical Romance™

## THE MARRIAGE TRUCE
### by Ann Elizabeth Cree

*A Regency delight!*

Relations between the Chandlers and the St Clairs had never been good. In attempting to rescue Sarah Chandler from a difficult situation, Devin St Clair had been forced to ask for her hand in marriage. What chance did such a marriage stand?

## AN INNOCENT MASQUERADE
### by Paula Marshall

*The Dilhorne Dynasty - Book Three*

Thomas Dilhorne was devastated by the death of his childhood sweetheart in giving birth to their only son. In desperation, Thomas's father sends him to Melbourne but when he doesn't return, the family becomes anxious. They don't know that Thomas has lost his memory...

### On sale 3rd November 2000

*Available at branches of WH Smith, Tesco, Martins, Borders, Easons, Volume One/James Thin and most good paperback bookshops*

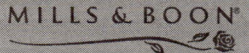

# Sensual Romance™

### A BABY FOR THE BOSS Jule McBride
*Bachelors & Babies*

Sexy, macho Rafe Ransom had to swap places with his assistant, Mackinley Leigh, for sensitivity training—he even had to look after her baby! Soon the baby had a hold on his heart and the mother a place in his bed.

### THE P.I. WHO LOVED HER Tori Carrington

Mitch McCoy, happily confirmed bachelor, couldn't believe it when his ex-fiancée, Liz Braden, turned up in town. But she needed his help and *he* needed to find out what he'd missed on the wedding night that hadn't happened!

### BACHELOR'S BLUES Leanna Wilson

Wade Brooks was looking for a safe relationship—with a nice, steady, reliable sort of girl. So he didn't expect to fall for Jessie Hart. The sultry brunette raised his blood pressure, making him feel all sorts of things he didn't want to feel...

### IN TOO DEEP Lori Foster
*Blaze*

Charlotte 'Charlie' Jones was used to fighting for what she wanted, and she wanted Harry Lonnigan—big time! Harry was doing his best to ignore the steamy attraction between them but, before he knew it, he was *in too deep*...

## On sale 3rd November 2000

*Available at most branches of WH Smith, Tesco, Martins, Borders, Easons, Volume One/James Thin and most good paperback bookshops*

# The perfect gift this Christmas from

## MILLS & BOON®

### 3 new romance novels & a luxury bath collection

### for just £6.99

### Featuring

## Modern Romance™

The Mistress Contract
by Helen Brooks

## Tender Romance™

The Stand-In Bride
by Lucy Gordon

## Historical Romance™

The Unexpected Bride
by Elizabeth Rolls